THE PEARL OF FRANCE

THE PEARL OF FRANCE

CAROLINE NEWARK

Matador
9 Priory Business Park,
Wistow Road, Kibworth Beauchamp,
Leicestershire. LE8 0RX
Tel: 0116 279 2299
Email: books@troubador.co.uk
Web: www.troubador.co.uk/matador
Twitter: @matadorbooks

ISBN 978 1788038 935

British Library Cataloguing in Publication Data.
A catalogue record for this book is available from the British Library.

Printed and bound in the UK by TJ International, Padstow, Cornwall
Typeset in 11pt Minion Pro by Troubador Publishing Ltd, Leicester, UK

Matador is an imprint of Troubador Publishing Ltd

For Natasha and Alexandra

LIST OF MAIN CHARACTERS

AT THE FRENCH COURT

The king	Philip IV
His wife	Jeanne of Navarre
His brother	Charles, count of Valois
His half-brother	Louis, count of Evreux
His half-sisters	Marguerite
	Blanche
His stepmother	Marie of Brabant

AT THE ENGLISH COURT

The king	Edward I
His children	Edward of Caernarfon (Ned)
	Joan, countess of Gloucester
	Mary, a nun at Amesbury
	Elizabeth, countess of Holland
His son-in-law	Ralph de Monthermer
His nephews	Thomas, earl of Lancaster
	Henry of Lancaster
Others	Henry de Lacy, earl of Lincoln
	Margaret de Lacy, his wife
	Alice de Lacy, his daughter
	Roger Bigod, earl of Norfolk
	John de Warenne, earl of Surrey
	Guy de Beauchamp, earl of Warwick

Humphrey de Bohun, earl of Hereford

Robert Winchelsea, Archbishop of Canterbury

Walter Langton, bishop of Lichfield

Piers Gaveston, a Gascon

John Gaddeson, a physician

IN SCOTLAND

The king in exile	John Balliol
The nobles	Robert Bruce, earl of Carrick
	John Comyn, earl of Buchan
	John "The Red" Comyn, lord of Badenoch
The bishops	Robert Wishart, bishop of Glasgow
	William Lamberton, bishop of St Andrews

Prologue

With a single sweep of his powerful right arm the king consigned five weeks of painstaking diplomacy to the floor.

'I will not be told what to do,' he roared.

Henry de Lacy, well-accustomed to his old friend's sudden explosions of rage, moved smoothly out of reach. He had no desire to be seized by the furred collar of his expensive new robes and shaken like a rat.

'There is nothing more we can do, your grace,' he said apologetically. 'You are fully aware of your situation.'

Of course he was fully aware. Why would he not be? He was *Edwardus Magnus,* king of England, warrior, crusader, conqueror; destroyer of Welsh princes, maker and un-maker of Scottish kings. All this yet his war chest was empty and the Holy Father was demanding he make peace.

The long years of hostilities had cost him the goodwill of most of his friends and if he had not been personally constrained by respect for the status of a brother monarch he would have strangled Philip in full view of his council. The turd might call himself king of France but he was nothing more than a lying, sanctimonious, duplicitous snake-in-the-grass.

'If you are to save Gascony, your grace,' said de Lacy, 'this is the only way. You must see that.'

Ah yes - Gascony, where once he'd taken his beloved wife, Eleanor. Bordeaux, the windblown marshes of the

Landes, the wide river valleys with their tiny walled towns and lonely monasteries. And the vineyards. English kings had held Gascony as dukes of Aquitaine and vassals of the kings of France for nigh on one hundred and fifty years and he was damned if he'd yield Philip a single foot. Losing Eleanor had nearly destroyed him but to lose Gascony would be beyond bearing.

'Tell me again,' said Edward, his anger giving way to a bone-sapping grey tiredness. 'Keep it simple and spare me your flowery embellishments.'

De Lacy struggled to recall the exact points of the treaty recently agreed with the French. He would have liked to retrieve his documents from their resting place amongst the rushes but thought it more politic to deploy his memory.

'It has been resolved that England and France will create a lasting peace,' he began. 'His Holiness will rule on the matter of Gascony, and your son will be betrothed to the Lady Isabella, daughter of the king of France.'

'So our two families are to live in perfect harmony?'

'That is what His Holiness desires.'

'What else? You said there was more.'

De Lacy shifted his feet uneasily. 'The French say their Lady Isabella is too young, your grace. They say the betrothal cannot be binding and in consequence are demanding something more proximate.'

The room vibrated with an ugly and ominous silence.

'Which one?' said the king in a still, cold voice.

De Lacy hesitated.

'By the blood of Christ!' snarled Edward. 'I know I must marry one of them. Which one is it?'

'The elder,' said de Lacy. 'The Lady Marguerite.'

Edward felt a momentary pang of disappointment. Plain and pious, his brother had said when he'd seen the sisters. Philip, of course, would never give him the Lady Blanche - a tasty morsel, dazzlingly beautiful but willful. Just the kind of girl to appeal to a jaded old man like himself.

Not that it mattered. He'd have the marriage contract dissected, sealed, nailed to the cross and signed in Philip's own blood. Then he'd wed his plain and pious bride, bed her, get her with child and return to his campaigning. Peace with France was what he needed. He didn't need a wife but it seemed he had no choice.

1

I was nineteen that summer when the English king sent his envoys back to Paris. They came from their damp little fog-shrouded island to our palace on the Île de la Cité when the bonfires were lit and my sister and I wore yellow flowers in our hair. We had returned from a visit to the abbey at Maubuisson and spied them at the cat-burning down by the river. Amidst the stench of charred flesh and wreaths of swirling smoke I saw their laughing faces and wondered why they'd come.

'To talk about my marriage?' said my sister wistfully.

There had once been a time when Blanche was betrothed to Edward of Caernarfon, the golden-haired son of the English king. She and I had new silk gowns and the family celebrated for a week. At the tournament, Blanche was placed on cushions in the women's pavilion and for three years she believed that one day she would be queen of England. But war had come and in the turmoil which followed we'd heard nothing more of the young Lord Edward. Someone said he was pledged to a daughter of the count of Flanders although Blanche swore such a thing could not be true.

'You cannot marry the son of your brother's enemy,' our mother had said firmly. 'So long as the English persist in their claim to our lands in Gascony they are not our

1

friends. Philip has torn up the contract of marriage. He refuses to honour the agreement and neither the lawyers nor His Holiness would expect otherwise.'

As good daughters of France there was nothing we could do but agree with our mother although in secret my sister wept hot bitter tears until her face became blotched and the tip of her nose turned horribly pink.

But now, after five years, war was over, the Holy Father's cardinals were busy making peace and the English king had sent his envoys back to Paris.

The summer twilight was fast disappearing and the evening candles already lit when I was summoned to my mother's presence. She was waiting for me in the room where she conducted her private business, a small casket of jewels placed on the table in front of her. She held up a string of rubies which, as they moved against the white of her gown, caught the flickering light and reflected a wash of colour across her face.

My mother was a handsome woman, with a broad smooth forehead. The eyes beneath her neatly arched brows were well set but her mouth had a perpetual look of discontent. She had been my father's second wife and gave him three healthy children but when he died it was Philip, the son of the first wife who became king and that did not please my mother. She didn't care for Philip. She didn't care for his brother Charles either.

'I have news for you,' she said, replacing the jewels reverently in their box and closing the lid. 'Good news.'

Her brow furrowed and I felt a well-accustomed pain as my belly twisted and knotted. I knew that compared to

Louis and Blanche, her other two children, I was a grave disappointment. No amount of effort on my part could change the look of aggrieved annoyance which clouded her face each time she saw me. I had few redeeming features. I was small and plain with hair the colour of mouse fur, a sort of miserable drab brown. Blanche said my ears were small and neat. But who bothers to look at a young woman's ears?

'Yes, *maman*,' I said, keeping my eyes fixed firmly on my slippers. I wondered what she could possibly have to say to me. I had done nothing wrong and besides she had said the news was good.

'Your brother, Philip, has seen fit to arrange a marriage for Isabella.'

Isabella was three years old. She was my brother's only daughter and his favourite child. He and Madame Jeanne had four sons but Philip didn't care much for them.

'Who is she to marry?'

My mother sniffed, a sure sign of disapproval. 'Edward of Caernarfon, the son of the English king.'

No wonder she was annoyed. It was Blanche, her own daughter, who was supposed to be crowned queen of England, not Philip's Isabella.

'It is a marriage designed to seal a treaty of peace between our two families,' said my mother in a cold voice. 'The choice is regrettable in many ways.'

'She's very young,' I ventured.

'Exactly,' said my mother, eyeing me with an unusual degree of interest. 'Too young for the betrothal to be binding so it has been agreed that a more proximate marriage will be arranged.'

'More proximate?'

I thought I would like to leave before anything more was said but that was impossible so I held my breath and waited.

'You should always remember, Marguerite, that the English are not to be trusted. Their ways are slippery and they are, by their very nature, treacherous. If we are not careful they will slither their way out of this treaty and all your brother's efforts will have been in vain. So to make certain of their compliance your brother has decided that you are to be married.'

'Me?' I said in disbelief.

'I see no other person,' said my mother. 'Unless some girl is loitering behind the arras. Of course I mean you. Philip believes you are clever enough to do this and I very much hope he is not mistaken.'

There was a moment of complete silence while I tried to make sense of what she had said. Who was I to marry? The English king had only one son. Perhaps there was a cousin I hadn't heard of, a cousin who might do for me.

I looked up, not quite meeting her eyes.

'*Maman*?' I whispered. 'Whom am I to marry?'

'Why, the English king of course. Edward of England. Who did you think you were going to marry? I have assured the English envoys that you are both obedient and fertile and it is all agreed. You, my dear Marguerite, are to be queen of England.'

Queen of England! The words were unreal. How could I be queen of England? Then I remembered my sister.

'What about Blanche?'

'What about her?'

'Surely *she* is to be queen of England?'

My mother shook her head.

'*Sainte Vierge*! Use your common sense, Marguerite. If Philip has chosen you he will have other plans for Blanche. In the meantime, this is your opportunity.'

She smiled in anticipation of my brilliant marriage for it truly was a brilliant marriage. I swallowed hard and tried to think of what it meant for me.

'*Maman*, how old is the English king?'

'What does his age have to do with anything?' she snapped. 'He is a king and you will be his queen. That is all you need to know.'

'Shall I have to live in England?'

My mother looked at me in exasperation. 'You could hardly expect the English king to live here, Marguerite. Don't be foolish. You will travel to England and once you are married, England will be your home.'

'But I can come back?'

My mother sighed. 'Listen child. When you marry, your husband becomes your lord and your master. You do as he says and go where he bids you to go. Once you have given him sons he may permit you to visit us but until then, you stay.'

I thought of the loneliness of being without my sister and prayed the marriage would be many years away.

'When will I be married?'

'As soon as possible,' said my mother happily. 'The English king is anxious for the wedding to take place by the end of the summer. Now smile. You are a very fortunate young woman.'

I didn't feel fortunate, I felt miserable. I walked slowly back through the palace rooms to our chamber where the other girls were mostly asleep. One or two were snoring gently but Blanche was sitting up in the bed we shared, fidgeting with impatience.

'Well?' she said as soon as the door was shut.

One of the maids slipped, shivering, out of the warmth of her pallet bed to help me undress. After she had drawn the heavy curtains round our bed, I clambered between the linen sheets and snuggled up against my sister's body hoping to warm myself.

'Lie down,' I said. 'And I'll tell you.'

She wriggled under the covers and put one of her arms around me.

'I am to be married.'

'You?' Blanche snatched her arm away. 'But I thought you were talking about *me*.'

She was annoyed, I could tell from the tone of her voice.

'Who are you going to marry?' she asked in a grudging tone.

'Our father's cousin, Edward of England.'

'What?'

She shot up in bed and grasped me by both shoulders.

'You can't marry *him*,' she said, shaking me roughly. 'You can't. He is the king. If you marry him you'll be the queen, and I'm the one who is to be queen of England, not you.'

There was a chorus of shushing from beyond the curtains.

'There's nothing I can do about it,' I whispered. 'Our mother says Philip has decided.'

'But what's going to happen to me?' Blanche wailed. 'I'll have to walk five paces behind you and sit on a stool at your feet. I won't be your poor relation and I'll never forgive you if you take my crown.'

'Our mother says Philip has other plans for you,' I said timidly.

'What other plans?'

'She didn't say.'

'Well, if you think I'm going to dance at your wedding you'll be disappointed because I won't.'

And with that she turned her back, pulled the covers over her shoulder and refused to speak.

I hadn't told her about Isabella but when I did I knew she would be even angrier. I sighed and thought how much more pleasant it would be if I didn't have to marry anyone.

'You know he's old, don't you?' said my sister next morning as we busied ourselves at our sewing.

'I know he's been married before,' I replied, threading my needle with a length of green silk. 'But he won't be very old. He would hardly want to marry again if he was, would he?'

'I've heard he's very, very old,' she said, stabbing the cloth with her needle. 'He's older than the oldest person we know.'

'He can't be,' I protested. 'They wouldn't make me marry him if he was.'

'Of course they would. All Philip cares about is his treaty. He's not interested in you.'

That was certainly true. Philip never so much as glanced my way. But then, why would he?

'Our mother won't let him marry me to someone like that,' I said doubtfully.

Blanche paused in her sewing and looked at me as if I was stupid.

7

'How can she stop him? If Philip wants to marry you to a man old enough to be your grandfather there's nothing she can do. And it's what you deserve for stealing my crown. You do realize there won't be any children, don't you? All he'll do is heave and grunt and paw at you with his wrinkled old fingers. He won't be able to give you a child and much good your English crown will be to you then.'

With that last bit of spitefulness Blanche jumped to her feet sending needles, silks and precious cloth tumbling onto the floor. The other girls pretended they'd heard nothing, bending their heads over their sewing, not wishing to be party to this particular quarrel and refusing to look me in the eye.

Naturally they envied me the honour - what girl would not want to be a queen? - but marriage to a decrepit old man was something to be feared. They knew the outward show of my marriage would be glittering but the shell would be hollow, the days and nights would be lonely and the future bleak. There would be no little children to brighten my life, just dutiful obedience and a cantankerous, ailing Methuselah dribbling at my side. It was no surprise there were no joyful congratulations.

We removed to Vincennes, my brother's second favourite hunting lodge, to make preparations for my marriage. When our mother casually mentioned the possibility of an imminent betrothal for my sister, Blanche melted into friendship once more.

By the end of the week Philip had taken a wild boar in the forest. The chase had been tremendous and we were still celebrating his success when the English envoys arrived. They had followed us along the road to our house amongst the trees, saying they wished to look over the person of the English king's proposed bride and between them decide if she was worthy. To be scrutinized by men I didn't know was bad enough but I dreaded more what Philip might do to me if they decided I was unsuitable.

'Measuring rod!' my mother instructed one of the maids. 'The king of England wishes to know the size of her feet.'

'My feet?' I gasped, lifting up the hem to expose my pale green hose. 'Why does he want to know the size of my feet?'

My mother smiled grimly.

'Not just your feet. He also wishes to know the span of your waist.'

I promptly clasped my arms tightly around my middle.

'Marguerite, stop being foolish. It is natural to want to know all about you. Any husband would be the same.'

'But what if he doesn't like what he's told? What if he calls off the wedding?'

'He won't do that. When a man asks questions about the person of his betrothed he has already made up his mind. He is firmly caught in the net. This is just the final struggle before he surrenders. It is to be expected.'

'And if he thinks your feet are too big he'll simply chop off your toes,' remarked Blanche.

I gave a shriek and my sister received a slap and a stern maternal rebuke which resulted in tears.

'We need to impress upon these men your good points,' said my mother, returning to the matter in hand.

I gave an inward sigh, for with my mother it was always the same. Beside Blanche I was found sadly lacking. Whereas my sister had grown steadily more beautiful, I had, if anything, grown plainer. My face had become narrower and my nose more pointed and my hair was the same unexciting shade of pale brown.

'You are pious,' said my mother firmly as if this was what my husband would value most. 'And you are well-formed.'

By that she meant I wasn't gap-toothed or hump-backed.

'And you are knowledgeable.' She paused. 'Although I'm not sure if that is an advantage as many men prefer a wife who is ignorant and will thus refrain from interfering.'

I had no idea how one might pretend ignorance but vowed I would not interfere with anything my husband might choose to do.

'You are docile, which is a quality highly prized by husbands,' she continued. 'They like a wife who is soft and yielding and agreeable. You have to admit, my dear Marguerite, that describes you perfectly.'

Soft, yielding, and agreeable. Was that really me? It made me sound like a comforting goosefeather pillow.

Now my mother was all briskness. 'The English envoys will have questions to ask but remember what I told you - if you don't know what to say, say nothing. A silent woman is always preferable to a foolish one.'

'But what if I give the wrong answer and the English king changes his mind?'

My mother sighed for the twentieth time that morning. 'He won't change his mind. His council has already agreed to the marriage.'

'His council?' I squeaked. 'What is it to do with his council? Are they going to want to inspect me as well? Why can't the king make up his own mind?'

'I don't know,' said my mother patiently. 'In England, it is the way.'

'They'll make you walk down their great hall in your shift to see if you're worth what he's paying for you,' said my sister.

'Blanche!' said my mother with ice in her voice. 'Be silent!'

It was stiflingly hot and the many elaborate layers of brocade, which my mother said brought colour to my cheeks, felt stiff and uncomfortable. I wore a simple gold circlet catching my hair on both sides so that it hung loosely down my back like a bride but I was only too aware of the beads of sweat trickling under my breasts and down my ribs.

I knew there were to be three of them carrying out the inquisition: the earl of Warwick, the earl of Lincoln and the count of Savoy who was married to my mother's niece. My mother said the count was widely respected for his wisdom so naturally His Holiness had insisted on his presence. She assumed the two earls were those the English king valued most but *she* considered the earl of Lincoln untrustworthy in the extreme.

The door of Philip's chamber opened and I walked in, keeping my eyes fixed firmly on the tiles, small lozenges of rose and cream with narrow borders of dark red. I sat on the stool placed ready for me and waited for my ordeal to begin.

The room was airless and crowded with dozens of people. Clerks in black stood hunched over their parchments and inks like an audience of wizened moles, and facing me, behind a long table, were my brother and an array of men I didn't know. Two of them, I noticed to my horror, were cardinals sent by His Holiness to witness my humiliation.

At first the conversation was about the intricacies of dowries and settlements and the possibility of annulments and papal dispensations. I found the words difficult to follow but knew agreement over these details was necessary to protect both my future husband and myself. It seemed as if my marriage was to be like a bargain in the marketplace where both sides had to be certain they were getting what they thought they were getting, and that what they were paying for was worth the coin. I knew the matter of who controlled Gascony and the other English possessions on this side of the Narrow Sea underlay my marriage, and I also knew how important this was both to Philip and to the English king. So I tried my hardest to concentrate.

'She is somewhat small,' said the count suddenly, peering closely at my face. 'Has she been unwell?'

'Her mother informs me she is never sick,' said Philip in a cold voice.

'And her womanly health?' enquired the count.

Philip's mouth twisted in distaste at the mention of such a private concern.

'You can be assured that she is fertile and will breed.'

'But what of the family?' asked the tall dark-haired English earl with the bushy eyebrows. 'Her mother? Her grandmothers?'

My brother gave the glimmer of a smile. 'Her grandmother, as you know, gave the blessed Saint Louis, eleven children, and her other grandmother came from good Burgundian stock whose breeding is impeccable. Her mother raised all her children. The family is strong. You see, *messires*, you need have no fear on that account. My sister will give your king healthy sons, provided of course ...'

Philip left hanging in the air the thought that a failure to produce sons would not be my fault but that of the English king.

'His grace has sired sixteen children and is still lusty,' replied the dark-haired earl testily. 'There will be nothing lacking in that department, you can be sure of that.'

'It has been a long time,' said my brother silkily. 'Nine years since his queen died.'

'Nine years is nothing to a man of such appetites,' the earl retorted. 'And the lady has a youthful charm which should lend spice to the encounter. Does she sing?'

'Like an angel,' said my brother. 'A sweet clear voice.'

'And has she skill with an instrument?'

'The lute.'

'Perhaps, in that case, she would care to entertain us.'

'I don't think we have time for minstrelsy, Sir Guy,' said the count, taking charge of the inquisition once more. 'We have not yet discussed the lady's education. Can she read? His grace is greatly interested in books and would not welcome an unlearned wife.'

'My sister has been excellently tutored in all the disciplines,' said Philip as if it was the most natural thing in the world for a daughter of the House of Capet to be able to read and write and understand the philosophies. 'I think my cousin will be pleased at her skill in these matters.'

So I would not be required to pretend ignorance after all, which was a blessing. Perhaps my future husband and I might find companionship in books?

'Our king places great store on piety in a woman,' said the stout little English earl, the one they called de Lacy. 'As you know, *monseigneur*, he has raised several foundations in memory of his beloved Queen Eleanor. He wishes for a wife who is equally willing to embrace the teachings of the Church.'

'My sister is properly devout,' said Philip. 'I do not think you can fault her teaching.'

'But she is *very* small,' said the one they called Sir Guy.

'Now come Guy, that is not important in a woman,' said the other Englishman jovially. 'Size doesn't matter, not like it does for a man.'

There were smothered laughs from the listening crowd and smiles from those at the table.

'She does speak, doesn't she?' said the count in a worried tone. 'She's not mute?'

Philip gave him a withering look which would have felled a lesser man.

'Sister,' he instructed me. 'Tell these men who you are.'

I opened my mouth but, horror upon horror, no words came out. I tried again and this time all I managed was a whisper.

'Speak up, my lady,' said Philip in his iciest voice.

'These men are from England and cannot understand unless you speak clearly.'

'I am the Lady Marguerite,' I said quietly. 'I am the granddaughter of Saint Louis of blessed memory, may God keep and preserve his immortal soul.'

Philip held up his hand for me to be silent.

'You see,' he said. 'A sweet voice with honeyed tones. What man would not be seduced by such a voice?'

Sir Guy coughed. 'Our king has a preference for a Castilian marriage. His interests are much engaged in that direction. You must appreciate the honour he does your sister by considering her as a wife.'

Philip threw him a look of such fury I was surprised the earl did not wince.

'My sister has numerous opportunities. She is young with many fruitful years ahead and it is a great sacrifice on her part to ally herself to your king who, at best, is past his prime.'

'Our king, let me assure you, is in full possession of his powers and is equal to any man on the battlefield, *monseigneur*,' retorted Sir Guy. 'You included.'

The count leaned forward to intervene.

'I do not think we acquit ourselves well by bickering,' he said firmly. 'Let us proceed to the next point - the lady's agreement.'

'I will answer for my sister,' said Philip.

One of the cardinals tapped the table.

'I am sorry, *monseigneur*, but that is not sufficient. The Church requires an assurance from the lady.' He turned to me. He had a lined face with fleshy jowls and great sad eyes.

'You are of age, daughter?'

'Yes, your eminence,' I said quietly.

'And you understand that a proxy betrothal will be binding in the eyes of the Church?'

'Yes, your eminence.'

I thought how gentle he was, how understanding, how kind. Then I became aware of a sudden silence.

'Is it your wish?' said the dark, heavy-browed Sir Guy whose long nose was quivering with impatience.

'I'm sorry,' I whispered. 'I didn't hear the question.'

'*Mon Dieu!*' said my brother.

The other earl, the kind one, smiled and said, 'Is it your wish, my lady, to marry our king, the great Edward of England, to be his queen? It is necessary for you to agree. The Church requires it.'

I looked from one to the other wondering if any young woman would dare to say no at a moment like this.

'Yes, *messire,*' I whispered. 'I agree.'

To my mother's satisfaction there followed a magnificent formal ceremony of betrothal after which my status as the English king's future wife was official. Everyone was very kind, praising my good fortune and telling me how lucky I was. But the more they made much of me, the more I feared I was nobody's idea of a desirable wife. No-one said that an old man such as my betrothed should be grateful for any young girl in his bed, no matter that she was small and plain. If only I could have been taller or prettier. If only I could have been more like Blanche.

The burning heat of July turned the roads to dust but the treaty was still not signed. According to my brother, Louis, the envoys were sailing back and forth across the Narrow Sea dealing with the finer points, trying to get both Philip and the English king to agree.

'It's not you,' said Louis, kindly, 'it's Isabella. Philip is terrified of arranging a marriage for her which will not be to his total advantage, and Edward of England is equally determined to have the best of the bargain. They say he wanted his son married to a Castilian Infanta but is having to agree to this marriage in order to save his lands in Gascony. His first wife came from Castile so he has romantic attachments to the country whereas, for us, he feels nothing but a desire for possession.'

'But they *will* sign, won't they?' I said, not caring one bit about Gascony or a Castilian Infanta but becoming more and more anxious for my marriage as each day passed.

'Yes,' said Louis. 'Neither of them is completely happy, but they'll sign. I'm sure of it. Philip is travelling to Montreuil tomorrow. He wants to make a grand gesture and he won't want to wait while the lawyers argue over side clauses.'

Madame Jeanne smiled at me over the head of little Isabella.

'My husband is talking of marriage between the English king's son and our daughter,' she said planting a kiss on top of the child's soft curls. 'Not yet, but soon. Think, my dear Marguerite, you will have your niece on the throne of England before long.'

I wondered at Madame Jeanne's carelessness in consigning my betrothed to an early grave, but said nothing. If it had been my nature to be jealous I would have minded dreadfully about the fuss over Isabella's marriage. It wasn't as if she was more royally connected than me. My blood was as sacred as hers. But I knew Philip would toss me over to the English king without a second thought if he could keep Gascony, whereas with Isabella he was insisting on guarantees and assurances, pledges under seal and promises made before God.

'You are a lesser dish,' said my sister spitefully. 'It is Isabella who is the haunch of venison and the roasted peacock. whereas you are simply a small bowl of wrinkled olives.'

Madame Jeanne patted my hand and said consolingly. 'You mustn't mind if there are no babies, my dear Marguerite. The English king is very old and can hardly expect to ...'

She stopped, clearly unsure which my betrothed would fear more - that he would fail in his attempts to father a child or that he would find himself unable to perform his duties as a husband should.

July drifted into August, the hay had been cut and soon it would be harvest time. The treaty was signed and Philip had taken his household to Chartres. My heart fluttered daily in fear that some new upset would result in the treaty being torn up but to Blanche's joy, the formal announcement was made of her betrothal. Rudolph, the eldest son of the king of the Romans, would travel to Paris next year, where in a solemn service and with all due pageantry he would marry the younger sister of the king of France.

'He is handsome, Marguerite,' enthused my sister. 'And young, only a few years older than me. He's a duke but his father has promised him a crown. I shall be queen of ... ?'

She wrinkled up her nose and pretended she was thinking hard.

'Louis says it will be the Bohemian crown for Rudolf,' I said kindly.

'I know that. You don't need to tell me.'

Now that her own future was settled, Blanche was more generous to me and refused to believe what the others were saying.

'Don't listen to those old pussies,' she said. 'You will have a lovely marriage. Think of the dreams we had: the gowns and the jewels and the furs.'

I forbore to remind Blanche that those were her dreams, not mine. She had also conveniently forgotten our childhood fear of marrying an old grey-beard with no teeth and a sagging belly.

The following day my mother sent a woman to instruct me on my duties as a wife. I thought she would be young, a married woman with a little experience who would settle my fears, but I was mistaken. She was old, her face hidden by her veil, but her eyes, sunk amidst pouches of wrinkled skin, were keen and noticing.

It was only a matter of days until I left for England and my chamber was full of chests overflowing with extravagant finery. I rose from the lonely contemplation of my precious books and bade her sit.

'Your lady mother has required me to talk with you,' she began.

I knew immediately that she was not one of us. Perhaps she came from my mother's home of Brabant on the far side of the River Scheldt where people spoke differently.

'You are to be married,' she said, seating herself heavily, smoothing the drab-coloured gown over her knees. Her worn boots peeped out from below the dark cloth and sat incongruously amidst the ribbons and girdles and embroidered slippers strewn on the floor.

'Yes,' I replied.

She gazed at me as if assessing me for the market.

'You are small for your age, I think, and narrow too. How old are you?'

'I shall be twenty before the year is out.'

'Old enough for marriage. Come!' she beckoned for me to approach. To my surprise and alarm she ran her hands over my hips, clicking her tongue and muttering to herself.

'As I thought, not good, not good.'

I felt I had failed in some degree but at what I didn't know.

'Your betrothed is not a young man, I hear?'

'No, almost sixty they tell me.'

'Tsk!' she clicked her tongue in irritation. 'Old fool! What are they thinking of? Now, listen closely to me and mark my words well.'

She told me what my husband would do to me on our wedding night and how I must submit, no matter what.

'It may hurt at first,' she said, 'but you will get used to it and if you are wise and do as I say you will learn to enjoy it.'

Then she told me what my husband might expect from me.

'Don't be afraid,' she said, her eyes twinkling. 'Most husbands wish their wives to enjoy what passes between them in the marriage bed.'

She explained how I could increase my husband's pleasure and what I should do to encourage his attentions.

'Old men do not have the energy of those boys who strut around making eyes at you girls,' she said. 'But they think of themselves as potent. You must never let your husband suspect you find his attentions lacking in any respect. You are his wife and it is your duty to make yourself available in such a way that desire will rise in him like water flowing from a spring. Do you understand? If he has no desire for you it is not his fault but yours. This Englishman - how long has he been without a wife?'

'Nine years I believe.'

'Let us hope he has amused himself with other women in the meantime.'

My thoughts must have shown on my face for she said, 'Oh don't look like that. Such women have their uses even for the most amorous of wives. But with a willing little creature like you in his bed I doubt your husband will have the energy let alone the inclination to look elsewhere.'

She then detailed the ruses a clever young woman might use to foster appetite in an older man who had long since lost interest in bed-sport. She talked of love potions which might aid desire and words I might whisper in his ear. This was not what I had expected of marriage and I was beginning to wish I didn't have to travel to England to marry their king.

'I know you girls gossip about men,' she said, smiling. 'Your friends will have told you stories. Some will be true, others will not, and you won't know which is which for you're a maid. But you can ask me. You can ask me anything and I will answer you honestly.'

I didn't like to say I never talked to the others about such matters. I knew Blanche did. She giggled in corners with the older girls, eyeing the young men in Philip's household, and I'd seen her in the dairy at Vincennes, gossiping and sniggering with the milkmaids.

'Will he like me?' I blurted out.

'Why would he not like you?' she said kindly. 'You are young, you are kind and you are willing.'

'Soft, yielding and agreeable,' I said dolefully. 'Like a goosefeather pillow.'

'What could be nicer for a husband when he goes to his bed than a soft, yielding and agreeable wife? Don't despise your good qualities.'

'But I want to be beautiful,' I cried. 'I do so want to be beautiful.'

'But you are,' she said, smiling. 'You *are* beautiful. You are thinking only of the outer shell, what you see when you look at your reflection. But look within and what do you find? A young woman of immense beauty of soul, someone who is kind and loving. It is not what is on the outside which makes a good wife but what is within. And a clever husband knows the difference.'

Before she departed she took my hands in hers, turning them over to look at my small white palms. She sighed deeply and kissed me on both cheeks.

'There, there, it is all done now. I shall not see you again. My face is not welcome here. There are too many who wish to forget me.' She gave a deep throaty laugh. 'Remember what I have told you and may God grant you a happy marriage and a clutch of little ones to brighten your old age. For a woman, a life without children is indeed bleak, as I know only too well.'

With that, she eased herself out of the door, shutting it quietly behind her. I sat and thought about what she'd said. I didn't know which frightened me more - that my husband might ravish me before he'd taken off his boots in his haste to prove himself a man, or that I would have to use one of the devices she'd described in order to stimulate his desire. Whatever happened I knew he would be disappointed and quite unable to see inside to the beautiful part of me.

'Did that old hag come and talk to you?' said Blanche as we went down to the hall for supper.

'Yes.'

'She came to me, too,' said my sister, tossing her head so that her golden hair rippled in gleaming waves. 'I told her I knew everything there was to know about pleasing men and it was pointless her trying to instruct me on matters about which I clearly knew more about than she did.'

'Oh Blanche,' I said. 'How rude of you. Have you no manners at all?'

'You know who she is?' said my sister, turning on the stair.

'No.'

'She is a woman who sleeps with other women's husbands. Although I cannot imagine anyone wishing to bed with her, can you?' Blanche wrinkled up her nose in disgust. 'She came from Brabant as one of our mother's

23

women and married a nobody. When he died she turned her talents to whoring. One of the girls told me she was the most expensive whore in Paris and there was hardly a husband in the city not seen with her on his arm.'

'I thought she was a midwife,' I said stupidly.

'Oh Marguerite,' laughed my sister. 'How will you manage without me? You are such an innocent.'

I wept all the way to Senlis. I told myself I would be brave but as our cavalcade clattered under the wall of the Châtelet and set off along the Grand Rue towards the north, I looked back and, at the sight of Philip's palace with its pointed rooftops and fluttering flags, I began to cry.

The women my mother had chosen to accompany me to my new life chattered gaily. None of them seemed to care about what we were leaving behind. It wasn't just the sights: the houses we knew, the churches where we worshipped and the turns in the road which we'd passed so often. It was the smells and the sounds of a life which would vanish forever. The pine-scented winter fires at Vincennes, my mother's musky perfume and the flowery fragrance of my sister's hair which reminded me of springtime in Clermont. And the accustomed ritual of bells, the rumble of carts coming through the gates at daybreak, the calling of men and women harvesting wheat in the blazing sunshine, and the shrieks of little children as they tumbled in the dust.

All these would soon be memories.

It took us two long weeks to cross the plains of Picardie and by the time we reached Boulogne I was almost weeping with tiredness. We partook of a final family meal. Philip spoke at length of his hopes for my influence on my English husband, the archbishop gave me his blessing and I said farewell to my many friends who would not be accompanying me. This was my last night. Tomorrow I would set out across the sea to a new life.

Now Blanche and I were alone in our tiny cramped chamber and there was nothing left to say. Everything had been said: all the promises, all the sorrows, all the words which would soon be lost forever. We held hands and looked helplessly at each other.

Tomorrow our paths would diverge and we might never see each other again. I would be on the other side of the Narrow Sea, the wife of an elderly man, living amongst people I didn't know. And before a year was out, Blanche would leave for Vienna and the high mountains of Austria, married into a family about whom everyone avoided saying too much. I wanted to be a good wife and I wanted Blanche to be happy, but I feared we might both be disappointed.

It was getting dark and the shadows were gathering when we heard a soft knock at our door. My mother wished to see me. I took a candle and ran quickly up the stairs to her chamber. She was sitting in her favourite travelling chair, her chin cupped in her hand. She patted the stool beside her and told me to sit.

'Well, my dear child,' she said. 'This day has come at last. Tomorrow we shall part and soon you will be a wife and a queen, but for tonight, for the last time, you will be my daughter, my dear one, my little Marguerite.'

'Oh, *maman*,' I said, tears beginning to gather at the back of my eyes. 'I shall miss you.'

'No you won't,' said my mother with a rueful smile. 'You will be far too busy making your new life and that is what I wish for you. I didn't ask you here for us to be unhappy. There is something I need to tell you which concerns your marriage and I want you to pay attention to what I am going to say.'

I nodded my head and listened carefully.

'You are going to marry a man who has loved before and I would not want you to be as unprepared as I was.'

She paused, purposefully fingering the rings on her left hand and I wondered what it was that was so important.

'When my brother told me I was to marry your father, I was overjoyed. I was twenty-one years old and proud to have been chosen. Brabant was not the wealthiest or most powerful of France's neighbours and your father might well have looked elsewhere for a new queen. On my wedding day I held my head high and enjoyed the attention. What young woman would not?'

I smiled. My mother was a woman who liked being at the centre of things. She disliked the way Philip never consulted her or sought her opinion. Only once had I known him seek her help and that had ended in such a furious row that he had never asked again.

But my mother hadn't finished with her story. 'My women escorted me to the royal bedchamber, scented and oiled and ready for my husband's delight. He arrived with his men and the jokes became bawdy which, as you can imagine, made me uncomfortable. Finally prayers were said, our union was blessed, and the curtains were drawn. My new husband and I were alone. And then, when I might have expected a tender embrace – there was nothing.'

I blushed in embarrassment. This was my mother's wedding night. This was a private matter.

'What you must understand about your father, Marguerite, is that he was an unhappy man. He had disappointed his parents and lost his first wife, the only person he believed who had truly loved him. He didn't want to marry again but he was the king and it was necessary. I had a little understanding of what went on in the marriage bed as my sister-in-law had told me what to expect. But nothing had prepared me for this awful hostile silence. I hardly dared to breathe.'

A flush of pink spread across my mother's high cheekbones and her voice became even quieter as she revealed the secrets of that night all those years ago.

'He kept the clothes she had worn. They were in one of his chests, carefully layered with rosemary and lavender to protect them from the moth. There was a special gown, one she had often worn to please him, a beautiful dark red silk embroidered with silver thread and stitched with tiny pearls. That night he made me put it on. I knew immediately it was hers. I could smell her scent within the folds. When he lay with me, he whispered her name over and over again into my hair as he made me his wife and when he had finished he opened his eyes and wept because it was me he held in his arms and not her.'

My mother paused.

'You see, my dear, there were not just two of us in our

marriage, there were three. She was there in his mind, in his eyes and in his heart. She consumed him entirely and he wanted nobody else. How do you think I felt to be so humiliated that he could only take me by pretending I was her?'

My heart was full of compassion for the hurt she had suffered at the hands of my father and I wanted to weep.

'If it had been a secret between the two of us, I could have borne the shame, but my humiliation was to be greater than that. Other than in my bed, he ignored me. Then he sent away my women, the ones I had brought from home, leaving me friendless. His mother had no kind words to say and found ample opportunity to show her dislike of me. I found myself shunned, even by his children. I hope you will never know how it is to feel so alone. I thought to tell my brother but what could I have said?'

She looked at me and I saw her eyes were clear. Her weeping had been done a long time ago and there were no tears left to shed.

I had never known my father and didn't know what to say.

'Do you know what I see when I look at Philip?' she said. 'Beyond the powerful king and the man who is Madame Jeanne's husband, I see an angry small boy. When I knelt down that first day to greet my husband's children, he looked at me with his mother's eyes and said, "My father doesn't want you here and neither do I." Then, he spat at me. I remember my shock and the wetness of the spittle running down my face.'

I put my arms around her, something I hadn't done

since I was a little girl, and laid my cheek against hers. With an intuition I didn't know I possessed, I knew how much it had cost her to tell me her secret.

'I love you, *maman*,' I said quietly. 'I love you.'

2

SEPTEMBER 1299

'Dover!' announced the captain of our ship with pride. 'And in record time, thanks be.'

I looked curiously at the little square harbour with its sheer white cliffs and felt a rush of relief at having arrived safely. There was an imposing castle set high on the eastern ridge and some low wooden houses strung out beside the quay. Leaning against a wall, quite distinct from the fishermen and merchants busy with nets and barrels and bundles of goods, were a group of richly dressed men. I stared hard but couldn't see anyone who might resemble my future husband so I presumed he wasn't there. Perhaps it was just as well because my women said I looked windswept and whey-faced from the journeying.

Several ships from our little flotilla had already arrived and I spied my brother standing on the quayside. By the time the drum stopped beating and our barge glided to a halt by the harbour wall Louis was holding out his hand, ready to assist me up the steps. As I placed my unsteady feet on English soil for the first time, trumpets blared loudly. Startled, I looked round to see where Philip was, then realised the fanfares were for me. I was being welcomed to England by a cheering crowd and a line of liveried men with gleaming instruments.

The gathering of people on the quayside swelled to a

multitude and I couldn't tell one person from the other. These were the English, my new fellow countrymen. At the front of the crowd were four men, two older and two younger, the youngest no more than a boy. He may have been tall and good-looking but his narrow shoulders and beardless chin betrayed his youth. He couldn't have been more than fifteen. After a brief introduction Louis came to escort me forward.

'Lord Edward, I would like to present to you the Lady Marguerite, sister of Philip, by the grace of God, king of France, king of Navarre and count of Champagne. Sister, this is Lord Edward of Caernarfon.'

So this was the young Lord Edward. I lowered my eyes, bowed my head and bent my knees. The boy bowed, pulling off his crimson bonnet and uncovering a head of magnificent golden hair.

'Welcome to the port of Dover, Lady Marguerite,' he said. 'Should I call you mother?'

I bit my lip in panic. It would not be at all proper for him to call me mother. Philip never permitted such familiarity. He always called my own mother, *madame*. But I didn't know how things were done here at the English court.

'I think my L-Lord Edward,' I stammered. 'I think you must ask his grace, the king, if it is suitable.'

'Oh,' he said, looking downcast. 'If there is any likelihood of unsuitability on my part, Lady Marguerite, you can be certain his grace, my father, will find it.' His face brightened. 'But you can call me Ned.'

This was worse. Surely he should be my lord Edward, or, when his father and I were married, perhaps stepson? But Ned? Such a vulgar and unsuitable name for the heir to the throne.

The young man at his shoulder gave a cough.

'I forgot,' said Lord Edward. 'This is Lord Henry of Lancaster.'

The young man inclined his head and made a small bow. This must be one of Madame Jeanne's two half-brothers, the sons of the English earl, Edmund, and his French countess, Madame Jeanne's mother.

'He is *my* cousin. But is he *your* cousin or your nephew?' Lord Edward cocked his head to one side and considered the problem.

'Both,' said Lord Henry. 'Greetings, Lady Marguerite. Welcome to your new home. My lady mother arrived at Canterbury a few days ago and is eager to reacquaint herself with you.'

He was about the same age as me, of middling build, brown hair, not particularly handsome, but looked good-natured enough.

'We must introduce you to the others before they feel we're doing them down.' Lord Edward leaned towards me and spoke in a low conspiratorial tone. 'Are they like this in Paris at your brother's court, always seeing slights and ill-feeling where none are intended?'

I didn't know what to say to this unasked for confidence and felt increasingly discomforted. To my relief Lord Edward turned towards the elderly grizzled man behind him and said, 'This is Roger Bigod, earl of Norfolk, Lady Marguerite. You must have him tell you about his battles. Ask him about the row he had with his grace, my father. It was a tremendous falling-out in the parliament at Salisbury two years ago and they almost came to blows.'

This boy, who would be my stepson, was like an undisciplined puppy, all large paws stepping where they shouldn't go, knocking things over, enthusiastic but untrained, loveable but dangerous and not someone to be encouraged in his careless talk. He spoke like a child in the nursery rather than a young man of rank. Did my betrothed know he behaved like this? Did he encourage it? The odd thing was that the others seemed unperturbed as if it was no matter that the heir to the English throne behaved in this way.

'My lady,' said the earl of Norfolk, bowing over my hand in a surprisingly agile manner for one so old. 'You are welcome.'

His voice was gravelly, as if he had demons plaguing his chest. I thought he'd be a fearsome opponent in battle and was surprised to learn he'd been at odds with his king. And in front of the parliament!

'And this fine fellow,' said Lord Edward with a careless sweep of his arm, 'is our gallant Sir Humphrey de Bohun.'

Lord Henry dug Lord Edward in the ribs. 'You've forgotten his title, Ned.'

I was horrified at the lack of respect shown to my betrothed's son in public. It was one thing for young men to push and shove in the privacy of the yards, but to do so on an occasion like this was unbelievable. Lord Edward was the second most important man in the land and the others were treating him like a kitchen knave.

'He's only just acquired it,' protested Lord Edward. 'How am I meant to remember everything? Sorry, Lady Marguerite, this is the earl of Hereford, and as you can see, by far the most elegant lord in the land.'

Lord de Bohun was attired in a tunic of azure and gold with an undershirt of fine white linen and was wrapped in a cloak of rich green velvet edged with fur. His bonnet was a darker green with plumes of some exotic bird attached to the bands, and his fingers were covered in an array of jewelled rings. With all this finery he easily outshone the others and was what my mother would have called a peacock, a man who cared for nothing but the impression he made upon others.

He swept me a magnificent bow, lifted my hand and pressed his lips to my gloved fingers. I felt the colour rise in my cheeks and a shiver run up my arm at the sudden touch of a man's mouth. It was all I could do not to snatch my hand away. The crowd had no such inhibitions and cheered loudly. It seemed all the English were as casual and lacking in proper formality as the men surrounding the Lord Edward. Realising they must think me very dull and solemn, I gave a little smile.

The elderly earl of Norfolk said something to me but spoke so rapidly I failed to grasp his words. I stood looking bewildered wondering what I was meant to do.

'My Lord Norfolk says you must be tired and we should repair to the castle for you to rest,' said Humphrey de Bohun slowly in his perfect French. 'If we leave our young friends to arrange matters you'll still be standing here with those pretty women of yours when the moon comes up and the stars prick the heavens.'

Lord Henry said something to the group of young men crowding behind him causing several muffled snorts and guffaws.

'Ignore them,' murmured Humphrey de Bohun. 'The young have no manners these days.'

Out of nowhere a black and white garbed cleric hurried forward and gabbled prayers of thanks for our safe arrival. From the disapproving looks given by the earl of Norfolk, I gathered the man should have been here earlier. It did seem as if the English party was ill-organised but I reminded myself this was a foreign country where the formalities were doubtless done differently. I must learn to accept things as they were and not be critical.

'We have a litter for you, my lady,' said the earl of Norfolk, assessing the size of my retinue and assuring himself that everything was being properly done.

'Thank you, my Lord Norfolk, for your care. I am grateful for your kindness.'

Blanche would not have bothered to thank the man, taking his concern as her due. I felt a sudden pang of home-sickness for my sister but I knew she'd be in a state of ecstasy planning gowns for her wedding to her Hapsburg prince and not missing me at all.

I was escorted to a curtained litter filled with cushions and furs for my comfort and with no further delays we journeyed slowly up the hill to the castle. As the litter bumped and jolted along the narrow track, the mules slipping on loose stones, I reflected that perhaps travelling by ship wasn't so dreadfully uncomfortable after all.

After brief prayers in the chapel where more thanks were given for our safe arrival, the castellan's wife led me and my women to our chamber. It was a remarkably comfortable little castle, every bit as fine as some of Philip's smaller hunting lodges. But I was certain it must have been built to defend the English coast from pirates rather then for the enjoyment of her princes. From the upper walls I could see all the way to Picardie and the road which led to Paris. Home was just a faint shadow on the horizon beyond the blue-grey waters of the Narrow Sea but I knew it was there and that gave me great comfort when later I lay trying to find sleep, disturbed by the alien sounds of an English night.

Next day as soon as we had broken our fast, we set off again.

'It's only a day to Canterbury, my lady,' said the earl of Norfolk who rode on one side of me. 'I think you will be glad to arrive. My wife tells me journeying can be exhausting for women. It's different for us men, we are born to the saddle. Some say we are wedded to it.'

I was accustomed to his manner of speech by now and could understand him provided I listened with all my attention. He was a big man who appeared ungainly on the ground with his huge girth and bowed legs, but once in the saddle looked as light as a feather, completely at one with his horse. I could easily imagine him riding off into battle.

'Does your wife rest at your *château*?' I enquired. 'Or will she be at Canterbury?'

'She will be there to greet you,' he said, smiling through his moustaches. 'She is a young filly like yourself, my lady. Nothing would keep her away from a wedding. To tell you the truth, marrying Lady Alix was a blessing. If we were on better terms I would have told his grace the same but he'll mellow now he's got you to keep him warm.'

A blush rose into my cheeks at his familiar talk of fillies and marital warmth. How strange the English were!

36

As we journeyed through this part of the king's realm, which I learned was called Kent, England began to work her charms on me. The air was soft and gentle, and the land undulated in little hills and valleys with small streams and deep woods of oak and beech. It looked a fair and prosperous country and I had yet to see a single bog.

We passed merchants and pilgrims making their way to Dover but when they saw our banners they moved quickly onto the crop fields to let us pass. We journeyed through small villages where huddles of dwellings had firewood piled high against the walls, and fenced gardens with hen coops and goose pens. The houses were very different from ours at home with huge thatched roofs covering the walls, coming right down almost to the ground.

'It keeps the rain out, so they tell me,' said Louis.

'Does it rain often?' I asked, looking up at the clear blue sky.

'Only when you command it, my lady,' said Humphrey de Bohun, bringing his horse up on my other side.

I thought the elegant earl of Hereford should learn to be less extravagant with his compliments but I was beginning to accept this new carefree way of talking. However, I was glad my future husband was not with us. Wives must be discreet, that much I knew from my mother's teachings, and while jealousy is a sentiment known well to all men, I thought an older husband might find it more easily than most.

At the first settlement, the villagers cheered as we passed by. There was a lot of shouting and laughing and words I couldn't understand. I longed to know what was being said but felt it would be impolite to ask so I kept silent.

'The English seem a happy people,' I remarked to Louis.

'It's no surprise,' he replied. 'Every village has an ale house and I've been told that when they're not toiling, the men spend their time drinking. They sit on benches with pots of ale even when they're supposed to be at prayer. It's no wonder our mother says they're an ungodly race.'

At the next village I searched for the ale house but could see nothing but ordinary dwellings and however much I stared at the people they seemed no more the worse for drink than our people in the alleyways of Paris.

'Do they not drink wine?' I asked Louis.

'Only the wealthy drink wine in England. The peasants consume ale. It is the drink of the Englishman.'

'His grace has a store of exceptionally fine wine from his lands in Gascony,' said the earl of Hereford. 'It's as smooth as anything your brother will have served in his palaces.'

Humphrey de Bohun seemed determined to make me realise how superior all things English were, from the weather to the wine to his elegant attire. He was just like my sister with her new-found love of Austria.

'At the top of this rise there is a view of our famous cathedral,' said the earl of Norfolk riding up to join us.

'Perhaps you have heard of it, my lady?' said the earl of Hereford, edging the earl of Norfolk's horse away from mine quite deliberately. 'The archbishop tells me the number of pilgrims who come to the shrine of Saint Thomas increases each year. It is a veritable industry and brings huge profits to the city as well as to the Church.

I'm sure your brother wishes he had a few bones of Saint Thomas to swell his coffers.'

'My brother has the most holy crown of thorns at Sainte-Chapelle,' I replied. 'He has no need of your saint's bones.'

That, I thought, would show the earl our family could not be outdone.

As we crested the hill we pulled up the horses to look out across the plain towards Canterbury. It was true the cathedral dominated the countryside around because everything else was very low and mean. I thought the great cathedral of Our Lady at Amiens was more magnificent.

'It's small,' I whispered to Louis.

The earl of Norfolk looked questioningly at my brother.

'My sister is not impressed,' said Louis with a laugh. 'She claims we have bigger in France.'

'The city of Lincoln has a cathedral with a spire taller than any in the whole of Christendom,' said the earl stiffly. 'Perhaps his grace will bring my lady to see it once you are wed.'

Sainte Vierge! I thought, how difficult it is to say anything. I laid a gloved hand on Lord Norfolk's arm.

'Forgive me, my Lord Norfolk. I sometimes speak without thinking. It is a habit of the very young and I should have outgrown such foolishness by now.'

I smiled at him as we rode down the hill and he seemed somewhat mollified.

As we passed under the gatehouse into the city it was like entering a prison. There was no way back to the girl I had once been and all I could hope for was a gaoler who would treat me kindly and help me do my duty well.

'Smile,' hissed Louis into my ear. 'You are about to meet your husband. Do you wish him to send you home?'

My eyes were misted by tears as I looked around me at the grey stone houses beyond the high city walls and the throngs of cheering people. Everywhere there was noise and commotion. Women waved ribbons and threw flowers, men tossed their bonnets in the air and dogs and little children ran alongside us in the mud. Then, out of the chaos ahead, winding their way through the narrow city streets, came a party of horsemen.

The palms of my hands felt moist, I swallowed hard and felt my heart begin to thump. I looked down. I looked up. I didn't know where to look for fear I might see this man I was to wed. I desperately wanted to discover what he was like yet was afraid in case I was disappointed. Once I'd seen him I could no longer spend my half-sleeping hours building imaginary pictures of my future husband. If a thing is known, it cannot be unknown.

There was no mistaking him. Even without the rich clothing and the gold circlet on his head, I would have known him for a king. This was not the withered old man of my nightmares, a dotard in the twilight of his life. This was a warrior. A straight-backed, powerful man who stared across the crowds with dark penetrating eyes. One eyelid drooped slightly, which gave him a dangerous look.

There was a milling about of horses as the two parties met. The king dismounted, not as I'd thought he might, heavy-bodied like a sack of corn thrown from a wagon, but lightly with the grace and ease of a youthful chevalier. He strode over to my mount and held out his hand. At close quarters I saw his hair and beard were threaded with silver.

'I bid you welcome, Cousin.'

His voice was strong, the accent strange and with a slight lisp which made him seem less frightening. My heart slowed down, for the unknown is always more frightening than what is real, and my betrothed was very, very real indeed.

He helped me dismount and I saw at once how much taller he was than me. He offered me his arm and together we walked to the welcoming party of worthy townsmen standing by the steps of what I was told was the hall for the guilds where the merchants met to talk business.

For what seemed like hours we listened patiently to an endless stream of addresses and letters of welcome, followed by choristers singing arias lauding my supposed virtues while small girls in white dresses danced for our delight. When at last I thought I couldn't stand upright a moment longer the king called a halt to the entertainments and I was allowed to retire to the lodgings which were mine for the night.

'Tomorrow we shall become acquainted,' said my betrothed looking across the top of my head and speaking to no-one in particular. 'I shall see you at the cathedral.'

And with that, he and his accompanying retinue were gone.

Tomorrow, I thought. Tomorrow everything would change. Tomorrow I would become a married woman. Tomorrow I would become a queen. I felt a shiver of what

I believed was excitement but of course it might just as well have been fear.

Once we were safely in our chamber my chests were unpacked and my clothing brushed and aired and hung on perches. My women, spurred on no doubt by thoughts of the attractive and, so I had discovered, as yet unwed earl of Hereford, were contriving last-minute improvements to their gowns. I thought it would be a poor man who would be seduced by a piece of crimson ribbon but, as Blanche had told me, I knew nothing of men. Perhaps Humphrey de Bohun was as susceptible to finery as any man.

As the long sleepless hours passed, I lay thinking of the next day. Tonight I shared a bed with one of my women. Tomorrow I would sleep with my husband. I wondered if he would be disappointed in me for I was no beauty. My breasts were too small and my elbows too sharp, and on the rare occasions I caught sight of my face in the curved surface of a bowl, I was disappointed by my plainness.

I squashed all thoughts of the conversation with my mother's friend as I didn't want to think of such things tonight. If I dwelt too much on the intimate part of this marriage I feared I might want to run home to my mother and sister and not get married at all. Yet I firmly believed this was the path God had chosen for me and it was my duty to tread it with a full and loving heart.

As I slipped over the borders of sleep, my last waking thought was - I wonder if he will like my hair?

Next morning I looked in the polished silver of my mirror and saw a different young woman, not myself but a radiant, beautiful bride. My women had bathed me in warm water scented with rose petals, dried me with fresh sheets and then rubbed sweet-smelling oils over my body till I tingled and shone. One garment at a time, they had dressed me in my finery: the delicate silk kirtle, the blue brocade gown - blue being the colour of the Virgin's robe - the green and gold surcote embroidered all over with seed pearls, the crimson mantle lined with yellow sindon, and the wide gold belt which was a wedding morning gift from my betrothed. On my feet they placed a pair of delicate silk slippers and on my unbound hair a golden coronet. I could not help but be pleased.

'Are you planning to spend the whole day gazing at your reflection?' Louis called from somewhere below. 'If you don't hurry, the celebrations will be over and your betrothed will have married someone else.'

My women giggled and with a rustling of gowns and swishing of mantles we swept out of the chamber and down the stairway. My wedding day was about to begin.

It was not many yards to the cathedral but as Louis and I walked on a carpet of flowers through the narrow street with a red cloth-of-gold canopy held high above our heads, it seemed like a hundred leagues. We entered the crowded square in front of the cathedral where I could see my betrothed and his friends gathered in the dark recess of the porch. Nearby was the archbishop who would perform the marriage. He was surrounded by bishops, their tall mitres dwarfing the white-robed boys in attendance. I climbed the steps with Louis's arm beneath my hand, our French party following behind like a trailing veil. No hill had ever seemed as steep as those six shallow steps.

The king and I stood beneath a golden canopy as the archbishop began the marriage ceremony. First, Louis passed me into the care of my betrothed and then stepped back leaving me alone with this stranger I was about to marry.

I glanced sideways and noted the furred collar and the richness of his robes. Through the open door I could see row upon row of English women waiting, pale and glittering in the pools of candlelight. Deeper into the nave would be the hundreds of invited barons, knights and other dignitaries, and beyond them the priests and the choristers who would sing the solemn Mass.

'I take thee Marguerite.' His voice was powerful, full of confidence. 'For fairer, for fouler, in sickness and in health.'

I heard the gentle whispering of the crowd below as if it came from a distant land. For me there was nothing and no-one other than this man who was pledging himself to me till death should part us.

'... and thereto I plight thee my troth.'

I held out my right hand. It was without a single tremor. The archbishop took the heavy gold ring from the silver salver held by the priest at his side and handed it to the king.

'With this ring I thee wed.'

He held it over my thumb.

'With my body I thee worship.'

He moved it to just above the next finger.

'In the name of the Father, and of the Son and of the Holy Ghost.'

He passed the ring over my other three fingers, finally sliding it onto my ring finger as he said, 'Amen.'

I was his wife.

Nothing could take this away from me. Henceforth and for evermore I would be his. There was nothing and no-one but God who could part us and I would not think about death on a day like today.

Now all that was left of the ceremony was the handing over of the deniers, the pieces of gold which symbolised the dower my husband was bestowing upon me. The details had been fought over tooth and nail by Philip's negotiators and the English envoys and I knew that somewhere there was a lengthy and precise inventory of every rent roll and manor, but it didn't detract from the spiritual element of the occasion, reducing it to a bargain of hard coin. It seemed to me these were, in truth, symbols of marital love and fidelity. My husband was promising to care for me and showing anyone who cared to look that he could do so.

Side by side we knelt on matching embroidered cushions at the altar rail as the nuptial Mass was celebrated, and side by side we processed slowly down the choir, through the nave and out into the sparkling autumn sunshine and a thousand cheering citizens of Canterbury. My husband waved at the crowds and I managed a small smile. Somehwere behind me I heard a familiar voice and out from the gloom of the cathedral came the little fat English earl, Lord de Lacy.

'Congratulations, your grace,' he said bowing to his king and then to me. 'May I be the first to welcome your wife.'

'Checking the inventory, de Lacy?' said my husband jovially. 'Is she what we agreed to?'

The two men laughed but I thought my husband's remarks unsuited to the occasion and remarkably unkind. We both knew our marriage was an arrangement but he didn't need to make it sound as if Lord de Lacy was a horse dealer and I, a sway-backed pony. He'd be wanting to examine my teeth next!

'It is good to see you again, my lady,' said Lord de Lacy. 'And I must say you look radiant.'

He was a kind man, a worthy man and would, I thought, be a good friend.

In the great hall, which was laid out for the wedding feast, we received the congratulations of my husband's family. The Lord Edward was magnificently clothed today. He outshone every other young man but appeared somewhat subdued in his father's presence. He welcomed me formally and then turned to introduce his sisters.

Only two of my husband's four daughters had come to see him wed, as the other two were married to men whose lands lay far across the seas in the Low Countries. It must be difficult for a daughter to see another woman sit where her mother had sat, receiving the adulation that her mother had received, but they both managed it well.

Joan, countess of Gloucester, was a tall middle-aged woman with the determined mouth and chin of her father. She was more than ten years older than me and had already been married twice. She eyed me coolly and, barely lowering her lashes let alone her head, made a slight curtsy and bade me welcome.

'I am pleased to make your acquaintance, Countess,' I said in a small voice. 'I trust we shall be friends.'

'His grace, my father, is only lately reconciled with my husband and me,' she said, looking sideways at the king. 'So I suspect friendship might be a trifle slow in coming, but I too hope our relationship will be cordial.'

I thought it a cold little speech but then she leaned forward and said, 'If it pleases you I shall bring my daughters to visit. I expect his grace, my father, will be off to war again soon and I doubt you will care to accompany him. Life is tedious under canvas and northern castles are horribly draughty. If you stay behind you may find yourself in need of company.'

She arched her delicate eyebrows enquiringly at me.

'Thank you, that would indeed be pleasant,' I replied in surprise. 'How many daughters do you have?'

'I have five: my three de Clare girls, Eleanor, Margaret and Elizabeth; little Mary, who is nearly two and a babe still in the cradle.' She turned to the young woman behind her. 'This is my sister, Mary. Doubtless you have heard she is a religious but I swear you wouldn't know it.'

Mary was dressed in a gown of the finest cloth and a distinctly fashionable headdress. I'd never before met a woman who had been veiled and yet went out into the world. I thought of the poor girls locked away in the abbey at Maubuisson with no vocation to give them strength, and was puzzled. How did Mary manage to acquire such freedom? Surely convent doors were locked? My thoughts must have shown plainly on my face.

'You are horrified to see me away from my devotions, are you not, my lady?' she said, smiling. 'You think I should be shut in the priory, praying on my knees for the happiness of your marriage to his grace, my father, instead of being here to welcome you into our family.'

I didn't know what to say at such outspokenness.

'I am pleased to make your acquaintance,' I said feebly, repeating the only words I could find. 'I trust we shall be friends.'

She looked at me out of her wide grey eyes.

'You are younger even than me, I think, and you may have need of friends. A royal life is a cold one for those who come late to the feast and there are many here who will not wish you well. But if you need a friend, I shall always be there.'

She had one eye on my husband who was conversing with Lord Henry and a man I took to be Lord Henry's brother, Thomas, earl of Lancaster.

'Thank you,' I replied, unsure of what to say to this supremely confident young woman. 'However I am well acquainted with a royal life.'

'Oh, I'm sure you are,' said Countess Joan, breaking into our conversation. 'But things are done differently here. Though what my sister knows of royal life I'm at a loss to imagine.'

With that she excused herself and drifted away down the hall. I was surprised at the spitefulness in her last comment. Perhaps the sisters were not as friendly as I'd first thought.

'You have a sister?' Mary enquired.

'Blanche, and she is dear to me.'

'That is a blessing. But I know what it is like to be imprisoned with a parcel of women. The life you will lead in our royal palaces will be little different to mine in the priory,' said Mary. 'And if you are troubled you may send for me. My brother and sisters often ask for my help when they are in debt or at odds with his grace, our father. I am called upon to be banker or peacemaker, whichever is required more urgently. And it's easy for me because I have no earthly husband to command me. I am my own mistress.'

I saw the trumpeters raise their instruments and knew the feast was about to begin. My husband came to my side and without a word took my arm and escorted me to our canopied chairs on the dais. My women seated me, twitching my mantle and smoothing my gown, before retreating to their places lower down the hall.

After my step-children's kind welcome I found my husband's continuing silence deeply worrying. We sat side by side throughout the wedding feast and if I'd put out my hand I could have touched him. But he didn't say a single word to me until he noticed I'd barely tasted any of the dishes put in front of me.

'I see you are not hungry, madam,' he said in a cool voice. 'Master Lovekyn will be sorely disappointed. He has spent many days and nights preparing this spread for your delight.'

What could I say? My appetite had vanished at the sight of the hundreds of guests, all the unknown English people who had come to stare at the plain little daughter of France their king had been forced to marry in order to buy peace for the realm. The feast was one fit for a king, or a queen, but when I tried to swallow, my throat was full of rocks. Each dish was more magnificent than the one before and everyone else ate greedily. I toyed with a slice of partridge dipped in sweet plum sauce but after a moment replaced the sticky meat onto my platter.

I saw curious looks from the younger women, unfriendly and pitying ones from their elders. The men paid me no attention whatsoever apart from an initial cursory glance, but men had never paid me much attention. I lowered my gaze and stared at my hands and the heavy gold band encircling my finger, a ring which bound me to this stranger beside me.

The king snapped his fingers and a man appeared at his shoulder to do his bidding. He disappeared only to reappear a few moments later carrying a large casket which the king indicated he should set on the table in front of me. I looked at the wooden box banded by silver with ivory inlay round its lid, wondering what it was.

'My wedding gift,' said the king.

Cautiously I lifted the lid and peered inside. The casket was full of wonders: gleaming emeralds and dazzling sapphires; a brooch of sparkling diamonds, a clasp fashioned from silver and decorated with topaz, stars of pearls and a narrow collar studded with deep-glowing rubies. I had never seen such a wonderful array of jewels.

'They belonged to your great-grandmother, the Infanta of Castile, mother of the blessed Saint Louis. I thought you would like them.'

His voice was soft.

I could find no words for my heart was too full to speak. Where there had been coldness, I felt warmth rushing in, flooding me with joy. He had thought of me and chosen a gift which he believed would please me.

I turned to him, my cheeks flushed and my eyes brimming with unshed tears.

'Oh, thank you, my lord' I whispered. 'They are beautiful, the most beautiful jewels I have ever seen.'

I picked out a brooch of sapphires which would have suited Blanche. I turned it over in my hand and wondered how my husband had possession of my great-grandmother's jewels. But of course, I had forgotten - his first wife was also an Infanta of Castile. They must have belonged to her.

'What of your daughters, my lord? Should these jewels not go to them?'

I had said the wrong thing. I knew it. At once his face lost that gentle expression and became shuttered and dark.

'If I had wanted to give them to my daughters,' he said in a hard clipped voice, 'I would have done so. I wished to give them to you but perhaps I was mistaken.'

He looked away. For a moment I had believed I was favoured but now I felt the full weight of his disapproval and ice slipped back into my heart. I was nothing to him and the gift was just a formality. It meant nothing either.

When the feasting was over and the dishes removed, the minstrels struck up their tunes and the gathering descended into an orgy of singing and dancing. I sat rigid with embarrassment, a small polite smile fixed on my face. No-one spoke to me, although my husband had conversations with his elderly friends. The men had wrinkled skin and grey hair and I was more than ever aware of the vast chasm of age between us.

I looked out across the hall at the young people

enjoying themselves and thought of my sister. Where was she? Was she thinking of me on my wedding day?

After what seemed a lifetime my husband rose to his feet, signalling for the music to cease. He held out his hand and helped me rise. Together we walked round the hall past the crowds of great men and their families. Some smiled knowingly, some sniggered, expecting a royal bedding to be as much fun as any other.

I'd been told that in England a couple would be teased unmercifully and a husband and wife who escaped into the marriage bed without some indignity being forced upon them were fortunate indeed. I couldn't imagine how anyone would dare to play a joke upon the king but I was nervous for myself. We walked up the stairway towards the chamber where we would spend our first night together but when we arrived at the door, my women appeared and whisked me away.

I endured another round of sponging and scenting and rubbing in of oils. Each part of my body was prepared for my husband's delight and I had to be as perfect as I could be. Pins were removed and my hair combed out so that it flowed over my shoulders. As I fingered the fine dun-coloured strands covering my breasts I wished for the hundredth time they could have been golden.

Once my women had me suitably clothed in the soft silk nightgown, I fastened a pale green mantle round my shoulders, slid my feet into a pair of fragile satin slippers and walked from my privy chamber into the bedchamber beyond. My women followed, smothering their giggles as they eyed the king's attendants.

My husband looked equally as frightening in his

nightgown and crimson bed-robe as he had in his wedding finery. His hair and beard had been neatly combed and I was glad to see he wasn't wearing his boots. But I was still terrified.

He took my hand and we knelt at the foot of the bed. The elderly bishop, raised his hands and there was silence in the chamber. Interminable prayers were said, our union was blessed and holy water sprinkled over the fine silk sheets where we would lie. Everything was done, which could be done by others, to ensure that our bedding would be fruitful.

We stood up and one of my women undid the gold clasp and helped me off with my mantle and slippers. In just my nightshift and holding my husband's hand, I mounted the steps and climbed between the sheets. He walked round the other side, handed his bed-robe to his valet and climbed in beside me. The mattress dipped and the bed ropes creaked at his heavy weight. As the curtains were drawn round the bed, I heard the first bawdy joke followed by gales of laughter. The king twitched the curtains aside and roared at the top of his voice. There was more laughter, more vulgar comments, a running of feet and a muddle of girlish screams disappearing into the distance. I heard the door bang shut and at last there was silence.

I looked resolutely at the folds of curtain pulled across the sides of the bed: green and bronze, darkest brown, almost black in the depths, heavy and ornate and, I was certain, exceedingly costly. Thick enough to keep out night-time draughts and weighty enough to keep whatever passed between us hidden within. I could hear my husband's breathing and my own heart beating.

I had known this moment would come and thought I was prepared but now it had arrived all I wanted was more time, more moments of waiting. I didn't want to be a wife. If my husband found me displeasing I would have nothing more to hope for. I would have to live the rest of my life knowing I had failed at the one task I had set myself - to please my husband and do my duty by him.

After a moment, when nothing was said, my husband sighed and swept back the curtains on his side of the bed. He heaved himself out and stood there with his hand out.

'Come!'

Memories of my mother's tale of her wedding night flooded into my mind and I sat frozen with fear.

My husband leaned closer and I shrank back against the pillows.

'Come, my lady,' he said gently. 'If we are to be husband and wife I think we shall be easier with each other if we are better acquainted. Let us sit by the fire with a cup of wine and talk.'

I stared at him, disbelieving.

'Don't you ...,' I said falteringly. 'Don't you wish to ...?'

'Wish what? To ravish you before you have even called me husband? No, my lady, I do not.'

He looked at me impatiently.

'Come on. Up out of there. Put on your mantle, it's not as warm in here as I would like.'

With that, he took the poker and stirred the embers in the hearth into life. Flames licked up round the charred logs and shadows danced about the room. I slid silently from the bed, pulled the mantle over my shoulders and pattered across the floor. As I settled myself in a chair on one side of the fire, I looked up at him. He was regarding me sombrely.

'You have nothing on your feet.'

'I couldn't find my slippers.'

He crossed to the bed and returned carrying them in his hands. He knelt down at my feet and, holding my ankles, eased first one foot and then the other into the delicate little frivolities.

'Thank you,' I whispered.

He looked up from where he knelt. His eyes were shadowed. The hem of my nightgown brushed the back of his hand where he still held my ankle and I felt the heat of his fingers as a shiver crept slowly up my bare leg.

'I shall fetch you some wine,' he said abruptly, rising to his feet. 'No, don't protest. You will feel better with some drink. And some food too. I noticed you ate little and I know just how hungry young maidens can be.'

As he fetched the wine and a platter of sliced capon from the side table, I thought - of course, he is the father of grown-up daughters. I also wondered how many other young maidens he had entertained in his chamber since his wife's death.

The wine was fierce and burned my throat.

'What shall I call you?' he said.

'What would you wish to call me, my lord?' I replied in a low voice. 'My given name is Marguerite but perhaps you would prefer to call me wife.'

'Marguerite,' he mused. 'The English daisy, the little French pearl. How apt.'

'*Monseigneur*?'

'Nothing,' he said. 'The word wife has a chilly ring about

it but that is what you are, are you not? You are my wife. How strange that sounds. I had not thought to say that word again but kings have their duties the same as other men.'

'My lord?'

'I have but one son, my lady. Just one and it is not enough.'

He sounded angry but looked sad.

'So many little boys but just the one grown to manhood. What use is a man who cannot father and keep living sons? Kingdoms fall apart without strong men to guide them and if anything should happen to Ned, which pray God it will not, men must know there is another son of mine to take the throne.'

I listened while he despaired, knowing he had no need of me other than to bear him sons. It was ever thus. As my mother had explained to Blanche and me countless times, a wife's first duty was to bear sons for her husband.

I put out my hand and touched his with the tips of my fingers.

'I am certain God will bless us with many children,' I said. 'I shall pray for a healthy son.'

He looked at me and smiled sadly.

'You are a good girl.' He patted my hand. 'Perhaps we shall make shift together in some way or other. Now, you must distract me from these dismal thoughts. Tell me of your life before you came here. What of your girlhood?'

What a strange question for a new husband to put to a wife but the English were full of surprises.

'I had a very ordinary girlhood, my lord. I was raised with my sister, Blanche. We did the things that all girls do and learned the things that all girls must. But they would be of no interest to you, my lord. They were merely women's things.'

'Ah,' he said. 'Women's things. How well I remember those.'

There was silence for a minute then he roused himself once more to speak to me.

'Are you pleased to be here?'

'I am surprised.'

I spoke without thinking and then wished I had not.

'Surprised? In what way, surprised?'

'I thought your grace would prefer to marry my sister,' I said in a low voice.

He looked at me curiously.

'And why would I prefer to marry your sister?'

'She is beautiful, my lord.'

'And you think, given the choice, I would have chosen her?'

'Most men made much of her.'

'And ignored you?'

'I don't think anybody noticed me but I am very small and very plain.'

'And do you think your sister, with all her beauty, would have made me a good wife?'

'Oh, I am sure she would. I love my sister dearly and she will be a good wife to her husband whoever he may be.'

He regarded me steadily while I wished the conversation ended.

'Do you imagine kings are ignorant of the charms of the girls who are paraded before them?'

'I don't know, my lord.'

'My brother, God rest his soul, told me everything

about the sisters of the king of France. He had observed them closely and spoken with their mother and their brother's wife, women who knew them well. He told me of the beautiful, delightful Blanche who could charm birds from the trees and a saint from the path of chastity; and he spoke of her quieter, more studious older sister, the kindly child who cared for others before herself. He told me of the jealous tantrums and selfish moods of the one and the generous nature and dogged determination of the other. He told me how the younger practised petty cruelties upon her sister and how that sister constantly turned the other cheek.'

'It was not like that,' I protested. 'He was mistaken. Blanche is truly good.'

'Hush,' said my husband. 'He was merely doing his duty. Peace was the requirement for both your brother and for me and I was not given the choice. And I am glad I was not, for men are vain and like to be admired as much as women do and I might have been tempted to choose your sister. Think how much envy there would have been from others to see me master of such a beautiful and desirable young woman, and the envy of princes is not something to be set aside lightly.'

I felt my spirits sink further. For all his kind protestations, I knew he would have taken Blanche rather then me.

He leaned back in his chair and looked at me thoughtfully.

'You are very young.' His voice was slightly slurred.

'I am nineteen.'

'Yes. But very young. Very untouched. Has your mother told you of what will happen between us?'

I blushed to the roots of my hair and lowered my face so that it was hidden from him.

'Yes,' I whispered.

He paused for a moment, then stood up and came behind me. I sat there, the cup of wine, almost finished, clutched in my hands. I could feel his eyes on my nightgown, where the neckline was cut low. I could feel him savouring the curve of my neck, the outline of my small breasts, the length of my legs pressed against the silk and I trembled even though it wasn't cold.

'Come to bed,' he said, his voice thick with a hint of what could have been desire or simply hunger for a woman. 'We must do our duty and make a prince for England.'

I awoke. He lay beside me, his face younger in sleep. One arm was cast loosely above his head, his hand laid against his cheek. The lines which surrounded his eyes were smoothed away and his mouth was softer. Above all he looked more vulnerable and less of a king.

I thought of the kisses he had pressed on me in the darkness, of the invasiveness of his lips and his tongue, the roughness of his beard and felt a stir of something deep within me. He had been extremely gentle, handling me like a piece of delicate finery as if unable to believe he had something so fragile within his grasp. When he lay on me it was with care and he had taken me with a tenderness I had not expected. It had been painful but he had held me close and stroked my hair until the tears subsided. Afterwards he had looked at me and smiled, his eyes bright and his teeth white in the half-light.

'Now I shall call you wife,' he had said.

I flushed to remember what we had done but reminded myself that our bodies were God-given and if God intended a man and a woman to come together like this then it was no sin.

'What are you thinking, wife?'

I started. I hadn't known he was awake.

'I was thanking God,' I replied quickly.

'I should thank your husband also for he is closer at hand.'

'Thank you, husband,' I said quietly.

He laughed and pushed himself out of bed.

'I shall send your women to you,' he said. 'And I shall see you later. Today we have a tournament for everyone's enjoyment and I trust it will amuse you.'

With that he let the curtains drop back and I heard him call briskly for his attendants. I lay back in the comfort of the bed, breathing in the unaccustomed stale warm smell of a man. It was hard to imagine that from now on, whenever he wished, I would share a bed with this large hairy man I called husband.

My women arrived, agog with curiosity. I could see they wanted to know the answers to a thousand questions they dared not ask. If I had been one of their own I would have been plagued until I'd told all: What was it like? Did my husband acquit himself well? And how often? But because I was who I was, and my husband was who he was, they dared not open their mouths. However their eyes betrayed them, sliding sideways to gaze at the bed, greedily noting every rumple of the sheets and displacement of the pillows. I would have liked to rub their prying noses into the depths of the marriage bed until they cried out for mercy but that would have been an unworthy act for the wife of a king.

As I stood naked in the privy chamber, they sponged me and poured warm water over my shoulders, chattering away, and all the while I knew they wanted to touch my skin as he had, smoothing his hard fingers over the length of me. The younger girls collected up my discarded nightgown and as the drying sheet was wrapped around me, I heard one of them whispering to her friend. I blanched at her words and remembered my mother's warning – "keep your women in order for it is the mark of a lazy mistress if her maids gossip and misbehave, and how can your husband be expected to rule his subjects if you cannot rule your women."

I turned and looked at the two girls. They couldn't have been more than thirteen and had been picked by my mother for their good families and suitable connections.

'I would like you to repeat what you just said.' My voice was steady.

They stood there, their mouths opening and closing like little fishes. They hadn't realised they could be overheard.

'Come along, we are waiting.'

'We were just saying,' said the braver of the two.

'Yes?'

'We didn't say it ourselves, it was what we heard.'

'Yes,' said her more timid friend. 'We heard someone.'

'And what did you hear? What was said?'

They looked one to the other, both desperately trying to avoid what they knew was coming.

'Hurry up,' I said. 'What did you hear?'

The taller one, the braver one, dropped her head and muttered a few words.

'If you can't speak up perhaps a touch of the rod will help,' I said sharply.

I had no desire to beat my women but I knew they must be disciplined or any authority I had would slide away as butter slides from the platter when the day is warm.

'One of the king's men said it.'

'Yes?'

'He said ...'

She looked desperately from side to side, seeking a way out but there was no escape.

'He said the king had bought a pig in a poke.'

'And he said, some hope there was for begetting anything with a poke from a grey-beard,' the other one rattled off quickly as if the faster she spoke the less the awfulness of what was to come.

I sighed. It was worse than I'd thought and I wasn't sure what to do. I could certainly keep order in my own household but should I tell the king what was being said by one of his own servants? Then I had the uncomfortable thought that perhaps it was not lowly servant's gutter talk but the gossip of one of the king's so-called friends.

The older women looked at me approvingly as I gave orders for the girls to be beaten and sent to spend the day on their knees. I hoped prayer would bring them to their senses and certainly to miss the tournament would be punishment in itself.

It was the very best place to be, seated high above the lists. There were thousands of people crammed into the arena and the scene was awash with golds and blues and silvers and crimsons. At each end of the grassy course were gaily coloured tents with flags flying from their pinnacles, and beside them, dozens of gorgeously arrayed knights and their horses. The noise was tremendous.

I sat beside by husband under the canopy in the royal pavilion and was very glad of the cushions at my back because the day was going to be a long one. Louis, seated on the king's other side, was conversing happily with an elderly grizzled man about the respective merits of the contestants.

I touched my husband's arm.

'My lord, who is my brother talking to?'

The king looked to see and then smiled.

'The earl of Surrey, John de Warenne. An old friend and one of my best commanders, though we've had our difficulties over the years. A bit long in the tooth these days, to tell you the truth, but he keeps a good stable.'

He patted my hand companionably.

'It is going to be a fine display for you today, my lady, and we have a weighty purse for the winner. There's Lord de Lacy whom you already know.'

I gazed at the noble earl hoisting himself into the saddle, ably assisted by his squire. His opponent looked an insignificant knight. The herald announced the combatants and at a signal the two men thundered towards each other. I closed my eyes and missed the moment when the earl tipped the younger man off his mount onto the grass. The crowd howled its approval. Lord de Lacy was clearly popular.

'Why do you close your eyes?'

The question came from behind my shoulder as my husband's son slipped into his seat beside me.

'Sorry, I should have greeted you properly, lady mother, but the sight of you with your eyes screwed up reminded me of my sister, Elizabeth.'

His father seemed to have no objection to him calling me lady mother and he really was a very charming boy.

'I don't like seeing them come together,' I said, smiling. 'I hate to see a man hurt.'

'There's not much damage done, not since his grace, my father, banned the use of pointed lances. He was losing too many good knights. The older men complain the fun's gone out of the sport. They liked the old ways when men got killed.'

'Are you not taking part?'

He frowned.

'His grace, my father, prefers me not to fight. He says the people cannot afford to lose me. So I have no skill.'

How odd! Every boy I knew loved to joust. Fighting was what turned boys into men.

'Where is your sister Elizabeth?' I asked in a low voice. 'His grace doesn't care to talk about his daughters.'

'I'm not surprised. A couple of years ago he was so angry with her he seized her by the hair and shook her like a pup. Then he threw her coronet into the fire saying she was not worthy to wear it. Elizabeth thought he was going to strangle her.'

'*Sainte Vierge*! What had she done?'

'Refused to accompany her husband, back to Holland after their wedding. She said Jan was a miserable little runt and she wanted to stay in England. His grace shouted she would do as she was told or she was no daughter of his. Everybody heard them. It was a spectacular row.'

'How old was she?'

'Fourteen. I advised a fine display of tears but it didn't work and in the end she had to go and live with Jan. She should have learned from Mary who always gets her own way.'

'Poor girl,' I said, feeling sorry for this unknown step-daughter of mine.

'She was foolish. She chose exactly the wrong moment because he was already in a fury over our sister, Joan.'

'The countess of Gloucester, yes, I remember. She paid her respects yesterday at the wedding feast.'

'Joan pays no attention to his grace and it annoys him immensely.'

At that moment there was another roar from the crowd and I looked up to see Humphrey de Bohun riding his great black horse slowly up the side of the course towards our pavilion. He looked very handsome dressed in azure and gold.

My husband leaned towards me and spoke softly. 'I think, my lady, you have a champion. It seems the earl of Hereford would care to fight under your colours.'

I had no desire to anger my husband by favouring another man but he appeared happy enough at the recognition of his wife. I knew what I was supposed to do and fumbled in my sleeve for a piece of pale green silk to fix to the earl's lance.

'Thank you fair lady.' Humphrey de Bohun bowed his head to acknowledge the favour then looked straight at me with his bright blue eyes before cantering away to the end of the course.

My husband shifted to get himself comfortable before inclining his head and whispering in my ear.

'He is a pretty young man, is he not, wife? I trust you do not have a penchant for pretty young men.'

He was amused, not angry, so I smiled politely.

'No, my lord, I prefer men with more maturity.'

It was clearly the right thing to say as he leaned back with a satisfied smile.

I touched my husband's arm.

'Does the earl of Gloucester not fight, my lord?'

'Hardly, he's been in his grave four years. I think it would take more than a summons from you for Red Gilbert to rise up and fight again.'

'Oh, but I thought ... the Lady Joan, is she not his countess? I thought her husband ...'

I stopped hastily. His face was darkening but I didn't know what I'd said to displease him.

'I do not care to discuss my daughter's so-called husband with anyone and if you value your position in this family, madam, you would do well to remember that. No bastard will ever win my approval and no child of his will cross my threshold. Do I make myself clear?'

I nodded dumbly. He turned his back and began talking to Louis. I sat numb with pain, bewildered by his lightening changes of mood. One moment he was as tender as springtime, the next he was in a fury. I would have to pray for patience and keep a watch on my tongue and remember he was my master in all things.

I did not dare question my stepson further about his

sisters in case my husband overheard. Instead I spent the rest of the morning staring at the competitors and trying to enjoy myself. This was a very splendid occasion and a celebration for my marriage. So why did I feel miserable?

The day dragged on with one exhausting event after the other. I changed my gown twice in order to appear an ornament to my husband's position and by the time the last song was sung and the minstrels finally laid aside their instruments, my feet were sore and my back ached. I had spoken with so many people, I could not remember one from the other and the smile on my face felt as though it was fixed on by nails. All I wanted was to be alone with my husband.

I was weary and only too glad to be dressed by my women ready for the night. My two young penitents were red-eyed and silent as they went about their duties and I noticed there was a more respectful attitude towards me by all the younger women. The same ritual was followed as the night before and after my women had followed me into the bedchamber and I'd said my prayers they put me between the sheets and scuttled out. My husband came in with just one attendant. I wondered if he would wish to sit and talk as we had the previous night or if he was as impatient as I was to close the curtains. Despite myself I could not help but feel a pleasurable shiver of anticipation for the feel of his long hard body on mine.

'I am tired,' he said crossly, handing his robe to his valet and clambering up the steps into the bed.

The curtains were drawn and we lay in silence. After

a little while he sighed deeply and turned on his side. In the gloom I could see lines of tiredness on his face and my heart filled with pity for him. I knew the coldness he had shown earlier today was my fault and I was determined to do better.

'Duty before pleasure,' he said wearily. 'I desire sleep like a starving man desires a crust of bread but the needs of kingship come first. Open your legs, my lady.'

Then without more ado he drew up my nightgown and hoisted himself on top of me. He was impatient and it hurt but when I cried out and tried to twist away he pinned me closer to the bed and covered my mouth with his.

'Pray for a son, wife,' he said as he rolled off me.

A few moments later he was fast asleep. I lay there, stunned by the roughness of his handling. This man, who the night before had professed to want a willing bed partner, tonight had not seemed to care if I was willing or not.

Tears seeped from under my closed eyelids as I lay weeping in silence. After a while I realised I was feeling sorry for myself which was a sin. My thoughts and concerns should be for my husband for my duty was to please him. My feelings were unimportant. I whispered in the dark to Our Blessed Lady to help me do better.

Next morning I woke bleary-eyed and heavy-hearted. My husband had risen early leaving me to sleep. I knew that he had matters of business to attend to each day and would spend time before Mass closeted with his councillors. This was a world which did not touch me. My mother had made it clear that wives should not meddle.

Husbands did not like it. I thought of Philip's injunctions for me to influence my husband for the advantage of my French family and realised how impossible this would be. But I was determined to be pleasant to all the elderly men who occupied our pavilion however tedious they might be and I would be brave and talk with some of the wives and daughters.

I found the earl of Surrey waiting for my husband.

'My Lord Surrey,' I said, speaking clearly for I'd been told the elderly John de Warrene was somewhat deaf. 'I have a question to ask which I've been told only you can answer.'

He preened himself as men do when made to feel important.

'My lady, I will do my best. What is it you wish to know?'

'Scotland,' I said. 'I do not understand. They say my husband will go campaigning there. But why? I understood he had brought peace. I know they don't have a king any more and that my husband has their great seal. So why would he need to campaign there?'

He regarded me with interest, clearly deliberating how much I needed to know about what was essentially men's business.

'If you read *The History of the Kings of Britain* you will see the book is quite clear on the matter and the lawyers agree. Scotland is an inferior country, merely a limb of the body, subservient to England.'

'So the Scots are my husband's vassals?'

'Yes, but John Balliol, their king, didn't behave as a vassal ought. Made an alliance with your brother. We had no alternative but to march in.'

'I am sorry, my Lord Surrey, but was it not an aggression to march in?'

'Aggression? Never! His grace was entirely within his rights. If your vassal don't behave, you teach him a lesson. And what a lesson it was! Balliol packed off to the Tower and his grace made plain to the others what would happen.'

'And what was that?'

He bellowed with laughter. 'No more king of the Scots! We carried off their sacred stone from the abbey at Scone. That showed them we meant business. We took their keys and demanded fealty. We left our men in their halls to see they obeyed and his grace did me the honour of putting the great seal of Scotland in my hands. Said it was a good day's business for him, getting rid of a turd!'

'If peace was restored then why is his grace campaigning?' This was becoming more and more muddling.

'Ah, my lady, there's always a Scotsman who don't know when he's beat. First that young fool Bruce, the lord of Annadale's son, and that sly bishop, Wishart. Then that brigand Wallace pops up from nowhere. Slaughtered my men at Stirling. Corpses everywhere! I shan't tell you what he did to my treasurer, Cressingham. The man was dead, but it was a heathen act.' A single tear ran down the earl's cheek and disappeared into his whiskery beard. 'You women have no idea what war is like.'

He was clearly distressed and I wished I hadn't asked. I tried not to think what might have happened to *Messire* Cressingham.

'Got the better of them the next season. Routed them at Falkirk, chased them across the country. Took Bruce's castles but the crafty bugger slipped the net. We'll get him though, never you fear, and we'll get that churl, Wallace too. Skulking round Paris, I hear, paying court to your brother. I hope I live long enough to see him hang in chains.'

I didn't wish to be drawn into discussions about my brother's perfidy and his support for these disobedient Scots so I thanked the earl and wished him good luck for the joust. I was concerned because my marriage was meant to create good relations between our two countries but it seemed that my brother was proving deceitful. I hoped my husband wouldn't blame me for my brother's sins. If Philip consorted with my husband's enemies it would be impossible to help my family.

I turned to find Ned slouching on a cushion looking downcast. 'Is something the matter?' I enquired.

'I have offended his grace, my father, again. That's the third time this week.'

'Is there anything I can do?'

He laughed ruefully. 'Not unless you can change his opinion of me. It seems I choose the wrong company.'

He scuffed his boots in the dust of the platform and stuck out his bottom lip. He reminded me of Blanche. How ridiculous for a young English lord to remind me of my sister but they both had the same rebellious look when they failed to get their own way.

'What do you do which so displeases his grace?'

'He doesn't like my friends. He says they're low-born and I spend too much time being idle and amusing myself. He says being king is a serious business. But I like my friends and don't see why he should dictate what I do.'

Poor boy, I thought.

'Does his grace not order your household?'

'Oh yes, he decides who will be appointed. I like many of them but I have other friends and he doesn't approve of them at all, says they are unsuitable. He wants me to be more like Cousin Thomas. And now he's threatening to cut off my income.'

I knew I was on difficult ground. I wanted to be kind to Ned for he was a pleasant boy and my stepson, part of my new family, but I was fearful of angering my husband who clearly had an awkward relationship with Ned as well as with his daughters.

'Earl Thomas seems pleasant.' Truthfully I knew nothing of the Lancaster brothers but certainly Lord Henry had seemed friendly.

'Thomas would like to be ruler of all England,' Ned said bluntly, 'not just his own domains.'

I drew a sharp breath. This was close to treason.

'I trust he doesn't say such things aloud.'

'No, but he thinks them. When we were younger he said he'd never bend his knee to me because I was a fool.'

'He didn't mean it. Boys often say silly things in the heat of a quarrel.'

'He was no child when he said it and he meant every word.'

I felt a frisson of fear and remembered hearing someone talk of the goose which walks over your grave in time of danger. I touched the back of my neck and whispered a silent prayer.

3

AUTUMN 1299

A few days later we left Canterbury to journey to a place called the Island of Thorns where we would stay before my husband and I set off on a progress to the north. To facilitate his campaigning in Scotland my husband had moved his officials to the city of York in the northern part of his realm. My heart sank at the thought. My women said the people there had tails beneath their tunics and spoke in a foreign tongue. I didn't believe them but the thought was very frightening.

Now the marriage celebrations were over I knew my life would be different. My husband and I would no longer share the same rooms. I would have my own household and my own apartments and my husband would visit me whenever he had a mind. This, I had been assured by my mother, was usual. Husbands and wives never shared apartments and royal women led separate lives. If a man found his wife pleasing he would seek her out during the day but if she was not to his liking he merely used her each night until she conceived a child. Then he would not visit her again until after the child was born and she was once more ready to receive his attentions.

Today would be the last day we would be together and it was clear to me that, as far as my husband was concerned, I had only one purpose - to bear him a son. There was to be no loving companionship or happy family life, no role as a helpmeet or confidante. I was not to be his intimate friend, merely a vessel for the carrying of another child.

I wanted to weep in my disappointment, for I knew I had failed. He had been forced to marry me and now that he had met me, he was no longer interested. My role was to carry a son, nothing more. I wished I was beautiful and accomplished, then perhaps he would want me with him. But what man would want a small plain insignificant young woman like me?

I had again fallen into the sin of self-pity.

The news that I was to have men in my household who had previously served my husband's first wife distressed me greatly. Of course I was being foolish. If I had bothered to raise my nose out of the trough of misery into which I had fallen, it would have been obvious. Of course I needed experienced people to help me and what better men could there be than those who had served the last queen. What seemed like a slap across my face was in fact a kindness, but it took me a long time to realise the care my husband had taken in making these arrangements.

He also appointed several English women to my chamber, women I didn't know and thought I might not like but I remembered my mother's words and tried to bear this burden with good grace.

As we rode out of the city, dressed in our regal finery, the crowds cheered calling out names I couldn't understand. I tried hard but in the end was defeated.

'What do they say, my lord?' I asked, tentatively tying to make some conversation.

He laughed, in high good humour now the merrymaking was over and he could get back to the life he'd had before I interrupted it.

'They are calling you a French pearl, a treasure. It seems they have decided to like you.'

I blushed, touched by the unexpected compliment. He rarely spoke to me and never with terms of endearment and I was becoming used to his rather brusque manner. I tried not to mind but my dreams of how we would be were fading fast in the face of the bleak, loveless reality of my marriage.

It was pleasant to be out of the stuffy rooms and on the road again in the clear morning air of early autumn. If it hadn't been for my feelings of failure I might have enjoyed the journey.

'Will you like being a French pearl?' my husband asked as we passed round a small copse of trees and out of sight of the walls of Canterbury.

'If it pleases you, my lord, I shall like it very much.'

'Oh yes, it pleases me,' he said. 'Eleanor was inordinately fond of pearls and I think the name suits you, my little French pearl.'

With that he threw his head back and laughed.

His humour had been better these past few days, but the nights were difficult for me. He was more considerate than he'd been that second night but he still didn't speak to me other than to order my compliance in our bed. Just once he stroked my cheek, running his fingers gently over my warm skin, and one early morning, with the cobwebs of sleep still in his eyes, he woke and gathered me to him in a wordless embrace. But every time I thought I was beginning to know him, he would retreat into a mood of indifference. He was unlike any man I had ever met and I was nervous of his moods and his temper. I was also very careful not to talk of his children as that seemed to be a subject which caused him particular annoyance. And I never mentioned his first wife.

I discovered later that on the day we left Canterbury he had issued a call for a mustering of troops at York in eight weeks time. This was to be the start of the next campaign against the Scots.

'I shall be leaving you, my lady,' he said formally. 'I must do battle again. This time, God willing, I shall conquer the Scots for good.'

'But it will be winter,' I cried in dismay. 'Surely, my lord, you cannot fight in the snow?'

My women said Scotland was known to be a harsh and barren land where snow fell from Michaelmas through to midsummer and beyond.

He laughed, brushing aside my concerns.

'I conquered the Welsh in the snow. Did you not know that, my lady? I shall do the same to the Scots. My army will chase them from the walls of Stirling and show them who is master. They are mistaken if they think I shall stand for their petty rebellions. Their so-called king is safely in the hands of His Holiness and now they are leaderless they *will* submit to me. With the army I plan to take this winter we shall defeat them and by next spring, all Scotland will be ours again.'

He looked at me seriously. 'I trust, my lady, that by the time I leave you at York, you will be carrying my child.'

'I trust so too, my lord,' I said. 'I pray every night for a son.'

Three days later we approached the Island of Thorns over a narrow wooden bridge spanning a muddy little stream.

'The Tyburn,' said my husband carelessly as we clattered across the planks. 'The Confessor chose this site to build his church, though, God's bones, I could have chosen many a better one. It is convenient for the river crossing and not far from the city but the ground is marshy.'

The Confessor was the English king made saint who ruled this land before the Conqueror snatched the crown. I knew all about him and his great piety as he was well remembered. My grandmother had told me he was so saintly he refused to lie with his wife, denying himself the pleasures of the flesh. "I wonder what his queen thought of that?" she had whispered in my ear. I missed my grandmother as I missed my mother and my sister and my home.

'And that,' said my husband, indicating the magnificent church ahead of us, 'is where my father chose to empty his treasury. The abbey church of Saint Peter. He spent most of his life and most of the Crown's money rebuilding it.'

'Is the Confessor buried there?' I asked.

'Yes. In the most beautiful shrine you have ever seen. It glitters like the morning sun.'

I looked at this church which my father-in-law, whom I would never know, had built.

'It's beautiful,' I said.

It was indeed. With its soaring walls, its arches, its great north window and its flying buttresses, it was a marvel, equal to anything I had seen at home. But it was not the only building on the island. Apart from the cluster of little thatched cottages by the bridge, there were two large halls built closer to the river and what looked like a palace which was yet unfinished.

Beyond the great abbey church were buildings where the community of brothers lived and worked and behind those the abbey gardens, neatly laid out and surrounded by high stone walls. There was also a tiny church hiding in the shadow of the abbey.

'What is that?' I enquired, pointing at the humble little building.

'The church of Saint Margaret,' replied my husband shortly. 'The workmen pray there.'

'I like it,' I said, smiling. 'It is my saint's name.'

My husband looked up in surprise.

'So it is. I had not thought.'

We rode towards the half-finished palace where dozens of men covered in mud and dust were hoisting great blocks of pale stone onto walls which were already dizzyingly high. Some parts of this maze of buildings seemed to be perfect, with cloisters and a galleried hall complete with great arched windows, but elsewhere I could see walls no higher than a man's knee and charred timbers, scorched stones and shattered tiles lying around in filthy heaps.

'This was my father's great palace of Westminster. That's what they call this place – the West Minster. As you see parts of the palace burned down. I am sorry, madam, I cannot offer you the luxury you have doubtless been used to, but as my wife you must go where I go.'

I reassured him that wherever he chose to lay his head would be sufficient for me but he wasn't listening.

'When we have more time I will show you the chapel I am building here. It will be dedicated to Saint Stephen and will outshine your brother's Sainte-Chapelle.'

He looked well pleased as he said it and I realised it mattered greatly to him that his building would be more magnificent than my brother's. We inspected the outside of the new palace and then my husband took me down to the muddy foreshore behind the halls.

We sat on our mounts looking out across the slow-flowing waters to the far bank where I could see nothing but mud and reeds and tussocks of marsh grass. There was a gap in the rushes where horses gained access to the ford but I couldn't see where the road went as it was masked by the grey sedge.

'When the tide is right and the river low you can take a horse across here, but you'll need to tuck up your skirts or you'll get wet.'

He chuckled at some pleasing memory then wiped the smile from his face. He was like an autumn day, one minute sunny, the next covered in cloud anticipating rain. He turned his horse and I followed. Together we left the Island of Thorns, crossing back over the bridge, making for a large building, half-hidden behind stone walls. The gate was guarded by several of my husband's men so I presumed this would be where we would rest.

'This is where I lodge when I am at Westminster,' said my husband. 'It belongs to my friend Thomas de Corbridge, archbishop of York. But he never comes here so he is happy for his king to borrow it.'

'How kind of him.'

'Kind? It isn't kind. It is his duty. Those dammed clerics in their own little worlds have too much money and too much power. All they do is to make trouble.'

Every conversation was like stepping across a meadow of thistles. I never knew what to say which would not annoy him. I thought perhaps I'd best be silent.

That same night, our first in the archbishop's house, he seemed returned to the husband of our wedding night. Instead of the perfunctory coupling of the past week he wanted to engage me in conversation as we lay in the semi-darkness, hidden behind the thick curtains.

'You will come with me to York.'

This was not a question but a command.

'I will follow you wherever you wish, my lord. I am your wife and desire to serve you well.'

He looked at me closely as if trying to understand meanings beyond my words. He hadn't touched me since he'd got into my bed, but was lying on his side looking at me, frowning slightly. I lay as still as possible not sure what he wanted of me and fearful of saying the wrong thing.

He sighed. 'A husband wishes for a dutiful wife, my dear, but he also wishes for one who is loving, one who cares for him as a man.'

'Am I not loving?' I asked anxiously. 'I try to be. I'm sorry if I have failed. I will try harder.'

He reached out and touched my face with his fingers, gently stroking my cheek. He pulled off my night cap and then slowly un-plaited my hair so that it fell across the pillows. With the utmost care he wound his fingers into the strands pushing them away from my face. Leaning across, he planted a gentle kiss on my lips, brushing them with his own. His face was only inches from mine and I could feel the warmth of his breath. With one of his hands, he lifted the hem of my nightgown and began to stroke my belly and my legs.

'Take it off,' he whispered into my ear. 'Then I can see all of you.'

I sat up, undid the ribbons and struggled out of the silk folds. I lay down again and waited, wondering if he found my nakedness pleasing to him. He lay watching me, idly stroking my breasts.

'Your skin is beautiful,' he said, running one finger up to the tender spot at the base of my neck. 'It is soft and smooth like velvet, and pale as a moonbeam. They named you well, my little French pearl.'

He carried on stroking me. 'Do you like this?' he asked, not moving his eyes away from my body.

'If you wish me to,' I said quietly.

I felt as tightly strung as a bow, unsure whether my paramount feeling was one of fear or desire. I wanted to respond, to melt under his touch, but something held me back. I was terrified of displeasing him.

'How about this? Do you like this?'

He was stroking the hair at the base of my belly.

'I don't know, my lord. Do you wish me to open my legs now?'

He sighed and withdrew his hand.

'Submission is not the same as love, my dear,' he said. 'I don't wish you to endure what passes between us, I need more from you.'

'Everything I have is yours,' I said in bewilderment. 'What more can I give you, my lord. You have my body. It is yours to command. I shall do whatever you ask.'

He looked at me in despair and I couldn't think what I'd said to displease him.

'I could command the bodies of a dozen willing women. Believe me, they'd tumble over themselves to share the bed of a king. And there are men who would further their own ambitions by thrusting their wives between my sheets in the hope of finding favour with me. So you see, my dear, I am not bereft of a woman to warm my bed. But you are not just any woman, you are my wife. We shall, God willing, share a bed for many years and I don't wish to pass my nights with someone who merely endures my attentions. I want a wife who desires her husband.'

'But I do desire you, my lord,' I protested. 'It is a wife's duty to desire her husband.'

'Duty?' he said harshly. 'Forget duty and all those pretences your mother taught you and look at me. Now, forget I am your husband and look at me as a man.'

His eyes glittered in the half-light. They were dark and devouring, almost frightening in their intensity. I saw lust there, lust for my body, but not love. Never love. For this was a man who, it was said, had loved his first wife devotedly and had sworn to love her forever. I'd been told by several well-meaning women how he'd shut himself away with his grief when she died, and how he had built magnificent monuments to her memory, one in every place where her body had rested on its final journey to the abbey on the Island of Thorns. She was lying there now, waiting for him to join her in death. I wanted to be a good wife but I knew I could never touch his heart. It was already safe in her keeping.

'I do desire you,' I said quietly, praying that God would forgive me the lie. 'You are the only man I will ever love. I knew it when I pledged myself to you on our marriage day. For as long as I live, you are the only man I shall desire.'

I closed my eyes as a panic rose in my breast. To be truthful, I had no idea how to show a man I desired him but if my marriage was to succeed I would have to be brave. I remembered clearly what my mother's friend had told me to do, how a wife could increase her husband's passion. My husband needed to know, not how much I cared for him but how much I desired him, and as the stirrings of desire were still only part-woken in me I would have to use subterfuge.

For the first time, I touched his body. I felt him shiver as my fingers caressed his skin.

'I want you,' I whispered, trying to make my voice sweet and honeyed but fearing I sounded foolish. 'I want you to hold me and touch me. I want you in every way that a woman wants a man.'

That night he was even more desperate in his lovemaking as if every thrust would take him closer to his total possession of me and closer to his heart's desire - another child, another son. And afterwards, when it was all over, he lay on his back with his eyes open, staring at the night lamp but not speaking. I wasn't certain if I had deceived him and was unsure if he was thinking of a child, or me, or the rebellious Scots and I didn't dare ask.

A week later, my husband left me at the archbishop's house with my women while he journeyed down river to the Tower, the old fortress on the eastern edge of the city. I seldom asked where he was going or who he was meeting. It was not my business. Likewise he showed no interest in my doings. My sole duty was to give him an heir and beyond that, provided I conducted myself discreetly and didn't bother him with trivialities, I could amuse myself.

He had not been gone half a day when I had a visitor. I was trying to learn a new song while my women provided some accompanying music, but it was going badly. My voice was not particularly tuneful and I was only too happy to lay aside the manuscript. To my delight, it was Lady de Monthermer with her daughters.

'I was visiting a friend and was told that his grace, my father, was at St Thomas's Tower and I thought you might care for some company.'

'You are very kind,' I said. 'And I see you've brought your girls to brighten my day.'

Lady de Monthermer inclined her head and signalled for her daughters to come forward.

'This is Eleanor, my eldest de Clare daughter,' she said holding the hand of a pretty young girl in a yellow gown. 'She's nearly seven. These are Margaret and Elizabeth, her sisters.'

The de Clare girls were very alike with their red-gold hair, pale skin and wide-set eyes, but they none of them looked like their mother so I presumed their father, "Red Gilbert" had been named for his hair. The youngest child, dark-haired and shy, peeped out from behind her nursemaid's skirts.

'And this is Mary, my de Monthermer daughter. There is another but she is still in the cradle and too young to come visiting.'

After I had greeted the girls and made a fuss of them, Lady de Monthermer bade the nursemaids take the children out to play in the gardens.

'Don't take them near the river,' she instructed.

'They are lovely girls,' I said. 'You must be proud of them. Eleanor is as sharp as a needle. She will be a clever young woman when she grows.'

Lady de Monthermer, laid her hand on my arm. 'I thank you, you are kind to praise them. But I came today because there is a favour I have to ask of you, well two favours really.'

I was intrigued. She was so poised and confident I wondered what she could possibly need from me.

'First, may I call you Marguerite? I wouldn't want to call you mother as I was not inclined to have warm feelings for my own mother, and my lady seems very formal when you are now family. And please would you call me Joan? I'm sure some would say I should wait for you to ask but as you're many years younger than me, I presumed to take the lead.'

'Nothing could give me greater pleasure - Joan.'

I gathered her hands in mine and then leaned forward and kissed her cheek. She flushed slightly but I could tell she was grateful.

'What is the second favour?'

'I need someone to speak for me to his grace, my father. He hasn't forgiven my husband for marrying me. He's still hostile and I'm not sure how to improve matters.

He'd like to be rid of Ralph completely but that would be an impossibility. He needs him as a captain for these interminable Scottish campaigns of his, and when all is said and done, Ralph *is* my husband and the father of two of my children.'

'I've not met your husband yet,' I said.

'No,' she said drily. 'He's not welcome here.'

'Why is his grace so unwelcoming?'

'Oh,' sighed Joan. 'It's an old story. Gilbert, my first husband was chosen for me. He was thirty years older than me and a hard and violent man. It wasn't a happy marriage and when he died I was determined to marry to please myself. Ralph was ten years my senior and a squire in my late husband's household. I'd known him all my married life and an affection had grown between us. He would not have been deemed suitable by his grace, my father, because Ralph is base-born. But I didn't care. So we waited a year for the sake of decency and then I married him.'

'And his grace was angry?'

She laughed, smothering the sound with her hand.

'Angry? He was incandescent with rage. He'd been planning to marry me to the count of Savoy. Negotiations for the marriage were well advanced and it must have been acutely embarrassing for him.'

'What did he do?'

'First he confiscated my lands so I had no income. Then he had Ralph arrested and thrown into prison.'

'*Sainte Vierge*! How dreadful! What happened?'

She gave a low throaty laugh. I could see what an attractive woman she was. It was no wonder her late husband's squire had been prepared to risk so much to marry her. It wouldn't have been only her worth as a countess which would have attracted him.

'I gathered up his grace's grandchildren and confronted him, prostrating myself on the floor and pleading for my husband. There is nothing like a penitent daughter and four beautiful wide-eyed innocents to melt the snow round a grandsire's heart. My son was six and a straight-backed little image of his father. I instructed the older children on what to say and with the bishop of Durham to give me support, I succeeded in having Ralph released.'

'And his grace accepted your marriage?'

She laughed and patted her belly.

'His grace could see I was well advanced with young Mary. He didn't want more of a scandal than he already had.'

'But all is not well?'

'No. His grace is ill-disposed towards my husband. He won't allow him to carry my title, so Ralph is not earl of Gloucester as he should be. He won't have him at our Christmas celebrations and worst of all he will have nothing to do with Ralph's children. I don't wish there to be a chasm between my de Clare children and their half-sisters. You've seen little Mary today and how well she does. It would be unfair if she was punished by his grace's stubbornness.'

I thought of young Mary de Monthermer, all dark curls and plump legs, and promised to do what I could to mend the rift between father and daughter. After that we spent the remainder of Joan's visit watching the older girls and idly gossiping. I learned a lot about my husband and probably more than I wanted to know about Eleanor, his first wife.

'She had eyes for no-one but her husband and ignored her children.' This was Joan's assessment of her mother. 'I was too young to know if it was coldness on her part or if desire for his grace occupied all of her affections but certainly she showed none to me. As an infant I was left with my grandmother who was kindness itself so I had no desire to return to England and see my parents. I was seven years old when I next saw either of them and what I remember of our meeting is my mother chastising me for my behaviour.'

'It is a mother's duty to show her daughters right from wrong,' I said. 'I'm certain she cared for you.'

'I am certain she did not,' replied Joan, shutting her mouth firmly as if to indicate the subject was closed.

She departed late in the day with a gift of some cloth and little trinkets for the girls. It had been a welcome diversion and I was sad to see her go.

My husband returned in a bad temper. I had no idea what had happened to cause his ill mood but he was shouting at the servants and finding fault with everyone. When it was time to retire I was unsure whether he would come to my chamber or not. No word had been given to expect him so my women prepared me for bed in the usual way. They were busy chattering of this and that, folding up gowns and tidying away books and games when a hurried knock at the door gave us only a moment's warning of the king's arrival. He burst in with a couple of nervous attendants. I could see he was very angry.

'Out!' he roared at my women. 'And you!' he barked at the hovering men behind him.

Before the door had even closed on his valet he had taken three strides towards the bed where I stood, still wrapped in my mantle. I expected a roar of fury instead his voice was icy calm and all the more frightening.

'Did I not give you instructions that I would not have that bastard's children in my house? I leave you alone for a day and what do I find? The minute my back's turned you open the door to them. How dare you forget yourself. This is not your brother's house where no doubt you did what you pleased. Here, you are *my* wife and you will do as *I* say. Do I make myself clear?'

I shrank back against the bed, frightened he would strike me.

'Yes, my lord,' I said softly, surprising myself at the calmness of my voice. Inwardly I was quaking with fear.

'Well?' he said. 'What do you have to say for yourself?'

'Welcome back, husband. You've been gone a while and I've missed you.'

He was so surprised he just stared at me. I think he expected me to crawl on the floor and weep at his feet in abject apology or be like his children and put on a show of defiance, and because I did neither he was caught off guard.

'Would you care for some wine?' I enquired. 'It is your favourite.'

'Wine? Yes. Thank you.'

He went to the chair by the fire and sat down heavily, rubbing his eyes and running his hand through his hair. I fetched the cup and knelt in front of him.

'Here, my lord.'

He held the cup to the candle, watching the jewels flashing in the reflected light, then emptied the contents in one go.

'What am I going to do?' he sighed.

'Do, my lord?'

'With you, with my barons, with those wretched children of mine? Everyone delights in defying me, and I won't have it.' He banged the arm of the chair. 'If I am ruler of this realm I have the right to be obeyed and those who cannot bring themselves to do so will feel my wrath.'

'Yes, my lord.'

He looked at me kneeling in front of him, and shook his head.

'I had at least expected obedience from my wife,' he said sadly. 'You, I thought, could be trusted to do as you were told.'

'I am dedicated to your grace's happiness.'

'And you think by defying me you will increase it?'

I weighed up my words carefully. 'I think if your daughters could show you how much they care for you, and how much they need your affection, you would be easier in your mind and happier than you are now.'

He eyed me suspiciously.

'You are like my friends. They use weasel words to try and persuade me to things against my will.'

'I would have thought they'd be more inclined to bang the table and shout.'

He laughed.

'You're right, they do.'

'And you bang the table and shout louder.'

'I do, yes. But it was not supposed to be thus. Somehow the discussion descended into an argument over forest rights. All I wanted was their agreement to fight the Scots. I didn't want to discuss the royal forests. I need my nobles because without them this war is lost before it is begun. It's difficult enough to find coin to pay foot soldiers and for provisions without having de Warrene and Bigod constantly fussing about charters and other such nonsense. Can't they see what is important?'

'Perhaps they don't have your grace's clear vision and single-mindedness. My brother, Louis, says most men swim around in a fog of indecision and uncertainty overlain with despair.'

'He's a wise man, your brother, Louis. However, I don't intend to repeat my father's mistakes and have this country riven with civil war, with over-mighty nobles believing they can dictate to an anointed king. I endured too many years of that when I was younger and I learned the necessity of keeping a tight rein on their ambitions. They need to know who is in command, who makes the decisions, and in whose gift all their wealth is held. We'll take on the Scots and we'll defeat them. I have sworn it before God, and when it's done I shall take up the Cross and go east to the Holy Land, to Jerusalem.'

I knew his first wife had been constantly at his side so I said quickly, 'And I shall accompany you.'

'You?' he said in a tone of utter amazement.

'If you will have me, my lord.'

We travelled to York by way of the towns of Nottingham and Lincoln, and I was glad of the carriage for the journey was arduous. I'd hoped to see much of this new country of mine, but the low mist and persistent rain kept me inside the queen's travelling coach, and I couldn't even tell if the outriders were still with us as they were lost somewhere out of sight. All I could see from the tiny curtained windows were countless roaring streams and all I could hear was the endless hammering of rain on the carriage roof.

When we stopped for the night, darkness was already upon us. Beyond a glimpse of forbidding grey priories and fog-shrouded manor houses, I had no sight of anything. Our lodgings were damp and despite their owners' attempts to provide a welcome for the king and queen, our rooms were uncomfortable. The grand progress, which was supposed to introduce me to my countrymen, disappeared in a morass of bad temper and miserable weather.

We plodded on day after day, our banners dripping and our men progressively more hunched into their cloaks and by the time we reached the outskirts of York we were all dispirited. Everybody's clothing was soaked and I had barely set eyes on my husband for days. But as the walls loomed up ahead of us, the sun came out as if in welcome to this, my husband's city of the north, and I could see the soaring towers of the great minster church.

It was still under construction, like so much of my husband's realm, but I thought that when completed it might be even more magnificent than the cathedral of Our Lady at Amiens. Louis would have been filled with wonder, but sadly my brother had already taken himself back home, laden with gifts and promising to write and visit again soon. He was my last link with my mother and sister and with his departure I felt truly alone. I was poised somewhere between my French family and my English one, fearing I now belonged to neither yet hoping I might remain bound to both.

It was seven weeks since our wedding day and although I'd not been counting, my women had. Each night they examined my linen and soon they were exchanging looks and staring at my belly as I stood naked before them for my bath.

'My lady, it has been two moons,' began the eldest, who had appointed herself as my mother's surrogate.

'I know,' I snapped. 'I am well aware of the passing of time. I need no reminder.'

The truth was I did not dare to hope, so said nothing to my husband. I ordered my women to keep silent with threats of dismissal and an ignominious return to their families if they disobeyed. Under no circumstances were they to gossip outside my chamber.

A week later when I noticed my breasts were plumper than usual and tender to the touch, I knew I must inform my husband. I wasn't sure how much men understood of these matters, this was something nobody had told me, but it would be unthinkable to let him suspect I'd kept hidden such important news. I barely liked to admit that part of my reluctance to tell him I was with child was the fear that he would desert my bed. I denied to myself that my feelings were anything other than wifely affection.

'My lord,' I began tentatively.

We were alone in my chamber sitting by the fire. He had come to visit me as he did most nights and was drinking a last cup of wine before we retired to bed to do our duty. I was staring into the flames and thinking of my sister, wondering how she did and whether she was thinking of me. I had received no letters but Blanche was not a good correspondent, finding the effort of putting her thoughts into words for a clerk to commit to parchment much too arduous.

'Yes?'

I hesitated. 'I believe I am with child.'

He looked at me for a long moment then laid his hand over mine. 'Thanks be to God. This is the best of news. You do not know how happy you've made me, my little pearl. A son, at last.'

'Perhaps it will be a daughter, my lord. I wouldn't have you gamble your every hope on a son.'

'No. You and I make sons together. I know it.'

'If you say so, my lord,' I said, smiling at him the way a woman does when she knows her husband could be mistaken.

I felt a sudden chill as he removed his hand from mine.

'When will our son be born?'

'In mid-summer, when the roses bloom.'

'By then we shall have the Scots bending their knees to him. They've quite lost heart at the news of our marriage. They fear your brother will no longer give assistance to their warmongering.'

'You are pleased, my lord?' I asked shyly.

'I am. You have done well.' His eyes followed every curve of my body beneath the folds of silk despite there being not the slightest swelling where the child slept. 'You have fulfilled your part of the bargain I made with your brother, my little pearl. Let us hope he, too, keeps his promises.'

He leaned back and stretched, easing his shoulders which often pained him in the latter part of the day.

'I shall journey easy to the borders knowing you carry our son.'

Apart from that one brief moment of holding my hand he hadn't touched me. He hadn't kissed me or embraced me as I'd imagined a loving husband would. It had all been words of gratitude when I so desperately wanted more.

'It's late,' he said, raising me to my feet as if this was something I'd suddenly become unable to do on my own. 'You must rest. Your duty from now on is to look after our child. I want no accidents.'

With the greatest of care he took my hand and led me to the bed, laying me down tenderly and pulling the covers up to my chin.

'You must ensure you don't take sick and harm the child.'

'But my lord?' I said, aware he was preparing to leave and return to his own room.

'Is there something you need?' he enquired. 'I'll call your women. You are carrying a royal child inside that belly of yours and they must take the greatest care of you.'

He stepped back from the bed and regarded me soberly as I lay obediently between the sheets.

'I pray you sleep in safety, my little pearl,' he murmured. 'May Our Lady watch over you and our child.'

He kissed me chastely on the forehead and left, chuckling to himself as he opened the door, surprising the grooms who were dicing on the floor outside. I could hear his voice joking with them as they collected up their winnings, and his footsteps as he walked briskly away.

It would soon be known to everyone in the castle just how pleased the king was with his getting of a child on his wife. From the chamberlain in the hall to the lowest of knaves in the kitchen everyone would be watching my belly with the same peculiar fascination as my husband.

After my women had fussed and fretted and finally left me, I lay awake into the small dark hours of the night, tossing and turning, unable to sleep, wishing my husband was by my side. I put out my hand to touch him across the wide expanse of cool linen sheet, wanting the feel of his long lean body under my fingers, but he wasn't there. And while he slept elsewhere, doubtless lost in a self-satisfied manly slumber, I lay awake, desiring him as he had taught me, until the bells rang for Matins and another day dawned.

I saw my husband each morning at Mass and we dined together in the hall, sitting side by side on the dais, but he didn't come to my bed. I became irritable and snapped at my women who merely laughed indulgently and talked of the peculiarities of women who were breeding. My husband was perfectly polite and solicitous of my care but showed no inclination to lie with me.

'It would be unwise, my dear,' said Lady de Lacy, the motherly wife of the earl of Lincoln, patting my hand with her heavily be-ringed fingers.

I hadn't known who to ask, and having dismissed the notion of consulting my physician who would be shocked, or my chaplain who would find a hundred reasons why the Church would be opposed to the idea, and knowing that none of my women were knowledgeable in such matters, I had decided to ask the countess.

She was a plump kindly woman, fair-skinned and brown-eyed. Her pedigree was impeccable if one ignored the baseborn royal ancestor and she bore the title of countess of Salisbury in her own right.

She listened carefully as I tried, with a great deal of embarrassment on my part, to explain the difficulties I was experiencing. But she completely misunderstood my dilemma.

'His grace will be understanding, my dear. He has been through this many times before. He knows the first few months are the most dangerous and he will do nothing which might damage the child.'

I shut my mouth firmly before I was foolish enough to tell her that it was not my husband who desired us to lie together, but me. I felt certain that she, too, would be shocked.

4

WINTER 1299

That first winter I spent in England was one of almost complete misery for me and if it hadn't been for the child growing daily larger within my belly I would have felt deserted by God. On a blustery late autumn day I watched my husband ride off to war with all his friends, except for the elderly earl of Norfolk who, pleading ill-health, had sent his senior household knight with the earl's army of followers.

They made a magnificent sight as they disappeared along the road and into the hills. Seeing their colourful banners and their lances decorated with fluttering pennants, their warhorses dressed in silks and satins, followed by an endless procession of wagons and pack horses carrying their provisions and their pavilions, I almost wished I was going with them.

'Don't be downhearted, your grace,' said Lady de Lacy. 'Our husbands will return before long and in the meantime we shall have to amuse ourselves.'

'Thank you Lady Margaret,' I said. 'Do I look miserable? I thought I was being brave.'

She turned her back on the last of the wagons rolling out of the courtyard and, taking my hand, led me back up the steps into the warmth of the castle.

'This is your first experience of your man going to war,' she said kindly. 'But it won't be your last so you must learn to bear it as we all do with a straight back and a smile on your face. Has his grace decided where you will reside while he is away?'

'He desires me to stay here or at one of the archbishop's houses south of the town but he said if I wished to visit with anyone I may do so provided I am careful and take sufficient of my household with me.'

'By which he means a dozen women to do your bidding and your physician and your chaplain, just in case,' laughed Lady de Lacy. 'His grace is behaving like a young lad with his firstborn. You'd never think he'd had sixteen before this, would you?'

I disliked everyone's constant allusions to the fruitfulness of my husband's first wife and the veiled inference that I would be unlikely to succeed as well as she had done. I wondered how long it had taken *her* to conceive a child after their wedding day.

'I know what we'll do,' said Lady de Lacy. 'We'll pay a visit to my daughter at Pickering on the edge of the moors. That should put the bloom back in your cheeks, my dear, for you do look dreadfully pale.'

Alice de Lacy, countess of Lancaster, dwelt at Pickering Castle, two days' journey away. As we travelled towards the high moors we left the flat fertile land behind. The countryside was wild and barren and by the time we reached our destination it was getting dark. This far north the days were short in November.

The castle was perched above a deep rocky chasm, reminding me of Philip's fortress at Pontoise which Blanche and I had found a frightening place. I wondered if

Alice de Lacy employed torturers in her dungeons like my brother did. I wasn't sure I would have liked to live here alone. I would have been afraid of bandits and robbers.

'They do not do well together,' confided Lady de Lacy as we approached the outer walls. 'She says he is uncouth and violent and he has other women.'

Lady de Lacy had been waxing loud and long on the subject of Alice's husband since we'd left York and there was now little I didn't know of her opinion of Earl Thomas.

'How difficult for you,' I said as we passed under the gatehouse into the courtyard. 'Are there no children?'

'No, nor likely to be. She has refused him her bed. I have told her time and again it is her duty to lie with him but my daughter is wilful. I fear my lord and I spoiled her when she was a child.'

Waiting inside, dressed in a green fine-spun woollen gown was the tall, nineteen year-old Alice. She looked very much in command of her household and I could easily imagine her standing up to her formidable young husband. I looked around the small high-roofed hall, noticing, with surprise, a distinct lack of grandeur and comfort. Alice was the wife of the third most important man in my husband's kingdom and should certainly have been able to keep a better house than this. There were some good tapestries but they were old and faded, and the board had only a few pewter and gilt cups and platters, and a single battered silver bowl.

'I don't keep a grand house,' she said, taking note of my wandering eye. 'But we have good food and wine and my minstrels are tolerably skilful. Do you like to sing, your grace?'

'I am not very tuneful,' I admitted. 'But I enjoy it.'

I thought Alice overestimated the skill of her minstrels, however they played with great enthusiasm and clearly had such respect for their lady that I was prepared to forgive them.

After we had eaten, we sat by the fire in Alice's tiny solar where draughts from the narrow unshuttered windows crept round every corner of the room and made me long for the comfort of my rooms at York.

'I am sorry,' said Alice. 'I spend so much time alone here I have forgotten how inhospitable it must seem to others.'

'Her grace will think I taught you badly, Alice,' grumbled Lady de Lacy, pulling a shawl round her shoulders and sitting forward to gain some heat from the smouldering fire. 'When I think of the years of training you had in running a household, not to mention the example I set you, and yet here you are allowing your servants to become thoroughly lazy. It's no wonder your husband complains.'

'My lord is not complaining about the standard of care I give to his castles,' said Alice placidly.

'Perhaps not,' sniffed Lady de Lacy. 'But nevertheless ...'

There followed a list of Alice's failings and the efforts which Lady de Lacy had made through the years to ensure she would raise a daughter fit for fussiest of husbands. At last, having exhausted her supply of maternal criticisms, Lady de Lacy took herself off to bed, complaining tiredness and aching legs, leaving Alice and me alone to gossip by the fire.

'My lord of Lancaster is devoted to his grace, your

husband,' said Alice. 'But he has no respect for his son. He likes him well enough, but thinks him unsuited to be king and I fear for what may happen when ...' She stopped. 'I beg your pardon, that was not polite.'

I smiled. 'It's hard to guard our tongues when we are young. I know mine runs away with me at times.'

She regarded me with her lovely brown eyes. She was not particularly beautiful, being rather narrow of face with an upturned nose, but those eyes with their golden flecks made up for her other deficiencies.

'May I ask your grace a question?'

'Please, call me Marguerite. We are cousins by marriage and I'm still unused to being called your grace.

She inclined her head in acquiescence.

'Do you know if the young Lord Edward favours my lord of Lancaster? They appear on good terms, and yet in private my husband speaks of him with contempt. I ask, not for my husband's sake for he's well able to take care of himself, but it would not benefit Lord Edward to make an enemy of my lord for he is a violent man when crossed. He has a quick temper as well as a foul tongue.'

She seemed genuinely concerned and I warmed to her.

'My lord is not like his brother,' she continued. 'Have you met Lord Henry?'

'Yes,' I nodded.

'He is charming, and his wife is a lovely young woman if a trifle ignorant of the world. Maud is with child. Did my mother tell you?'

'No, she has said nothing.'

'I'm surprised. She believes in spreading our family news far and wide. I'm not sure if I envy Maud.'

'Would you like a child?'

'Not if it means sharing a bed with my lord.'

'I was raised to believe it is a wife's duty to share her husband's bed,' I said cautiously.

'So was I,' said Alice. 'And I believe should be so. But a husband has duties too, would you not agree? And if he is like my lord of Lancaster then I'd not find fault with any wife who barred the door of her bedchamber.'

I was surprised her husband tolerated such behaviour.

'I never understood what it was to hate,' she said quietly, her eyes fixed on the pool of light lying between us where her words floated and disappeared. 'Until my marriage I was treated with kindness. I was thirteen and my lord was three years older and although my parents were anxious in case I was too young, it was agreed we should bed on our marriage night.'

She sat very still.

'He was not kind me,' she said flatly. 'I liked him well enough before but afterwards ... and of course it was the same every night. After a week I went crying to my mother but she reprimanded me and sent me back, telling me I must do my duty by my husband. I'm sorry, Marguerite, I shouldn't burden you with this. It isn't as if there's anything you can do. There isn't anything anyone can do.'

'You must have been very frightened,' I said, thinking Lady de Lacy should have prepared her daughter better and silently thanking my own mother for the care she'd taken.

'If I was frightened, I learned not to be,' she said. 'I don't think he was a particularly cruel man, as men are often inclined to violence if thwarted, but we made each other very unhappy. So now I prefer not to share his house.'

'But surely he wants sons?'

I thought of my own husband's preoccupation and knew Earl Thomas must want an heir, one to carry on his name and inherit his titles and vast estates. All men wanted sons.

'I think I am barren,' she said. 'After six years there has been no sign of a child, not even once, so perhaps in this one thing I have defeated him. He is not pleased, in truth he is furious. He says it makes him look a fool. But what can he do?'

'Have you tried potions to help you conceive?' I asked.

She smiled. 'You sound like my lord. He accused me of visiting a wise woman to prevent a child and beat me soundly for that supposed disobedience.'

'Surely you cannot continue like this?'

'I see no reason why not. For all his supposed virtues, my lord is greedy. He has three earldoms already but has eyes for those of my parents which should be mine by rights. Together with his grace, the king, he has arranged that my inheritance shall remain within his family no matter what should happen. In the end he will take it all but if he dies I shall get nothing. So, he will be content and I shall stay here. What better arrangement can there be than that?'

She laughed but I could see she was bitter. There was no escape from her miserable marriage and she would be shackled to her husband until God saw fit to release her.

'Besides,' she said. 'What choice do I have? My lord pays for my household so long as I reside at Pickering but

I have no money of my own. How would I live if I did not live here?'

When the fire died down to glowing embers, we prepared to retire. As we were rising from our chairs, she put her hand on mine.

'Be careful my dear Marguerite. Not everyone rejoiced at your marriage and there are some who wish it had never been. If you should conceive a child there may be those who would wish to do you harm.'

I hadn't told Alice I was with child and obviously Lady de Lacy had not yet shared the news with her daughter.

'Who would wish me harm?' I said, looking fearfully into the darkness beyond the firelight for an assassin lurking in the shadows. I felt that same cold, slithering feeling within me that I'd felt once before and an immediate need to protect the fledgling life in my belly.

'I know no names but my mother told me that before the old queen died an agreement was reached as to who should take the throne if anything happened to the king's son.'

'And who would it be?'

'I don't know, she wouldn't tell me. But I know my husband covets power and a son of yours would lie in the path of any would-be usurper. So please be careful. Men are greedy. They know your husband is old and some, like my lord of Lancaster, think young Lord Edward an unsuitable candidate for the throne.'

As I lay in bed that night I wished she hadn't spoken. The mattress was lumpy, the castle draughty and rain seeped through the shutters. While the winds howled round the castle walls, my three women tossed and fidgeted through the long hours of darkness, and I lay awake worrying.

Despite the enjoyment of Alice's company I was not sad when it was time to leave. With promises to see each other for the Christmas festivities, and exhortations to improve the running of her household, her mother and I waved farewell to the lady of Pickering and set off back down the road towards York.

Now the days were dark and short and we spent our waking hours inside, unwilling to brave the relentless cold and rain. We attended to matters of business, we sewed, we read, we made music and we played games. I wrote letters to my family and wished I had heard from Blanche.

I had two letters from my husband who was a dutiful correspondent. He told me of the failure of his men to raise enough foot soldiers, how he had delayed their advance in the hope that more would be recruited, but how, when they finally reached Berwick on the Scottish border, he had less than a quarter of the men he had been promised and fewer than a tenth of the nobles who should have turned out to fight for their king. His people had let him down just when he most needed them. I could feel his despair and my heart bled for him.

Even with a prolonged visit from Alice we passed a subdued Christmas. My husband promised that once he had passed New Year at Berwick he would come south and we would return to his castle at Windsor where he would set about planning a new campaign for the summer.

I was standing at the top of the steps worrying about how I looked when the first man rode in under the gatehouse. I wanted it to seem as if I had just drifted out wearing my best gown to greet my lord but in truth I'd been in and out of the hall ever since noon when the harbingers had arrived to tell us my husband was on his way. My girth had increased since November and I so hated feeling fat. It was as if I had eaten too much at dinner.

I wanted to run down the steps and throw myself against him and envied the castle hounds who raced into the courtyard the moment they heard the horns. I stayed where I was, twisting my hands into knots, my heart knocking hard against my ribs.

A groom held his horse by the head and one of his servants helped him onto the ground. He looked around at the gathering crowd and then raised his head. When he saw me he acknowledged my presence but stayed where he was. He didn't come to greet me and he certainly didn't run up the steps into my arms. I watched as he issued instructions and drew his senior men around him. I began to feel cold. Lady de Lacy touched my arm.

'Come inside, my dear. He is safely returned and it won't do for you to be shivering out here. His grace will have important matters to attend to now he is back. There are bound to be messages waiting for him and people who must be seen, so come upstairs and wait.'

I trailed back and up into the solar feeling a sense of despondency when I should have been feeling joyful. My husband had returned safely and soon we would travel south to where it might be warmer.

After what seemed like hours, while I sat half-listening to one of my women read a text on the temptations of the saints, my husband came. The doors were flung open, his men lined the entrance, my women moved back so that he could see me sitting beautifully in my chair, and there he was.

'She's at it again,' he stormed, waving a letter in his hands as he crossed the floor. 'Doing exactly what she wants. Here! Read what she says. Off to visit her sister indeed!'

I rose and made a reverence. 'My lord.'

'The child is well?' he asked taking note of my new rounded belly.

'Yes, my lord.'

'Good. Now what am I going to do with my daughter?'

The offending parchment came from The Hague, from Elizabeth, my husband's youngest daughter, the one who had dared to defy her father.

In the end, our reunion, which should have been joyful and tender, was tarnished by his anger at the news. It transpired that Elizabeth was now a widow. Her husband, fifteen-year-old Count Jan, had succumbed to one of his frequent illnesses and died. Elizabeth wrote that she would travel to visit her sister, Margaret, in Brabant, and would return in the summer to see her father and the rest of her family.

'Poor Elizabeth,' I said. 'A widow at seventeen.'

'I shall have to find her another husband,' growled her father irritably. 'As if the news from Stirling isn't bad enough, now I have to deal with this as well.'

'What has happened at Stirling?' I enquired, trying to remember where Stirling was.

'They've surrendered to the Scots. The moment my back was turned.'

His mood was dark and he continued to grumble about the difficulties of finding another husband for Elizabeth.

'Where will you look?' I asked, realising that there was to be no pleasant rekindling of warm feelings until he had resolved his numerous problems.

I knew he would consider the usefulness of another alliance with the counts of the Low Countries or possibly with the kings of Castile or Aragon. The closer my husband could bind these powerful men, the stronger his own position would be. Of Elizabeth's feelings in the matter he gave not a single thought. Like all men he believed women were there to play their part in the furtherance of their men's ambitions. It was only because I had been where Elizabeth stood that I considered her at all.

'Perhaps she is with child,' I said hopefully to Lady de Lacy when my husband had left.

'I think it unlikely,' she replied. 'I suspect she is still a maid. They were betrothed when very young and he was always a sickly little boy.'

After two days we began making plans for our return south. My husband spent every waking hour closeted with his officials and I barely saw him other than at mealtimes. Sometimes he even missed Mass which surprised me for he was usually diligent in his devotions. In the end I decided I must be brave. He was my husband. What could he do to me?

'My lord,' I said quietly as we dined together in the

hall. 'It is cold and lonely in my bed without you. Will you not come to visit me?'

He stopped with a slice of venison half way to his mouth. He turned, a look of intense surprise on his face, then replaced the meat on his platter and leant back in his chair, his elbow on the arm and his chin on his hand. He regarded me with great interest but said nothing. A flush was rising into my cheeks and I began to wish I hadn't spoken.

My mother would have been horrified at my presumption and I imagined Blanche saying how stupid I was, insulting my husband for his neglect. I felt foolish for having spoken but after that one long hard stare my husband ignored me and continued to eat and drink as if I'd said nothing amiss.

That evening as my hair was being tucked up into my nightcap there came a rap at the door. It was one of my husband's servants come to inform my women that the king would sleep with the queen tonight. There was an immediate flurry of activity while the women scurried round, whispering to each other, making sure everything was tidy.

I was sitting upright against my pillows when the door opened and in he came, striding across the floor, dressed in his nightgown and crimson bedrobe. He waved everyone away except for his personal valet who helped him off with his robe and assisted him up the steps and into my bed, pulling the fur coverlet over his legs. Once the curtains were drawn I heard the man leave the room.

'Are you well?'

'Yes, my lord.'

There was a long pause.

'I'm sorry your time in the north came to nothing and your barons let you down,' I said.

He grunted.

'Lady de Lacy was very concerned.'

No answer.

'Our Christmas festivities were very sombre when we heard the news. We had the countess of Lancaster with us but nobody had the heart for singing and dancing when there was nothing to celebrate. Even my fool found it hard to raise a laugh from the company.'

I was talking too quickly but was more frightened of the silence than of filling the void with nonsense.

'My women were pleased to see your men returned. It brightens their lives and gives them an excuse to dress in their finery.'

More silence.

'Will you try to engage the Scots next summer or will you wait to see what they do?'

He put his head back and eased himself against the pillows.

'When the Scots stop slinking off into the hills and finally issue an invitation to do battle,' he said, 'I know exactly what they will do and how they will conduct themselves because they are easily read like most men.'

I wondered why he was instructing me on the military strategies of his enemies.

'An invitation to do battle means just that - to join our forces in a show of strength.'

'Naturally,' I said. 'What else would it mean?'

'As I said, men are easily read. However I am not so sure about the daughters of Eve. Are they also as transparent as a pool of clear water? I used to think they were. But when my wife invites me to her bed and then prattles inconsequentially and gossips of people in whom I have no interest, well, then I wonder if I have misread the signs. Was it a conversation she was after or a treatise on difficulties within her chamber? What does she really want?'

He raised his eyebrows, a small half-smile curving one side of his mouth, making him look less severe.

'I ... I thought.' I found myself unable to go on.

He leaned over and stopped my words with a kiss.

I felt his beard brush my face and the heat of his mouth on mine.

'You thought?' he said quietly, untying the ribbons on my nightcap and starting to unbraid my hair. 'Or you desired?'

I looked up into his eyes as he unwound the long fine strands. I was betrayed by my body for how could I hide the quivering of my limbs and the trembling of my lips.

I breathed the words he wanted to hear. 'I ... I desired you.'

'And do you still? Or was this just a passing fancy to do battle?'

I slid into his arms and pressed myself against him.

'I think it is a lifelong campaign.'

'That,' he said, 'is what every commander likes to hear.'

At the last moment he drew back. 'It is alright? Your physician is not concerned this will harm the child?'

At that moment I wished my physician consigned to the farthest reaches of the universe.

'No,' I lied. 'No he is not. My lord, please don't stop.'

How easily won is a battle when the antagonists realise they are both fighting on the same side and wish for the same end. So it was with my husband and me. If in our marriage bed we had not both found love we had at least found passion and mutual desire. We were each filled with a hunger for the body of the other and if on my part it was more than just passing lust, I was certainly not able to tell him so.

5

SPRING 1300

I was in the garden at Langley, the pretty little manor house on the hill where Ned and his household spent most of their time.

'What in the name of Our Lady are you doing?'

My stepson, clad in a tattered shirt and hose, was standing up to his knees in mud and earth in a ditch, wielding a large spade. Beside him, several other young men, swarthy and mud-spattered, were throwing out mounds of evil-smelling soil and debris. Robert the fool capered around while a small crowd of onlookers, mainly the richly dressed young men of Ned's household, laughed and jostled each other. The chamberlain was mortified at this total lack of decorum and begged me to return inside.

'I am sorry, lady mother,' said Ned, scrambling up onto the grass. 'We are constructing a new type of garden which requires an immense parterre here to the east of the wall. Do you like it?'

He was trying, unsuccessfully, to brush the mess off his clothing.

'But why are *you* doing this?' I said. 'Surely you have men to do work like this? His grace, your father, cannot mean you to spend your days grubbing about in the earth.'

At the mention of his father, Ned scowled.

'I don't see why I shouldn't work in the gardens if I like. This will be my manor one day and if I choose to dig a ditch rather than spend my time sword-fighting I don't see that it's anyone's business but mine.'

I sighed. I had come to Langley to see Ned as I knew my husband was concerned. He wished his son to accompany him on campaign this year and I wanted relations between them to remain cordial. The plan was to go north in early May, well before our child was due. I would remain at York while my husband and his army would ride on to Carlisle, which I now knew to be close to the border with Scotland.

'But Ned, you are a king's son. Kings do not dig ditches. They command armies and make policy and give orders. My brother doesn't dig ditches. His men would laugh at him if he did.'

I had a sudden impossible vision of my cold, fastidious brother, Philip, clad in his finery, wielding a spade in a ditch. It was an amusing thought but I could not encourage Ned in such foolishness.

'It would be most unbecoming for a king to dig ditches,' I said firmly. 'His nobles and councillors would have no respect for him, and if they had no respect how could he be master of them?'

But Ned was not convinced.

'I don't see why a king can't dig ditches and be respected,' he protested. 'I'm as good a fighter as anyone else and my friends would follow me to the death, which is what a king should want. Perhaps his grace, my father, would have more success with his barons if he dug ditches with them.'

I could see no point in discussing matters further,

so I linked arms and suggested we went to see his latest acquisition - a beautiful white greyhound bitch. She had whelped ten days earlier and I was anxious to see the pups.

'I must ensure my friends have everything they need,' he called as he loped over towards the chaos. He leapt into the ditch and put his arm over the shoulder of some menial, a man so covered in mud I doubted his own mother would recognize him. The churl looked up and laughed into my stepson's face with a familiarity I found decidedly disturbing. After a few words, Ned slapped the man on his back and scrambled up the bank.

'They're fine fellows,' he said, smiling broadly.

I made some doubtful comment.

He sighed. 'Dearest lady mother, take that frown off your face. You're beginning to look like his grace, my father, and that will never do. I know you don't approve of my pastimes or my friends but weren't you young once? Didn't you long to run your hands through the warm earth and feel the softness of leaf-mould beneath your fingers? And on summer days, didn't you wish to leap into a river and splash in the shallows or, better still, swim in the deep cool water? Were you not as impatient for these joys as I am?'

I thought of my upbringing in Philip's palaces. There had been no earth, no leaf-mould, no swimming in rivers for Blanche and me, just very correct behaviour overseen by a series of our mother's women. Somehow I felt an unaccountable sense of having lost some part of my childhood. Did I really wish I had revelled in the mud like Ned?

'Come on,' I said briskly. 'Let me see Melisande and her pups.'

We stood in a corner of the sunny courtyard, watching the new mother curled up in the straw with her squirming offspring. All around I could hear the sounds of Langley: tiny wrens singing loudly from the depths of the bushes and in the warmth of dusty corners, insects buzzing, busy with their secretive concerns. The walls of the courtyard were alive with small creatures scuttling in and out of shadowy cracks, and on the roof of an adjoining stable, a sleepy cat was too comfortable or too lazy to be bothered with an easy meal. There were rumbling carts and the shouts of men but over and above it all was the merry laughter of my stepson's friends frolicking happily in the mud.

'She is very fine,' I agreed, scrutinizing the recumbent bitch. I longed to pick up one of her tiny bundles but she regarded me with such a fierce expression, I thought she might bite.

'May I have one if they are not all bespoke?'

'Of course,' he said, pleased to be generous. It was his most endearing quality that he wanted his friends to be happy. I was considered a friend but I wasn't sure about my husband.

Ned's joy was uncomplicated and I wished it was as easy to please my husband. He was having difficulties with his parliament. He needed money and support for his planned campaign but said the demands made on him undermined the very essence of his kingship. His northern knights were particularly intransigent.

'I'd hang the lot of them,' he growled.

'Will they not fight?'

'Half the country is saying it won't fight. In Durham they claim they're Saint Cuthbert's folk and are not obliged to fight beyond the Tyne and Tees.'

I didn't know what the Tyne and the Tees were, but I gathered they were not sufficiently far north to please my husband. Perhaps they were not even as far north as Carlisle.

'But surely they owe you service?' I said.

'I have no idea what my subjects will do. Apparently they wish to be *invited* to fight, not *told* to fight. By Christ! Do they think I am a child? Sometimes I think the country has become mad and they've forgotten who is king.'

He was beset with problems and in the end decided he would leave preparations for the muster to his councillors and their recruiters while he would make his annual pilgrimage to the holy shrines of East Anglia, a part of my husband's kingdom I had yet to visit.

'But it is still Lent,' I said in some surprise, when my husband told me we'd be leaving for St Albans in two days.

'It could be Christmas for all I care,' he shouted, working himself up into another fury. 'I don't expect you to criticize my arrangements, madam. If I say we are leaving you will issue instructions to your household and get yourself to St Albans.'

This was the pattern of our life. There would be weeks when he was working hard when I would hardly see him, and sweet moments when we were close, playing chess or reading to each other by the fire. These times were interspersed with furious rages when bowls would be thrown, servants kicked and everyone became the target for his tongue. It was exhausting and I longed for the peacefulness of my previous life with my mother and my sister.

I had heard nothing from Blanche who by now must be swept up in preparations for her wedding day. I longed to be with her but with our child due in the summer there was no possibility of my going. I often thought of our life together and every night I said a prayer for her just as I had promised.

We arrived at the busy town of St Albans in time for the Easter festivities. It was a scant day's ride in the carriage from the Island of Thorns but nevertheless I was glad to see the abbey on the hill which signalled our journey's end.

It was the day following the feast of the Resurrection of Our Lord and in the churches at home, in the cathedral of Our Lady on the Île de la Cité, canons would be chanting the Kyrie Eleison and our people would be on their knees. We had celebrated much of Eastertide on our knees whereas here the festivities were taking a most peculiar path.

'Make sure you are well clothed,' my senior lady had said, finding the subject of my night attire one of great embarrassment since the morning she'd discovered me naked amongst the rumpled sheets.

I could hear the comforting sounds of a castle waking to a new day. I glanced over to see if my husband was asleep. He had elected to spend the night with me. He had said it was safer!

'Are you awake?' he whispered out of the gloom.

'Yes, my lord.'

'You'd best prepare yourself.'

'For what?'

'A surprise, my little pearl. Just one of our quaint English customs. It will give you something to write about to your mother. You can tell her what a heathen your brother has married you to and, if you exaggerate a little, perhaps he will come and rescue you from my uncivilised clutches.'

It was one of his continual jokes that my brother was not happy about the man to whom he'd given his sister in marriage, whereas I knew full well that Philip didn't care about me or the man, only about the treaty.

There was noise beyond the curtains, a creak of a door, a muffled giggle, a patter of girlish feet across the floor. Suddenly the curtain was flung back and there were my women, fully dressed, grabbing at my husband and pulling him out of bed. They were shrieking with laughter and clutching the king and exposing his legs in a way I'd not have thought possible. I had a sudden horror they would see parts of his naked body which only his body servants saw. But I needn't have worried. My husband swung himself quickly out of the bed and was upright, wrapped in his bedrobe, before most of them even caught sight of his nightgown.

They dragged and pulled him across the floor and into the outer chamber leaving me sitting alone amongst the sheets feeling rather foolish. Through the open door I could hear the grooms and the younger women screaming with laughter.

I scrambled out of bed as quickly as my large belly would allow, shrugged on my mantle and crept down the stairs to the great hall where our households were waiting with the captured king. Everyone was chanting and banging with feet or brooms or pans brought from the kitchens. My husband was tied to his chair by a long golden cord and was laughing uproariously.

My life at Philip's court had not prepared me for vulgar displays of horseplay and part of me was truly shocked at the indignity. But I also half-wished it could always be like this.

'I yield,' cried my husband above the din. 'Have mercy! Treasurer, a handful of coins for my captors if you please. Now if you will kindly release me, we shall begin the festivities.'

Those were the good times but they were few. Matters were easier between us now that I had proved my worth as a wife but he still held me at arm's length. When we sat together he would talk of his hopes for the Scottish campaign and would occasionally mention his children, but I'd had little success in raising the subject of Joan's husband. I might persuade myself we were close but there were whole parts of himself he kept hidden from me and in many ways I knew him no better than the day we first met in Canterbury.

I'd been warned by my mother of the dangers of being a second wife but she hadn't considered that I might love my husband. I had expected to feel gratitude and wifely devotion to the man I married but I was totally unprepared for love. Naturally he didn't love me, that would have been impossible. I was not the kind of young woman to inspire love in a man.

Our child was another matter entirely and now that I had passed what the midwife called "the dangerous months" my husband shared my bed as often as he could. He took pleasure in stroking my swollen belly and of course Eleanor had given him sixteen children so he was well-accustomed to swollen bellies. But I wondered if she had given him access to her body when she was heavy with child in the way I did. I rather hoped not.

6

SUMMER 1300

It was June and I was as plump as a partridge. Our army was encamped near the archbishop's house at Cawood, a little place south of York, where my husband was to leave me. The day dawned with breaths of thin mist rising from the woods and the surface of the river but by the time we ventured outside the sky was a clear piercing blue without a cloud in sight. The sun was shining as if it was already midsummer. It was a fine day for a hunt.

With my husband's permission I was allowed to ride in the queen's litter drawn by the quietest of horses accompanied by an escort of my women and a dozen strong men. I was feeling in good spirits and the lethargy of the past few days had vanished with the morning mist.

We set off along the shallow valley and up into the woods. Ahead was the sound of horns as horses and riders plunged through the thickets. It was at the furthest point of our expedition that I felt a sudden shaft of pain as if my back had been spiked by a dagger. I thought one of the horses had stumbled and was about to say something when another pain shot through me. Before I could do more than gasp and hold my belly, a deluge of wetness gushed from between my legs.

'*Sainte Vierge!*' I cried. '*Le bébé!*'

It was too soon! My midwife and my astrologer had

both agreed it would be after mid-summer and it was nearly four weeks until then. I couldn't be losing my baby. Not when I had carried it for so long.

'I shall ride for his grace,' shouted one of the men, spurring his horse in the direction of the absent hunting party.

'Where shall we take my lady?' cried one of my women. 'It is too far to Pontefract. The baby won't wait that long.'

'The archbishop's house at Cawood is even further,' said another.

'The queen cannot give birth in the woods like a peasant woman,' sobbed a third.

'There's a house beyond the trees,' called one of the men. 'But go carefully. His grace won't thank you if you tip my lady onto the ground.'

The pain was unbearable and I feared I was screaming. I prayed to Our Lady. Save my baby. Please, Blessed Lady, save my baby. I am not afraid to die but please let my baby live.

As those around me panicked I felt the pain mount to a pitch where I think I must have fainted.

I was running with Blanche through the wheat fields at St Germain. The sun was hot on my face and a thousand glittering fragments splintered in my eyes as a heated skewer pierced my body.

I chased up the narrow stairs of the tower at Vincennes with black hounds gnawing at my belly. Their snarls filled my ears and their slobber wetted my face. I felt them rip the flesh from my back as the screams of my sister tore through the air. 'Marguerite!' she shrieked. 'Marguerite!'

I couldn't breathe. I was suffocating beneath a heavy blue curtain. Its braided cords looped around my throat, my chest, my belly. They pulled tighter and tighter and I screamed.

Somebody shouted, 'Push hard, hinny!'

It couldn't be Blanche. Blanche was getting married. She was dancing, her gold and azure gown swirling and flashing in the candlelight, faster and faster and faster. She would come if I called. She would drop her golden girdle, her jewelled crown, and come running. 'Blanche! Blanche!'

'Nearly there, hinny!'

Someone was screaming. I shook my head from side to side to escape from the sound but the noise went on and on and on.

The sun was on my face but this time it was gentle and warming. This was God's welcome to Paradise.

Then, as a blade sliced through my body, I screamed and remembered nothing more.

Later they told me I had been carried to the manor house at Brotherton. I believe a priest was called before someone had the wit to find a midwife. I swam in and out of a fog of pain and my women believed I would not survive. I don't know who found the midwife or where she came from, but I'm certain she saved my life and that of my child.

'It is a boy, my dear.'

Kind Lady de Lacy was bending over me, wiping the sweat from my brow. 'You had us worried. The midwife said you were narrow. I think she despaired of birthing your son but she was skilled and here we are, everything done. We can thank Our Lady for a safe birth.'

'My husband?' I whispered, my lips thick and dry.

'He has been told. He's as pleased as a young lad with his first. You'd never think he's seen this before and so many times. Once we have you pretty again he will come and see you both. Now, would you like to greet your son?'

He was beautiful. Pink crumpled skin and a crown of fine dark hair; his fingers, little starfishes with translucent nails, and as I unwrapped his shawl I saw he was perfect in every way. His legs so thin and red, his feet, tiny imitations of my own, ten minute toes curled together. His eyes screwed tight shut and his rosebud mouth pursed as if waiting for a kiss. They placed him in my arms and I couldn't stop gazing at him. When the time came I was very reluctant to give him up.

My husband came as the sun moved round and the smell of grass and wild flowers crept through the narrow window. Had I not promised him our child would come with the roses?

He held my hand and smiled. 'Well done, my little pearl. Did I not tell you we should make a boy?'

'You did, my lord. And is he not perfect?'

'If you say so.'

My husband gave a cursory glance at the cradle. Unlike me he showed no desire to examine every aspect of our son from the top of his soft downy head to the little pink soles of his tiny wrinkled feet. He was more concerned with other matters.

'He will be Thomas which will please our host, the archbishop. It is a good solid name and carries echoes of the day of our marriage.'

Little Thomas. Named for a cleric and a saint. God would surely watch over him.

'The baptism will be tomorrow. De Corbridge will be there. This is an important child and it is our duty to see he is well-protected. If anything should happen to Ned, which God forbid, young Thomas would rule after me.'

With the dust motes dancing lazily in the late afternoon shafts of sunlight and my husband standing by my bedside, I felt a goose step softly over my grave.

After ten days my husband and his household departed. He had spent the final hours issuing instructions for more men to assemble at Carlisle while I had lingered in my bed unaccountably weeping at the slightest thing. He kissed me but his mind was already far away in the wilds of the border country while mine was immured here with our son. We were two people bound together, with hearts pulling in opposite directions. I could no more think of doing battle with the Scots than he could contemplate the domestic life of our child.

One morning about three weeks after I had given birth, when I was still as weak as a newborn kitten, there came a hesitant knock at the door. It was the chief nursemaid. She was a small woman, the wife of one of my husband's men. Instead of her usual placid smiling face, she looked frightened.

'The wet nurse is concerned, my lady. The child is vomiting. She says he has kept nothing in his belly since yesterday.'

Fear clutched at my heart and I knew that this was what it meant to love.

I insisted on going to my son. My women fussed but eventually threw a warm mantle over my shoulders and helped me through to the nursery. Thomas lay in his cradle screaming. His face was red and his body rigid. I looked at him helplessly. I put my hand on his cheek. It wasn't burning but I knew so little of babies. Perhaps a fever in such a tiny infant was different to that in a grown woman. I felt panic rising.

The wet nurse was a French woman, one of my mother's choosing. She had given birth a few weeks ago. She looked healthy enough but perhaps her milk was too rich and lay like a morbid confection in his tiny stomach. Or perhaps it was not rich enough. Could this be a malignant disease working its way through his little body? Or - I shivered at the thought - could it be the work of an evil spirit?

'Yesterday he was vomiting, my lady,' said the wet nurse.

'He was vomiting and I was not told?'

She looked guiltily at the chief nursemaid.

'I thought nothing of it, my lady. Babies often spit out their milk if they have sucked too much.'

'You are not paid to think,' I hissed at her. 'You are paid to feed my son. Pick him up.'

She bent over the cradle and lifted Thomas out. He stopped screaming almost at once.

'Feed him,' I ordered.

She sat down and put him to her breast but after a couple of sucks he twisted his body and began screaming again.

'Perhaps it is the milk,' said the youngest nursemaid, a plump girl, unafraid to voice her opinion.

'There is nothing wrong with my milk,' protested the wet nurse. 'My own child thrives.'

'Perhaps your own child steals all the milk and leaves nothing for my son.'

She cowered away from my temper. She knew if she was dismissed and returned to her husband he would likely beat her.

'My mother knew a woman whose milk curdled in her child's belly, m'lady,' said the youngest nursemaid.

'What happened to the child?'

There was a pause. 'God took it,' she whispered.

'*Sainte Vierge*! *Vite*! Fetch me Lady de Lacy.'

Lady de Lacy came at a run, her face full of concern. I clung to her arm.

'What shall I do?' I cried.

'We shall get another wet nurse,' she said firmly. 'We'll send to Pontefract or York if necessary. There must be a local lass with milk enough to spare for the king's son. This wretched woman has proved herself unworthy. Look how her breasts droop. I'll wager there's only thin gruel in there. No wonder the mite is crying. He's an English prince and what he needs is good English milk.' She put a comforting hand on my arm. 'You mustn't worry.'

But that was impossible. My heart was held hostage by my son and telling me not to worry was like telling the sun not to rise or the moon to fall out of the sky.

While the nursemaids pacified Thomas with rags soaked in honey water, I paced up and down my chamber waiting for the men who'd gone to find a wet nurse, to return. At noon my women insisted I lay on my bed. I should not be walking the floor, they said.

I was beginning to despair when, just after the chapel bell rang for Vespers, the chief nursemaid came running.

'She's here, my lady,' she said, trying to catch her breath. 'They've taken her to the nursery.'

She was a well-built young woman, fair-haired, wearing a shabby gown and cap. She carried her own child in her arms and looked bewildered by her sudden translation into the nursery of the king's son. I looked at her healthy cheeks and breasts the size of melons and felt reassured, but Lady de Lacy was taking no chances. She pulled the girl's clothing aside and squeezed her breasts as you would a cow in the marketplace.

'Milk aplenty for two,' she pronounced. 'Put that child down and feed the king's son. If you do this well it will be the better for you.'

'But my baby?' the girl said with a look of blank incomprehension on her face.

'You may keep your child with you,' said Lady de Lacy. 'Have you a husband?'

'Yes, m'lady. He's gone to Carlisle.'

'He will be well paid for your work here.'

'But my little boys?'

'Your other children can do nothing but benefit from your association with the queen. And when the king's son is grown and has no further need of you there will be a purse and you will return to your husband. Be assured, he will be well pleased.'

With some reluctance the young woman handed her own baby to one of the nursemaids and sat down on a stool beside the cradle. She lifted Thomas up and held him to her breast. My son hiccupped twice and then fastened his mouth onto what she was offering. He sucked noisily. After a while she put him to the other breast and a few moments later he was asleep, his eyelids fluttering in contentment. She held him against her shoulder and rubbed his back but he didn't wake. His small chin was smeared with milk and his head lolled heavily against her neck.

'Give her a bed near my son,' I said to the chief nursemaid. 'Find her a clean gown and some water to wash. She stinks and it's not good for the king's son to inhale odours of the farmyard.'

I smiled at her. 'You have done well and I thank you.'

After that, Thomas thrived. He grew bigger and his voice became louder and more demanding. The new wet nurse said he sucked twice as long as her own child. She wondered if a king's son might need more milk than an ordinary child and I thought how pleased my husband would be to know his son had a royal appetite. And six weeks after the birth, when the aching pain had gone and the blood had ceased flowing, I was blessed with due ceremony and we went to Cawood.

We settled down to long summer days governed by the demands of the royal tyrant in the nursery. I saw the nursemaids bite their tongues when I insisted for the twentieth time that day that Thomas should be brought to me. I was enchanted by him. He was utterly perfect and every day I noticed something new.

I called to Lady de Lacy. 'He's looking at me. He can see me.'

'So he can, the little mite. What a fine royal son you have there, my dear. His grace will be proud of you both.'

The letters I received were a distraction from my life with my son. The doings of our army plundering through the towns and villages north of the border seemed less important than the fact that Thomas had smiled. My husband wrote with triumph of the success the army had at Caerlaverock, a small fortress across the Solwaeth, how they had taken it with ease. He rejoiced at such an early success but wrote of his concerns that the Scots would not come to battle as they kept disappearing into the hills.

I received a letter from my sister. Her wedding had been three days before Thomas was born. Surely a fortuitous time for them both? She wrote at length of her gown which had taken twenty tailors forty-three days to sew, her jewels which outshone even our great-grandmother's treasures, and of the richness and elegance of her new wardrobe. She wrote of the kings and queens who had attended the celebrations and of the gifts she had received. She told me of her excitement at the honour done to her by the great men of Austria but she didn't mention her husband at all. It was as if Rudolf did not exist.

In early August we were surprised by Archbishop Winchelsea. He rode up one early evening with what looked like a suspiciously large retinue.

'I am commanded by His Holiness to deliver a letter to his grace,' he said pompously as he greeted me. 'I am led to believe his grace will be somewhere across the border.'

'I believe so, your grace,' I said politely. I knew my husband had made an enemy of this man and he certainly was a rather unpleasant individual. I knew one should not dislike God's elected representatives, but it was hard to find much to favour in this fat man, with his loud voice and ingratiating manner.

'I have no desire to go tramping about in the wildness of that accursed land,' he grumbled. 'It would be more convenient if his grace had remained at Carlisle. I have been told the water crossings into Scotland are treacherous, even in the summer.'

Luckily his mission was urgent and next morning it was with little regret that we watched his party disappear under the gatehouse on their road to the north.

'I hope he gets his feet wet crossing the firth,' said Lady de Lacy uncharitably.

The archbishop had been gone a week when I had a much more welcome visitor. My husband's youngest daughter, Elizabeth, came like a breath of springtime, full of joy for her rediscovered freedom. She was tall and fair with the look of her father and all his mannerisms. To my surprise at least thirty horses followed her under the gatehouse.

'Lady Elizabeth, greetings. Are all these your people?'

'Yes dearest Marguerite, my new lady mother,' she replied gaily, stripping off her cloak and gazing round the hall her eye alighting on my favourite tapestry. 'Oh look! King Arthur and the swans. When I was a child I thought the swans were real and would one day flap their wings and fly away. But you see what happened? I was the one who flew away.'

I was less concerned with the swans than with how we would manage to house and feed so many people.

'I hope you don't mind if I call you Marguerite,' she said, smiling engagingly. 'I can't possibly call you mother.

You're only a year older than me. It would be ridiculous, wouldn't it? I told Margaret you and I were certain to be friends. Of course, my other sisters ignore me. Mary is always on her knees and Joan is absorbed in her love affair with that old knight she married, and she's got all those children. I know children can be perfectly adorable but they are such a burden. And how is my new brother? Can I see him?'

I called for one of my women to bring Thomas.

'Oh, isn't he lovely,' Elizabeth enthused. 'You are so lucky, Marguerite. He's the sweetest little thing I ever saw. Just look at his tiny hands. Oh do look, he's smiling. *Bonjour* little Thomas.'

She touched him with the tips of her slender fingers, talking baby-talk, but showed no desire to hold him.

'Margaret's son is not nearly so handsome,' she pronounced. 'He's got big ears and looks just like his father. Did you know her husband has three concubines? There are little bastards everywhere. Margaret is miserable but there's nothing she can do about it and her women are almost as dreary as those I had to endure in The Hague.'

I felt a pang of sympathy for this step-daughter I had yet to meet. I thought of the humiliations I would endure if my husband kept a concubine, parading his lack of fidelity to anyone who cared to look. At least my husband was faithful to me, in body if not in mind. And a dead wife didn't really count, did she?

'You don't know how wonderful it is to be away from those stuffy women at Jan's court,' she yawned. 'They were so dull and so prim. You'd have thought I was wanton when I expressed a desire to do something other than embroider endless cloths. We would sit there day after day stitching away, listening to the most tedious of religious texts. There was nothing else, not even a hint of singing. And as for dancing? They thought it the invention of the devil. At the funeral I think they wanted me shut up in the vault with poor Jan.'

'I'm sure that's not true, Elizabeth.'

'My dear Marguerite, you have no idea how dreadfully flat and dispiriting and dreary it was. It was a grey place full of dull, grey people. But I love England. We have sunshine and trees and hills and little valleys. I am so pleased to be home.'

She prattled on like this all day. By the time we retired to bed I was exhausted even though I'd barely spoken a word. Elizabeth had described every aspect of her extremely dull life in The Hague and had talked incessantly of the superiority of England and all her English friends who she was simply longing to meet again.

Next morning she started on her father. I discovered her sitting in the solar leafing through one of my new romances.

'I like this one,' she said, putting it down. 'All those knights doing such brave deeds. Now, Marguerite, you must tell me - has my father said anything to you about a husband for me?'

She never called him his grace, my father as the others did and I was beginning to have some sympathy with my husband over the episode of the coronet flung in the fire. I could see how annoying Elizabeth might be to him. But I liked her. She reminded me of my sister, my dearest Blanche.

I sat down beside her and picked up my book which was in danger of falling off the edge of the table.

'He has mentioned it,' I said cautiously. 'I am sure he has discussed it with the council but they are very busy with the campaign in Scotland at the moment. But you don't need to be worried. I'm certain he will choose wisely. He has all our best interests at heart, including yours.'

'If he had my best interests at heart he would never have married me to that awful boy,' she said, sticking out her bottom lip just like Ned did.

'It was a good marriage, Elizabeth,' I said gently. 'A very good alliance for your father.'

'For him perhaps but not for me.'

'Marriage is not intended for the benefit of young people. Don't be foolish. You have to play your part in advancing the fortunes of your family just like everyone else and your father did what was best.'

She shrugged her shoulders and then held out her hands. 'Oh, don't let's quarrel. Let's walk in the garden and I'll tell you my secrets and you can tell me yours.'

The summer had been warm and the Persian lilies and gillyflowers were flourishing. We sat on a turf bench shaded from the sun by a sweeping willow tree whose leaves trembled at the slightest movement of the air. I could smell the delicate scent of the apothecary's rose drifting in the noonday heat.

Elizabeth spoke in a small voice. 'Jan was a whiny boy and I truly do not want to marry someone else like him.'

I inclined my head, not sure exactly where this conversation was leading.

'Dearest Marguerite,' she said, edging closer. 'Would you persuade father to let me choose my own husband?'

'Elizabeth!' I was quite shocked.

'Oh, don't look like that,' she said crossly. 'Father arranged my first marriage so I think I should be allowed some choice this time.'

'Young women don't arrange their own marriages,' I said firmly. 'Not even if they are widows. It's a family matter. You know that.'

She pouted and looked sulky. I wondered if she'd been indulged as a child. Perhaps Eleanor had spoiled her youngest daughter.

'You see, Marguerite, I don't know if he still wants to marry me but if he does ...›

It appeared Elizabeth had lost her heart to some unsuitable man and was hoping I could persuade my husband to let her marry him.

'Who is it?'

She turned away from me and put her face up to the sun. She may have been a widow of seventeen but at that moment she looked more like a thirteen year-old maid. It was possible Lady de Lacy was right in her assessment of Elizabeth's marriage.

'Perhaps there's nobody,' she said coyly. 'You'll have to wait and see if you can guess.'

I sat with the letter from my husband in my hands. The messenger had arrived late in the day but I had waited until Elizabeth and I were alone to read the letter. He began very formally and correctly.

My very dear Companion, I trust you are well and fully recovered. I trust also that our son, Lord Thomas, does well and is in good health. The days have been many since I last enjoyed the pleasure of your company and I have long desired your presence. We shall return across the firth as our work here is done for the moment. I shall endeavour to pass the days peacefully after our tribulations until I see you again, which the Good Lord may permit to be soon.

There followed a lengthy description of the trials he had undergone and a sarcastic mention of Archbishop Winchelsea, who had arrived at Sweetheart Abbey where my husband's army was encamped. Apparently Lady de Lacy's wish had been granted as the archbishop had enjoyed a very unpleasant encounter with the quicksands on the Solwaeth.

I read it twice, trying to divine my husband's intentions because he would often write one thing but mean something else.

Elizabeth was fiddling with her embroidery. 'Is that a letter from my father?'

'Yes,' I replied. 'He is returning.'

'With his men?'

'He didn't say.'

Two weeks later we were in the garden when we heard a distant horn. Elizabeth clapped her hands together.

'Who do you think it is?' she said excitedly as we hastened back to the house.

I don't know who she thought it might be but by

the time Lord de Lacy and his retinue arrived she was resplendent in a fresh gown.

'It is your husband, Lady Margaret,' said Elizabeth in a disappointed voice. 'How very pleasant for you.'

Lord de Lacy heaved himself off his horse, landing on the cobbled courtyard with a thud. We greeted him formally and then went up the steps to the hall.

I took him to my chamber away from the noise and commotion below as he was still puffed and red in the face from his exertions. Fumbling in his pouch, he retrieved a sealed packet which he handed to me. It was another letter from my husband. I tucked it into my sleeve to read later.

'Is his grace well?' I enquired.

'His grace is in a fury which is why I am here,' he said jovially. 'The archbishop is never his favourite person at the best of times, as I'm sure you know. But when he brings a letter from His Holiness informing his grace that our intervention in Scottish affairs is unhelpful and not to the Holy Father's liking, well, you can imagine what he said.'

'So our armies are quitting Scotland?'

'Yes, but we'll be back. We've not caught Bruce or Wallace and there are scores to settle. His grace is sending me to Paris and then to Rome. What do you think of that, my dear?' he said, turning to his wife.

Lady de Lacy looked relieved. I could imagine her thoughts. Paris was safer than Scotland and Rome even safer. Campaigns, no matter who you were, could be dangerous.

When I was alone, I opened my husband's letter. He was at Carlisle and likely to remain there for some little while and he required my presence. My heart sank. My time with Thomas was to be ended.

I didn't want to leave him. Naturally I knew it had to end one day, but not yet, not when he was so small and so vulnerable. I thought perhaps I would delay a bit longer. I would wait until the harvest was finished.

Two days later Lord and Lady de Lacy left, but still I delayed. Day followed day and I failed to give the order for our removal to Carlisle. I told myself that Thomas needed me more than my husband did. My son was growing bigger and every moment with him was precious.

On the Feast of the Confessor another letter arrived. This time the instructions were quite clear. Thomas was to be despatched to Woodstock and I was to come to Carlisle without delay. The king commanded it.

7

AUTUMN 1300

The journey to Carlisle took two weeks in those dark days of an early English autumn. The terrain was difficult with steep-sided hills and narrow valleys and paths which petered out in front of our eyes. We found rivers flooded and bridges washed away. Twice the road became so deep in mud, the carts carrying our belongings got stuck. I longed to be back in the comfort of my chamber at Cawood with Thomas only a few steps away but my son was on his way south to Woodstock with his nursemaids and I didn't know when I would see him again.

In the fading light of the afternoon the enormous granite castle on the hill looked both imposing and sinister.

'It's very impressive, isn't it?' said Elizabeth, doubtfully. 'Oh but look! That tower is in ruins. Are you sure we're expected? I wouldn't want to sleep in the shelter of a wall.'

'Lord de Lacy said the Scots ravaged the castle last year,' I replied. 'But his grace, your father, is making repairs. Don't worry, he wouldn't have asked us to come unless there were apartments for us. He's not expecting us to sleep beside our horses in the heather!'

Elizabeth giggled.

As we rode under the inner gatehouse, I saw him waiting on the steps. My heart turned over with a sudden shock. His hair was whiter than I remembered. We'd been separated for five months but I hadn't expected him to change.

Beside me Elizabeth was fidgeting with excitement.

'There's Ned,' she cried.

Not waiting for the groom to take the reins or the lad to offer her his hands, she slid from her horse and ran to her brother. Forgetting their manners they greeted each other like little children, with hugs and laughter.

Ned was taller and browner than when I'd last seen him. His hair was still golden and his eyes a brilliant blue. He was growing to be an extremely good-looking young man and would surely break a dozen hearts before he was wed. I hoped Philip's daughter would appreciate such a handsome husband.

It was one of Blanche's prerequisites when we'd played the game of choosing husbands. Hers had to be handsome and wealthy and important and young and ... I couldn't remember the other conditions, I just knew she'd never found anyone who matched her ideals and, judging from her letter, Rudolf had also failed the test.

I didn't long for someone young and handsome like Ned or Humphrey de Bohun. I was perfectly happy with the husband I'd been given - an elderly man with nearly white hair who must once have been handsome but was so no longer.

I stared at my husband who stared back at me. I dismounted prettily and walked towards him.

'My lord,' I said, inclining my head and extending my gloved hand.

'Greetings, my lady,' he said formally. 'I see you have brought my daughter. I trust she has been a pleasant companion for you while you idled your days away.'

I had forgotten how frightening he could be. He wasn't smiling and I realised that by delaying I had seriously displeased him. I should have set out the moment he'd asked me to come. I remembered my good intentions at the beginning of our marriage, how I had promised that any feelings of mine must always be subservient to his. Yet the moment there'd been a conflict, when I'd wanted to stay with my son rather than be at my husband's side, I had failed him.

We were escorted through the great hall and up dark winding stairs to our chambers. Despite the ever-present noise of masons chipping away at the outer walls, the rooms were comfortable.

My women were delighted to be somewhere new and even more delighted by the presence of my stepson's household: dozens of dangerous young men newly returned from campaigning who would be anxious to recount stories of their exploits to any pretty woman who cared to listen. These were men who had been without the company of women for many months and in my chamber there was a frisson of excitement as the younger girls planned their dalliances and discussed their prey.

As for me? I was dreading the moment when I would be alone with my husband.

We finished unpacking the chests and I washed and changed out of my travel-stained garments. I was sorting through my jewel casket planning what to wear for the feast, when, with no warning, my husband arrived. With a sideways nod of his head he cleared the chamber. My women scuttled out like frightened hens. I'd never seen them disappear so quickly.

I turned to face him, my back hard against the table, the golden belt studded with rubies, which he'd given me last New Year on his return from Berwick, still in my hands. The light from the fire and the spluttering candles threw huge back shadows across the room.

'You disobeyed me,' he said abruptly. 'I ordered you to come and you delayed.'

'I'm sorry,' I began.

'I gave you an order.' His voice was rising. 'I thought you understood a wife's duties.'

'I do, but ...'

'So why did you not do as you were bid?'

'I thought to stay with our son.'

'You thought? You thought? I want none of your French manners here, madam. I have no interest in how you behaved in your brother's house but here you will do as I say. Is that understood? And when I tell you to come you will drop everything and pack up your household and come. I thought I made myself plain last time we had this discussion. You must obey me. You are not a child any more. I have quite enough disobedient children and I will not tolerate a disobedient wife. Now that you have a child of your own you are fully a woman, and women are obedient to their husbands. Do you understand?'

He was looming over me and I tried not to feel afraid. He was very much taller than me and considerably stronger. If he wished, he could knock me over with a single blow of his fist, and yet in the fourteen months we'd been married he had never lifted a finger against me. There were times he'd been sorely tempted because I'd seen it in his eyes.

If he had loved me I would have felt safe but I knew any

kindness was born of a regard for my position as his wife rather than any particular feelings he had for me. A fleeting thought ran through my mind and was gone - had he and Eleanor quarrelled? Had he ever struck her in anger?

'Our son needed me,' I began lamely. 'I thought to stay with him.'

'Our son is a babe and it is no part of your duties to care for babes. He has a household of women for that, women whom I pay well. Your duty is here by my side.'

'A child needs his mother,' I said stubbornly, beginning to feel stirrings of anger.

'Phaw!' he said. 'Peasant talk! If you want to grub around in a hovel with a bunch of brats then you can go for you have no place in my life. I didn't marry you to acquire a nursemaid. I married you to get me a wife.'

His anger was misplaced and by then I was feeling thoroughly self-righteous. I had only done what I thought was right. But a little worm of doubt was already wriggling at the corner of my mind. Deep within me I knew I hadn't done what I thought was right, I had done what pleased me and that was to remain with Thomas.

'Have you no understanding of your position?' he thundered. 'You are my wife and a husband needs his wife more than a child needs his mother. What would you have me do if you're not here? Take a woman? Is that what you want? Shall I select one from your chamber? I'm sure there are some who would be happy to share a bed with their king. Is that what you think I should do?'

'Of course not,' I cried. 'But you are a grown man and can reason. Thomas is just a baby. He can't understand why I have left him.'

'That is ridiculous. Thomas doesn't even know you. What you wanted was to idle your time away playing with him, wasn't it? You never once thought of your duty as my wife.'

'How dare you say Thomas doesn't know me,' I shouted. 'He knows I'm his mother. You haven't seen him for five months. How would you know anything about him? Just because you don't care for him there's no need to assume I don't. He is my son.'

'He is my son too.'

'I know just what store you set by your sons, my lord.'

There was a deep well of silence into which you could have dropped a bucket.

'What do you mean by that?' His voice had a dangerous edge to it.

'I know what you said when they brought you news of your little son's death.'

'And what did I say? Think carefully before you speak, madam.'

If I had been sensible I would have heard the note of warning in his voice, but I was beyond sense, beyond reason. I was speaking from my heart and the heart is the most unguarded of speakers.

'They told you your father was dead and your son, John, also. And you said "I can always make another son but God has given me only one father." That's what you said, my lord - you could make another son. Is that what Thomas is? Just another son? One that might die but it doesn't matter because you can always make another. How could you be so callous?'

He was white around the mouth and his eyes were

narrowed in fury. I had heard the same story both from my step-daughters and from Lady de Lacy.

He put out his hand and held onto the back of one of the chairs. He said nothing while I tried to get my temper under control. I was trembling because I hadn't realised how angry I was.

'If you really think that of me,' he said with a dangerous calm, 'then our life together has been a waste of my time and yours. I thought you understood my feelings and my aspirations, but clearly you have a perverted view of me as some soulless monster. Naturally you are far too young to understand a world where men are killed and children die. You didn't fight to be who you are so you've not the slightest understanding of what my kingship means to me. I saw my father nearly lose his throne through being weak and vacillating. I saw him beaten into the ground by his barons. I had to fight for my crown. I nearly died for it. And then I had to watch my wife lose child after child and despair of ever keeping one alive. Just because they were small and just because we were not with them, do you think we loved them any the less? Do you love Thomas less because you are here and he is elsewhere?'

At that point I did what I'd promised I would never do, and what any sensible woman would have done sooner - I burst into tears.

'You don't understand,' I sobbed. 'I'm torn in two. I want to be with you and be a good wife but I also want to be with Thomas. I know he has to have his own household, and I know it's best for him to live at Woodstock where he'll be safe, but I feel so alone without him.'

'Don't you think it's the same for a man? Do you

think my men like being away from their wives and their families? But it's part of their duty. Perhaps, contrary to what you believe, men know their duty better than women.'

By that point I was blinded by tears. All the sorrow at parting from my son and the exhaustion of the journey combined to fuel the flood of weeping. I covered my face with my hands in a vain attempt to hide the tears. I sniffed and hiccupped while a torrent of tears ran down my face. It was then, in the lowest moment of my despair, I felt his hand on my shoulder.

'I'm sorry,' I sobbed. 'I'm sorry. I've tried so hard to be a good wife.'

'Hush,' he said. 'Hush, don't say any more. We've both said far too much.'

He pulled me against him. Through the veil of tears I could see the deep red of his velvet robe where it brushed against my cheek and worried I was making it damp. Slowly I stopped crying.

'Time is too short to spend our hours fighting,' he said. 'I thought once I had finished with the Scots I was done for the season. I hadn't expected to encounter another assailant in my own castle.'

As an attempt at a joke it was rather feeble but it was what I needed. I smiled and laid my hand on his chest. It was reassuringly solid and comforting.

'Oh my lord, I'm sorry. My words were cruel and I shouldn't have spoken them.'

'Sometimes it is better to speak one's thoughts than to suppress them. Men like to know where they stand.'

'Yes, but ...'

'But what, my dear? You heard I was cold and heartless

and you believed it. They were dark days but they are in the past and I do not care to remember them. The past is the past and cannot be reclaimed and we must live for today. So dry your eyes and let me see you smile. We will say no more for we are man and wife and it's well known Adam and Eve quarrelled in the garden, so why should we not do likewise.'

I dried my eyes on my sleeve and let him seat me in the chair. He sat opposite and began to tell me of the last few weeks, of his unpleasant meeting with Archbishop Winchelsea, of his difficult journey back across the firth in foul weather and of his despair at ever persuading his council to grant him sufficient money to gather an army large enough to deal with the Scots.

I listened with half my attention, horribly aware that we had only postponed the discussion of our differences not solved them and that neither of us really understood the other at all.

For the feast I wore my pale green brocade gown with the rose-coloured surcote and my dark green velvet mantle lined with lambswool to keep me warm. The November rain was finding its way through windows and under doors, and the stone walls felt cold and damp to the touch. All I wanted was to huddle round a fire.

With my husband's present of a new gold circlet on my head, I took my place beside him in the great hall. We were flanked by Ned and Elizabeth and my husband's senior nobles. I could see the earl of Warwick, Guy de Beauchamp and my husband's half-cousin, Aymer de Valenece, the Pembroke heir. Humphrey de Bohun was there, as sleek and good-looking as ever, along with the two Lancaster brothers.

After my encounter with his wife I paid particular attention to the earl of Lancaster. I wondered how loyal he was and wondered how Ned would cope when the day came for him to take the throne. Through the brightness of the flickering candles and the talk and the music there was an undercurrent of danger. It was hard to know who was a friend and who might, one day, turn out to be an enemy.

When the acrobats had finished cavorting for our amusement and the minstrels were playing a last low melancholy tune, I noticed Ned further down the hall in earnest conversation with a dark-haired young man. Ned was seated sideways on the bench listening intently to what the young man was saying. After a moment he burst out laughing and clapped him on the shoulder. The young man grinned, his dark eyes dancing with pleasure.

'Who is that?' I asked my husband. 'The man talking to your son.'

He glanced down the hall and smiled.

'One of mine. A promising young fellow, name of Piers Gaveston. Father's a Gascon noble in Béarn but fell foul of your brother and fled to England, bringing the boy. I've agreed to transfer him to Ned's household. They seem to get on well and I think he'll be a good example for my son. He's a talented soldier and Ned has much to learn in that department. It should work out well.'

The fire had burned low but with so many people feasting and merrymaking the hall was still warm. There was no reason why I should suddenly have felt cold, no reason at all. I was surrounded by my family. The food and wine had made everyone happy and sleepy, and all seemed well with our world. It would be many years before I would remember this moment and by then of course it would be much too late.

8

SPRING 1301

I poked my nose out from under the fur covers. The air felt cold despite the heavy curtains and the warmth of my husband's body. I moved closer. He was lying on his side facing away from me, his gentle breathing telling me he was still asleep. Being careful not to wake him, I laid my cheek against his back, loving the feel of his solid presence. As long as he was here beside me I knew I was safe and I could pretend I was loved.

Ever since our quarrel before Christmas he had been especially kind, visiting me nearly every night. Our togetherness had brought me great joy and when I told him of my suspicions that I was again with child, he had held me close, the smile on his lips pressed against my hair, the strength of his embrace warming my heart.

'I think it will be towards the end of the summer,' I said, thinking of practical matters. 'Will you mind if I am not with you?'

'The safety of our second son is more important than my desires,' he replied. 'I shall send you to Woodstock. I want no repeat of your near disaster of last time and you can spend time with young Thomas.'

I was amused at how he assumed it would be another boy.

'What about the safety of our daughter?' I moved away from his exploring fingers.

He laughed, and pulled me tightly against him.

'We make sons, my dear. It will be another boy and we shall call him Edmund in honour of my brother.'

'But if it's a girl?' I persisted.

'Then you may choose the name. But I should warn you, if it's a girl, I'll have you back in our bed in two shakes of a lamb's tail to make another boy.'

'My lord,' I said in mock horror, removing myself to the far side of the bed and thinking of Eleanor's sixteen babies. 'How many sons are you planning for us?'

He looked at me, all the laughter gone from his face.

'As many as God gives us, my little pearl, and let us pray it will be many. A man can never have enough sons and you have to admit the making of them is very enjoyable.'

And so saying, he grasped my wrists and pulled me back into his arms. Later, when he lay grunting gently in his sleep, I compared my own pleasing fruitfulness with that of his first wife. We'd been married for barely seventeen months and already had a son in the cradle and another safe in my belly. I wondered how long it had taken Eleanor to produce two children and if they had both been sons.

Beside me in the bed, I felt him stir as he woke. He rolled over on his back and turned his head to look at me. His skin was creased and his eyes still heavy with sleep and now that he was awake, I could see the frown lines on his face.

'What is the matter, my lord? Are you unwell? Shall I send for something to ease the pain?'

'Not unless you can bring me a potion to bewitch my council.'

'Ah,' I said. 'Are they still proving difficult?'

We had come to Lincoln for a gathering of all the great men of my husband's realm, a parliament which was to sanction money for the campaign in the summer. I knew my husband needed agreement to raise a tax and no settlement had as yet been reached.

He pushed himself further up onto the pillows.

'I've told them I am without money and the country must provide if we're to recommence war with the Scots and I've told them I need a fifteenth of their goods but all they do is mutter and grumble and offer me a twentieth. They don't understand. If we can't hold Scotland then my dream of a greater kingdom is at an end.'

'But my lord, your kingdom is already great. Would it matter so very much if Scotland was not won?'

He looked at me with distaste and I felt the whole weight of his displeasure in the silence which followed. I should have heeded my mother's warnings and not meddled in matters which didn't concern me.

'I would not have expected you to say anything quite so stupid,' he said as he got out of bed. 'You clearly have not the slightest understanding of what you're talking about. Eleanor had more sense in her little finger than you have in the whole of your body. You'd better return to your spinning or whatever else it is you young women do.'

And so saying he walked out, slamming the door behind him, leaving me to ponder the wisdom of trying to be a good wife. I wondered how much Eleanor had interfered in his business and whether he'd welcomed it or if he had shouted at her the way he sometimes shouted at me.

While my husband made preparations for his war I spent mornings in my privy chamber with my clerks answering letters and dealing with the dozens of petitions which came from all parts of my husband's realm. I was constantly surprised at how knowledgeable his people were about the law, being quick to appeal to their lord if they believed their rights breached. And many understood they were more likely to receive satisfaction by petitioning a soft-hearted queen than bothering a busy, battle-hardened king.

I had a letter from a woman in a village near Norwich complaining of injuries done to her business by her bishop, and one from a man in St Albans whose house had been unjustly occupied by another. There were complaints concerning licenses for mills and breweries, dowries unpaid, mothers prevented from seeing their children, requests for cases to be adjourned and for sanctions to be lifted as fines had been paid. It was never-ending.

And after that I had to write letters to my husband's chancellor requesting monies due to me to be provided for how else was I to finance my household. There were many people to be paid, probably near fifty, and my women needed new robes for the summer. I tried not to worry but I could see why my husband was constantly in debt and perpetually harassed by his shortage of coin.

But the parliament was not the only reason we were in Lincoln. My husband had decided it was time to honour his elder son.

Ned stood before me clad in a truly sumptuous outfit. His embroidered satin robes were covered in pearls and sapphires, so much so that he glittered from head to toe.

'How do you think I look?'

'I think you look magnificent and every inch a Prince of Wales.'

'Piers says earls shine with the reflected glory of their own exalted opinion of themselves and princes glitter but only because of the inordinate amount of jewels they wear upon their person.'

I laughed and clapped my hands. Master Gaveston could certainly provide an amusing turn of phrase for each and every occasion. It was no wonder Ned enjoyed his company.

It was not only expedience which had led to today's grand ceremony but my husband's realisation that his son was no longer a difficult boy to be ignored or chastised, but a young man of promise, one of whom he could be proud. Ned was tall, good-looking and manly, and at seventeen, his father's son in every respect, except for his rather peculiar pursuits. I wondered if he bore any resemblance to Eleanor.

'Have you seen my coronet?' he said, removing himself to a seat by the fire.

'I have, and it's very fine. With that on your head you will bear the weight of the many Princes of Wales who have gone before you.'

'Oh lady mother,' he laughed. 'Llewelyn ap Gruffudd's head is on a spike above the entrance to the Tower so I'm not sure there is any weight left to be reckoned with. But from today Wales is mine and I shall enjoy having its men bend their knees to me.'

'Are you nervous?' I asked.

'No.' He paused. 'But you know why his grace, my father, is doing this, don't you?'

'You're his eldest son. As a father he naturally wishes to give you lands of your own.'

'Nothing his grace, my father, does is ever natural. Everything has an ulterior purpose. I had to think long and hard as to why, and why now. Then I remembered the prophecies of Merlin'

I frowned, trying to remember what I knew about the Welsh magician.

'There's one, saying my father's line will be ended by a prince who comes out of Wales and takes the crown.'

'Yes, I remember.'

'So if I am Prince of Wales it's not possible for me to end our line, is it?'

He smiled at his solution to this conundrum.

'How clever of you,' I said, patting his shoulder in what I hoped was an appropriately maternal way.

Yes, he really was an extremely handsome young man with his golden hair and smooth bronzed skin. He possessed a masculine appeal which wasn't wasted on my women who spent fruitless hours sighing over him, but I thought I would do well to remind myself occasionally that he was my stepson.

The cathedral church of St Mary the Virgin on the hill was, as the earl of Norfolk had once told me, the most magnificent church in England. Three towers with pointed spires rose high into the winter sky dwarfing the drab little houses below. The central spire was, according to the good citizens of Lincoln, the highest man had ever made and closer to God than anywhere else in Christendom.

In the vast nave where great white columns rose ever

upwards and pale arches soared high above our heads, hundreds of candles burned steadily. I knew my husband's memories of this church were sad for it was here he had prayed at the shrine of St Hugh to save his first wife and yet God had taken her.

The day before I'd watched as Ned was endowed with his new title and lands but today we'd come for a more private and personal reason. Yesterday the sun had shone in a sky of perfect blue but today rain came early and now louring clouds threatened yet more inclement weather.

'You will accompany me,' my husband had said when he planned the aftermath of the celebrations for Ned's day. 'As my wife you will assist me in the remembrance of one who was so dear to me.'

Since coming to Lincoln Eleanor's name had been on his lips all the time. It was as if she was living in the next chamber, someone to be mentioned casually in conversation. He wondered what she would have thought, what she would have done, recalling places they'd visited and happy times they'd spent together. I tried to be kind but found it difficult. Even though I would never have dared criticize my husband, I was very tired of hearing what Eleanor had thought and done and said.

I must, in one of my more unguarded moments, have said something unwise to Lady de Lacy, for she looked at me shrewdly out of her wise old eyes.

'He cares for you too my dear.'

'Does he?' I said rather crossly. 'Sometimes I wonder.'

'You must remember he was married to the queen for more than thirty-six years, a lifetime for most men. He is bound to have happy memories. She was only a girl when he first knew her and they were extremely close. You can't alter that.'

'Did you know her well?' I asked, curious to know what someone other than my stepchildren thought of this woman my husband idolised.

'As well as any.'

'What was she like?'

Lady de Lacy paused to think. 'She went everywhere with his grace. They were seldom apart. It was impossible not to see how they loved each other and how their minds worked together. It was a joy to observe them hand-clasped. Certainly there were those who thought she had too much influence over him, but, you know your husband, he's a strong-minded man and likes to have his own way. He would never have allowed her to interfere in the governing of his realm.'

I wasn't sure if this told me anything I didn't already know.

'But there *were* those who thought her too foreign, an unlucky queen, and some people considered her greedy,' continued Lady de Lacy.

'Greedy? In what way?'

'She liked to acquire land. The bishops were very unhappy about her methods and so were the people whose lands she took.'

'Did my husband know what she was doing?'

'Oh I'm sure he did. There nothing those two didn't know about each other. But what king would object to his queen enlarging her own lands? I suspect it would have pleased him. It just didn't please everybody.'

So the perfect Eleanor had not been perfect in everyone's eyes, only in those of my husband.

As we knelt in the chantry chapel where the late queen's viscera were buried, I recalled what Lady de Lacy had said about this woman and wondered if this was truly Queen Eleanor I saw in front of me. The tomb was ornate and her golden effigy chilling. Finely sculpted features depicted a strong, proud face, one full of nobility and womanly suffering. Her hair was unbound, her hands clasped in prayer where they would remain forever resting on the gilded folds of her gown. She was prettier than me.

The church had felt warm but the chantry chapel was cold despite the multitude of candles which burned day and night in everlasting memory of this woman who had been my husband's first wife.

'*Domine, Jesu Christe, Rex Gloriae.*'

I bowed my head and tried to remember the words of the Mass.

'Lord Jesus Christ, king of Glory.'

My mind kept sliding away into thoughts of this woman who had died so long ago. Our prayers begged for the soul of my husband's dead wife to be delivered from the pains of hell, from the deep lake and the mouth of the lion, not to fall into darkness but to be guided into holy light. And while we prayed I pondered on the strangeness that her children rarely mentioned her name. It was as if her death had expunged all memory of their mother from their minds.

And my husband? He couldn't let her go. Each time he said "Eleanor and I" or "the queen and I" I felt stabbed to the heart by a now familiar shaft of pain. At first I hadn't recognised this feeling for what it was but now I almost welcomed the pain. It was like biting on a sore tooth.

Jealousy was a sin. I knew that. And a sin for which I had not been prepared. I hadn't realised I could commit such a grievous sin when I'd been unaware of the temptation. How could I possibly be jealous of a shade?

'*Agnus Dei qui tolis peccata mundi.*'

'Lamb of God, who takes away the sins of the world.'

The Mass was nearly over but my mind, which should have been full of prayer, was tortured by unwelcome thoughts. I looked at the tomb and the thoughts came unbidden. She may have been the first wife, but I would be the last. I would be the one who would soothe his brow in old age and whisper of our long years together. Her children no longer cared for her but they liked me, they needed me. I gave them the love which she had denied them. They may have been *her* children but *I* was the one who cherished them. *Her* sons had died but *mine* would live. *I* was young and alive and in his bed and *she* was old and dead and lying in a tomb. She could never have what was now mine.

'*Dona eis requiem.*'

'Grant them rest.'

'*Agnus Dei, qui tolis peccata mundi. Dona eis requiem sempiternam.*'

'Lamb of God ... Grant them everlasting rest.'

My ears were full, my senses swimming in a sea of smoke and incense until at last we were done.

'*Pie Jesu Domine. Dona eis requiem. Amen.*'

'Merciful Lord Jesus. Grant them rest. Amen.'

As I rose from my knees I looked at my husband's face, at the pain etched in every line, at the depths of sorrow in his eyes and knew at once I was mistaken. I had taken nothing of hers because she held him still. She had been dead for more than ten years but it was as if she still lived and breathed and smiled, as if her absence was just for a moment, and then she would be amongst us again. She would touch his arm and he would turn, his face lighting up in the way a man's face does when he sees the woman he loves. She was his reality, and I was nothing but her shadow. He might bed me and enjoy me, welcome our children and have me at his side when he required the companionship of a consort, but she was his true wife and she was his only queen.

I had known when I married my husband that I would be a second wife. My mother had warned me of the difficulties I might face and I had accepted my place in his life with no complaints. I'd even said I would not be jealous. But I should have taken care and heeded my mother's warnings.

This was my first visit to the castle at Kenilworth and we were supping *en famille*. I never enjoyed being on display and it was pleasant for once not to sit in the great hall. I much preferred the quiet domesticity of moments like these. Not that our meal was entirely domestic as my husband was discussing strategies for his campaign. The dishes on the table were designated as various Scottish castles and our cups were armies. I thought my own cup was in danger of being swept onto the floor along with the disobedient Scots.

'The prince's army will attack in the west. He'll secure the Bruce castles at Ayr, here, and at Turnberry, here,' said my husband, moving my cup of wine to his left. 'My men will come in from Berwick and we'll head by Selkirk forest to Glasgow. '

'Pincers,' said Earl Thomas.

'As you say. Then we turn our attention to Stirling and the access to the north.' He moved the dish of perch in gudgeon sauce to the centre of the table. 'It's well defended and we'll need every bit of our firepower.'

Joan yawned, her handsome face flushed and pretty in the candlelight. My intercessions on her behalf had at last borne fruit and Ralph de Monthermer sat amongst us, fully restored to royal favour. But my husband kept eyeing his daughter as if somehow she'd got the better of him, perhaps by trickery or other underhand means.

'Are you weary?' I asked.

'No,' she replied. 'Merely bored. I shall be glad when they've gone, at least then we can discuss something other than the failings of the Scots and their raggle-tailed armies.'

'They quarrel amongst themselves like scavenging dogs,' said my husband. 'The Bruces and Comyns would tear out each other's hearts rather than fight together. If old man Bruce had supported Balliol it might have been different, but he didn't. He thought the crown should be his. Now he's dead and the Comyns know his son's not the stuff of kings.'

'The Comyns will never give up on one of their own,' said Ralph de Monthermer quietly.

'How is Balliol one of their own?' I asked.

'John Comyn's mother was Balliol's sister,' explained Lord Henry. 'They're bound in blood.'

Elizabeth, who sat on my husband's other side, talked very little. She was wearing her best blue gown and looked a picture of loveliness with her rosy cheeks and red lips but I noticed how she was alert to every footstep.

This was the last day before my husband headed north but when I suggested a stroll in the garden he said there was no time for idle amusement. Elizabeth refused saying she was otherwise occupied but I discovered Mary who was happy to accompany me.

'Let's go to the tiltyard causeway,' she suggested. 'We can watch the birds on the mere or if we're in luck the canons might be out fishing in one of their rickety boats.'

The causeway stretched all the way to the great gatehouse at the far end. To our left lay the lower pool and to the right, curling round to the west, the great mere, its waters stirring slightly in the morning breeze.

'It's enormous,' I said in admiration. 'His grace, your father, said that when his brother besieged the castle in the days of de Montfort's Great Revolt it took six months to capture it.'

'Did he tell you how the captain of the garrison cut the hand off my uncle's envoy sent to demand the surrender?'

'No, he didn't tell me that.'

I shuddered at the cruelties of war. We passed under the little gatehouse which protected the inner courtyards and walked out onto smooth hard surface of the causeway.

Mary frowned. 'Who's that?'

About thirty paces ahead of us a man was leaning over the wall at the edge of the causeway. His body was half way over the stone parapet, his feet barely touching the ground. He was dressed in my stepson's livery and was clearly trying to reach something in the water.

'It's Master Gaveston,' I said in surprise.

The young Gascon pulled himself back over the wall and pushed himself upright. He was a trifle shorter than Ned, pleasant-looking with dark curling hair and a mouth which smiled easily. He was flushed and his eyes were merry. When he saw who we were he gave a deep bow. Flamboyant good manners, I thought, and definitely not an Englishman.

'What are you doing out here, Master Gaveston? Why are you not preparing for tomorrow?'

'Greetings, your grace,' he said in his familiar Gascon accent. His voice reminded me of home and made me feel more kindly towards him. He was definitely an attractive man.

'Well?' I said severely.

'It's Lord Edward, your grace.'

I frowned. If he was waiting for my stepson why was he hanging over the wall?

Before I could say more, Mary cried out, 'Look!'

Swimming towards us along the great mere were two people, shouting and splashing.

'Is that Lord Edward?'

'Yes, your grace.'

'What's he doing?'

'He's trying to see how fast he can swim the mere.'

'He's making a great commotion about it. Who's that with him?'

Master Gaveston laughed. 'Robert the fool, your grace. Always one for a challenge. He said he could swim the mere there and back before dinner and faster than anyone else, so Lord Edward pulled him in. Of course Robert changed his mind but Lord Edward would have none of it and has been chasing him the whole way. I volunteered to haul Lord Edward out when he reached the causeway wall but it's too far down. He'll have to make his own way ashore.'

I put up a hand to hide my smile.

Mary pulled on my sleeve. 'I think it might be wise for us to retrace our footsteps.'

'Why? This is very diverting.'

'Because, if I'm not mistaken, my brother is clad in rather less than you might think.'

I laughed. 'You mean he has no shirt on.'

'I'm not sure he has his hose on either,' said Mary.

'In that case, Master Gaveston,' I said, trying to conceal my amusement. 'We women will leave you alone to rescue your two water sprites.'

As we hurried back along the causeway we heard Ned calling from the water. I looked back. His arm was upraised in greeting. I waved back. The sight of his firm young body rising from the mere with droplets of water sparkling on his bronzed skin was very pleasing, yes very pleasing indeed. But my gazing at my naked stepson was not something which would please my husband and besides, Mary, as an unmarried woman, should not be allowed to witness such a thing.

As we approached the keep we parted company. Mary had letters to write but I wanted to see the private garden which Lady de Lacy had said was a delight. I wandered past the stables with my two women idling slowly behind me. A couple of young maidservants were loitering outside the garden but scuttled away as I approached. I pushed the door open slightly, then quickly closed it again.

'Wait for me here,' I instructed my women.

I reopened the door and quietly slipped inside. At the far end of the pebbled path, not more than ten paces away, was my step-daughter Elizabeth in the arms of a young man. At the sound of the door closing they sprang apart. I think I was as surprised as they were for Elizabeth's erstwhile lover was none other than Humphrey de Bohun, the glamorous, eligible earl of Hereford.

'Holy Mary! I thought you were my father,' said Elizabeth.

I walked up the path towards them.

'What if I had been? What if his grace had found you manhandling his daughter in this fashion, Lord de Bohun? What would your chances of his favour be then? Or do you consider yourself too great a man to be cast down by your king?'

'Marguerite, you don't understand,' cried Elizabeth.

'I understand what my eyes are telling me.'

'Your grace,' began Humphrey de Bohun.

I put up my hand to silence him. I was surprised how powerful I felt despite this man being several years my senior and not the insignificant young squire I'd imagined entangled with my step-daughter.

'Don't say a word.'

I looked from one to the other. Elizabeth was tousled and defiant while Humphrey de Bohun hid his thoughts behind a face which betrayed nothing. I had no idea what he was thinking or what his intentions were.

'First you, my lord. Why are you are here? I presume this is not your first tryst with my step-daughter. I can hardly believe she would encourage such liberties upon so brief an acquaintance.'

'It is not what you think, your grace,' he said smoothly. 'My intentions towards the Lady Elizabeth are honourable. I want her for my wife. I always have.'

Elizabeth seized both my hands in hers.

'We've loved each other for so long, Marguerite. I thought it was hopeless, but now ...'

'We hope to persuade his grace our marriage would be to his advantage,' continued Humphrey.

'If his grace didn't favour your marriage before, he's hardly likely to do so now.'

I suspected my husband was negotiating another foreign marriage for his daughter and I wanted no part in encouraging these two lovers to hope for his approval.

'But everything is different now,' pleaded Elizabeth. 'When I was young my father insisted the betrothal contract with Jan had to be honoured even though I didn't want it. And he disliked Humphrey's father.'

Humphrey de Bohun took over the story. 'My father and the earl of Norfolk quarrelled badly with his grace. Harsh words were spoken and the dispute almost came to a show of arms. I could do nothing. I was merely my father's son and there was no possibility his grace would approve our marriage. But now my father, God rest his soul, is dead and I have come into my lands. I'm the earl of Hereford and I want the Lady Elizabeth for my countess.'

He gazed at Elizabeth with a look of total devotion.

'Very prettily put,' I said tartly.

I regarded the two of them. Standing amidst the tumble of orange and yellow gillyflowers, with the currant bushes in full bloom, they looked like a pair of star-crossed lovers. I had sympathy for their plight. I knew what it was like to be in love and their hearts were young, like mine.

'Tomorrow, Lord de Bohun, you leave for the north. I suggest you say nothing until the Scots are defeated and his grace is in a more generous mood. Then, and only then, I shall help you.'

Elizabeth threw her arms around my neck and kissed me.

'Oh Marguerite, thank you, thank you. You are the kindest, sweetest mother to me.'

Humphrey stood with his arms behind his back, a smile lighting up his handsome face.

'Your grace, I don't know what I can say.'

'Say nothing. We've not cleared the first fence, and *you* still have the Scots to defeat.'

I smiled at the two of them.

'I shall leave you to say your farewells but I shall expect you in my rooms very soon, Elizabeth.'

As I slipped back out of the garden, I could not resist turning back to see them clasped once more in each others arms.

Elizabeth ran into my chamber, rosy pink and breathless.

'Straighten your clothing, Elizabeth,' I said severely. 'You look as if you've been tumbled in a hedgerow.'

She smoothed the folds of her gown. As she ran her hands across her hips I had a dreadful thought. I took her by the arm and pulled her into the window embrasure.

'I want you to answer me truthfully, Elizabeth. Do you understand?'

'Yes.'

'Jan, your late husband?'

'What of him?'

'Did you lie together?'

'Did we what?'

'You heard,' I said. 'Did you lie with him? Were you man and wife together?'

She looked me straight in the eye and answered quite coolly, 'No. Not even once.'

'So you are a maid still?'

She blushed a deep red, and fiddled with her plaited girdle. 'Jan never touched me. He was too sick. He was always too sick.'

'That is not what I asked. I asked if you were still a maid, still *virgo intacta*. Or have you and the handsome earl of Hereford anticipated the delights of the marriage bed?'

She looked cross, like a child caught stealing cinnamon cakes.

'What business is it of yours?' she cried petulantly. 'You're not my mother.'

'No,' I said quietly. 'I am not your mother but my duty is to protect your honour and care for you as she would have done.'

'She never cared for me,' muttered Elizabeth, tears beginning to trickle down her cheeks.

Young women who cried were annoying. For pretty

young women it might prove a successful strategy but it wasn't going to work with me.

'Don't talk nonsense,' I said firmly.

'It's not nonsense. If she'd cared for me she wouldn't have left me.'

'Oh, Sweet Mother Mary, Elizabeth,' I said as she began to weep in earnest. 'It was God's will your mother died. She would no more have wanted to leave you than I would. But when we are called we have no say in the matter. She was sick and God delivered her from her misery. I am certain she loved you.'

I put my arms around her and tried to think like a mother. What would Eleanor have done?

'Listen to me. If your marriage with Jan was not a true marriage then we must protect you. Girls do not make assignations with handsome young men no matter how much they may yearn for them. If your hopes for this marriage come to nothing then your reputation as a maid must be unblemished.'

She lifted her tearful face to mine.

'If I can't marry Humphrey, I shan't marry anyone.'

'It is not for you to decide who you marry. I shall do my utmost to help but the decision is not mine and it is not yours either. Now dry your tears and come and help me finish putting away my things. Tomorrow the men leave and you don't want Lord de Bohun to carry the image of a miserable face all the way to the border.'

The day went too fast. By evening the men were packed and ready to depart. They would go at first light as soon as they had broken their fast. The courtyards were full of loaded wagons and through the upper windows I could see the flickering lights of camp fires in the park beyond the causeway. Tomorrow they would be gone and I would be on my way back to Woodstock and my son.

'I think I shall miss you, my little pearl,' said my husband as we lay in bed. This would be the last time he would be with me for many months.

'I shall miss you too, husband,' I said, my mind half on our son, wondering how much he had grown and hoping he remembered me.

It was stuffy behind the curtains and I thought idly of how pleasant it must be to lie encamped under the stars feeling the soft night air on one's cheeks. I wondered if my husband would hold me tightly in his arms if we lay out there together amongst the grasses looking at the stars.

'De Lacy said something today,' he continued.

'What was that, my lord?' I said, bringing myself back from my dreams of a nocturnal tryst.

'He talked of a coronation. His words reminded me how remiss I've been in not offering you a crown.'

A crown! The prize I had dreamed of for many months ever since I realised how much I cared for him. It was true everyone called me your grace and referred to me as my husband's queen, yet it must be obvious that without a coronation, an uncrowned, unanointed wife would in truth be no such thing. Eleanor had been crowned. *She* had been a true queen.

I waited for the rush of excitement but it didn't come. Coolly I examined his offer but knew before I counted the advantages, that I would refuse. I had imagined I would fight tooth and nail to acquire this ultimate symbol of my importance to him. But his casual offering of my greatest dream in the same way he would cast a bone to one of his hounds, disappointed me. If he had implored me to accept, if he had pledged his devotion, told me how important I was to him and his realm, or if he had said he cared for me, then I would have accepted. But it was another woman's leavings and I didn't want it.

I looked at his face. The lines of worry had grown this past winter, and his hair was now completely white. He might be old, he might be bad-tempered but I loved him. It ripped me apart sometimes knowing how much I loved him and how little he truly cared for me. I knew he had worries, not least his perennial problems with money. He was in debt to several of his nobles as well as the Italian bankers, and Ned said that Master Lovekyn had still not been paid for our wedding feast.

'I don't need a crown, my lord,' I said staunchly. 'It would not make me any more your wife nor would it make me care more for your realm or your people. I told you once I was yours for as long as I live and a crown was not part of my bargain. And a coronation would be an unwarranted expense when you are so short of funds.'

He took my hand and kissed it.

'Ah, my sweet little pearl. What a good bargain you were: a son in the cradle, another in your belly, and now an economical goodwife as well. I think I shall put you in charge of my treasury and that way I'll never run short. If we're not careful your brother will demand further concessions from me saying I have more than I was entitled to under our marriage contract.'

'My lord, I shall always do what is best for you. And

my brother knows nothing of our marriage. As I am sure you know, I do not correspond with him, only with my mother.'

'I'm sorry, my dear,' he laughed. 'You are such a delight to tease. You take everything so seriously.'

He was already removing the ribbons and unbraiding my hair. Having thus undone a large part of my women's night-time efforts, he turned his attention to my nightgown. While one hand played with strands of my hair which now lay fanned out across the pillow, letting his fingers trail through the tendrils, brushing any wisps away from my face, his other hand began gently stroking my breasts. Any thoughts of annoyance faded as I felt the accustomed pleasure at his touch. But however much I had him caught, and the nets of our passion did indeed hold him tightly, I too was a prisoner. And I was trapped more securely than he was because by tomorrow his desires would have faded while mine would still be alight, fuelled as they were by love.

'Will you come to me at Christmas?' he murmured, moving closer and planting kisses on my neck. 'After our son is born.'

'I will come whenever you command me,' I whispered, all thoughts of my child banished from my mind as the joys of passion took over.

At that moment I truly believed I would cross the oceans for a single night in my husband's bed. It was only later as he lay sleeping that I realised I would always have to be the one to take ship because he could never bring himself to quit the shores where his beloved Eleanor lay. She held him tight in her cold, dead arms and he had no wish to leave. He desired me, he lusted after me but he didn't love me, not the way he loved her and certainly not the way I loved him.

The time had come. My husband gave a nod of his head. 'Take good care of yourself and our son, my lady. I shall see you at Christmastide.'

I wondered for the hundredth time why he never asked me to accompany him. Eleanor had travelled with him on his campaigns, a constant helpmeet at his side, a pair of loving arms to comfort him each night. But I was only fit for sending back to the nursery, to sew and spin and be with our son. I was of no importance to him, of no worth. In truth, I felt undone.

'God speed, my lord,' I said, trying to keep back the tears. 'May Christ and His Saints ride with you.'

We watched them, a long line of men and horses strung out along the causeway, disappearing into the mist, their brightly coloured banners held aloft, the pennons limp in the damp morning air. They were followed by hundreds of heavy wagons piled high with the necessities of war, the horses already heaving under the strain.

'No tears this time, your grace,' said Lady de Lacy as I stood dry-eyed watching my husband ride away.

'I'm learning, Lady Margaret,' I said, too miserable to cry.

9

WINTER 1301-2

I could see nothing but dark swirling waters beneath my feet and was frightened I would fall into the chasm below. A hand stretched out of the gloom and grasped mine.

'Nae worry, lady,' said a gruff voice. 'You're safe now. Just a wee bit further. I'll nae let you fall.'

He was a burly man, wrapped in dark cloth, with a bonnet pulled low on his brow. I could barely see his features, hidden as they were by a beard and a mass of dark-red hair, but his words were kind and his grip was strong. I climbed up the slippery steps to the wharf, thankful to be on firm ground once more. I looked around me: grey mist, grey sea, grey walls and grey land.

'A thousand greetings to you, my lady,' said my rescuer. 'Welcome to Blackness. We'd nae expected you so soon. I've sent the boy to Linlithgow to tell them you're come. Oh my, but there'll be celebrating there tonight. Away inside now, out of the damp. The lassie will make you comfortable till your companions are ashore.'

The dark-haired girl who opened the door stared at me with large round eyes. She couldn't have been more than six years old. Her gown was grubby and far too small, showing her bare legs and feet. She stood aside for me to enter. I found myself in a small stone chamber hardly big enough for two of us. The girl was too over-awed to speak but seeing a low wooden bench I sank onto it. Gradually the world stopped swaying and my belly returned to its normal state. It had been a long and uncomfortable journey but it seemed we were nearly at our destination.

The message had come two days before the feast day of St Martin. My husband had instructed his officials at York to organise my removal to the north and would in due course inform them whence I was to travel to meet him. I was further informed that his grace had requested the Lady Elizabeth and the Lady Joan should accompany me as it would give his grace much pleasure to see his daughters.

To my regret Thomas and Edmund had to remain at Woodstock where the air was clean and the danger of illness small. Dear Edmund. Such a good baby. He had arrived shortly before the feast day of Our Lady on a morning full of sunshine and the promise of a good harvest. This time, although there was pain and fear, it was short-lived. Lady de Lacy said the birth was nothing compared to those dreadful days at Brotherton when they thought I would die. When she told me it was a boy, I remember thinking how pleased my husband would be. He had been proved right - again!

Thomas was walking now, unsteady little steps, but each day he grew bolder and I was sad, knowing that when I saw him next he would probably be talking as well. He could make a few attempts at "Mama" but his favourite word was "no".

I spent hours on the floor with him to the despair of Sir Stephen and Lady Eveline, the couple who managed the nursery household. I knew they thought it undignified, but Thomas enjoyed having me on a level with his own small self. He was not greatly enamoured with Edmund, shouting at him when he cried and trying to hit him with his tiny fists. But they were so close in age I was sure they would become friends. it would be a delight to see them as they grew together and I couldn't wait for my husband to meet his youngest son.

I'd written informing him of Edmund's birth but it was weeks before I received a reply and then it was polite but curt: yes he was pleased, yes he was glad all was well, but no, he would not be returning, there was far too much to be done.

The days were drawing in fast by the time Joan, Elizabeth and I had arrived at York. The autumn mists were cold this year but there had been little rain. We wanted nothing so much as to rest but the letter from my husband ordered us to proceed north without delay.

'I have decided to remain in Scotland through the winter for it will annoy my enemies. We shall be here at Linlithgow for the Christmas festivities and it will give me much pleasure to receive you. It is only a small palace but there is a pretty little lake and a church built of many-coloured stones, the like of which I have not seen before. Our Prince of Wales will make haste from Carlisle where he is at present and will be with us for the celebrations. This I know will please you for I am aware of how much care you have for my eldest son.'

By the time Joan and Elizabeth were safely ashore the dank little room in the old stone tower was crowded with too many wet, dispirited, shivering women. All I could hear was a profusion of snuffling and coughing and muttered complaints.

'We must leave, your grace,' said the captain of our guard, as he stood in the doorway. 'There's little daylight left and I'd not suggest a stay in this benighted place. We must press on to Linlithgow. The man here says it's only a short journey.'

I acquiesced happily for I too did not fancy a night by the shores of the Scottish Sea in the damp little fort.

We rode in single file as the track was narrow and strewn with branches wrenched from the trees by a recent gale. There were puddles, deep enough for a man to drown in, and no sign of people or buildings. It was a bleak place indeed.

We must have been travelling for about an hour when the man at the front shouted. I peered out from under the hood of my cloak. I could make out lights wavering in the distance. This must be the palace of Linlithgow.

Never was a place less well named. It was not a palace, rather a poor manor house, but I had to admit it was preferable to the fort at Blackness. As we rode up I could see neither the pretty little lake nor the church built from many-coloured stones but I had no doubt they were there. As my husband had amply proved to me time and time again, he was never wrong.

The torches flared wildly as we entered the hall. My husband was there to greet us looking, I thought, tired but happy. I hoped it was our arrival which had cheered him rather than his successes with his armies.

'My lady,' he bent and took my cold little hand in his.

'My lord,' I said with a smile on my lips, a smile just for him.

The hall was full of people. Ned was there, exuberant as ever, and I could see Humphrey de Bohun, his eyes alight with what I took to be love at the sight of a tousled and very weary Elizabeth. Joan's husband greeted her with muted enthusiasm, always unwilling to show too much affection to his wife in front of my husband. And the men of my stepson's household were barely noticed by my damp miserable collection of women.

'I had not hoped to see you so soon,' said my husband.

'Nor we,' I replied politely. 'But we were blown all the way on a south-easterly, no matter whether we were at sea or on horseback. I think we shall crave your indulgence and remain here till the wind turns, if it pleases you, my lord.'

He laughed.

'It does, my lady. It pleases me greatly.'

We stayed several weeks and they were amongst the happiest of my life. It isn't necessary to have grand castles to be content but it was strange that this mean little place on the edge of a barren land in the middle of an inhospitable winter should have been where I carried some of my fondest memories. Perhaps it was because his first wife had never been there.

I told my husband about Thomas and Edmund, and he told me about his fury at being unable to take the castle at Stirling because "those fools" had failed to provide him with the necessary means. I told him of Thomas's first words and he told me of how my brother had brought pressure to bear on His Holiness to release John Balliol, the one-time king of the Scots. I told him how Edmund could smile and how like my husband he looked, and he told me of his plans to call my brother's bluff and force the remaining rebellious Scottish nobles to make peace.

In our different ways we were both content.

'A Scottish pearl I have within my grasp this time,' said my husband, stroking my cheek that first early morning in the privacy of our bed. 'What do you think, wife? A boy again?'

I smiled at him, too lazy to contradict him.

'Perhaps I'm being selfish,' he said, sitting up and twitching the curtain back. 'Would you prefer a daughter?'

I struggled to raise myself from the depths of the fur covers.

'God has been good to us, my lord. I fear to ask for more.'

He regarded me soberly.

'God will always be good to you, my little pearl. You are truly one who deserves God's blessings.'

'I am not always deserving,' I protested.

He leaned over and silenced me with a kiss.

'Remember what you said, my dear. Your husband is never wrong. Now I must up and prepare for the day. I have much to organise.'

I noticed with a rush of pleasure that he hadn't mentioned Eleanor once.

Joan and I were accompanied by Joan's husband Ralph de Monthermer when next morning we strolled down to the lakeside.

181

'His grace, my father, was right,' said Joan. 'It *is* a pretty little lake.'

The water was dark and ruffled with small white waves. Personally I thought it sinister. Perhaps the sun had been shining when my husband first saw it and thought of me. I shivered and pulled my cloak more tightly around my shoulders.

'In the native tongue it is the loch of the black hound,' said Ralph de Monthermer. 'They say a man hereabouts, having offended his lord, was tied to a stake on one of the islands and left to die. But the man's faithful hound swam out each day carrying food to his master. When the lord was told he ordered the animal chained to a post on another island.'

'And is that the hound?' I asked, as we heard baying in the distance beyond the trees.

'A nonsense!' scoffed Joan. 'A tale to scare children and simple folk. I don't believe a word.'

'But one to strike fear into people on dark nights,' insisted her husband.

'It would have been more sensible to use a boat,' said Joan briskly. 'Why a hound?'

She turned her head away and stared at something.

'Look, Marguerite! I do believe that's Ned. What is he doing? God's bones! The fool!'

Bobbing up and down on the choppy waters was my stepson, his golden hair flying in a sudden squall. He was trying with great difficulty to navigate a small boat across the lake. He was stripped to the waist and beside him in the tiny craft was none other than his favourite companion, Master Gaveston. Judging by the waving arms and shouts of laughter they were enjoying themselves but I shivered at the thought of freezing spray on bare skin and decided it was not a pastime I would care for.

It was odd how Ned relished these easy rustic pleasures which my husband thought wholly unsuitable. Fooling about in boats or swimming the great mere at Kenilworth were not activities expected of a prince who would one day be king but I could only feel a wave of affection for my difficult stepson who so delighted in being different.

'Why does Ned think it amusing to be out on the water in the middle of winter?' said his sister crossly. 'And why can't he dress properly? He complains his grace, our father, treats him badly but he makes no effort to behave.'

'He's young,' said her husband mildly. 'Young men are notoriously wild.'

'Were you wild, Lord de Monthermer?' I enquired with a smile.

He laughed. 'No, your grace, I never had the opportunity. But it's said your husband, his grace, the king, was very wild in his youth.'

Aha! I thought, certain that bit of information might be useful one day.

It was impossible in a place such as Linlithgow, with its cramped little hall and small chambers, to have much privacy. Even my husband gave up trying to conduct his business and relaxed and enjoyed the Christmas festivities. For twelve days we feasted, we exchanged gifts, we sang, we danced, we listened to the minstrels and laughed at the tumblers and play-actors. But towards the end of the celebrations I decided the time had come to broach the subject of Elizabeth's marriage. Naturally I chose our bed as the only place where we could not be overheard.

'My lord,' I said as he lay beside me, shadowed in the half-light.

'Mmm?'

'Have you made any decision about your daughter's marriage?'

'Elizabeth?'

'Yes.'

'Is this your business?'

'No, my lord. It is not but I have a care for the girl and wondered if you were considering another alliance with your friends overseas?'

'I do not think I have many friends overseas at the moment,' he said dryly. 'The only person it would benefit me to marry my daughter to right now would be His Holiness. And as that is most unlikely to happen I think you can safely say I have made no decision on the matter.'

He shifted himself and heaved one of the fur covers over his shoulder.

'Have you a plan in mind, wife?' he asked curiously.

'I wondered if you would consider one of your nobles, my lord; one who would be of use to you. You said to me once that marriage fosters good relations.'

He gave a smothered laugh.

'Who are you planning to marry her to, my little pearl? I trust it is not poor John de Warenne. He's been a bachelor for many years and is not used to a woman in his house. I can't see him taking a wife.'

'No, my lord,' I said carefully. 'I was wondering about the earl of Hereford. He is unwed is he not? And he is wealthy.'

My husband laughed out loud this time. He seemed to find my suggestion amusing.

'I cannot see why you should laugh, my lord. I thought it a sensible idea.'

He pulled me into his arms and held me tight.

'I've often thought I should sack the lot of my council and have you sitting at my right hand, whispering policy in my ear. Just think, not only would I always make wise decisions, but how amusing it would be when we disagreed. Instead of the shouting matches we have in the council chamber, you and I could retire to bed, draw the curtains and settle our differences in the best way possible.'

'And what way would that be?' I asked innocently, knowing I had sown the seed and must now be patient and leave the plant to grow.

After the Feast of the Epiphany we removed ourselves to Falkirk where my husband had ordered a tournament to celebrate the end of the campaign. After four wonderful days of jousting with my husband arrayed as King Arthur and me as Guinevere there was an entertainment about which my husband would tell me nothing. It was, he said, a surprise.

The candles were lit, the hall was crowded and on the shallow dais was a great circular table of blue and gold. Round the table sat my husband, my step-son and twenty-four specially selected men, all dressed appropriately in the colours of King Arthur and his knights.

There was a blare of trumpets, the steward called for silence and in she came - the ugliest woman I had ever seen. She was riding a mule, not a well-groomed animal but probably the oldest and most moth-eaten creature in the whole of the kingdom. Its head was lowered in the way mules have and the woman was finding difficulty in making it move. She gave the animal a good kick and a lad from the kitchens whacked it from behind.

There were huge cheers as she rode slowly up the hall swaying slightly in the saddle. She wore a dirty drab-coloured gown and a dark woollen cloak, and dangling down over the mule's flanks were two long shapely legs clothed in black hose and stout leather boots. On her head was a russet-coloured cloth and peeping out from this, two coarse braids. At first I thought her hideously deformed but then I realised she was wearing a mask. This gave her huge bloodshot eyes and a nose about half a foot long.

'It's the damsel!' cried Ned, jumping up from his seat.

A great cheer rose from the body of the hall and shouts of 'A-welcome! A-welcome!'

'Cowards!' shrieked the damsel in a high falsetto voice. 'Cowards that would let a wronged maid be so put upon. There she is, imprisoned in a tall tower by a lake. Or perhaps we should say "lochen" to please our newly welcomed friends, those who at last know right from wrong.'

At this there were smiles from the Scots newly come into my husband's peace and more banging on the tables by the Englishmen.

She pointed at my husband's knights.

'What then, Sir Bedivere? Too afraid she'll take one look at you and beg her father to bolt the door?'

The earl of Lancaster flushed, but called good-naturedly, 'Stay mistress! No-one calls me a coward. I'll answer your challenge. Where is the maid? I'll release her from her bonds.'

It took me a while to identify the damsel on her mule. She was none other than Ned's friend, Master Gaveston. He made a very fine woman and I wondered whose idea it was that he should play the role of the loathly damsel in this evening's charade. The guise was brilliantly done.

'So brave Sir Bedivere wishes to release this lady from her tower, does he? Now let me see where it might be for methinks I have forgotten.' She stroked her whiskery chin and put her head to one side. 'Might it be the castle at Pickering?'

The words were hardly out of her mouth when the hall erupted with laughter. There were very few who were ignorant of the earl's problems with his wife.

The damsel wagged her finger. 'Nay I am mistaken, for the lady there, needs no father to bar her door. It must be the tower at Linlithgow. I've heard there is a likely lady chained there. It must be she. How say you, Sir Bedivere? Will you release her from her torment?'

I felt sorry for Earl Thomas. He was not a man with a ready wit. While he was trying to think what to say, Guy de Beauchamp, the tall black-haired earl of Warwick whom I had first met in Paris, leapt to his feet, and bowed courteously to the damsel.

'Sweet damsel,' he said as the hall was again rocked by a gale of laughter and the damsel bridled at the compliment. 'If my fellow knight-in-arms is too bedazzled by your beauty to take up the challenge, then I most certainly will. On the morrow I will ride for Linlithgow and seek out the lady.'

The damsel slipped off her mount and, using a stout stick which had been concealed beneath her cloak, approached her new victim.

'What!' she cried in her high cracked voice. 'Another brave knight. Who comes here? Why Sir Galahad, you wish to unchain the lady do you?'

'I do,' said Sir Guy.

'What could be more fitting? A black hound in search of a black bitch! A cold swim it'll be for you in search of your mate. I wish you well, Sir Knight, and trust the lady learns to put her tail aside for you.'

By the time we had finished laughing and a red-faced Sir Guy had sat down, the damsel had taken apart two further knights. My husband was laughing so much I thought he might choke on his wine. This was the kind of evening the men deserved after the privations of the campaign and they were determined to enjoy it to the full.

'What have we here?' she said, pointing at the elegantly reclining figure of Humprey de Bohun.

'Pretty Sir Perceval, I do believe. Now, what have we got for you? Another maiden? Nay, I've heard you hunt for royal quarry in the greenwoods. I'd not presume to offer you less.'

I thought our damsel was risking my husband's wrath. It was one thing to mock the men but this sort of jest could land Master Gaveston in a great deal of trouble. However my husband was mellow this evening and in no mood to be irritated and let it pass.

'And what of you, Sir Knight!' said the damsel, pointing at Ned. 'Sir Gawain. A goodly knight, if I am not mistaken, close in kin to our lord, King Arthur.'

At the cheer which greeted these words, my husband waved his hand to the crowd to acknowledge their applause, and gave Ned a friendly push.

'What would you have of me, wench?' Ned enquired politely.

There was a lewd comment from the back of the hall which was drowned out by some table-thumping.

'Why, Sir Knight. Surely you have been told? Has your father not tickled your fancy with tales of my beauty? I am renowned from Falkirk all the way to Berwick and beyond and I believe you are still unwed.'

She pushed her fearsome face right up to Ned and laid one hand on his chest.

'I am indeed without a wife.'

'Then look no further,' said the damsel. 'For here she is, ready and willing and able.'

Raucous waves of laughter filled the hall and two of my women were in such a state of merriment they disgraced themselves by falling off their bench.

'Have you a challenge for me, my lady?' said Ned, stepping back.

'Indeed I have, my fine one. A problem to test the keenest of minds.'

'I am waiting then, my wife-to-be.'

'It may have come to your notice, Sir Knight, that I am not so fair of face.'

'Who says?' shouted a voice from the back of the hall.

'A knight never comments on a lady's looks,' said Ned gallantly, desperately trying to keep a straight face.

'But suppose on our wedding night I was transformed?'

'Impossible!' cried out another voice.

'Changed to a beautiful maiden, soft of skin, fair of face with lips like cherries and silken tresses falling down my back. All yours for the taking.'

'That would indeed be a miracle,' said Ned with a grin.

'Ah,' said the damsel. 'But in the morning I would again be as you see me now. Not so pretty, eh, Sir Knight?'

She paused, assessing the mood of her audience.

'Or, you could have me sweet by day and my true coarse self by night.'

'No choice!' called a man from the side of the hall. 'Take the pretty one by night. Who notices a wench in the daytime?'

'Nay,' called another. 'Beauty by day! When the sun goes down all cats are grey and you can always close your eyes.'

My stepson stroked his chin, pretending to give proper consideration to the question.

'Lady,' he said. 'Who am I, a mere man, to know the mind of a woman? I will give *you* the choice. *You* decide.'

This was, as we all knew, the correct answer.

'In that case, Sir Knight, my beloved, my sweet one, my betrothed,' simpered the damsel, nudging herself up against my stepson in a very provocative manner. 'I shall see you anon in the bedchamber. By giving me the choice you have broken the evil spell under which I have laboured these many years. From henceforth I shall be a beauty both by day and night.'

And amidst a gale of cheering and clapping and many more bawdy jokes she leapt onto her elderly mule and with a couple of lascivious glances over her shoulder at Ned, trotted off down the hall and out of sight.

'God's nails!' said Joan, wiping her eyes. 'I don't think I've ever seen anything so funny in my life. I wonder who she was?'

Elizabeth leaned forward and said, 'I don't think it was a woman at all. What do you think, Marguerite?'

'I think,' I said slowly, 'that some mysteries are better left unsolved.'

The great tournament was over and soon the men would disperse. The foot soldiers had already departed and now the knights would leave, some to their homes, others to castles in Scotland held by the English, and many accompanying either Ned or my husband back into England. All swords would be sheathed and war banners furled because my husband had announced a truce to last until the autumn. We could look forward to a summer of rest.

'I shall be sorry to leave,' I said to Elizabeth.

'And I,' she said mournfully.

'Be patient,' I counselled her. 'There is nothing more we can do for the moment. You must wait and so must Lord de Bohun.'

As we went down the stairs we were met by one of my husband's clerks, a fussy little man with ink all over his fingers.

'Your grace, my lady,' he said, bowing courteously to us both. 'His grace, the king, requests your presence and that of the countess, in the great hall.'

'Is there some problem?' I enquired.

'One of the rebels has come to submit to his grace. Everyone is gathering. Of course it's been an arduous task these past weeks for us, hammering out an agreement. There is so much paperwork with the lawyers changing their minds at every turn. And then there is the matter of delay in the delivery of parchment. We are quite overburdened.'

He was still muttering away to himself as we reached the hall. The vast space was full of people. Three chairs draped in blue cloth had been placed to one side for Elizabeth, Joan and me. My husband's carved chair with the pointed back was central on the dais. He was surrounded by his friends, looking extremely pleased with himself To one side stood the senior members of his household and lining the length of the hall, hundreds of knights.

There was a noise of shouting at the door and in came a tall dark-haired man followed by six others. They were bare-headed. There was a collective gasp from the crowd as the leader strode up the hall towards my husband.

'Who is it?' I whispered to the man at my shoulder.

'The earl of Carrick, your grace. Sir Robert Bruce. The lord of Annandale's son.'

I saw men finger their daggers and felt my stomach flutter. This man was our enemy. I'd heard my husband talk of him and how he had defied his father to fight against the English. I wondered what had made him change his mind.

My husband sat forward in his chair. He fixed the earl with a look which would have made a lesser man quake. The hum of noise in the hall ceased and you could have heard a pin drop in the silence.

'You have come to see me, Sir Robert? I have been told you are ready to lay down your arms and return to my peace.'

'Edward of England, I have come here to do homage for my lands in Carrick and to swear fealty to you as my overlord,' the man announced in a strong clear voice.

'Very well,' said my husband. 'Come close.'

Sir Robert approached the dais and knelt on the rushes. Clasping his hands together, he offered them to my husband. Then he spoke.

'I Robert Bruce, son of my father Robert de Bruis, and of Marjorie, in her own right countess of Carrick, do swear to you, Edward of England, in the presence of this company here, that I will be faithful to you with regard to your life and the members of your body, in good faith and without deception. I acknowledge that I hold from you, as a fief, the lands in Carrick ...'

I was surprised. I thought he'd speak roughly but his voice was cultured and his command of language was perfect. He spoke without hesitation.

'... for each and all of which I make homage and fealty with hands and with mouth, to you, my liege lord. I promise to be a faithful vassal to you in all things in which a vassal is required to be faithful to his lord, and I will do you no harm. I promise to observe this homage I do here for my lands against all persons, in good faith and without deceit.'

My husband leaned forward and covered Sir Robert's hands with his own, accepting the homage. The earl of Carrick was now one of our men and no longer an enemy.

When I looked more closely at our newly welcomed friend, I could see, beneath the dust and grime of travel, he was an attractive man. He was young, his eyes were dark and evenly spaced, his skin sallow, his face well-shaped and his forehead high. He was without a wife but it was said he had a way with women and with those dark good looks and forthright manner I could almost imagine being caught in his coils myself. Almost, but not quite.

10

THE YEAR 1303

It was the feast day of the Circumcision of the Lord and I entered the chamber where the gift-giving ceremony was to take place, full of apprehension. Each year it was the same. I could not rid myself of the memory of Philip mentally weighing and costing each gift as it was presented, fixing the giver with an appropriate icy stare or imperceptible curve of his lips. As I stood next to my mother my belly had lurched in terror lest my meagre gift was not sufficiently worthy to meet with his approval.

I seated myself beside my husband, aware that between us, as always, hovered the shadow of his first wife. My husband welcomed her presence and sometimes misremembered himself and called me Eleanor. But she never acknowledged my existence, bending her whole attention to the man she loved though she was as real to me as any other woman in the room.

My husband was not the most imaginative of men in the matter of gifts and I suspected he delegated the task to one of his officials, giving no serious thought to the matter. This year I received another gold cup to add to my collection, beautifully decorated with leaves and flowers like the others he'd given me on previous occasions. At this rate my aumbry would be full and I'd have to commission the carpenter to build me a second one. I ran my fingers over the embossed surface and thanked him prettily for his kind thought, hearing the silent whisper at my shoulder - "Is that all?"

Ned's gifts were received with shrieks of excitement from his little nieces and smiles of appreciation from his sisters. To my boys he gave wooden toys and to his father, a jewelled clasp which merited a nod and a formal speech of thanks. Against protocol my stepson had left my gift to the last and now that his servant's arms were empty of intriguing silk-wrapped packages, he placed himself squarely in front of me. Eleanor's shadow had melted into the darkness at the sight of him as if she couldn't bear to meet this son she had abandoned to me.

In his palm lay a small velvet bag. His fingers burrowed inside seeking what lay within and with a flourish he produced an enormous cabochon ruby set cleverly on a golden band.

'This is for you because you are my dearest and most precious lady mother,' he said, giving me one of his truly engaging smiles.

His sisters gave a collective gasp and even Lady de Lacy's eyes widened at the magnificence of the jewel. Ned took my hand in his and looking into my eyes, slid the ring onto my finger. The polished stone gleamed in the candlelight, casting splashes of shimmering pigeon's blood onto the folds of my white velvet gown. I was speechless. It was the most beautiful and costly jewel I possessed and far outshone any of those in my great-grandmother's casket.

'A handsome gift,' said my husband dryly, a slight edge to his voice which most people would not have noticed. But I knew him too well to miss the jealous undertone.

'Oh let me see,' said Elizabeth, with undisguised envy. 'I do think it very mean of you, Ned. This is much finer than my brooch.'

'But you have a husband to buy you rubies.'

No-one said a word but the meaning was there for all of us to hear: Elizabeth had at last married her Humphrey and had a husband. But so did I. Luckily at that moment Thomas pushed his brother onto the floor. There was a resounding howl from Edmund and the awkwardness of the moment was broken as embarrassed nursemaids rushed to scoop up my little boys and bear them away to the nursery.

Later that night my husband came as usual to my bed and, saying nothing about the gift-giving, proceeded to claim his rights as a husband. He was not rough or unkind, in truth the pleasure he gave me was as great as ever, but the thought was fixed in my mind and therefore probably also in his that his son might give me jewels of unimaginable value but only he had the right to my body.

Soon after the Feast of the Epiphany, news arrived from the north. The Scots had attacked my husband's new castles and the one at Selkirk had fallen. It was a long time since the days of the great round table tournament and the coming in of the earl of Carrick and peace could still not be taken for granted. It was an ever-repeating cycle of campaigning and success followed by victories draining away which I feared would last for as long as there were Scots who would not accept the king of England as their overlord. But my husband was not deterred and immediately began preparations for a new campaign which he believed would defeat the Scottish rebels once and for all.

'My lord,' I said cautiously, not liking to interfere but greatly curious as to how the money could be found for his expedition when I knew he was deeply in debt. 'How will you pay for this army?'

'God's teeth, wife!' he shouted. 'Do you think I keep a tally of every debt owed to the Crown? Go and ask my treasurer if you want to know but I warn you, you will not like the answer.'

I supposed he was squeezing those to whom only a few years ago he had been generous and thought it wiser not to enquire further. From a petition presented to me by a London merchant I discovered dues had been raised on goods brought in by foreign merchants, and Ned said the treasury was clawing in the marriage aid not collected on his sisters' marriages. It seemed every barrel was being well and truly scraped. It was as well I had refused a coronation otherwise my husband's debts would be even greater.

He set out in the late spring while thousands of men were gathering on the border: men from Wales, from the north and from Ireland where the earl of Ulster had gathered a vast fleet to transport his army. This time the English were accompanied by the earl of Carrick who, my husband informed me, was bringing two thousand foot soldiers and as many men on horseback as he could muster.

All through the summer months I visited my manors and enjoyed precious days with my children, pursued by letters from my husband telling me of his progress. The English army had bypassed Stirling and were plunging deep into the furthermost parts of Scotland but the Scots retaliated, first by laying waste to castles in the south-west and then by marching across the border to attack the castle at Carlisle.

In August I received a furious letter which looked as if it had been chewed and trampled underfoot in frustration.

'There were no supplies waiting for us here at Perth which there should have been, not a single sack of wheat, and no coin to pay the men. It is monstrous how incompetent my officials are once my eye is off them. I have instructed those fools at Westminster to arrest whatever ships are needed to ferry grain north for how else can I feed my men. We have waited a full month and it is only now we can advance. From now on there will be no mercy shown to those who oppose us and once my armies have passed through I doubt the rebels will find a single stook of corn or living animal to give them sustenance.'

There were no kind thoughts for me or his two sons which showed how distressed he was by his situation and his lack of coin.

In early September when I reached Pleshey, the great de Bohun castle in Essex, another letter awaited me. My husband was advancing towards Aberdeen while Aymer de Valence together with the earl of Carrick, had struck out for the south-west to give aid to Ned and the newly-arrived men from across the Irish Sea.

I stayed two weeks with Elizabeth, admiring her new daughter, before taking ship north to Tynemouth, to the cliff top priory overlooking the Northern Sea where I had been ordered to wait for instructions. The days were tedious but at last I received news. My husband had decided to overwinter in the midst of his enemies at the abbey of Dunfermline.

'This is where they bury their kings, so I will sit and wait. They will bury no more kings of Scotland here, for I will have every one of them on their knees before the year is out, and I will have the traitor Wallace in chains. If there is to be a king in this land from now on, it will be me and mine. The body of my dearest sister lies in the abbey, beside that of her husband, so I shall bide my time here, while I wait, in praying for her soul. I would like your presence by my side this Christmastide, my dear companion, and will ask my officials at York to make arrangements for your journey. My new son-in-law would also care for sight of his wife.'

11

THE YEAR 1304

Our horses plodded onwards, their heads turned from the light flurries of snow blowing in off the sea. It was thawing and by now the track was a morass of mud and soft ice. On our right the waters were unsettled and brooding, the distant shore a mere dark line between grey sea and sky. As we rounded the headland and turned down into the shelter of the valley I saw the village.

At first I thought it was deserted but as we drew nearer I realised the appalling truth: almost everything had been razed to the ground. There was blackness amidst the blanketing snow, a blackness of man's doing. Houses destroyed, torn down, their thatched roofs burned. Barns which had once sheltered animals, in ruins, nothing but piles of rubble. Even the church stood roofless and bare, arched windows shattered, roof beams destroyed, the great oak door ripped off its hinges.

The ground all around was littered with debris: splintered bones of dead animals, half-charred baulks of timber, blackened stones, and drifts of snow which covered the Good Lord alone knew what. We rode through in silence. The only sound apart from the noise of our horses was the soft slap of sea on the lonely shore and the raucous cawing of black crows circling above. Everything else was mute in a pall of white and grey and black.

At the end of the settlement near the ruined church was a small clump of trees. As we approached my sense of dread grew. At first I didn't know what they were but as we drew closer I saw they were corpses, twelve in all, swinging slowly from the snow-covered branches, the ropes creaking to and fro.

They must have been dead some while as the lower limbs had been attacked by animals, some gnawed away completely leaving nothing but white bone and tattered cloth. Round each neck was a stout noose against which a head lolled and on the bodies themselves, the skin was not yet putrid but firm with frost, features still clearly visible, the faces twisted in those last dreadful moments of life.

'What awfulness has happened here?' I asked the captain of the guard.

He eyed me impatiently as if I ought to know.

'Our army came through in the early winter, my lady,' he said. 'The villagers sheltered the enemy and our men made an example of them - burned their houses, hanged their leaders. You have to teach these people a lesson.'

'But nobody has shriven them and they should be buried. And what of the others? The women?' I asked, my voice faltering. 'And the children?'

'Killed. Gone. Disappeared into the hills or starved. Who knows?'

It was clear I irritated him with my questions. I pulled my thick cloak more tightly around my body. The cold wind had sneaked under the furred lining and was chilling my bones.

Just then I caught sight of a child. He stood by the ruined church watching us. He was ragged and small, thin and bare-legged, about the same age as Thomas with something of the same look about him. It must have been the dark hair and eyes because in no other way could he possibly have resembled my son. There was no sign of the other villagers. In truth we had seen no-one since we had left Dunfermline.

'What about that child?' I pointed to the boy.

'Vermin,' said the captain dismissively.

We rode on but I couldn't get the thought of the swinging corpses and the silent, watching child out of my mind. I didn't realise it then, but I was noticing for the first time, truths which I should have known all along.

I had thought of war as men fighting on battlefields. I hadn't known it touched the lives of ordinary men and women going about their daily business, and I hadn't known it left children abandoned in the middle of a wasteland with no food or shelter and no-one to care for them. I was foolish and blind. My husband had said as much to me that day at Carlisle when we had quarrelled after Thomas was born. He said I had no idea what the world was like, how brutal it was. And he was right.

As we rode on, I wept for that child and all those, like him, who were alone and afraid. I wept for the women who had seen their men strung up in front of their eyes and their homes destroyed by my husband's army. And last, and least of all, I wept for myself and my pitiable folly and ignorance.

We had come to St Andrews for the parliament and for the submission of the rest of the Scottish landowners. Last year, in the damp and chill of a Scottish autumn, the English army had marched into the heartland of the Comyn clan, and forcefully persuaded the lord of Badenoch, John Comyn, and his friends to cease fighting and make their peace with us.

Wisely, my husband was merciful, but he decided that every Scot must now bend his knee and swear fealty to their overlord. No matter how little land they held, no matter how small and mean their house, homage must be done. There was to be no-one left outside my husband's peace except for the traitor Wallace, and he was to be hunted down like the dog he was.

The second day was bright and sunny but the cold persisted and patches of snow still lay in crevices on the bare hillside above the town. The sea out to the east was the colour of amethyst with silver streaks where sunlight caught the swell. White foam frothed over the foreshore, slipping away leaving gleaming black rocks behind in its wake. The gulls shrieked and wheeled, swooping for riches as the sea retreated.

I stood just outside the castle walls, looking down at the harbour where dozens of ships bobbed about in the water. Casks and boxes which had been off-loaded onto the quay were being stacked in piles, ready for bringing up the track for the feast later in the week. The town was crowded and this parliament was going to be a long one because my husband said there was much work to be done.

'Is it wise for you to be here, my lady?'

My heart fluttered in surprise and I turned round. The voice seemed familiar but it was two years since I'd seen the earl of Carrick at Falkirk and I barely recognized him.

'Sir Robert!'

He bowed and straightening up, smiled at me.

'I'm sorry, my lady. Did I frighten you? I was concerned at you being out here, unattended except for your women.'

'But I am quite safe, Sir Robert. We are at peace now, are we not?'

He looked beyond me, towards the north, to where I could just make out hills in the distance, a long snow-covered line of blue and grey.

'Peace?' he said quietly. 'Yes. We are at peace. We need to stop fighting. A land soaked in blood is no good to any man.'

'I agree,' I replied. 'I'd not seen war before this and didn't know how cruel it could be.'

He paused a moment before replying.

'My grandfather would weep were he alive.'

'Was he a fighting man, Sir Robert?'

'He should have been king of the Scots, my lady. He pitted himself against the others because he knew his claim was stronger.' He stopped again. 'But they chose Balliol.'

'He must have been a disappointed man.'

'They were like cocks on a dunghill both wanting the crown. But we made a terrible mistake.'

'What mistake was that?' I asked curiously.

'When you are a cock in the chicken coop, my lady, it is unwise to invite the fox into your house. We asked the fox to help us decide who should stand on top of the dunghill.'

'My husband?'

'It was the bishops. They feared a bloodbath and thought the king of England would prevent one. Instead he rewarded us with an endless subordination of Scottish pride.'

I fell silent. It occurred to me that, no matter that he had made his homage at Falkirk, the earl of Carrick was not wholeheartedly one of my husband's men.

'And what of your father?'

'My father is a good man but not one for fighting. He doesn't have the stomach for it.'

'And your mother?'

His eyes softened.

'A wonderful woman, a Scot through and through, unlike my father who is more of an Englishman than Scot with his southern manors and his books. She was the daughter of an earl and I take my title from her, not my father. If it would please you and you have the time, my lady, I would like to tell you the story of how they met. It may not be the truth but it pleases me, and she and my father would never say.'

'Tell me your story, Sir Robert. I am content to listen.'

He smiled at me. Yes, he was undeniably a handsome man and I could imagine what was said about him was true.

'There was my mother all alone living in her castle at Turnberry. It was many years ago and she was waiting impatiently for her husband to return from the Holy Land. He had taken the cross and gone to fight the Saracens. She waited a long time but he didn't come back. Instead my father returned bringing sad news of her husband's death to the lady of Carrick. They say she took one look at this handsome young knight, for my father was a good-looking man in his youth, and having given him hospitality, she kept him in her castle until he agreed to marry her.'

I thought if Sir Robert's father was anything like his son it was no wonder the lady of Carrick was determined to have him in her bed.

'I like to think it is true,' he said, smiling broadly. 'It is how I remember them together: my mother wild and impetuous, my father decent and honourable. Having been compromised by the fascinating young widow in her castle by the sea, naturally he married her. What else could he do?'

I laughed. 'What else indeed? I think if I were you, I too would want to believe the tale, and maybe it *is* true.'

He laughed with me, his eyes sparkling like sunlight dancing on the sea.

'My mother was a woman of the western seashore,' he said dreamily. 'They are different, you know, the people of the west. They think differently to the men of the east; they are wilder, fiercer and less forgiving and yet kinder, softer and more mysterious.'

'And you?'

'Oh me?' he laughed. 'I am part my mother and part my father. I have the stomach for a fight, my lady, and the heart for it but I also have the sense the Good Lord gave me. And good sense tells a man there is a time to fight and a time to make peace.'

'And now is the time for peace.'

'Yes.'

All of a sudden he looked sombre.

'Too many have died and too much blood has been spilled. And for what? I sometimes wonder what my grandfather would have made of this. Poor man. He was sadly disappointed in my father. He wanted a fighter for a son.'

I thought of Ned and my husband.

'Men are often disappointed in their sons, Sir Robert. They wish for a replica of themselves, someone to fight the fights they have left unfought, and are frustrated by what they have. But that does not mean the sons are worse than the fathers, merely different.'

'You are right, my lady. Of course you are right.'

He looked thoughtful, and I wondered if he was thinking of his father or of my stepson. Seeing my husband impose his will on these people, I could not imagine Ned doing so, and I suspected the earl of Carrick thought the same.

We walked a little way along the grassy cliff, side by side. It was very companionable. I was curious about Sir Robert Bruce. He was clearly a man who loved his country but I sensed there was more to him than a simple soldier.

'Are you married yet, Sir Robert?' I asked, remembering he had been unwed last time I had seen him, and thinking it would be a lucky woman who had him in her marriage bed.

'Yes, my lady. These two years past.'

'And your bride?'

'The daughter of Lord Richard de Burgh, the earl of Ulster. The one they call the Red Earl.

I was surprised. The Red Earl was one of my husband's staunchest allies. Sir Robert smiled, knowing instinctively what I was thinking.

'His grace's man,' he agreed. 'A wise move for me.'

'Yes,' I returned the smile. 'A good marriage for you both. I trust you are content?'

'Content enough, my lady. My wife is a pleasant young woman and she cares for my daughter.'

'You have a daughter?'

'Yes. Marjorie. From my first wife; she's nearly nine.'

It was hard to imagine him the father of a girl-child. He was turning out to be very different from the man I had supposed him to be.

'And you have brothers and sisters?'

'We are a large family. As I told you, my mother was very enamoured of my father and would seldom spare him from her bed. One of my brothers serves in the prince's household and I have a sister married to the king of Norway. We are close-knit yet spread far and wide, but one thing we have in common - we would give our lives for each other. See, my lady, we have almost reached the caves.'

I suddenly realised how far we had walked.

He smiled at me, showing his white teeth. 'I think we should return before your husband believes I have run off with you, or worse.'

I looked at him considering his words carefully. Less handsome than either Humphrey or my stepson, yet Sir Robert Bruce, the man of the western shores, possessed something they both lacked, something I could not readily identify but which I thought might well be prove to be dangerous. He was the kind of man a young woman could easily fall in love with, a man who would throw you across his saddle and ride off with you into the night, a man over whom a foolish woman could break her heart. I was no foolish woman but I did wonder if he was faithful to his wife.

My husband took my hand in his.

'What do you think of your new quarters?'

The pretty little pavilion with its fluttering flag looked sturdy and I felt sure it was big enough. I peered inside. The floor was covered in fresh heather and rushes, and there was plenty of room for my bed. I looked up to make sure there was no gap in the roof. I'd heard tales from Lady de Lacy of leaking tents and rain pouring through in the middle of the night, but my pavilion appeared sound. I turned to my husband.

'It is beautiful. Thank you. You have gone to a great deal of trouble.'

He waved away my thanks.

'I want you to enjoy the next few weeks. It will be a diversion for you. Our army will not be long in persuading the garrison here to surrender.'

We were encamped outside the great castle at Stirling which stood fair and square in our path on the journey back to England. It was the only castle left to be brought under my husband's control. Sir John Soules, the lord of Stirling, was in France and had declined to return and swear fealty, so my husband had decided to take Sir John's castle for himself.

'I have informed the commander of our intention to besiege the castle unless he surrenders forthwith,' he said, rubbing his hands together with gleeful anticipation.

The castle perched high on the hill at Stirling had guarded the crossing of the river for as long as anyone could remember. Other than by sailing the hostile waters of the Scottish Sea, an army wishing to gain access to the valleys and flat lands beyond the River Forth must cross the bridge at Stirling.

Next morning as we broke our fast, a messenger arrived from the castle. My husband's gaze ran down the parchment and as he read his frown grew deeper. He cast the message aside and said, 'You can tell Sir William Oliphant that I am not inclined to allow him the enjoyment of a leisurely correspondence with his master as to whether or not he should defend his master's castle. Tell him to make his preparations for tomorrow we shall attack.'

And with that my husband fell to devouring his bread and cheese with great gusto.

At first I thought little of what was happening. As my husband said, this was war and men knew what to expect. A castle which refused to surrender should prepare to be starved or bombarded into submission. It was barbaric but at least I didn't have to watch as day after day our army used their war machines against the walls.

'Where does it all come from?' I said to Ned who had paused in his duties to pay me a visit.

He laughed, wiping the sweat from his brow.

'We've stripped the lead off church roofs from here to St Andrews. There's not an ounce left. We have the heaviest counterbalances and finest war machines anyone has ever seen. I've bet Piers a shilling we'll get that south tower within the week. We're using Beelzebub today. Don't you think it's the best of the lot?'

I felt wearied from the noise and the shouting and the incessant banging and crashing.

'Why do you give them names? They're only machines.'

'You are not in harmony with war, are you, lady mother?'

'No,' I said crossly. 'I hate what it does to people.'

'If you worry about that, you'll have to make sure you are the victor.'

'Even victors do not return unscathed. Men's consciences are scarred by war,' I said firmly. 'It does them no good at all.'

It was nearly the feast day of St Anthony and the walls were still unbreached. I tried to compute how many days the garrison had been without fresh supplies. Was there still water and what did they find to eat?

My husband was thoroughly enjoying himself. He was like a small boy with new toys in the nursery and I felt a heaviness in my heart at his glorying of war. Before Stirling I thought perhaps I was beginning to understand him but now I realised I didn't know him at all. It saddened me to see how he enjoyed destroying other men.

Down the slope at the foot of St Mary's Wynd a ferryman was dozing in the shade of a clump of willows, waiting for people who wished to cross to the abbey church of St Mary at Cambuskenneth. As I perched in his rickety craft, with the water running a bare hand's width below the rim, the pretty bell tower came into full view. Behind me at the top of the hill our men were using every ounce of their might to reduce a single castle to rubble and destroy those left inside, while here was this peaceful house of God.

'Ye're nae the first this morning,' said the ferryman, helping me out onto the bank. 'The brothers have a deal of visitors these days. And with fair women like ye, I've a mind to put on a robe and cowl myself.'

I smiled politely and passed him a coin.

The church was a fine one, much used in the past, so my husband said, by Scottish kings and queens when staying at the castle. It was smaller than our grand cathedral churches but well-decorated and pleasing to the eye, though beauty was not what I sought that morning. More than anything I wanted peace.

I told my women to wait outside. They could wander the gardens at will or sit by the river but I would enter the church alone and they were not to follow. The oak door was heavy but yielded easily to my hand, the hinges well-greased no doubt by the ever-vigilant brothers.

Inside all was hushed. Thin morning light filtered through the high windows but there were few candles lit, just two on the altar and another in the little Lady Chapel on my left. The floors were not tiled but stone-flagged with no wool rugs to soften the cold. I stood perfectly still, breathing in the familiar scent of beeswax and the lingering traces of incense, as the deepening silence settled around me like a cloak.

Moving down the shallow step into the Lady Chapel I was aware of a profound sense of peace. I knelt in front of the statue of Our Lady and began to pray. Just at that moment I heard a noise. It was a chink, like the ring of a sword striking stone, followed by the muffled sound of a door closing. I didn't move. I wasn't frightened, at least not at first. I presumed it was one of the brothers entering on abbey business.

There were no more sounds and for a moment I thought I had imagined them, but then I heard the whispers. There were two of them and they stood beyond the rood screen, near the altar. They must have come in by the side door but they were not brothers from the monastery, I could tell that from their voices.

After a while they walked back up the nave and I could hear them more clearly even though they were still speaking quietly.

'It is agreed?' said the first.

'Written in blood,' said the second.

'And sworn on the Holy Book?'

'Yes.'

'If the time comes for a Scottish kingdom ...'

'*When* the time comes for a Scottish kingdom.'

I recognized that second voice. It belonged to the earl of Carrick, Sir Robert Bruce.

'Naturally,' said the first man. 'Before the old fox dies?'

'That depends on Comyn. If he's with us, then yes.'

'But for the moment this lies between us and Almighty God.'

I could see them both now. The light from the windows cut across their faces. The earl of Carrick looked tired. His accomplice, a youngish man with fair hair, seemed vaguely familiar. I tried to recall where I'd seen him. Then I remembered. Without his bishop's vestments he looked different. This was William Lamberton, bishop of St Andrews, a man I'd last seen at the parliament. I frowned, trying to recall what my husband had said. I'd been told he was a Balliol man, wedded to the ex-king and his Comyn allies, yet here he was having dealings with their sworn enemy, Sir Robert Bruce.

I shrank back into the hood of my cloak, pulling it across my face. I didn't want them knowing who I was if they happened to look my way. Shrouded like this I could be any woman come to pray at Our Lady's feet. But they carried on up the nave without looking to left or right.

'You have counted the blood money due if you don't live up to our bargain, Sir Bishop?' said Sir Robert quietly.

Lamberton laughed, then stifled the noise. 'I've made my decision, Sir Robert. You've no need to fear I'll change my mind and loss of money would not sweeten the folly if I did. Balliol won't return. We're certain of that. So if it is your desire, the crown is yours. Just be sure the lord of Badenoch agrees. We don't want more killings.'

'And Wishart?'

'Ah, the good bishop of Glasgow, my brother in Christ. Never fear, he's in agreement. But it must be all of us so make certain of the Comyns. You may not like them but we need them and their kin.'

I held my breath afraid they'd hear me. No mouse could have been as quiet as I was and no cat could have posed as much danger as these two men.

'We must decide on a sign,' said Lamberton.

'I'll think on it,' said Sir Robert, his voice growing fainter as they disappeared up the nave.

'Then it's to King Robert.'

'Nay. It's to the kingdom of Scotland.'

'And the early death of unwelcome intruders,' laughed the bishop.

I heard nothing more. I stayed where I was, shivering. It was treason but what should I do? Should I tell my husband or should I keep silent? My husband already knew how fragile was the loyalty of men like the earl of Carrick. He had once described Sir Robert as a man whose allegiance changed with the wind, but I felt sick at the casual way Bishop Lamberton had wished my husband dead.

I stayed where I was for a long time, too frightened to move, but eventually, when I was sure they were gone and would not return, I rose and took my leave. All the way back along the path to the river, despite the sheltering group of women giving me the illusion of safety, I looked fearfully about me, wondering where the two men were and what they were doing.

Late that afternoon when supping with my husband I noticed how weary he was. He was no longer a young man but somehow this last campaign had drained him of his remaining youth. In private, when we were alone the lines down the side of his mouth seemed deeper and made him look dispirited. His eye, which drooped when he was tired, appeared permanently half-closed, and his hair and beard were now completely white. Yet five years ago, at our marriage how young he had looked.

'Did you hear what I said?'

I jumped out of my reverie.

'No, I'm sorry, my lord.'

'The earl of Carrick is back with us. The father's dead and Bruce has come to do homage for his English lands. I wish I had more like him and fewer like that weasel, Lamberton, who looks you in the eye, mouthing a prayer while all the time he's planning to knife you in the belly.'

'Is the bishop not to be trusted?'

'I'd sooner trust a scorpion. But Bruce is sound and

soon we'll have Wallace strung up on a gibbet and that will be an end to it.'

'My lord, there is something I must tell you.' I began to speak of the overheard conversation when my husband gave a sudden groan. His face twisted in pain and he clutched at his belly.

'My lord?'

I had a sudden vision of Blanche, mimicking the old men at Philip's court who moaned of aches and pains. "Always whining about their bellies," she'd mocked. "If I was married to one such, I'd slip him a potion of devil berries. That would stop his complaints."

But I didn't want my life to be that of nursemaid to an ailing husband. I was young enough to want more from a husband and I most certainly desired another child.

'Shall I get you something to ease the pain, my lord?' I asked.

'No, keep me company. You may sing for me. A wife's duty is to entertain her husband, not to talk to him of war.'

'But ...'

'Sing!'

I picked up my lute and, as ordered, began to sing.

It was mid-summer and towering above my head was a monster built from wood and ropes. This was my husband's latest war machine and it looked like the work of the devil himself. The sack for the rocks lay limp under the axle, yet I was told this engine could hurl its missiles right over the walls of the castle.

'I've named it Warwolf,' said my husband, admiring his latest toy. 'I'll teach that young puppy, Oliphant, a lesson in warfare. Show him what it means to defy the king. Before the week's out he'll be crawling out with his tail between his legs, begging for mercy.'

I thought of the men trapped inside the castle who'd been nearly three months without supplies. I had rarely been hungry in my life and could not imagine what it must be like to starve. Were they eating rats? I'd heard this is what men did, but I couldn't imagine it. My brother Louis said men, *in extremis,* ate their dead comrades but I refused to believe any Christian man would commit such a foul act.

At that moment we heard a cry from one of the guards. A young man holding a torn white pennant was coming out of the castle gatehouse.

'Aha!' said my husband, rubbing his hands together with glee. 'The garrison wish to parley.'

The man looked half-starved. He was about twenty and thin to the point of emaciation. His cheeks were hollowed and his tattered garments hung on arms and legs which were like sticks. He was covered in grime yet despite his privations he held himself erect.

'Well?' said my husband. 'What does Sir William have to say for himself? Does he still wish to write a letter to his master or has he realised who his master is?'

The young man looked my husband in the eye and began to speak.

'Sir William Oliphant, captain of the garrison of Stirling Castle, wishes to convey to you, Edward of England, his wish to surrender the castle into your hands. He expects you to honour the code of chivalry and treat the garrison honourably. There is to be no loss of life or limb, and no retaliation is to be caused to our people. We acknowledge your superior power and have no wish to prolong our agony.'

He swayed and looked as if he might collapse.

My husband smiled.

'A shame he didn't think of this three months ago. I might have been inclined to accept. But now ... well, now I think we shall continue a bit longer. I'm sure Sir William has eyed my Warwolf and wondered what damage it can inflict, how many it can kill. I'm minded to let him discover for himself what happens to those who defy me. Return to your captain and tell him I decline his offer. Tell him to ask again in a week's time - if he's still alive.'

Not a flicker passed over the young man's face. He bowed courteously, turned, and walked slowly back up the hill, eventually disappearing under the gatehouse. In the shadows the gate opened a fraction to let him slip through and then slammed tight shut again.

'My lord,' I protested. 'You can't refuse their surrender. They're starving.'

He rounded on me.

'I can refuse anything I like. I am the king and overlord of them all. And, I would remind you, madam, your overlord as well. So get back to your sewing and leave men's work to men.'

'But my lord ...'

He lost his temper. I was completely unprepared for the sudden onslaught. It had been so long since I'd seen him like this I had completely forgotten how frightening he could be. Grasping hold of my wrist, he dragged me through the crowd of men to my pavilion, shouting at the three women sewing shirts for their menfolk to get out. They scuttled away like frightened beetles, dropping garments in an untidy heap on the chest.

Once inside, he grabbed hold of my arms with such force that he crushed the fabric of my gown and bruised the skin beneath. I could feel the imprint of his fingers against the bone as he pushed me backwards.

'Why do you do this? Always prodding and poking at my decisions with your sharp little tongue. Eleanor never behaved as you do. She knew what war was and how a royal wife should behave. In all our years together she was a constant support in everything I did, not like you, a continual prick to my conscience.'

I was frightened by his brutal handling of me but not so much so that I was prepared to ignore his insult. And he should have known better than to mention *her*: this paragon of virtue, this flawless wife, this shining example of queenly perfection whom I could never hope to emulate.

I had lived with him for a long time and had had to suffer too many casual reminders of my failure to live up to the example of his beloved ideal companion to accept this latest rebuke. His unjustified attack on my fruitless efforts to make him a better king and a more merciful lord unleashed all the years of unspoken resentment and we were back again in that tower room at Carlisle the year Thomas was born, eyeing each other across a chasm as wide as the Narrow Sea with not the slightest understanding of each other.

I pulled away from him and stood perfectly still, my hands gripped tight in fury.

'Perhaps your first wife had as little conscience as you

seem to have,' I replied sharply, my voice rising in anger. 'Perhaps a woman who prefers to ride off on crusade rather than care for her children's welfare has little idea of God's teachings.'

'Don't you dare speak of her like that,' he shouted.

'I'll speak of her in any way I want,' I screamed. 'You seem to forget who *I* am. I am not just a vessel for bearing your sons, I am your wife and I'm tired of always coming second in your thoughts, always being compared to her, and I'm tired of being expected to save you from yourself. Don't you understand the virtue of mercy?'

'I never asked you to save me from myself and mercy is the province of weaklings. A king needs to be strong.'

'So strong you bombard half-starved young men to death? What sort of king delights in crushing men who are already on their knees? '

'One who wins, madam. That is what war is about – winning. Grinding your enemy into the mud and if he won't surrender, putting a sword through his gullet. Or would you rather I let the Scots ravage our country unchecked: thieving and killing and violating our womenfolk. Is that what you want, madam? A lusty Scotsman in your bed?'

'How dare you,' I retorted, appalled by his insinuation. 'That is a disgusting and degrading thing to say.'

'As disgusting and degrading as war itself. You are no soldier and war, as I have told you before, is men's business. Women do not interfere. Didn't your mother teach you that? I should have known better than to marry you. No king of England has had any joy from a French wife. My grandfather's slut of a wife took so many lovers he ordered them hung from her bedrails, and *his* father shut his wife away, for interfering in his business. He let her rot for twenty years. So don't think you can defy me, madam. You were supposed to bring peace and you didn't. You were supposed to secure me Gascony and you didn't. Perhaps I'd better return you to your brother - used goods which were not what he promised.'

My blood ran cold at the thought of Philip's anger if I was sent back to Paris.

'You wouldn't, my lord. Not after all this time. You couldn't.'

'Oh I could, believe me, I could. Isn't that what one does with French whores? Send them back when you've finished with them.'

I swung my arm back and slapped him as hard as I could across his face. I don't know which of us was the more surprised.

He grasped my wrist. 'So you want a fight do you, my lady?'

I snatched my hand away and stood there, shivering in anger and fear.

He stared at me for a moment, then walked over and deliberately laced the tent closed.

'It is best we are not disturbed. Quarrels between a man and his wife should be private, and this time, as you requested, madam, I shall remember exactly who you are. You are my wife and we both know what a wife's duties are, don't we? Or have you forgotten what it is to be a wife?'

I clamped my lips together and said nothing. I was terrified at what I had done and even more terrified at what he might do in return. But simmering beneath the fear was an anger so huge I was not sure it could be contained.

'I told you clearly at the beginning of our marriage what your duties were as my wife and they didn't include rebuking me in front of others. If you were one of my children I would have you whipped.'

'Why don't you?' I cried. 'Go on! If it will slake your bloodlust I'd rather you beat me than make those poor wretches endure another day of your bombardments. Go on! Have me whipped. Strike me with your fists.'

'Listen to me,' he hissed, coming close and putting his mouth to my ear. 'If I thought that beating you would make you see reason, make no mistake I would do just that. But I have lived a long time and have never yet raised my hand in anger against a woman. If I want to bend you to my will there are far better ways.'

I was foolish and didn't see the danger but as my husband had just told me, I was no soldier.

'If there are better ways then perhaps you'd better use those,' I spat back, shoving him away from me.

He grasped the tops of my arms and pushed me slowly back against the bed. 'War makes a man thirsty for conquest, madam, and I've not yet had satisfaction of that castle. Now cease struggling and raise your skirts.'

'My lord!'

I was horrified. I could not believe he meant it and yet it was obvious what he had in mind. This was the behaviour of varlets and churls, of men in their cups, not of a king and certainly not of my husband. I had never refused him and he had never taken me in anger, it was not the way things were between us.

Despite our occasional quarrels he had never behaved towards me other than with the utmost propriety and I did not recognise this monster who had arisen out of nowhere. He moved his hands to my shoulders and with one swift movement ripped my surcote down the front. I tried to free myself, twisting this way and that, but he was determined and much stronger than me. He grasped my wrists with one hand while with the other forced up my chin so that he could look into my eyes. Then he pushed me till I was half bent back.

'Make no mistake, madam. This time you will do as I say.'

He pinned my body with one arm while, with his other hand, groped at the folds of my skirts.

'My lord,' I cried. 'This is unworthy of you.'

'As were your words,' he grunted.

'Stop!' I cried. 'Stop it! You can't do this.'

'I can,' he said, fumbling at his own clothes. 'I can do anything I like. I am your husband and your king. And you are my wife.'

His beard was rough and his breath hot on my face as he pressed his body against mine, and for the first time I realised just how powerless I was. He could crush me with a single clench of his fist if he wished and there was no tenderness, none whatsoever. I could have been a street whore.

'Look at me, madam, and remember this: I will not be defied. Now, stop fighting me for this is a battle you can't win. Besides which, I thought you wanted another child.'

'I do,' I sobbed. 'I do, I do. But not like this.'

'So be quiet,' he said, covering my mouth with his hand. 'You need to be taught a lesson in obedience.'

Afterwards, when he was done with me, he stepped back and watched impassively as I vainly tried to repair the damage to my clothing. I was crying. I saw rents in my gown and my kirtle and, all over my arms, bruises and scratches which he had inflicted upon me. I wouldn't look at him but could hear his rasping breathing slow down until at last there was silence. Whatever demons had driven him were now at rest.

'I shall send your women to you,' he said stiffly. 'And I shall instruct two of my men to stand guard outside your pavilion. You are not to leave without my permission. I would prefer not to have you criticise my every move nor sully the name of Queen Eleanor in front of my men. Do I make myself clear?'

And with that he unlaced the door and went out, leaving me to weep in the dust and heat of the afternoon amidst the ashes of my love for him.

Warwolf was completed five days later and, accompanied by much jubilation from my husband's men, commenced its awful work. Rock after rock was hurled at the walls of the castle. Even if I wanted to look, I could see little through the small window in our pavilion. The dust rose in clouds from the breached walls and the attendant crashes masked any shrieks or cries from within. I wondered how men could survive such an onslaught. If the attack carried on all the men would be dead and there would be no castle left for either side to possess.

After two days of having their fortifications pounded with increasing ferocity, the garrison sent out their messenger. This time, with me quietly obedient at his side, my husband made the man stand in the morning sun for over an hour while he debated whether or not to accept their surrender. He sat in his chair stroking his chin while he made a great show of contemplation.

He lifted his cup of wine and drank deeply, keeping his eyes fixed on the garrison's representative. Then he called for a platter of cold meats and proceeded to nibble at them. The young man's eyes couldn't leave the sight of the food. He stood rigid without trembling but his tongue licked his cracked lips as he watched my husband eat and drink.

After a while my husband tossed the remaining food to the hound which lay at his feet. I wanted to scream at him to stop the torment but I didn't dare say anything. The livid bruises on my body were an aching reminder of the fragility of my position. At last he flicked his fingers then one at a time with infinite care he sucked the grease from them.

'Very well,' he said. 'I have considered the matter and I agree to the terms of surrender. You may go and inform your commander. But tell him I insist it be done properly. He will understand what I mean.'

At midday we were seated waiting for Sir William Oliphant and his men. I was ordered to be present and sat silently beside my husband. My gown was fastened high on my throat with a jewelled brooch for I'd no wish for others to see evidence of our quarrel. Of course my women knew. How could I have hidden such things from them? But we were well-used to keeping secrets and our life together in our overcrowded rooms was probably more intimate than that of many a husband and wife.

The main gate opened and out they came. There must

have been about thirty of them. They were stripped down to their under-shirts and were barefoot. Their hair was covered in ashes and round their necks each man wore a noose of coarse rope. Despite this abasement and their obvious pitiable condition they held their heads high and our men raised a cheer for their bravery.

They walked down the castle approach to where we sat. The men knelt on the muddied grass while Sir William Oliphant went down on his knees at my husband's feet. He looked him straight in the eye and, with hands which shook only slightly under the weight, held out the great iron keys of the castle.

'To you Edward of England,' he said in a clear voice. 'I surrender these keys and this castle and I offer myself and my men into your custody and care.'

He was younger than I had expected. Somehow I'd thought he would be a grizzled old captain but he couldn't have been much older than me. My husband put his shoulders back and regarded the man at his feet.

'Better late than never, Sir William.'

He turned to Aymer de Valence who stood at his right shoulder.

'Have them in chains. They can go to London, to the Tower.'

I gasped. 'My lord!'

'You wish to say something?'

He fixed me with a look which made my whole body tremble.

'No, my lord. It's just that ...' I bit my lip, afraid to go on and wishing I'd not spoken.

'Just what?'

'What will happen to them? To Sir William and his men?'

'Oh, I'll not hang them if that's what you're worried about, my soft-hearted wife.' He laid great emphasis on those last words, delivering them with a slight sneer in his voice. 'Failure to submit to your overlord is treason, but on this occasion I am minded to be merciful. They can endure a spell in prison for their sins.'

The kneeling men were dragged up and hustled away. My husband gazed after them, a look suspiciously like regret in his eyes.

'Well,' he said to those around him. 'A pity that's all over but there it is. Let's go and celebrate. Ralph! Guy!'

He called to his men. A search would have to be made of the castle and any bodies buried and there would need to be an inventory. I despaired to think of the unnecessary loss of life.

'And the day after next,' said my husband, rubbing his hands on his thighs with enthusiasm for the task ahead, 'we shall have a tournament to celebrate.'

In the arena, trumpets sounded and gaily coloured pennants flew in the breeze. The men were as cheerful as I had seen them since the feast at Falkirk more than two years ago. They challenged each other in the lists, thundering down the course, lances pointing, shields at the ready, either shouting victory or pulling themselves up out of the dirt.

There was laughter and cheering and why should they not be joyful? We had prevailed. The castle was ours, the war was over, Scotland was part of my husband's realm and at last we had put an end to the spilling of blood. The two lands were now one: one throne, one crown, one king. All the Scottish nobles were safely within my husband's peace and if there were any dissenters they wisely kept their thoughts well hidden.

I kept my eyes on the earl of Carrick but he seemed as merry as the others. Watching him on that late summer morning, I could almost believe I had imagined those moments in the abbey church at Cambuskenneth, the two men in the shadows and the whispers of treason. But I knew I hadn't.

That night I dreamed of the delights of the marriage bed. I sighed, as a man's firm hands stroked my breasts and my belly. I saw the whiteness of my skin and his rough brown fingers tracing the curves of my body. I moaned as he pressed his lips against my neck, nipping the skin slightly with his teeth. I gasped as he held me closer, crushing me against his chest, forcing my head back. I looked into his eyes and saw ... the steady dark gaze of the earl of Carrick.

I woke in terror. It is said the devil sends dreams to women who have neglected to guard themselves against sin and certainly it was an evil spirit which sent this one. I lay awake, whispering prayers, pleading with Our Lady to protect me from whatever demons prowled out there in the darkness, yet all the while aware of the surging waves of desire sweeping through every part of my body.

12

AUTUMN 1304 - SUMMER 1305

We left Stirling at the end of the summer and crossed back into England. The heat had faded the grass to the colour of bleached linen and everywhere the trees were turning to their autumn livery of brown and gold. We skirted the high moorland country where crisp branches of heather purpled the ground and descended to where flat green fields stretched out towards a distant shimmering sea. A half-day's journey from Beverley we reached the royal castle at Burstwick where my husband wished to rest and regain his strength. And it was here in the wilds of Holderness that he and I at last made our peace.

Since that dreadful day at Stirling our estrangement had continued, neither of us prepared to apologise and admit to being in the wrong. But in the long quiet days at Burstwick, we found the words and the feelings to repair the damage we had wrought. I knew I had been too full of pride and self-importance and he admitted to selfishness and bad temper.

'I am a fool,' he said. 'I sometimes forget what a pearl I have in you, my dear. You have a purity of heart which puts me to shame.'

'No, my lord,' I protested. 'I am the one who is fortunate. Look at what you have given me.'

He patted my knee companionably.

'What have I given you but the sight of war and the opportunity to share an old man's bed?'

'You're not old,' I protested. 'You're just stubborn and foolish.'

'Ah, my dear. If I am foolish in war, am I not also foolish in love?'

He took my hand in his. He had never before spoken of love. How strange it was after we had endured a quarrel so bitter and hurtful and I had seen the worst of what men can do to each other, that he should speak those words. I laid my head against his chest feeling the thud of his heartbeat and thought once again how fortunate I was.

We stayed at Burstwick for three months. Part of me wanted to rush back to Woodstock to see our boys but my husband's needs came first and weekly letters reassured me that Thomas and Edmund were well. I sent instructions to Sir Stephen for winter cloaks, fur-lined with silver buttons, and for beaver-skin hats to keep my sons' heads warm when travelling.

We wandered in the gardens, did a little hunting and some hawking and gradually my husband began to feel stronger. We rode by the shore of the estuary where the slippery mud gleamed silver in the morning sun and a hundred different birds poked and pecked in the glistening, oozing marshes.

'Look!' I whispered. 'A heron.'

There he stood, solitary, hunched and grey, his feathers ruffled. Then with no warning and a mighty flapping of wings he was up and gone while my husband cursed the lack of his hawk.

As the autumn days grew shorter and the winds began

231

blowing cold off the Northern Sea we received sad news - the earl of Surrey, my husband's friend, John de Warenne, was dead.

'I could weep for the death of my old comrade,' said my husband bleakly. 'We didn't always agree but he was a good, loyal man. They're all dying, wife, every one of them, all my old comrades-in-arms. Soon only I shall be left and what will become of us then?'

But his grief at the death of his friend was blunted by the news of two new grandchildren: a son for Joan and a daughter for Elizabeth. I tried not to mind that that Elizabeth had named her daughter, Eleanor. It was natural to honour her mother but an evil worm whispered, "She didn't choose *your* name, did she?"

After a happy Christmas gathering at Lincoln we journeyed through the cold winter countryside for the happiest of reunions with our boys. But the happiness had not lasted and by the time we reached the Island of Thorns my beloved sister was dead.

I wept and wept until I thought I might drown in my tears. Mary sat on the settle and took my hands in hers.

'Dearest Marguerite, please stop crying. You will harm yourself.'

Tears seeped through my fingers and dripped onto my woollen gown.

I heard her say to some other person, 'I can do nothing. She is destroyed with grief.'

The news had come by messenger, a man with the red lion of the royal house of Hapsburg emblazoned on his tunic and a letter for the king of England. My husband came to me. I don't remember what he said but I remember crying out, falling to my knees and covering my head with my hands.

'No!' I screamed. 'No! It can't be true. It's a mistake. She can't be dead. God wouldn't take her away from me. Not now. Not like this.'

He knelt beside me. I saw his robe, crimson red, the fur trimming brushing softly against my face, as I pressed my forehead against the hard cold tiles on the floor.

'Come, my dear,' he said. 'Remember who you are.'

I beat my fists against the ground.

'I am her sister,' I sobbed. 'That's who I am. I am her sister. She didn't have anyone except me and I have no-one but her.'

He raised me up and held me in his arms. Then he placed me gently on a chair and held a cup of wine to my lips.

'Drink. It will help, believe me.'

I looked at him through the veil of my tears. I took the cup but my hands shook too much so he held it to my mouth. The metal was cold against my lips and I choked as the liquid burned my throat.

'I lost both my sisters,' he said, with the utmost kindness in his voice. 'And Edmund, my dearest brother. I understand.'

But no-one could understand. Blanche had been everything to me. She had been my only companion, my only friend, my only confidante. She had gone to her marriage with such high hopes but from my mother's letters I knew she had been unhappy. Rudolf was not the husband she'd imagined and indeed no man could have lived up to the dreams she'd woven for herself. And the babies who might have been of comfort to her had in the end destroyed her.

She died in a distant place I had never seen. I'd imagined travelling across the Narrow Sea to visit her, flying up the steps of her fairytale castle, the two of us dancing across the floor as we'd done in our long-ago childhood days at Vincennes. But there had been my babies and the Scottish war. My husband could not spare me from his side and I had let her die alone and without me.

The letter said she was to be buried in the church of the Greyfriars near her husband's palace but by the time we received the news she was already in her tomb. I was not even there to say farewell.

'The sister was lost to her years ago,' I heard my husband say. 'She never knew but it was obvious. A Hapsburg wife? Not a marriage to which I would have condemned one of my daughters.'

I thought of those happy days at Fontainebleau: long drifts of grasses, green leaves stirring gently as we sat weaving crowns from brightly-coloured flowers. I thought of the bitter winter nights, skies heavy and dark, when snow grew high in the courtyards and Blanche lay quietly curled in my arms. And the New Year gift of a pair of lovebirds in a gilded latticed cage. I had wept with joy at her kindness and with sorrow for the plight of the small trapped creatures and she had laughed and called me foolish.

I heard a voice from far away. 'Marguerite, please dearest, stop crying.'

I thought of her carefree laugh, her sparkling eyes, her rose-coloured lips and her tumbling shining hair. The days spread out before my eyes in a never-ending tapestry of joy. But it was all gone.

Mary called my physician, and when the cordials and potions failed to stop the tears, she called my confessor.

He had come with me in the days when I was a new bride. 'You will need someone you can trust,' my mother had said, 'Someone who will be *your* man, not your husband's, someone who has your spiritual welfare as his first concern, not the machinations of your English court.'

And so it had proved. In the months and years which followed he had listened to my halting confessions, to my admissions of sins which his cloistered life could never have allowed him to imagine, and his advice had brought me closer to God. He was small, round-faced and elderly, a man who cared nothing for the trappings of palace life, who spent his days in prayer and contemplation. He was a good man and he helped me to be good.

'God listens to you, my child,' he said, sitting close. 'He hears your cries and sees the sorrow in your heart.'

'Why has God taken her?' I wept. 'I cannot live with the thought of her gone.'

'You are thinking of yourself again. Remember what we said before. The self must be set aside in the care of others. Only then can you achieve true salvation. It is not for you to pit yourself against the will of God. If He has taken your sister, it is not for you to question why. Your sister does not need your tears. Pray for her soul. Do not spend your time indulging your own sorrow.'

At that I stopped weeping and began to think of my family: my two little boys, my husband, my stepdaughters and their children, and my stepson - all so dear to me.

And my friends: Lady Margaret and Alice. I had much for which to be grateful but the thought did little to assuage the pain in my heart. People were kind, but where my sister had been there was an emptiness which could never be filled.

I learned to live with my grief and one warm afternoon as I walked in the gardens of the archbishop's palace, I tested my bruised heart and found it less painful than before. A line of clerics in dark robes were hurrying across the bridge towards the abbey and nearby some young men were fooling about in the dust. They were screaming with laughter and rolling on the ground in a show of vulgar horseplay. To my horror I recognised one of them as Master Gaveston and another as my stepson.

'You look sad, my lady.'

I jumped. I'd thought I was alone with my thoughts.

'Sir Robert. You delight in catching me unawares.'

'I doubt you'd make a good soldier, my lady. Those who sleep in the heather make easy prey for their enemies.'

Remembering my dream of last summer I blushed, and found myself unable to meet his eyes.

'What are you doing here, Sir Robert?' I said in a voice which was a little unsteady. 'I thought you were in Scotland.'

He smiled. 'I was. My castle at Lochmaben is in a sorry state after the fighting and I had a mind to rebuild it in stone.'

'Does it look well?'

'Well enough. There's much still to do but a man who wants something badly enough must be prepared to wait.'

'And are you good at waiting?'

'Yes,' he said looking directly at me. 'I have learned to bide my time.'

If he was accustomed to getting what he wanted however long it took and whatever he had to do to achieve his ends, then he was a very dangerous man indeed, and not just to his enemies.

'You haven't said why you are here?' I said gazing at the toes of my shoes.

'I'm here, my lady, because his grace needs three good men to advise his council on his new possession.'

'And he chose you?' I looked up and then wished I hadn't.

'And Bishop Wishart and one of the lord of Badenoch's men.'

'Not the lord of Badenoch himself?'

He laughed. 'John Comyn and I find it hard to sit down together. It's better he sends one of his men. This way we shall make progress not spit at each other across the table.'

'And Bishop Wishart?'

'A fiery man and a patriot.'

'Like yourself.'

'Yes, my lady, like myself. I am a Scot and I love my country.'

'But you are a man of the border too so surely you have allegiances on both sides.'

'I do. I have houses in many places: in your husband's northern counties, in my wife's homeland where the earls of Carrick have long held land, and here in the south. I have a house at Tottenham. So you could say I belong nowhere.'

'But *you* know where you belong and where you are at peace.'

He regarded me thoughtfully, weighing his next words carefully.

'I do. But you? Where do you belong, my lady? This was not always your country.'

'No,' I said quickly. 'But that is the lot of women. We are married and leave behind what was once dear and familiar. I was born a daughter of France but now England is my home.'

'We belong where our hearts lead us,' he said softly.

We stood side by side watching my stepson and his friends cavorting on the grass. Sir Robert appeared thoughtful but his mouth was curved in the tiniest of smile as if seeing my husband's son behave like a fool gave him pleasure. My husband might breed fear in the hearts of men but I feared my stepson raised nothing but contempt.

With the parliament over, my husband decided to visit some of his favourite castles and holy shrines. We sang as our brightly coloured procession made its way along the road to the little town of Chichester. To one side were low rolling hills of short-cropped grass and on the other a myriad of silent rivers in reed-lined channels and shingle banks cut off by stretches of shimmering silvery water.

Ahead of me rode my stepson and his friends. They were in high spirits but an angry voice floated back on the breeze.

'They are my parks, Lord Edward, and you did not ask permission. I resent your intrusion.'

The voice was that of my husband's treasurer, the bishop

of Lichfield, Walter Langton, a man who saw things the king could not see and heard things the king did not hear.

'Your parks, indeed, Sir Treasurer? Why are you making such a fuss? We only took a few deer. How many was it Piers?'

'Seven, my lord,' Master Gaveston replied.

Bishop Langton's eyes bulged and his face turned a violent shade of red.

'You poached seven of my deer? That's a hanging offence. I'll have you in the courts, prince or not, and I shall inform his grace, your father, of this outrage.'

Even at this distance I could sense my stepson's anger.

'Oh fuck off, you little turd,' he shouted. 'Take your miserable arse elsewhere. I've no wish to have you near my person.'

'My lord!' said the bishop. 'I protest.'

'Protest all you like. Go and bugger a few of your deer. That should keep you amused.'

My women, who were riding beside me and could hear every word, tittered and covered their mouths in mock horror. Unfortunately for Ned they were not the only ones who heard and before we reached the next village someone had told my husband. The procession halted, Ned was ordered to his father's side and one of my husband's men was sent to fetch me.

'His grace requires your presence, my lady,' he said politely.

Reluctantly, I rode to where my husband sat rigid with fury on his high black horse with Ned beside him scowling at his hands.

'You will apologise to your stepmother,' snarled my

husband. 'She does not expect to hear such language in her presence.'

'It wasn't in her presence,' muttered Ned. 'She wasn't there.'

'Apologise!' roared my husband.

'I wasn't…'

He raised his hand to stop me.

'Apologise,' he hissed, 'or I'll be forced to teach you some manners, here, in front of everyone.'

Ned's lips were tight with suppressed fury. 'I crave your pardon, lady mother,' he said stiffly. 'My words were not meant for you and I'm sorry if they offended your ears.'

'Your apology is accepted,' I said graciously, not daring to say anything else.

My husband sent me back to my place and later I saw him in deep conversation with the bishop. Ned, looking surly and rebellious, took up his previous position. Nobody spoke of what had happened but I knew there must be plenty of whispered speculation.

That evening my husband came to see me.

'I am sending him to Windsor,' he said, lowering himself heavily onto one of the seats by the fire. 'I can't have him insult my treasurer in that fashion. It was unforgivable. You heard what he said, I presume?'

'Yes, every word. It was not what my women and I are used to but men often curse and swear when they are provoked.'

'Men can do what they like in private but no son of mine will use words like that to a servant of the Crown on the king's highway. I despair of him. He behaves like a churl. His friends are louts from the alleyways, labourers, ploughboys. He has no idea how to foster bonds with the men he'll need when he's king. And he spends too much money on extravagances.'

'I'm sure he'll learn prudence,' I said gently but my husband wasn't listening.

'I have reduced his household. Some of the least desirable have been dismissed. They're a bad influence. Particularly Gaveston. That was a mistake. I thought he'd set my son a good example but instead he has corrupted him. They are far too close. They spend their time playing the fool and making mischief. So I've cut my son's income and removed his seal. That'll put a stop to his profligacy. He can sit at Windsor and think on his misdeeds.'

'He's only young, my lord,' I said hesitantly. 'You were wild in your youth, so I heard.'

'Who told you that?' he snapped.

'I forget, my lord,' I lied.

'Well whoever it was has a very poor memory and the circumstances were entirely different. I had to fight for what I have. Ned is being handed his inheritance on a silver platter and the boy isn't even grateful. God's nails! Why couldn't it be young Edmund? He'd make a much better king.'

Two days later we set off, leaving Ned behind. The meadows were flushed with the vivid colours of late spring and everywhere creamy-white drifts of meadowsweet crowded the damp valley bottoms. I should have felt joyful but I was miserable whenever I thought of Ned's banishment. My husband refused to speak of his son but before long letters began arriving from my stepdaughters.

Elizabeth wrote,

'Poor Ned is distraught. He is so unhappy now that my father has removed Master Gaveston from his household. You know how attached they are to one another. It really is not deserved. I am certain Ned never meant the words he spoke to my father's treasurer, who, when all is said and done, is only a servant. Dearest Marguerite, lady mother, please, please see your way to make representations on Ned's behalf. I know my father, will listen to you. He is always kindly disposed towards you and will surely listen to your pleadings.'

She carried on in much the same vein for several more lines, claiming that only I could heal the breach.

Five days later I had a letter from Joan.

'I have had to lend him my seal so that he can purchase his necessaries. It is monstrous that his grace, my father, has treated him like this. To have one's household reduced in such a peremptory manner is nothing short of persecution. It is the work of the very worst sort of tyrant. It is not that I am particularly enamoured with Master Gaveston, I find him rather too fond of his own opinions and Ralph says he is a conceited young fool, but he is Ned's friend.

My brother tells me he is short of funds. I have had to make him a loan. You would think his grace, my father, desired to reduce him to a state of want, begging for alms at the gate. Next he will have him in sackcloth.'

The following week, one came from Mary at Amesbury.

'I have written to his grace, my father, asking permission to write to my brother. I am aware there has been some great disagreement between them and my brother is very unhappy. So I wish to do what I can. Apparently my brother is also in need of monies as he does not even have sufficient for his household. Certainly in this particular I can assist him as I have more than enough for my own requirements. I do not like to ask you, dearest lady mother, but it would be pleasing to us all if you would see your way to plead with his grace to see reason in this matter. He is always concerned with assuring himself of your happiness and would I am sure indulge you in this small difficulty in which my brother finds himself. I do not know if it is wise for my brother to be so attached to Master Gaveston but surely the affection in which they hold each other can only be strengthened by keeping them apart.'

And if that was not sufficient to melt my heart and drive me to intervene on my stepson's behalf, I had at least five letters from Ned himself, each one more desperate than the last. It was difficult to know which distressed him more, the loss of his money or the loss of his friends. He spoke of the anguish he suffered at being parted from Master Gaveston and implored me to take his pleas to my heart and pursue his cause with his father. He spoke of the love he bore me, playing on my heartstrings as cleverly as any minstrel, and I found him quite impossible to resist.

It was a sunny day when we arrived at Leeds Castle and I knew it was time to say something. I hoped the luxuriant beauty of the surroundings would work their charms on my husband because this was an enchanted place, an Isle of Avalon, a Camelot, where spells could be woven and dreams could come true.

The lake, which encircled the castle, was a perfect mirror to our colourful progress across the bridge. The abundance of greenery glistened and shimmered like some fairie magic, casting a mysterious emerald light over the water's edge. I thought I was half way to being bewitched.

That evening we made merry with some tumblers and a group of fiddlers from Genoa who entertained us with a medley of songs. By the time we retired for the night my husband came to my room intent on keeping me awake a little while longer. Since banishing Ned he had sought my bed more frequently and I wondered if it was the seasonal warmth or if a man found strength in the quelling of his son.

Louis once told me the story of a fabulous white stag in the forests of Clermont who had fought the younger beasts for his right to the hinds. He roared his challenge through the shortening autumn days and drove away his own sons, proving his superiority with magnificent clashing antlers. Louis said the stag must remain dominant for if he was defeated he would be driven out to die.

'I don't think your mind is with me, little pearl,' said my husband, softly. 'Are you thinking of tonight's minstrelsy or are you distracted by other matters?'

I cursed myself for my straying mind. I knew my

husband well enough to know he needed to be soothed into a mellow mood if I wanted to succeed in helping Ned.

'You would be wrong, my lord,' I said quietly. 'I *was* thinking of your well-being.'

'That makes me very suspicious for you *always* have my well-being uppermost in your mind. So what is special about tonight? Are you planning some entertainment in our bed, something we have perhaps seen performed by the acrobats?'

I smiled. He could be very amusing when he chose.

'When we met first at Canterbury, my lord, did you think me suited to be your wife?'

He regarded me with even greater suspicion.

'When I first saw you,' he said slowly, 'riding towards me on that September afternoon, I remember thinking, dear God, it is forty-five years since I last married a child and here I am marrying another.'

'I was nineteen,' I replied tartly. 'Hardly a child.'

'To a man of sixty, my dear, you were a mere babe. But you have proved an agreeable companion and if you are asking if I regret our marriage then you already know the answer. However, if you wish to give me further reassurance as to your desirability and obedience, you know what to do.'

He slid his hand up inside my nightgown and whispered in my ear, 'Open yourself up to me, my little pearl.'

Later, as we lay in each others arms, he stroked my hair and said, 'Now, what was it you wished to ask me?'

'Did I wish to ask you something?' I replied sleepily, groping for my nightcap.

'I may be old, wife, but I am not completely gone in my senses. When a woman asks her husband what he first thought of her you can be sure she is after something. So out with it! What do you want?'

There was no deceiving him so I told him the truth.

'I want you to make peace with your son. It grieves me to see you estranged from each other and it would please me to have you reconciled. I do not ask this only for myself, my lord, but for you also. I know it hurts you to be on bad terms with the prince and I believe your mind would be greatly eased if you could find it in your heart to forgive him. Has he not been punished enough?'

'The trouble with you, my little pearl, is that everything you say makes such perfect sense. Yet why do I feel I am being put in the wrong?'

I touched my fingers to his lips.

'My lord, you are not in the wrong. It is not a matter of right or wrong. It is a matter of forgiveness.'

He looked at me and I could read tenderness in his eyes.

'I wish my brother were alive today to see the wisdom of my choice. I could not have a better companion than you, my dear. You keep our family together and attend so well to my many sins. I sometimes wonder what would have become of me if I had not chosen you.'

Like a wise wife I said nothing. The decision that I should be given to him was not his, nor mine. For him, if he wanted peace, it meant accepting me as his wife. But if it pleased him to believe otherwise, who was I to put him right?

My husband wrote to Ned soon afterwards and I

received no more letters from my stepson other than
a formal and very charming note thanking me for my
efforts.

*'I regret any distress you have endured on my behalf
and thank you dearly for the goodwill you have shown
to me when dealing with this difficult matter.'*

13

AUTUMN 1305

On our return to the Island of Thorns we were greeted by the news that Sir William Wallace, the captured Scottish traitor had been brought in chains to London and was now imprisoned in St Gabriel's at Fenchurch. There was an undeniable sense of excitement in the air as this last of the Scottish rebels was finally in my husband's hands.

Londoners enjoy a good spectacle and next day they turned out in their thousands to jeer the Scottish traitor. His gaolers placed a circlet of laurels on his head and people in the streets pelted him with rotten eggs. He was a miserable and sorry sight, dirty and bespattered with all kinds of filth, yet he bore himself with a dignity which surprised me. It was only the thought of his many evils, the hundreds of our men he had killed and the foul deed committed on the body of the earl of Surrey's treasurer, which prevented me from feeling sorry for him.

'So much for the one who boasted he would wear a crown at Westminster,' said my husband jubilantly. 'He is nobody, my dear. Just a common man, a Scotsman who thought he could defy me. Don't give him another thought.'

He rubbed his neck with his weather-browned fingers, a self-satisfied smile on his face. He looked remarkably well for a man of his years and I was pleased our time in the south-east had done him good.

'I have given my instructions to the mayor and the justices, they know what to do with traitors. Meanwhile you and I will go hunting in the forests of Essex. I have a fancy to seek more prey for clearly at the moment I am favoured by Dame Fortune.'

I never spoke to my husband about what happened to Sir William Wallace but shortly before Michaelmas I asked Ralph de Monthermer. We were seated together at one of the interminable dinners during the parliament and had exhausted the subject of our children.

'A traitor's death, your grace. Not a pleasant way to die for a man. Half-hanged, crawling about in his own blood with his guts pulled out before his head is cut off.'

'Where is he buried?' I said, trying to ignore the sudden waves of nausea.

'He has no grave. His head is spiked on London's Bridge and the quarters were sent north as a warning. I believe some part of his remains is pinned to the bridge at Stirling.'

He turned to me, his long face looking more mournful than ever.

'Are you alright, your grace?' he said gently. 'You do not look well.'

'I feel somewhat faint.'

I excused myself to Sir Ralph and followed by one of my women, hurried back to my chamber where, with no ceremony, retched noisily into a basin. As I wiped my lips she said, 'Is it?'

'Is it what?' I asked, raising my eyes from the disgusting mess of my dinner.

'You were vomiting last time,' she said obliquely.

I hardly dared admit to myself that I might be with child. I had waited so long and suffered so many dark moments. I had missed my last course but had thrust the knowledge to the back of my mind, not wanting to hope and be disappointed.

I thought back to that time in the summer, to those magical days at Leeds, to the shining castle and the silver lake, to a place where even a queen could dream and her wishes come true. I thought of the soporific warmth and comfort of our marriage bed and the lazy, languid nights of our passion. I smiled to myself and decided to keep my secret a little while longer. Just in case.

'It is a miracle,' said Alice, gazing at what had once been a vast open space. 'A city of tents sprung up overnight.'

'Hardly overnight,' I said with a wry smile. 'The air has been choked with dust for weeks and we've endured the noise of those carts rumbling across the Tyburn day and night. The carpenters start at dawn and judging from the hammering, I doubt they sleep at all.'

Alice shrugged. 'It's necessary. The men must have somewhere to stable their horses.'

It was true. Hundreds had been summoned to this parliament to agree the arrangements for the governing of the king's new lands. The halls would be full and everyone of any importance would be there.

'How is your marriage?' she asked, tucking her arm into mine as we wandered slowly back to the gardens where the air was clearer and we might even be able to hear the birdsong.

'Are you still content?'

She was my only confidante now that my sister was gone and Lady Margaret became daily more like my mother. I knew Alice's own marriage was unhappy whereas I who had been sold to my brother's enemy for the price of a treaty and thrust into the bed of an elderly man who might have been dead before I was out of my wedding garments, was ... what? I thought perhaps I was content.

'Marguerite?'

'I have a secret, Alice. But you mustn't tell anyone.'

'A secret?'

'Yes.'

She looked at me expectantly and when I didn't say any more her gaze dropped to my belly.

'You're not?'

'I am.'

'Oh Marguerite!'

'But you mustn't speak of it for I haven't told my husband.'

'Oh cock's bones! This is women's business. What have husbands to do with it?'

I patted my belly. 'I think my husband would dispute that.'

Alice began to laugh. 'I pray God will give you a daughter.'

I thought of my boys and how much they would enjoy a sister.

'My husband desires more sons,' I said quietly. 'He

cannot forget what happened to Eleanor's sons and fears a repeat of the past.'

'I will not have it called a realm,' thundered my husband. 'It is a land. From henceforth it is part of my kingdom, a lesser part, a limb. However, I am a merciful man and I will allow the Scots whose lands were given in war to my men, to buy them back. Is that not fair to everyone?'

I was told they had all nodded in agreement; nobody dared gainsay the king of England, though one or two had looked anything but happy.

The king of England's position as overlord was undisputed and his kingdom would stretch from the northernmost tip of the lands of Scotland to the shores of the Narrow Sea. But matters had to be arranged to everyone's satisfaction because my husband knew only too well how fragile this peace might prove to be.

There were men who were consistently loyal to my husband, men like the earls of Buchan and Ross who, with John Balliol gone, saw no profit for themselves in a Scottish king. But I suspected others, like the earl of Carrick and the Scottish bishops, were only biding their time.

The air reeked of smoke and roasted meat and from the body of the hall drifted the unmistakeable stench of men and wine and sweat.

'Would you like my husband to escort you back to your apartments?' whispered Joan. 'These first months can be most uncomfortable.'

'You know?' I said in surprise.

252

'Of course I know,' she laughed. 'I'm sure every woman in the hall knows.'

'I must tell his grace, your father,' I said in panic. 'He mustn't hear this from someone else. And yes please, I should like to leave if it is no trouble to your husband.'

Joan looked at me in despair.

'You are the queen, Marguerite. Of course it is no trouble to him. You are such a goose.'

Ralph de Monthermer helped me from my chair, solicitously taking my arm as he led me out into the humid afternoon air. The early autumn was airless and the continuing heat made my nausea worse. I longed for a cooling shower of rain.

As we crossed the dusty yard we met the earl of Carrick hurrying from the opposite direction looking less than pleased.

'Do you know my good friend, Sir Robert?' enquired Ralph.

'Yes,' I said, lowering my head. I found it difficult meeting Sir Robert who seemed to have the knack of reading my innermost thoughts.

'My lady,' said the earl of Carrick, bowing and taking my hand. 'We meet again.'

I wanted to snatch my hand back in case he should feel how much I was trembling but with a great effort of will I left it where it was.

'I am escorting her grace to the archbishop's palace, Bruce,' said Ralph. 'I'll see you later.'

'Her grace should rest awhile,' said Sir Robert, casting a look at my body with a practiced eye. 'Standing too long cannot be good for her. You should take the greatest of care, my lady.'

I blushed further. How could he tell? How did he know?

'I shall,' I muttered. 'Thank you for your kindness, Sir Robert.'

'It is nothing,' he said, finally relinquishing my hand. He smiled slightly, one side of his mouth turned upwards as if he found our conversation amusing.

Ralph gazed after him as he strode away.

'Are Scottish matters safely resolved?' I enquired.

'No,' he said. 'They are not. The earl of Buchan and his cousin the lord of Badenoch are sworn enemies of the Bruces. They cannot forgive Sir Robert's grandfather for disputing Balliol's right to the crown.'

'His grace will keep their quarrel under control.'

'It has already come to a fight with swords drawn.'

'*Sainte Vierge*,' I whispered.

'Sir Robert has accused the earl of Buchan of whispering in his grace's ear.'

A cold thought slid into my mind and I wondered if this might have something to do with that day at Cambuskenneth when I'd seen the bishop of St Andrews and Sir Robert talking. I'd never told anyone what I'd heard and I'd tried to put the memory aside but it kept returning, an unwanted reminder of my concerns about Sir Robert's loyalty to my husband.

When we reached the inner walls of the palace. I disengaged my arm and turned to thank Ralph for his care of me.

'Does my husband think well of Sir Robert?'

'He did but now his grace is inclined to doubt him. He is asking for sureties for Sir Robert's castles.'

'But Sir Robert is not in danger, is he?'

Ralph looked at me curiously.

'Not yet. But I've warned him to be careful so he's on his guard.'

He waved to one of my husband's men, bidding him escort me up the steps into the palace.

'I trust you will be recovered soon, your grace,' he said bowing slightly.

What a pleasant man, I thought. How lucky Joan was in her marriage.

That evening, once we were alone in my chamber, I told my husband my news. He pulled me against him and for a moment said nothing.

'You are certain?'

'Yes, my lord. I am quite certain. It will be in the spring.'

He gave a deep contented sigh as if I had given him what he desired most in the whole world.

'I can think of no better celebration of our marriage than another child,' he said gently, 'and though I pray for more sons I think you deserve a daughter.'

He looked immensely pleased. He would delight in showing his enemies how potent he was and if any of them thought his powers were waning, the sight of his wife's swollen belly would silence them at once. I pushed away the niggling doubts I had about his regard for me. Behind the bed curtains he was a vigorous lover but I believed his desire was for more sons, not for me. At other times he displayed the placid affection of a man for a young mistress whom he kept to satisfy his carnal lust rather than the all-encompassing passion and devotion he would feel for a beloved wife. But after our reconciliation at Burstwick I had never again asked about Eleanor and he had never once mentioned her. If placid affection was to be my lot then I must be grateful for what I had been given and not keep wanting more.

Sheen was one of my husband's favourite manors, built in a pretty spot on the water's edge, a small fair palace half-circled by meadows with a low hill rising up behind. From the topmost mound the smoke of London was clearly visible and, high above the chimneys, the spire of St Paul's at the top of Ludgate Hill. My husband liked to keep an eye on the city. He said if trouble broke out in Kent or Essex you could be sure the seeds had been sown by some prating cleric in a London pulpit. The one thing he knew for certain about Londoners was that they couldn't be trusted.

On the first day of our visit, before I had even finished unpacking my gowns, I had a visitor. It was Ned. He breezed into my rooms while my women and I were discussing plans for the Christmas celebrations causing a flutter of excitement. I turned at the sound of his feet and clapped my hands.

'Oh! How wonderful. Lord Edward!'

'My dearest lady mother.'

He bowed, greeted me formally and then swept me up into his arms.

'How good it is to see you again,' I cried. 'But you must put me down, Ned. I am not supposed to be tossed about.'

'But I feel like tossing you about.'

I blushed. He looked at me closely and then smiled.

'Another child?'

'Yes.'

'What fun. Thomas and Edmund are wonderful little fellows and this one will be just as fine. Am I allowed to kiss you or is that forbidden too?'

'Of course you may kiss me,' I said, 'but only if you tell me why you are here. Have you reconciled yourself with his grace, your father?'

He yawned. 'I have just come from a very lengthy and particularly painful interview where I abased myself in the most humble way possible. You would have been proud at how contrite I was, dear lady mother. I crawled across the floor on my belly and licked his boots so now he is pleased with me and has accepted me back as his son.'

I tried to look disapproving at this mocking of his father but failed because I was so pleased to see him again.

'And now, may I kiss you?'

I offered him my lips and closed my eyes as he placed his mouth on mine feeling a little frisson of recognition but of course he was my dearest stepson and it was perfectly natural for us to kiss like this.

'Piers said it was the dullest three months he'd ever spent. But now all is forgiven and forgotten and I am the prodigal son returned.'

I laughed. He truly was the most delightful company. My women, who had slunk away to the far end of the chamber with their embroidery, were craning their necks and cocking their ears. There was precious little amusement for them at the moment and Ned was someone who brightened their lives. Of course they loved him. I loved him. Who could not love my stepson? Only his father it seemed.

'And is his grace to kill the fatted calf in your honour?' I enquired.

'In no way. I am to give the feast. We have settled a day and a place and we will celebrate my father's new realm and our newly happy family.'

He sat down beside me, stretching out his long legs and half closing his eyes. I could sense my women sighing over his well-made body and handsome face. His hair had darkened slightly over the years but the summer sun had bleached it golden again. He was more handsome than ever. In truth he was probably the best-looking man at court, a shining handsome prince who only needed a radiantly beautiful lady to complete the romance.

There was no need to search the families across the Narrow Seas for a suitable bride because my husband had already found one. The peace treaty when I became his betrothed and the one he had made with my brother's negotiators two years ago which finally brought an end to the fighting, had sealed the marriage contract for Ned with Philip's little daughter.

I remembered Isabella as a beautiful blue-eyed four year-old but she must be ten now, nearly old enough for the marriage bed. They would make a marvellous couple: two golden angels set together, and I was sure their children would be perfect, just like them, golden and blessed.

Ned tipped his head against the back of his chair and looked sideways at me.

'Now, my lady mother, you must tell me the news. What's been happening since I've been away? Who has done what and what scandals have I missed? And what about you, lady mother? Have you been good?'

'Of course I have. What possible mischief could I get up to shut away in your father's palaces? I've been at the archbishop's house entertaining my friends. I suppose you heard about Wallace?'

'I did,' he said. 'His grace, my father, must be pleased it's all finished.'

'Are you not pleased?'

'Oh of course, but I didn't consider this a personal matter like my father did. I think you could say that, for him, it has been an obsession, this war with the Scots. If I were to have an obsession it certainly wouldn't be war. There are far more enjoyable things to expend one's energies on.'

'Such as?'

'Music, singing, building.'

'Building?'

'Yes, building: palaces, walls, gardens, churches, anything that takes your fancy. Now that's something my grandfather was obsessed with too.'

'But he didn't do the building himself, Ned. He didn't lift the stones and thatch the roofs and paint the walls, and he certainly didn't get down and dig in the mud with the workmen and get himself covered in filth like you do. Your grandfather commissioned palaces and helped design them. He decided what he wanted and others did the work.'

'You are beginning to sound like his grace, my father,' said Ned nastily, pulling back his legs. 'I must lighten your days to stop you from being such a bore.'

He said it with a smile in his voice yet I detected a note of warning - don't trespass into my private life, keep out!

As he sat there smiling and joking, I wondered what he really thought, what made him the man he was? He was unlike his father in so many ways. My husband was a man of duty and determination whose friends would never desert him, while Ned, despite his outward piety, was like Blanche: frivolous and pleasure-loving. And I feared he had no desire to be a leader of men unless he was leading them down a primrose path.

I had no time to be alone or to worry about my stepson for next morning Alice came upriver in a small boat with just a couple of her women and two of her husband's men-at-arms. I was overjoyed for I thought she'd returned to Pickering.

'No,' she said, shaking her cloak to be rid of the spray from the river. 'I could not possibly miss one of Ned's entertainments. He is so talented at organising feasts, much cleverer than my husband who leaves everything to his steward, a man with no imagination at all. I wonder who will be there? Have you heard the new viol-player, Master de Roos? He is very skilful. I wish I could play an instrument with such passion.'

'I think everyone will come because one day in the future Ned will be king and they won't want to offend him.'

Alice pursed her lips but my mind was already racing ahead to thoughts of which jewels I would wear. The rubies suited me but I had a fondness for the emeralds and pearls my husband had given me.

'You know they talk about him?' she said.

'Who?'

'The prince.'

'Who talks about him?'

'My husband and his friends: Guy de Beauchamp, Humphrey de Bohun, and the others.'

'Of course they talk about him. He's the king's eldest son.'

'Marguerite, listen to me. You of all people need to understand the dangers. I pray your husband lives for many years, but there will come a time when the prince will be king.'

'Everybody knows that.'

'Yes, but not everybody thinks he will be able to command. They look at him and find him wanting, and it worries them. They whisper in the shadows trying to decide what they should do. They talk of his unsuitable friends. I shouldn't like to tell you what they say about the closeness of the prince and Master Gaveston.'

'Why should they mind about his friendship with Piers Gaveston?'

'They think he is besotted with him. They don't trust Gaveston and they think he is dangerous. They see how the prince uses his time and they don't like the things he does or the people he consorts with. You must believe me, Marguerite. I've heard them in my husband's castles, and by God's truth, it frightens me.'

'He's still young, Alice. He will be wiser as he grows and a wife will steady him. When he marries all will be well. My niece will solve all Ned's problems.'

Alice looked at me with pity in her eyes.

'He doesn't want her.'

'What do you mean he doesn't want her? Of course he wants her. He pledged himself two years ago and so did she.'

'The last thing the prince wants is a marriage with your brother's daughter. If he has to marry he would prefer a Castilian bride and who can blame him. From what I've heard I wouldn't care for your brother Philip as my father-in-law.'

I knew little of my stepson's feelings for his friend Master Gaveston. I knew they were close but Alice was hinting at a closeness that was, what – unsuitable? Unnatural? I thought back to the feast at Carlisle long ago when I'd first noticed Piers Gaveston, remembering the feeling I'd had, the sensation that danger lurked around hm. But I couldn't believe ill of my stepson and was sure Alice was exaggerating what she'd heard. Yet wriggling away at the back of my mind was the uncomfortable thought that much of it might be true.

Ned had never shown any particular interest in the women who fluttered like butterflies around him other than taking their adoration as his due. I'd never seen him steal a kiss or slide his arm around one of my maids the way other men did when they thought I wasn't looking. I was the only one to whom he was overtly familiar but of course I was his stepmother and there was no impropriety there. He could kiss me and think nothing of it and if occasionally I felt a quiver of something else, I carefully ignored it.

His sole pleasures involved the men of his household and what my husband referred to as his gutter churls. Previously I'd merely thought of him as too young and too interested in boyish escapades to respond to silly girls making calf's-eyes. But he was no longer a boy, he was a man, and men, as I was well aware, desired women.

But who was I to know about desire? I who had eyes only for my husband. I knew some men preferred young boys to their wives and I also knew this was a sin. The Church was quite clear on this matter. There had been an elderly lecher at Philip's court, well-known for his fondness for pretty pages. He'd kept a stable not of smart palfreys but of young lads fresh from the countryside. Blanche used to giggle, wondering what delights they could possibly offer. I thought it disgusting. Certainly one or two of my husband's comrades showed more interest in the well-made bodies of their squires than they did in those of their wives but I had never taken much notice.

Ned could not be like those men. As for Isabella? I refused to believe he wouldn't want her. She was everything a man could desire in a wife: beautiful, gently-raised, sweet-natured if she was anything like her mother, and compliant. And the treaty had been sealed. Of course it would happen. I could see nothing that could possibly prevent it. Just another few years to wait until Isabella was ready for bedding and then everything would be alright.

A week later we skimmed downstream over the swirling waters towards the palace of Westminster for Ned's feast. The river was crowded with people making their way to the city for the Confessor's Fair where according to my women there were bargains aplenty if you cared to look.

The hall was full to overflowing. All my husband's friends were in attendance: Earl Thomas, Aymer de Valence, Guy de Beauchamp and the elderly earl of Norfolk who had brought his frosty little filly. There were hundreds of others whose names and titles I didn't even know. It was a glorious, glorious celebration.

Every so often Ned's eyes slid down the hall to where his household sat on their benches and he would exchange a smile with Master Gaveston. I was glad he had a steadfast companion and dismissed Alice's warnings as malicious and spiteful gossip. Ned would need friends in the years ahead but nothing would give him as much comfort as a good wife.

I was full of fine food and wine and ready to enjoy Ned's entertainments. First were the minstrels with the bells and then everyone's favourite, Matilda Makejoy, the famous acrobatic dancer. She threw herself about with the utmost ease but how could a woman do such things? And in front of a company of men?

Afterwards was a quiet interlude with Guillame the harper, whose patron was my husband's old friend, the bishop of Durham, Anthony Bek. My husband liked Bek as much as he disliked that perpetual thorn in his side, Archbishop Winchelsea. There was complete silence as Guillame fingered his plaintive melodies and in case we had been lulled to sleep by the music we were woken up by the exotically foreign Leskirmissour brothers performing a lively sword dance. They stamped and shouted, leaping and thrusting, their scimitars flashing wildly in the light of the torches. My heart leapt into my mouth as a wickedly curved blade slashed close to a head or an arm. No-one was hurt but it looked extremely dangerous.

The entertainments continued for hours until the torches burned low and we were all sated with wine and food and music. My husband formally thanked his son, and Ned replied, enjoining us all to drink to the health and continued glory of his father. Tears gathered in my eyes. I was always weeping these days.

Later my husband and his friends disappeared to the king's privy chamber to discuss private matters. The others sat or lay around in various states of insobriety. Ned went with his father although I was sure he would rather have spent the evening gambling with his friends. Lady de Lacy struggled off to bed muttering about too much wine, leaving Alice with my three stepdaughters to compare notes on what people had been wearing.

I had no desire to discuss the latest fashions and decided instead to visit my mare in her stall. She had strained her foreleg and Ned had recommended a new ointment which was said to yield marvellous results. I thought I would suggest it to my groom.

I hurried down the steps and out into the courtyard, followed by two of my women who had showed no desire to leave the warmth and companionship of the hall for a walk in the cold. I could hear them fussing and grumbling as we made our way across the yard.

Dusk was falling and the torches were already lit but even with the wavering flames there were patches of shadowy darkness where danger might lurk. My husband's men guarded the gates and there were watchmen everywhere, nevertheless I was nervous.

I picked my way along the wall to the stables. The grooms were crowded round a travelling storyteller who must have been admitted to the royal precincts on my husband's word. My women lingered by the glow of the lantern to listen while I wandered along the stalls looking for Griselle.

The mare whickered gently, recognising my voice and pushed at my hand with her soft velvety nose. I stroked her glossy neck, then felt her leg, pleased to find no swelling.

'Good girl,' I whispered, resting my head against the sweet-smelling warmth of her body.

Further into the gloom, I saw a man leading out his horse. He was wrapped in a cloak with a large hat pulled low over his brow. As the two reached the end of Griselle's stall, he stopped.

'My lady!' he said in surprise. 'What in God's name are you doing here?'

I started at the sound of his voice.

'I might say the same to you, Sir Robert.' My heart was beating so fast I was almost stammering.

'For myself, I am leaving,' he replied with a smile.

'Leaving? But it's dark. You cannot leave in the dark.'

Sir Robert looked at me in a way which made my legs tremble and my throat tighten.

'The dark can be a man's friend, my lady, when he doesn't wish to be seen.'

I couldn't understand why I was so discomforted by this man I barely knew. This man who was implacably opposed to my husband's vision of uniting the kingdoms and whom I knew to be involved in treasonous business. Why did I feel this way when he was nothing to me?

'Where are you going in the dark?' I said, my lips finding difficulty in forming the words.

'Home.'

'Home?'

'To Scotland.'

I felt panic well up inside me.

'Scotland?' I repeated stupidly.

'Yes, my lady,' he said gently. 'To my castle at Lochmaben.'

A shout of laughter echoed down the passageway from the group by the door.

'The one you were rebuilding?'

'Yes.'

'With stone?'

'You remembered. Yes, with stone.'

'But wouldn't it be more sensible to wait till morning, when it's light? You cannot want to risk the dangers of the night road. I wouldn't... I wouldn't want anything to happen to you.'

He looped the horse's reins over the post at the end of the stall and stepped closer to me. Far too close. I wanted to step back but there was nowhere to go. My escape routes were all blocked. He lowered his voice to a near whisper.

'The night road may be perilous, my lady, but the danger here is greater. I have been forewarned.'

He reached into his battered pouch and held up a pair of spurs. There was nothing special about them, they were just an ordinary pair, the same as any man might use.

'I received a gift from a friend.'

I was puzzled.

'A pair of spurs?'

He leaned closer. His face was near to mine and in the half-light I could see the glint of his eyes, the beads of sweat on his forehead and the dark tendrils of hair against his cheek. I could feel the warmth of his breath on my face and the brush of his cloak against my sleeve.

'It is a warning,' he whispered. 'The meaning is clear. Flee for your life.'

'But who sent them?'

'I cannot tell you that. He has risked much to give me this chance to escape and I won't prejudice his position with your husband.'

I had no need to ask where the danger lay for I already knew. His enemy, the earl of Buchan, had whispered once too often in my husband's ear. I wondered if Buchan knew of the meeting at Cambuskenneth and, if so, what he had told my husband.

'So you will go?' I said miserably, suddenly unable to bear the thought of his leaving.

He turned back to his horse and undid the reins.

'I must.' He paused. 'I shall return to my castle and to my wife.'

'Yes, 'I replied dully. 'Of course, to your wife.'

He looked at me with his dark hooded eyes which saw more than they should. The moments passed as he stood there, half ready to go, looking at me while I looked at him.

'Don't misunderstand me, my lady,' he said gently. 'I have a greater loyalty than that which I bear to your husband or to my wife; one that binds me closer.'

I lowered my head so that he couldn't see my face.

'We are all bound, Sir Robert,' I whispered.

'Yes, my lady. Duty binds us hand and foot. And you are tied to your husband and his lands as you once told me.'

The horse at his shoulder shifted its powerful body. He put out his hand to take mine.

'Will you say farewell, my lady?'

I didn't want this moment to end so I hesitated. Then, forgetting my promises to God and my duty towards my husband, I took two steps across the void and slipped my hand into his. Mine was small and pale and trembling, his, firm and all-encompassing. I felt a shiver pass through my body as he tightened his grip.

'Farewell, my lady,' he said softly. 'May you be happy and live long.'

I blinked back my tears.

'You too, Sir Robert. May Christ and His Saints be with you on your journey.'

He raised my hand to his lips and kissed it lightly, his lips barely brushing the skin. He gave me a brief smile, held my eyes for a moment, then turned and led his horse away, disappearing into the gloom.

There was silence. I could hear no sound but the gentle movements of the other horses. Where he had stood a moment ago there was nothing but the slight imprint of his boot in the straw. There was no longer anyone here, no-one of importance, just the grooms and my women and the storyteller.

As I stood alone in the darkness, not knowing who I was anymore, I realised that we were both wrong. It was not just duty which bound me hand and foot to my husband. My heart was bound by something stronger; it had always been so, right from the beginning. As my breathing slowed and my heartbeats became steady once more, I reminded myself I was not a woman to throw everything aside for an illusion. Blanche had been the impetuous one. I was sensible. So with one last glance behind me, I counted my blessings and tucked the memory of a tall dark man, who for a few brief moments had touched my heart, safely away where it could not be found. Then, drying my eyes on my sleeve I went back through the stables to collect my women and return to my husband's care.

As we walked quickly through the courtyard I looked up. There was no moon and already wracks of dark clouds were rushing swiftly across the night sky bringing the first welcome signs of rain. I thought of a lone rider galloping through the darkness, a ship somewhere waiting, moored close by, ready to cast off, its lanterns covered. A good night to hide one's flight from one's enemies. I was certain he would be safe.

At the door I met Alice. She was standing in the shadows, wrapped in her dark-green cloak, and looked as if she had been weeping. I hurriedly waved my women away.

'The countess will bear me company,' I said to them. 'You can run back to the others.'

As they disappeared up the stone steps, I took Alice's hand.

'What's the matter?' I said softly.

'I saw him leave,' she said.

'Who?'

'Don't play with me, Marguerite. You know who.'

I remained silent, waiting for her to say something. I wasn't sure what she had seen or what she meant to do.

'I don't know what game you're playing,' she said angrily, 'or what you intend, but as you are my friend, please be careful.'

'Alice, it is not what you think. Not at all.'

'I don't know what I think,' she said. 'But I know his reputation. And you are the king's wife.'

'Alice, please believe me. I have done nothing. I have said nothing.'

'And he?'

'Nor him. We were saying farewell, that is all. Nothing more, just farewell.'

'So why have you been crying? Don't pretend you haven't. I can see tear stains on your face. You'd better wipe them away before someone else notices.'

I rubbed my eyes again on the end of my sleeve.

'Is that better?'

'Yes.'

She looked at me bleakly.

'Oh Marguerite, I do understand. I know how lonely a marriage can be, you know I do. But you cannot be seen like this. It is very dangerous. What if someone should tell his grace?'

I felt a moment of complete terror run through me and a chasm open up beneath my feet.

'There is nothing to tell,' I said stoutly, fear making my voice tremble.

She seized my hands and pulled me closer.

'He has many women,' she said. 'Everyone knows what he's like. He is a seducer. I could tell you the names of a dozen women who've shared his bed: good women, women with husbands and children, women just like you. To be seen in his company is enough for people to start talking. And you are so very loving.'

I put my arms around her.

'Alice, there is nothing amiss. Believe me. I went to

see my mare because her leg was strained and found he was leaving. We said farewell, that was all. Nothing more. Nothing sinister, nothing underhand, nothing which I could not tell my husband.'

I told myself it was not a lie. Nothing outward had happened and my innermost thoughts I would confess to God, not to Alice or my husband. I told myself to cease thinking of the man with the dark eyes and the castle of stone, to cease thinking of him and put our encounter behind me, not to think of it again.

14

If only one knew. If only God had granted me the gift of foresight. If only I could have known that this was to be our last truly happy time together. Would I have done anything differently?

It was the feast of Candlemas and my husband and his men spent the morning hunting. They rode through snow-covered copses of tangled thickets and bare-branched trees, but there was little to be found. I, of course, was not permitted to hunt so contented myself with re-reading the precious letters from my mother and keeping an eye on my younger women.

There had been no new wandering players for weeks and although the women were not complaining, I could tell they were fretful by the petty quarrels which kept breaking out in my chamber. The day before, two of them had fought like cats over a hank of green silk, and that morning there had been disagreeable words over who had cleaned my best leather boots and failed to remove the white marks caused by the snow.

My husband returned to the manor, red-cheeked from the cold and not the slightest bit dispirited. But later, as we sat in the hall, he bewailed the lack of fresh meat, complaining a coney from the abbey warren was not the same as a haunch of venison. There were very few at our tables these winter days other than our own household because the inclement weather kept people away. Nobody travelled unless it was essential.

The snow had arrived shortly before Christmas. At first the soft flakes dancing and twirling in the sky had given me a childish joy but the snow became heavier and by dusk everything was engulfed in a thick, ghostly shroud. Now, weeks later, highways were blocked with snowdrifts, bushes laced with frost and everywhere I looked, woods and hills were covered in cloaks of perfect shining white.

I sat there, thinking how happy I was, how fortunate we were, when I suddenly had that indefinable feeling that something was wrong. My immediate thought was for my unborn child. I placed my hands on my belly but all seemed as it should.

'You feel unwell?' enquired my husband, leaning towards me.

'No, my lord,' I said doubtfully. 'I am perfectly well. But something is wrong.'

I shook my head as if trying to rid myself of a voice telling of misfortune.

'The rabbit pie,' he said. 'I knew it.'

'No, my lord, the food was excellent. It is not that.'

'What then?'

'I'm not sure. Something is amiss. I know it. A peculiar sensation.'

'Aha!' he said smiling. 'It is the goose walking across your grave again.'

'Don't mock me,' I said. 'I know something has happened, somewhere.'

'Be careful, wife,' he whispered in my ear. 'Winchelsea will have you burned as a witch if you say such things.'

'He will do no such thing and you are only trying to frighten me, my lord. It isn't kind.'

He laughed and patted my hand.

'Come along my plump little goose. Let us retire to our chamber where it is warmer and I can stroke your feathers.'

Throughout the rest of the day I fretted. I didn't know if these feelings were sent by God or the devil, whether I should pay heed to them or pray they would leave my mind. Eventually I told myself there was no point in thinking of disasters which might never happen and when, next day, Lord de Lacy arrived through the snow in a bustle of braying horns and sweating horses, I laughed to think I had mistaken his visit for trouble.

He came from the papal court bearing letters from His Holiness. Last autumn, there had been another falling-out between my husband and Archbishop Winchelsea and I knew part of Lord de Lacy's mission to His Holiness had been connected with this.

'Well done, old friend,' said my husband, clapping Lord de Lacy on the back. 'I knew my sending you to Lyon was a clever move. You and Bishop Langton have succeeded beyond my expectations.'

He hurried over to me, waving a roll of parchment.

'See my dear, what I have here.'

He thrust the lengthy communication from the papal curia under my nose. 'His Holiness agrees with me.'

What a wise man His Holiness must be, I thought. It was always advisable to agree with my husband.

'He has absolved me from the oaths I gave at Lincoln

four years ago, and believes the Crown's rights should be restored. This is the best of news. I wouldn't give Winchelsea much hope of holding on to Canterbury now. His Holiness will have him out of his archbishop's robes before Easter.'

I could read the workings of his mind. With Scotland won, he and his son reconciled, with the Crown's rights regained and his bitterest critic silenced - what more was there to wish for? He had everything. And I too, I had everything my heart could desire: an affectionate husband, two healthy children and another, snug and safe in my belly.

How foolish we were. We sat at the top of fortune's wheel, drinking in the heady nectar of success, never thinking of what would happen when blind fate spun the wheel once more and we were pitched down into disaster. We were careless of the future, heedless as any wantwit, and at God's own tribunal we would be found guilty of hubris.

A week later, in the midst of a dripping thaw, we bade farewell to our friends in Dorsetshire and set off for Winchester and the parliament. We were in good spirits but had we known what awaited us there, I doubt if our joy would have been so unconfined.

In my upstairs chamber in the bishop's palace at Winchester, I was arranging my books and my chess pieces on the small table by the window while my maids unfolded and shook out my gowns. I was feeling well-pleased. Thomas and Edmund were safely installed in their own apartments not far from mine and were happily exploring their new home when all of a sudden a violent banging on the door brought one of my women running across the floor. She spoke hastily to someone outside then turned back to me, her face white and frightened.

'One of his grace's men is here, my lady. He has been sent to fetch you.'

I dropped the book I was holding and ran to the door.

'What has happened?' Like every mother my first fear was for my children.

'He has c-collapsed, my lady,' said the lad, fingering his cap and stuttering over his words. 'He was sh-shouting and s-screaming at his council like a man possessed. Then he fell as if struck by a hammer.'

A moment of blessed relief that it was not one of my boys but a leap of fear for my husband. I ran as fast as I could, my feet almost flying down the stairs.

They had placed him on the bed. His eyes were closed and his face was grey but he was breathing. I took his hand. It felt cold and clammy.

'What happened?'

'He had a letter from the north, and then this.' Lord de Lacy gestured with distress at my husband.

'What letter? What did it say?'

'The lord of Badenoch has been murdered, your grace,' said Aymer de Valence, stepping forward to stand beside Lord de Lacy. 'At Dumfries. In the church of the Greyfriars.'

My hand flew to my mouth. The lord of Badenoch murdered! John Comyn, the lord of Badenoch! A murder on holy ground! This was sacrilege.

'Who killed him?' My heart was full of fear.

'We don't know. The letter didn't say. His grace read the message and flew into a rage. Then he fell.'

'We've sent for his physician and the surgeon,' said Lord de Lacy looking more worried than I'd seen him look before.

The two men arrived, my husband's physician carrying his various bags and vessels. He prodded and muttered, sniffed my husband's breath, rolled up his eyelids and looked at his eyeballs.

'The humours are unbalanced,' he said gravely. 'The surgeon will bleed his grace.'

My husband's surgeon consulted his tables, then delved into his pouch and produced a small silver basin and a little blade. One of the servants held the basin while the surgeon incised my husband's arm. I watched the blood run freely, thick and red.

'Will he recover?' I whispered to the physician.

'If God so wills,' he said. 'The surgeon has done his best. His grace's heartbeat is strong.'

He looked at me more closely. 'And you, my lady, should rest. It will not serve his grace well if you should faint.'

I nodded my agreement, and sat down again.

All day I stayed by his side, watching and waiting. Before nightfall he began to stir and toss his head to and fro. Soon his eyelids fluttered and he opened his eyes. He looked about him, searching for someone. His eyes briefly rested on me and he frowned.

I smiled at him. 'My lord, you are returned.'

He looked at me more closely, wrinkled his brow again and turned his head to study the others in the chamber. He saw the familiar faces of his body servants and gave them a weak smile. He closed his eyes but a little while later he opened them again.

'Don't be alarmed, my lady,' said the physician. 'This is quite usual. Soon he will be as he ever was.'

I drew some comfort from his words but was afraid my husband didn't recognise me. Perhaps he was looking for Eleanor and didn't know who I was.

'Wife?'

The voice was quiet but perfectly lucid.

'Husband,' I said, my voice faltering.

'I've got the devil of a headache,' he said. 'What did you give me to drink?'

'Oh my lord,' I cried, unable to stop the tears from falling. 'I thought you were going to die.'

He looked at me curiously.

'Die? God's teeth! I may feel a bit out of sorts but I'm not going to die. Here, boy!' he summoned one of his body servants. 'Help me upright. Why am I lying here like some feeble girl? Move the pillows. Now, what was I doing?'

'My lord, you mustn't do anything. You must rest.'

'Nonsense,' he said, looking about him again. 'Ah yes, I remember. That accursed letter.'

'Please, my lord.'

'You understand what this means?'

I shook my head. 'No.'

'It has started again. The killing, the strife.'

'Maybe it is nothing. Just some ruffians. You don't know yet who killed the lord of Badenoch.'

'Don't I?' he replied. 'I can think of only one man who could have done this, only one man who has the inclination and the temper. I cannot believe he would turn against me. I thought he was too much in my debt, but the earl of Buchan warned me. He said Bruce was not to be trusted.'

He put his hand to his head and closed his eyes for a brief moment, then opened them again.

'Why were they there? What were they doing? This can have been no carefully planned murder, it must have been a sudden squabble. To kill on holy ground condemns a man to excommunication at the very least. The stakes would have to be very high to make a man commit such a deed, and he would need to be sure of his bishops.'

I thought of the abbey church at Cambuskenneth, of the two men in the shadows. Sir Robert *was* sure of his bishops. They had told him they were with him in this.

The next few days were constant turmoil. My husband had men rushing hither and thither. Letters were dispatched to the north: to Carlisle and Newcastle, to Berwick and Dumfries, to Edinburgh and Stirling. He bit his nails in fury at not knowing what was happening.

'Those fools at Dumfries! How could they have let such a thing take place right under their noses? They must have known what was afoot.'

Letters arrived telling different stories. The castle at Dumfries had been taken by Sir Robert Bruce's men. The castle had *not* been taken but the terrified justices inside had surrendered to a rabble fearing someone would set it on fire. The earl of Carrick's men had killed both John Comyn *and* his uncle on the steps of the high altar. The lord of Badenoch was not dead at all, merely wounded and being cared for by the brothers. The stories became wilder and more horrific, but whatever was true, of one thing there was no doubt - the town of

Dumfries was in uproar and the English were fleeing for their lives.

It was difficult to keep my husband quiet and rested. The chamber was full of his council raking over the embers of past mistakes and planning revenge for the loss of the English castles which had fallen to the earl of Carrick's men. Hotheads like Earl Thomas wanted to unleash a torrent of fury on the miscreants but the peacemakers like Lord de Lacy preferred to talk rather than fight. Some were for dispatching an army straight away but the older and wiser said they must wait for more news.

While my husband slept, I drew Ralph de Monthermer to one side. He looked worried as well he might. It had not taken me long to realise he must have been the man who had sent the warning to Sir Robert at Westminster last autumn. Both of us had failed my husband.

'Tell me what will happen, Sir Ralph. What will the earl of Carrick do?'

He looked at me sadly. 'It is God's own truth, my lady, I do not know.'

'But you are his friend. You must know what is in his mind.'

His shoulders slumped and I felt sorry for him.

'He will revive his grandfather's claim to the crown. He wishes to be king, my lady. Not so much for his own glory but because he is a Scot. He might have waited until his grace was no more.' He stopped in embarrassment.

'It is alright,' I said. 'I understand. He would not deliberately go against my husband but the prince is a different matter.'

'He admires his grace. He says it will be easier to take

a whole kingdom from the son than a foot of land from the father.'

He had no need to say more. We both knew my stepson was not the man his father was.

'He cannot have done this deliberately,' I said, repeating what my husband had told me. 'John Comyn was killed on holy ground.'

Sir Ralph stared out of the window at the darkening sky.

'Wishart will not excommunicate him,' he said slowly. 'He will support him in whatever he move he makes.'

Inwardly I thanked God. It would be a lonely existence outside the Church.

'What of the others?'

'There are many who will take to the heather with Bruce but by no means all. Those who fear losing their lands under an English crown will fight. But Buchan and Ross hate Sir Robert. And don't forget John Balliol still lives. In the eyes of many he is the rightful king and, even if he never returns, he has a son. These men regard Sir Robert as a usurper. Dear God, let us hope he sees sense.'

We stood together, lost in our fear of what was to come, both of us thinking of the same man and how, because of our faith in him, we had betrayed my husband's trust.

I fled through the darkness, up the steps of the watch tower at Vincennes with the demons howling at my heels, their leathery wings brushing my hair, their foul breath stinking in my face. I burst out into the freezing cold of the tiny platform where Blanche was laughing. "Jump!" she cried. "Jump!" I grasped the edge of the parapet to steady myself, but the worn stone crumbled to dust beneath my fingers and, with a clarion call from the lone horseman flying towards me through the snow, and a thousand silent screams echoing in my ears, I fell headlong into the void.

I woke to a flickering candle flame, a hand on my shoulder and an urgent voice. The woman's eyes were rounded in fear and her face was deathly white.

'What is it?' My mouth was dry, my heart racing. The dream was still horribly real.

'The Lord Thomas, my lady. The physician is with him. He said you should be called.'

I was out of bed before she had even finished speaking and out of the chamber by the count of ten. At the door to my sons' rooms their personal physician stood waiting. In the flaring torchlight his elderly bulk loomed large, his face hidden in shadow, his arm outstretched to bar the door.

'You cannot go in, my lady.'

'Out of my way.' I tried to walk past, expecting him to move back, but he stood firm.

'The Lord Thomas has a fever,' he said, lowering his voice. 'And there is variola in the town.'

'Oh *Sainte Vierge*!' My knees sagged and I fell against the door post. My women grasped me and held me tight. 'Variola? The little pox?'

'Yes, my lady. There is a possibility it is just an ordinary fever but we dare not take the risk. We must assume the worst.'

'Variola,' I whispered. Thomas had the little pox. He might die. Children died of the little pox and if they did not die they were hideously scarred. My firstborn. My

Thomas. The tiny baby I thought would not survive. God would not have let him live only to snatch him away now. Thomas! Oh Thomas!

'You must do something.' I was babbling in my panic, clutching at the man's sleeve. 'You must save him. You can't let him die. Oh please, don't let him die.'

'I shall have the surgeon bleed him, to bring down the fever, my lady, and there are potions to restore the balance of the humours. A purgative may be beneficial. But I have heard there is a man in London, a doctor of physic, an Oxford man, who has had some success with the variola. New treatments.'

'Fetch him.'

'He is not greatly experienced, my lady, not like myself, but he does seem remarkably gifted. I have heard good reports of his methods.'

'I don't care if he is as old as the hills or a babe in arms. If he can cure my son, fetch him.'

'Of course his so-called miraculous cures may be nothing other than self-aggrandisement, as is often the case with young men. Perhaps it would be better to try another remedy first.'

'Fetch him!' I screamed. 'Get me my clerk. I'll write a command this moment and you can tell the messenger where to go.'

We waited three days by which time I was a wreck of a woman. They wouldn't let me see Thomas because of the miasmas which might damage both me and the baby. Edmund, we sent to safety, to a house outside the town, protesting loudly as he was bundled into a litter together with his nursemaid. He had to be kept away from Thomas at all costs, for in my worst moments I recalled other children taken together in death. I cried and I prayed. I couldn't sleep. I couldn't eat. My women tried their best, reminding me of the life I had inside my belly which must be nurtured.

Thomas's fever continued. He complained of pain in his arms and his legs and he vomited frequently. The light hurt his head and his eyes. Dark curtains were hung across the windows and only a single candle was left burning.

On Thursday the messenger returned bringing with him the doctor of physic from London.

'John Gaddesden, your grace.' All I noticed were the hands which were slender and firm, long fingers stained with something blue at the tips; and his eyes: hooded, piercing, intelligent. All I could see was my son's saviour.

'What can I do?' I pleaded.

'Pray,' he said kindly, noticing my trembling hands, my swollen belly and my distress. 'My place is with the child. Yours is on your knees. Between us we shall do our best.'

That evening he came to me.

'The fever is abated.'

'He has recovered?'

'No, my lady. The fever dies as the variola takes hold. Tonight the lesions will occur.'

'Lesions?'

'Yes. In the mouth and on the tongue and then the forehead.'

'And if there are no lesions?'

'The lesions *will* come. Tomorrow we shall see the first signs. I have charged your men with covering the room in red cloth. We shall swathe the bed and the shutters with crimson velvet which I believe is to hand, and the child himself will be wrapped in scarlet linen. He will be given red liquids - wine or cordials. But they must be red.'

'And that will cure him?'

He smiled a thin little smile.

'Our lives are in God's hands, my lady. All we physicians do is to aid the Good Lord in his tasks.'

'But the red cloth, the red drinks? They will help?'

'I have had some success with patients in Oxford and London, particularly with the young.'

He was strong; I could feel his strength. And he was clever. He would save Thomas. God and Master Gaddesden would save my boy.

The next day the rash appeared and word spread throughout the palace. I had to tell my husband before he heard it from someone else. As I stumbled over the words, he turned his face to the wall and didn't speak.

'He is a clever man,' I said with fear in my voice. 'He is only twenty-five and already a doctor of physic. If anyone can save Thomas, he can.'

He turned back to me, his face etched with lines of pain.

'It is no use. I thought I could outrun the past. I thought I had done with dead children. Eleanor wept over so many dead babies and when our son Alphonso died, it destroyed her.'

'Don't say it,' I screamed. 'Thomas is not Eleanor's child. He is mine and he is not going to die. He is going to live. Master Gaddesden is going to save him and I won't have you or anyone else say otherwise.'

I wrapped my arms round my head and wept. My husband had given up on our son. He believed he was going to die and had already prepared himself for the inevitable. I wanted to howl. Oh God, please save my son. Oh Blessed Lady in Heaven, please, please, don't let my Thomas die.

He didn't die. He recovered. In his red-swathed room he opened his eyes, and gradually returned to the Thomas I knew. When Master Gaddesden said all danger was past, I was permitted to see him.

'It hurt, Mama.'

He had reverted to his baby self and cried easily, but he wasn't going to die.

'Oh Thomas, I love you, *mon petit*.'

He gave me a little smile and permitted an embrace and a gentle kiss on his forehead where the last of the variola pock marks were fading. His hair would soon grow to cover them and no-one would ever know he had been afflicted.

As March gave way to April, the green buds swelled to welcome the warmth of spring and the child within me grew larger. Thomas's recovery was slow but eventually he was well enough to accompany Edmund back to Woodstock. With my undying gratitude, Master Gaddesden left for London. He said he must return, not just to his patients in the city but to his *Rosa Medicinae*, a treatise on medicine he was writing, which, he said, would excel all others. If I had owned a kingdom, I would gladly have given it to him for saving my son, but as it was, a large purse of gold was all I had to offer.

In my concern for my child I had almost forgotten my husband's problems in the north. Two days after saying farewell to our sons we received the news I had been dreading. Sir Robert Bruce's fiery cross had been raised and marched across the land, calling his followers to action. English castles had fallen and men had flocked to the banner of their new leader.

The bishop of Glasgow had exhorted his flock to support the rebellion, and the bishop of St Andrews had slipped away from Berwick in the dead of night. The word was that he had taken the pilgrim ferry to Elie. When a letter finally arrived with news of the events at Scone Abbey, my husband flew into such a rage he threw a basin across the floor and cursed and swore until I feared for his sanity.

Lord de Lacy picked the message from the stone flags where it lay amongst the rushes, and read what it said.

'On the feast of the Annunciation, a great multitude of men gathered at the ancient abbey of Scone. In the presence of more than half of the noble men of Scotland, together with the bishop of Glasgow and the bishop of St Andrews, with all due ceremony and with regalia suitable for the occasion, Sir Robert Bruce was crowned king of Scotland. He has let it be known that from henceforth he shall be known as King Robert.'

'My clerics said it could not be done,' shouted my husband. 'They said he didn't have the coronation stone, he didn't have the vestments, he didn't have the crown, and he didn't have the earl of Fife.'

'That is so, your grace,' said Bishop Langton. 'No king of the Scots can be crowned but by a member of the House of Fife. That is how it has always been. And we have earl in our possession.'

'And now what do they tell me?' screamed my husband, 'Wishart had hidden the regalia. He had a banner with the royal arms secreted in his bishop's treasury in Glasgow. Why didn't we find it? Why didn't we know it was there?'

'It would be impossible to know such a thing, your grace,' said Humphrey uneasily. 'The bishop would have many such hiding holes.'

'And that bitch, Buchan's wife - a McDuff of Fife. Why didn't we have her under lock and key? It's well-known she's Bruce's whore, and now you tell me she put the crown on his head.'

I flinched at the words. Alice had told me of the man he was so why did I feel such hurt?

'The earl of Buchan assured us she was held safe,' said Aymer de Valence. 'He had her locked in a tower room with men on guard. But it seems the earl has vipers in his love-nest for someone smuggled the lady out. She took his finest horses and the earl is furious. I wouldn't give a shilling for her safety if her husband catches her.'

My husband began to hammer his fists on the bed and to keen and tear the sheets in his fury.

'My lord,' I said. 'I pray you to be calm. You can do nothing about what has happened and it will not help to rail against it.'

He looked at me in disgust.

'Go away,' he hissed. 'You're a woman. You could never understand. Bring me my son. He will be with me in this.

We will grind them into the dirt. Bruce will rue the day he turned his hand against me, Bruce and all those involved in this treason.'

I returned to my bed exhausted by his anger. I felt the child move within me and thought how pleasant it would be to stay here in my own chamber, away from all the horrors, until my baby was born.

She came with the may blossom on a beautiful spring morning when the sun's first light had barely touched the sky above St Catherine's hill. Stealing in through the ill-fitting shutters, was the night scent of the may, the delicate pink and white flowers which grew against the walls of the palace. My old friend Lady de Lacy was in tears.

'Oh my dear, just what we have been praying for, a little girl. And so perfect, so lovely. Some people say all babies look alike but I swear you can always tell a girl. She looks just like you, I can see none of his grace in that tiny nose and rosebud mouth. And as for those eyes. Oh my dear, I'm going to weep again. I am so happy for you.'

I smiled at her through my tangled hair. She was truly a very kind woman.

Elizabeth and Joan had both been with me for the birth and I could not thank them enough for the help and prayers they'd given me during those long frightening hours when I'd clung to them and cried with the pain. Afterwards, Elizabeth had kissed my sweat-drenched forehead and whispered that she too was again with child.

Joan leaned over to admire her new half-sister. 'I'm glad she resembles you Marguerite. Let's hope she doesn't have our father's temper.'

I smiled. Joan found it very hard to forgive my husband for his treatment of Ned the previous summer.

There was a knock and Alice peeped round the door.

'I've brought you something,' she said. 'For you, not for the baby. Everyone makes so much fuss of babies and forgets about the mother who has done all the work.'

She thrust a small bunch of flowers into my hands.

'Our Lady's Tears. I found them in the garden this morning and thought of you.'

The tiny white bells lay snugly amongst the long slender leaves, their sweet perfume filling the air.

'Dearest Alice,' I said, holding her close and kissing her. 'I am blessed to have you as a friend.'

I lay and thought about my beautiful, longed-for daughter. I forgot the worries of the outside world: the horrors of the coming war, the quarrels, the endless arguing as to what should be done, and lived for this moment, here with my beloved child.

The wet-nurse returned her to my arms where she lay fast asleep. I should have been reasting but I couldn't take my eyes away from this tiny scrap of perfection. How could something so small bring such joy?

Later in the morning, my husband came. He looked tired and worried but had a smile on his face for me. He sat on the bed and took my hand in his.

'All is well, my little pearl. God has granted you your heart's desire.'

'Yes, my lord. He has.'

'And have you decided on a name for our daughter?'

It had been a long and painful journey over the years since our wedding day. I had fought my way through snarled torments of jealousy. I'd ignored my mother's warnings and had hated and despised a woman who had caused me no harm. My husband's first wife had done nothing other than love him, and if she loved him she would want him to be happy. In her shadowed world she wouldn't want to possess him, she'd want him to find companionship and love again. If I were to die that is what I would want for my husband - for him to be happy again.

Ever since our time at Burstwick I'd come to think of her differently, not as a rival but as someone like me, someone who loved him. I should have realised when Edmund was born that love is infinite. God has made it so. My love for Thomas was not diminished one bit because I loved Edmund. The heart always has room for more and if my husband loved his first queen, and loved her still beyond the grave, it did not mean he did not also love me.

I took my eyes away from the sleeping baby and gazed at my husband with tenderness.

'If you have no objection, my lord, I should like to call her Eleanor, in honour of your first wife.'

There was a moment of almost complete silence. All I could hear was the far-off twittering of birds outside my window and the distant sound of men and horses beyond the outer walls of the palace. His eyes filled with tears. I had never seen him weep before and didn't know what to say. He leaned forward and put his head on my shoulder, one hand laid gently against our daughter.

'Thank you,' he said, his voice muffled by tears and the silk of my nightgown. 'If I ever forget to tell you how much you mean to me, how much I care for you, remember this moment.'

We stayed like that for a long time, both our hearts too full to speak. It was only when the baby mewled that he lifted his head and looked at her with such an expression of love on his face.

'Greetings little Eleanor,' he said softly. 'My queen of the may.'

My eyes were closed in that half-land between waking and sleeping. I had been dreaming of Blanche and when I awoke there were tears on my cheeks. Beyond the bed curtain I heard one of my women say, 'She is still asleep, your grace.'

I pushed myself up and twitched the curtain open.

'My lord, I wasn't expecting you. I thought you were with your council.'

'I was and that is why I've come to see you.'

He turned to my women who were hovering about with armfuls of clothing and bits of sewing, and bade them leave us alone.

'Is something amiss?' I asked, arranging myself tidily amongst the pillows.

He paused a moment before he spoke. 'I have come to a decision,' he said slowly. 'It is time for things to change. I no longer have the stomach for campaigning and yet there is much still to be done.'

I put my hand on his. I noticed how wrinkled and spotted his had become this past year, and how the pouches beneath his eyes were dark and bruised. The skin of his face was grey. He looked what he had become - an old, sick man.

'I have given Gascony to my son.'

I gave a little gasp. Gascony was one of the symbols of his kingship, the last of the English lands in Aquitaine, and the source of much of the Crown's wealth. It was possession of Gascony which had been the reason for our marriage.

'Ned will lead our royal armies. Not that he is ready. He is too young, too untried and although it pains me to say it, he is not a leader of men. But I have to work with what I have and I shall do my best to give him men who see the vision just as I do, friends of mine who will advise him if he will heed their words. I've sent Aymer de Valence north. He will secure the border and attend to matters until we can amass our armies at Carlisle. He is a good captain and I have complete confidence in his ability to do my bidding. I've told him to give no quarter and, who knows, by the time we arrive he may even have that piece of scum, Bruce, skewered in a ditch.'

Despite everything, despite my devotion and loyalty to my husband, I felt my heart turn over.

'I shall make a new army of knights for my son. The young are feckless these days, but I shall inspire them, just as I have always done. I've sent out word that all those who are not knights but would wish to be, should come to Westminster for the feast at Whitsuntide. I know how men's minds work and I wager there will be a veritable horde.'

He put his hand on mine and slowly his eyes lost that fevered look they had when he talked of war.

'But now, my little pearl, we come to more intimate matters.'

'Yes, my lord.'

'I have started negotiations for a marriage for our daughter.'

'No, my lord!' I cried. 'You can't. She's only four days old, and you haven't consulted me.'

The easy tears of the new mother rolled down my cheeks and I clutched at his sleeve.

'Please, my lord. Don't take her away from me.'

He put his fingers up to my face and gently wiped away the tears.

'Hush,' he said. 'No-one will take her away. Listen to me carefully. I have done this to protect her. I am arranging a marriage for her with the young count of Burgundy. You know who his mother is?'

I did. The dowager countess of Burgundy was aunt to my brother Louis's wife, and sole possessor of the huge Artois inheritance.

'The little count's sisters are betrothed to two of your brother, Philip's sons. So you see what a good marriage this will be for our daughter.'

'Yes,' I whispered. 'I do see.'

'There are other reasons why this must be done now,' he said, lowering his voice. 'If anything were to happen to me, how much care do you think my son would take over a marriage for our daughter? He's as likely to marry her off to one of his unsuitable friends. You wouldn't want that for our little queen of the may. Can you imagine her as the bride of someone like Master Gaveston?'

He chuckled at his own joke but I sniffed miserably, still unhappy at the thought of my daughter ever leaving me.

'Dry your eyes,' he said, 'and I will tell you of my plans. I had in mind a pair of gilded swans.'

He talked enthusiastically of the ceremony and how he would first knight Ned, then let him do all the hard work of knighting the other men. He expected there to be well over two hundred who would come forward.

'It will take days,' he said with satisfaction. 'There are men who have never been knighted, like old Mortimer of Chirk, and his nephew, Roger, and there's Arundel's son, Edmund Fitzalan, young Hugh Despenser, Roger d'Amory and my old friend de Warrenne's grandson. The roll-call is endless.'

He talked of the feast afterwards when he would make his speech, where I knew from experience, wine would flow and men would be carried away with what I liked to call war fever. They would be reckless in their ambitions, and vows would be taken. They would believe they were invincible and could conquer the world, and perhaps it would be true. I was sorry to miss the excitement but I'd not forgo these precious days with my daughter for all the feasts in Christendom.

'It is time my grand-daughters were married,' continued my husband who was clearly in an arranging mood. 'The eldest de Clare girl is to wed young Hugh Despenser. I have talked with his father and it is settled. She is fourteen and Joan tells me she is ready for marriage. And I shall offer my granddaughter, little Jeanne de Bar, to my old friend's grandson, young de Warrenne. And the earl of Fife can have Ralph de Monthermer's girl, Mary. That should stop any future nonsense with the Scots. The boy has been in my son's household for years so he'll not be minded to crown any kings of Scotland in the years to come.'

'Oh husband,' I said with a smile in my voice. 'You are becoming quite the matchmaker.'

'It is part of a king's duties, my dear,' he sad seriously. 'Marry up these families and tie the knots good and tight. New blood is all very well but one needs to choose carefully. That is what worries me about Ned, he is careless.'

Yes, I thought sadly, Ned was loving and generous but he lacked the care and attention to every detail that a king needed. And most of all he failed to recognise the power of others, men who might turn their hands against him in the years ahead.

Ten days later the men departed for Westminster leaving me and my daughter in the peace and quiet of our togetherness.

'Till the feast of St John the Baptist, my dear,' said my husband, kissing me on the cheek, his mind clearly on his war, not on his wife and daughter. 'I shall see you at Westminster and we shall go north together.'

15

AUTUMN 1306

It was past mid-summer when we departed from the Island of Thorns and headed north but the horrors didn't start until we reached the town of Durham. It was here we first heard what was happening in the north and where, later, I had to live with the consequences.

My husband's old friend, the bishop, had generously offered his magnificent palace to us during our stay.

'It's no hardship for him,' growled my husband, trying to ease the pain by shifting his position against a cushion. 'Bek prefers his other palace. God's bones! What luxury these prince bishops live in, wife. You'd think he was the king himself.'

'He is your friend, my lord,' I said. 'He fights for you.'

'Ha!' he replied. 'Bek fights everyone. If he's not hunting he's squabbling with some prior or other. And who has to sort out his messes? Me!'

And with that he threw the costly velvet cushion onto the floor and demanded more wine.

Aymer de Valence had done his work well, retaking several castles and hounding Sir Robert's followers. His letter said dozens had returned to the English side, refusing to fight for their so-called "summer king". Those who did not, and were captured had been sent south to face my husband's justice.

'My instructions were that no quarter was to be given,' snarled my husband, upon being told of a group of prisoners awaiting his judgement in the castle dungeons. 'Our army was to burn and slay and raise the dragon, and everybody knows what that means. No-one is to be spared if they take up arms against me. No-one. Is that not clear enough?'

The captain who'd brought the news nodded in agreement, not daring to say a word.

'These scum should have been slain on the spot and those who took part in that farce at Scone will be put down like dogs. How dare they think to crown a Scottish king!'

'It was very wrong, husband,' I said quietly. 'Very wrong indeed.'

He gazed at me and smiled a singularly unpleasant smile. 'I have reserved a particular punishment for those who killed the lord of Badenoch at Dumfries.'

I wondered what torments he was planning to inflict on Sir Robert and his friends if they were caught. I said a quick prayer for the man who would run through the heather. I prayed the nights would be dark and the seas calm.

'And the prisoners?' said Ralph de Monthermer.

'Take them to Newcastle,' said my husband. 'Drag them through the streets and then hang them. Let them dance in the air to a different tune.'

'Surely we will keep the titled men for ransom?'

'Hang all of them,' growled my husband, his chin sunk on his chest, his back bent against the pain. 'Every last one of them. They've borne arms against their sovereign king. Whoever they are they will die.'

It was unheard of to treat knights captured in battle as common criminals. They were always treated honourably. My husband's men exchanged worried glances. The rules of war were being flouted and it put everyone at risk, including themselves. But no-one dared speak. With clenched fists and impassive faces, they left the chamber without a word, knowing better than to argue with my husband. The prisoners were taken away and within a week the killings began.

The following day the bishop of St Andrews was brought in under armed guard, together with the elderly abbot of Scone, a pitiful scrawny man of God. They were dirty and unkempt but the bishop seemed certain his ecclesiastical privileges would protect them. He stood upright in the centre of the chamber amidst a crowd of his captors, defiance shining out of his eyes.

'Well, Lamberton?' growled my husband. 'So you think that one moment you can kiss my ring and swear to uphold our agreements for peace, while the next you slither away like the snake you are and urge your followers to take up arms against me.'

The bishop said nothing.

'How wrong you are,' said my husband, menace lacing his every word. 'Let me tell you, Sir Bishop, if it wasn't for your cloth I'd have you strung up with the rest of them. I'm almost tempted to do so anyway but I'm told it would most likely imperil my soul. Instead I shall let you rot in one of my deepest dungeons. You can spend your remaining days, and I pray they be many, chained to a wall in a stinking pit and we'll see how much you regret your actions.'

William Lamberton's eyes didn't even flicker. He must

have known what would happen to him the moment he was taken.

'And take your creature with you,' shouted my husband, indicating the poor shivering abbot who was cowering behind the younger man's cloak. 'Did he think putting a metal circlet on a traitor's brow would make the man a king? If he did, he is a fool and deserves his fate. Take him away. He can be locked up elsewhere.'

He turned to the captain of the guard.

'Keep them close and fetter them. The clank of chains as they ride south will remind them of their sins.'

He laughed as they were taken away.

'I hear we have Wishart, wife,' he said to me as he rubbed his hands together. 'Is that not good news?'

I murmured my agreement. I'd heard that morning from one of my women that the bishop of Glasgow had been taken at Cupar Castle where he'd fled from the English army. Aymer de Valence's men had caught the Scots unawares near Perth and slaughtered them in their thousands. It was said the Scots were asleep and not expecting the English to venture out before daybreak. I remembered Sir Robert's words last summer about men who slept in the heather and wondered how he could have allowed such a thing to happen.

The remnants of the Scottish army had scattered and were being picked up in ditches and gullies by the victorious English but of the so-called Scottish king there was no sign. Although I knew it was wrong, I breathed a sigh of relief that he was still alive. Whatever he'd done I didn't want him to die a traitor's death.

I was surprised by the bishop of Glasgow. He was in

full armour, his hands bound and his face bloody. My husband surveyed him grimly.

'I see you are ready for celebrating Mass, Sir Bishop. Do those garments help you in your spiritual duties or is it perhaps that you fancy yourself still on the battlefield? You do know the difference, don't you?'

He thrust his face close to that of the elderly bishop, who looked back at him with hatred burning in his eyes.

'Silent for once, I see Wishart,' said my husband. 'Frightened we might take you for a common soldier and string you up on the gibbet alongside your countrymen? I must consult with my lawyers and see if you have removed yourself outside the protection of your cloth by donning that chain-mail. I have a suspicion it might be so. Then I can treat you like a treacherous churl without incurring the wrath of His Holiness. Think what I can do with you then.'

The bishop's face flushed red with rage.

'You thought to take me for a fool, I see,' said my husband. 'I heard what you did with my royal gift. That timber I gave you in the spirit of peace was intended for your cathedral roof. It was for the glory of God, Sir Bishop, not for you to build siege engines.'

He eyed the bishop with venom. They were like two fighting cocks, but my husband wore the spurs while the bishop was sorely wounded. There could be no doubt as to who would be the victor, just the method with which he would effect the *coup de grâce*.

'Take him south,' said my husband. 'The deepest dungeon in the Tower. Make sure he is chained and there is no need to be gentle.'

Sainte Vierge, but I was tired of this violence. I was swamped by a ceaseless tide of hatred and revenge, wallowing in a mire of bloody gore, a never-ending glorification of one man's might over another. I could not believe God intended for us to act thus, yet our English bishops said nothing. They donned their armour, summoned their men and led them into battle, following the banners of their earthly king.

My husband was a stranger to me in those days. He commanded my presence by his side but barely noticed me. I steeled myself to feel nothing as he consigned young men to their hideous deaths and old men to die in chains, but my heart rebelled.

The next day a young Yorkshire knight, Sir Christopher Seton, was dragged before my husband. He was mud-spattered, his clothes in tatters, his face bruised and bloody. He'd been taken at Loch Doon two weeks previously and brought here to face justice at my husband's hands. With his wrists bound tightly behind his back, he was thrust by one of his guards into a kneeling position below the huge carved chair in which my husband sat.

'Ah, the brave Sir Christopher,' sneered my husband. 'We have heard much of you. You should have taken more care over your loyalties, Seton. A Bruce for a wife was not a sensible choice.'

I wondered if it was one of Sir Robert's sisters he had married.

'I hear you felled one of my good men in battle,' continued my husband.

'I was defending my king,' said the man, speaking with difficulty through his swollen lips.

'Your king is here before you,' said my husband in his coldest voice. 'Do you not recognise him?'

There was a long silence where neither man spoke.

'The lord of Badenoch?' queried my husband. 'What of him?'

He had risen, pushing himself up with his arms and was standing full height looking down on his prisoner. He was wearing his emblazoned tunic and furred robes and looked every inch a powerful leader and a man bent on revenge.

'Do you recall the strikes you made that day in Dumfries or were you just defending your so-called master? Did Comyn draw first? Was that it? A sharp little dagger unsheathed against his enemy? Or did you butcher him in cold blood on the steps of the high altar?'

Sir Christopher Seton said nothing. My husband was going to have him killed whether or not he admitted to the murder of John Comyn.

We didn't know who had wielded the swords that day in the church of the Greyfriars. Two men had died and there were plenty of witnesses to say that a group of Bruce's men, and Sir Robert himself, were there. But as to what actually took place inside the church, nobody knew, or if they did, they weren't telling.

I looked at the young man's fair hair which fell in lank strands across his forehead, and thought to myself - it could be Edmund. In twenty years time my son would look like this: young, fresh, at the start of his grown-up life. I wanted to weep for these young men and their lost futures, but I didn't dare.

My husband sat down again. I knew he couldn't stand for long, it was too painful.

'It matters not which it was, Sir Knight. Whether you struck the death blow or not, it was murder most foul and you will pay the price. To take up arms against your king is treason and that is the death you will have, a traitor's death.'

Sir Christopher's face betrayed little. He was a brave man and would, I felt sure, go to the gibbet with his head held high.

'Take him to Dumfries,' said my husband to the guard. 'If my memory serves me right there is a small hill outside the town. You can hang him there.'

He turned back to Sir Christopher.

'Not just hanging, Sir Knight. We will have your guts pulled out while you are still alive to feel the agony, and then your head will be severed from your body and your body sliced in four. What price your support for the traitor Bruce then?'

But the young man still said nothing. He stared ahead, looking beyond my husband into a distant future, to a life which would never be his.

Our progress through the wilds of the north was painfully slow. My husband's litter managed barely three or four miles before we had to stop. He had exhausted himself at Durham and I was afraid for him. I had no idea what would happen to my children if he should die.

Not far from Hexham Abbey, at Newbrough, Ned

joined us, fresh from his triumphs in the north-east. He arrived clad in full armour, riding his huge black warhorse. His months in the saddle had burned his skin a ruddy brown and lightened his hair to a gleaming gold. He looked like a prince and I had to admit it was a relief to have him with me. He was someone to share the burden of my husband's illness.

'You will be pleased, father,' he said as the three of us sat together that first evening. 'Aymer and I have taken Kildrummy. We thought it might take some months, but they had a turncoat in their midst.'

'Were they there? Did you capture them?' said my husband eagerly, a slight flush of pink on his cheeks.

He was asking about Sir Robert's women: his wife, his sisters and his little daughter. The word was they'd been sent to Kildrummy because it was the strongest castle in the north-eat and considered safe. Obviously it was not strong enough or safe enough.

'We thought they'd be in the tower,' said my stepson. 'But they must have slipped away down the ravine in the dark. Aymer thinks they'll head north to the ports and take ship to the Orkneys or more likely Norway.'

I remembered Sir Robert had a sister married to the king of Norway. Doubtless they'd be safe there as I didn't think my husband would go to war with the king of Norway over a parcel of women.

'The north-east is loyal,' murmured my husband, assessing the situation through narrowed eyes.

'Yes,' said Ned, easing his neck after his long day in the saddle. 'The earl of Ross will bring them in.'

I thought of those poor women fleeing through the

heather, hunted down like animals by my husband's army and by their own countrymen just because of who they were. Women are blameless in these matters. They are mere shadows of their husbands and yet they suffer. I wondered where they'd sleep, where they'd find shelter and what they'd find to eat? Ned didn't say if kinsmen or friends of Sir Robert were with them but I hoped for their sakes they were not alone.

'My father doesn't look well,' Ned said to me when we sat together in my small draughty chamber at Thornton Manor where we'd halted for the night.

'No,' I said sadly. 'The bouts of pain are more frequent and he suffers from the flux but refuses to rest.'

'The bloody flux is a cursed disease,' said my stepson, pouring himself another cup of wine. Then he gave a short laugh. 'Your brother Louis told me your grandfather once had to cut a hole in his breeches he had it so bad.'

I sat there in the dying light thinking of the horrors and indignities of war. I knew war was brutal but I hadn't realise it would brutalize my husband.

'Are we headed for Carlisle?' asked Ned, sipping his wine.

'Yes.'

'Do we winter there or are we returning south?'

'I don't think your father is well enough to make the journey south. I think we shall have to winter in the north. He can summon a January parliament at Carlisle.'

'Five months,' he said thoughtfully.

'What are you planning?'

'Oh nothing of any importance. I was just thinking.

Soon we'll be finished here and I don't fancy kicking my heels in this benighted part of the realm until January.'

At that moment there was a wild knocking at the door and one of my husband's attendants burst in.

'His grace!' he cried. 'He's dying!'

I thought he was dead. He lay motionless in his bed, not moving, while his physician prodded and poked and sighed.

'It is the same as before, my lady,' he said mournfully. 'He has expended too much of himself and will not rest. I've had him bled but each time he endures one of these attacks he becomes weaker. What with the bloody flux soon he'll have no strength left.'

I looked at my husband, lying as still as a corpse. His breathing was so shallow I would have thought him gone to God if it were not for the slight flush of colour on his cheeks. What would I do without him? Since our marriage he'd been my whole existence and I was not sure if there was another.

Together the physician and I kept our vigil throughout the night and through the next day. Time ceased to have meaning and my world shrank to the confines of this small undecorated chamber in the wild border country and the man who lay silent and still beneath the covers of the bed.

At the end of the third day he stirred, his eyelids fluttered, and my husband returned to me.

'You frightened me,' I said, wiping away tears of relief.

He smiled weakly. 'I'm tough. You won't get rid of me yet, not while there's work still to do.'

'I do not want rid of you, husband. What would I do without you?'

Perhaps it was my pleas, but the next afternoon he called for his clerk and began to make provisions for our children. There was a lengthy document giving the Norfolk inheritance to Thomas once Roger Bigod was gone, and one granting lands of seven thousand marks to Edmund, and another which provided for the care of his youngest daughter, our little Eleanor. Ned signed the guarantee to care for his sister should my husband die before she was married. I was well dowered. Everything had been agreed before my marriage in that lengthy wrangling between the French and the English envoys, and I already knew which castles and manors I would receive in my widowhood. My husband had thought of everything.

'Norfolk will go before me, wife,' he said. 'Of that you can be sure. I shan't leave this world until the rogue is safely in his tomb. He's been a thorn in my side these past ten years, always defying me, always making trouble with the others. But I'm pleased with the deal I did, for now our boy can have his estates and title. Thomas of Brotherton, earl of Norfolk - how does that sound?'

'And Edmund?' I asked anxiously.

'I'm not sure yet,' said my husband pondering the future of his favourite child. 'Perhaps my late cousin's title. earl of Cornwall? What do you think?'

'Whatever you decide, my lord,' I said. 'These are your gifts and you must bestow them as you think fit.'

'True, but I'm tired now and my mind is befuddled. I'll think on it some more tomorrow.'

But next day there were other matters to attend to. If

I'd known I would have pressed him, I would have urged him to settle Edmund's future there, that moment. But I didn't know for we none of us can see the future, and in not knowing the die was cast and the uncertain future made.

In the worst of nightmares there is always an end, a time of waking, a realisation that one's fears are of the darkness and not of the day. But at Lanercost Priory on the edge of the windswept border country there was to be no cessation of pain and grief as my husband's personal vision of hell engulfed us all.

We arrived shortly before Michaelmas. We were ten miles short of the castle at Carlisle but my husband had a preference for the austere surroundings of the lonely priory just a stone's throw from where the great wall had once been. He said he would go no further.

To the south-west there was nothing to see but bare rolling hills and occasional clumps of stunted trees. Above us to the north stood dark forests and beyond that, I was told, the wilds of the Cheviot Hills which guarded the Lothian, a county loyal to the English Crown. The priory had suffered grievous attacks by the Scots ten years ago but little damage had been done.

'They burned some of our houses, my lady,' explained the prior, 'but, thanks be to God, our church was unharmed. They sneaked away through the forest when the English armies returned. Even that ruffian Wallace came with his men, but as you see, we are still here. God and our blessed Saviour protected us well. And it is a rare treat to see his grace again.'

'He has been here before?' I said, surprised, for my husband had said nothing.

'Oh yes, my lady. Many, many years ago, with the queen, the Lady Eleanor. That was a fine visit for his grace. He took over two hundred deer from the Inglewood. Those were good days, not like now. Now we fear the killing and burning will never end.'

We'd not been there a day when a man, who looked as if he'd been travelling for days without stopping, arrived with news.

'We have the women,' laughed Ned. 'They were caught by the earl's men.'

And for the rest of the day my husband went round with a smile on his face.

It was a miserable day when they brought in Sir Robert's women. Up from the south-west, swathes of torn cloud carried the first fat heavy drops of rain and by midday we were marooned in a clammy sea of low-lying fog.

It was out of this blanket of mist that a group of men and women trailed into our midst. There must have been at least thirty of them, wrapped in thick dark cloaks with Earl Ross's men in armour with swords at their sides. I caught a single glimpse of the women as they were roughly bundled into one of the priory buildings.

My husband chose the priory's chapter house to use as his place of business. It was a bare, circular room with no decoration, rather cold and forbidding, which only added to the feeling of oppression. After some whispered discussion, the first captives were brought in. They were two men. I looked towards my husband. He was enjoying this. I closed my eyes against the realisation that this man to whom I was bound could be tender and loving to me yet so vindictive and cruel to others.

'Ah,' said my husband. 'Who have we here?'

'Sir Niall Bruce,' said the clerk, consulting his list. 'Brother of the traitor, Sir Robert Bruce, caught with certain women at Tain, attempting to buy passage out of the land.'

My husband looked at the dishevelled, bruised figure, in front of him. The man's clothes were filthy, his boots in shreds and his cloak torn. He shared a likeness to Sir Robert but looked younger. He seemed quite calm, knowing there was no escape and that all he could do was meet God with dignity.

'I'll not waste my breath on you,' said my husband. 'Doubtless you acted on the orders of your brother, but that is little excuse. Take him to Berwick and hang him. A traitor's death.'

By now my husband's men were used to his peculiar desire for vengeance in this matter. The second man was forced to the floor. His hands were bound tightly behind him and his face was a bloodied mess, one eye half-closed, a huge purple bruise extending over part of his face. His nose was broken but he was defiant, I could see it in his one remaining whole eye.

'John of Strathbogie, earl of Atholl, your grace,' said the clerk in my husband's ear. 'Plucked from the wreck of his ship, attempting to flee the land.'

My husband eyed the man with particular venom.

'You knelt in front of me a twelve-month ago, my lord earl, when you made homage for your lands in Kent. You swore a liegeman's oath. Clearly promises made in the sight of God and your king mean little to you, if they are so easily cast aside. You took up arms against your king, and that is treason.'

'I owe allegiance to only one king here in this land, to King Robert,' said the earl through his swollen lips.

My husband leant forward and lashed out with his hand across the earl's mouth.

'Traitorous words,' he hissed. 'You condemn yourself.'

He looked round the rest of the chamber, his eyes noting each man of his who was there.

'Take him to London,' he said.

I thought he was going to say, 'to a dungeon in the tower', but he didn't.

'Hang him like the traitor he is.'

There was a gasp from around the chamber. Earls were not executed. It was unheard of. No king had ever executed one of his earls. Ralph de Monthermer, braver than the rest, stepped forward to my husband's shoulder.

'Your grace,' he said softly. 'Royal blood flows in this man's veins. You cannot hang him. Your grace's grandfather is his ancestor.'

I had been told by Lady de Lacy that the earl of Atholl was descended from a royal bastard of King John, a kinship of which, at one time, the earl must have been justly proud.

My husband turned his head slowly to look at Ralph.

'As you should know well, my lord of Gloucester, a baseborn connection is never quite as good as the real thing.'

Ralph flushed a dull red. Few people these days

commented on his illegitimacy, in truth most people had probably forgotten, but not my husband. He forgot nothing. Ralph's example was noted by the others and Humphrey went to my husband's other side.

'He is an earl, your grace,' he said as if explaining matters to a small child. 'He is highborn. It would not be right to hang him as you would a lowborn man.'

My husband smiled.

'You are quite correct, Lord de Bohun, as always. It would not be right. We shall hang him thirty feet higher than the rest so that all may see and marvel at this traitorous earl who dared to lift his sword against his king. Take him away.'

I felt like screaming. My head was bursting with the noise and the horror and the stench of sweat and fear. But there was to be no escape for me or for any of the prisoners.

As soon as the guards had hustled the two men away, the women were brought in. There were four of them, and with them came two small children, a boy of about seven and a girl who could not have been more than ten. For some reason I'd thought the women would be old, but they were young, like me.

I thought the youngest must be Sir Robert's wife. She was pushed forward onto her knees. Yes, I was sure this was Sir Robert's wife. She had fair skin and reddish-gold hair and was less ragged and filthy than the others.

'The Lady Elizabeth de Burgh,' said my husband's clerk. 'Wife to the traitor, Sir Robert Bruce, taken at Tain in the company of Sir Niall Bruce, attempting to leave the land.'

'Madam,' said my husband. 'You have been unfortunate in your father's choice of marriage for you. I regret you did not leave for the south while you had the opportunity but chose to follow your lord and master.'

'It is a wife's duty, your grace,' she said, looking somewhat boldly at him.

She clearly believed her father's friendship with the king would save her from any punishment. I wondered what my husband would do with these women and why he'd been so insistent on their capture. Perhaps he believed he could lure Sir Robert back to rescue his womenfolk. If he did, I was certain he was mistaken. Sir Robert's only care would be for his child, of that I was sure.

'Indeed,' said my husband, smiling at the Lady Elizabeth. 'How very correct. I like to hear of obedient wives. I also hear you chided your husband at Scone for playing kings and queens. That was far-sighted of you, madam, for his so-called kingship has not lasted the summer, as you foretold.'

She returned the smile, relaxing her shoulders slightly. She believed she was safe.

'But,' he said more severely. 'I cannot have you free.'

He turned to his men.

'Have the Lady Elizabeth conveyed to the manor at Burtstwick, in Holderness. She may have two women to care for her but they should be elderly and sober, certainly not of a joyful nature. And she is to be closely confined.'

A severe punishment for a young woman who had no say in her marriage, but by now I was used to my husband's wrath and the way it was being visited upon his captives.

'The Lady Christian Bruce,' said my husband's clerk

lifting his head from his parchments. 'Sister to the traitor...'

As he read out the details of her capture, I looked at Sir Robert's sister. Older than me, I thought, but not by much. She resembled her brother: dark hair and eyes, the same nose and cheekbones; a woman who under other circumstances would be considered handsome. I wondered who her husband was.

'I have sent your husband to hang, Lady Seton,' said my husband. 'Did you know that?'

Sainte Vierge! I thought. This was the wife of the Yorkshire knight, Sir Christopher Seton. The face of the woman on the floor was white and her eyes were blank with pain.

'He died at Dumfries. Would you like to see his body? No, I thought not, for to tell the truth there is not much of it left after my executioner finished with it.'

Christian Bruce's eyes filled with tears. She lifted up her bound hands and covered her face.

'Too late for tears, my lady,' said my husband. 'Take her south.'

He turned to his clerk. 'Where did I say?'

'Sixhills, your grace. In Lincolnshire.'

'Ah yes. The Gilbertine Priory of St Mary at Sixhills. It will be a good place to dwell upon your sins, madam. I hear the walls are very high, and the food scant and plain, but you won't notice that as you do penance for your sins. Take her away.'

I thought of the girls at Maubuisson and my heart felt squeezed with the pain of it all. It was not just fathers and brothers who would imprison girls behind convent walls but vengeful kings. How could my husband do this to these poor women who had played no part in this rebellion? It was not their fault if their husband or brother took up arms against my husband. Nobody would have consulted them in the matter just as my husband didn't consult me when he went to war.

The guards pushed the little boy forward. He was probably not old enough to understand what was happening but he sensed the women's fear and was crying. He was of tender years, perhaps not out of the nursery. His hair and eyes were dark and he looked a picture of complete misery. As he was pushed forward he turned to clutch at a woman's gown, but the guards wrenched his hands free. He crouched in front of my husband like a small dog, whimpering in fear.

'Donald, son of the late earl of Mar, nephew to the traitor, Sir Robert Bruce,' intoned my husband's clerk. 'Taken at Tain, in the company of Sir Niall Bruce and others.'

My husband stared impassively at the pathetic scrap in front of him. Poor child, I thought.

'Take him to Bristol, to the castle. Confine him there and make sure he cannot escape, for he is close kin to the traitor, Bruce, but there is no need to fetter the child, he is too young.'

It was the first sign of compassion I'd seen in my husband since this nightmare had started some three months ago. Perhaps the other three, the two remaining women and the little girl, would also be treated leniently.

How very wrong I was.

'The Lady Isabel McDuff, countess of Buchan.'

My heart leapt. This was the woman my husband had

described as Bruce's whore. She was small and dark-haired and rather beautiful in a wild way. Her lips were full and her eyes wide-spaced. Beneath her filthy gown she was small-boned, her breasts high, her hips slim. Her legs, which were bare and half-exposed for all to see, were long and well-shaped, her thighs gleaming white where the skirt had been split in two. One of the guards eyed her with interest, his tongue flicking across his lips.

Had these women been violated by Earl Ross's men? I was certain no-one would have defiled Sir Robert's wife for the Lady Elizabeth had an untouchable air and her captors would surely have stopped short of abusing a lady of high estate. But what of this woman who was an acknowledged whore? One part of me hated her, but the other, the better part, felt only pity. I couldn't imagine how it would feel to be in the power of such men, to be defenceless against their lust.

My husband looked particularly pleased to have the countess of Buchan in his power. I wondered if he had consulted with the earl on her punishment. Perhaps she would be returned to her husband who would doubtless whip her for her disobedience. Perhaps he would imprison her in one of his castles. I didn't know how a husband would behave to a faithless wife but I was sure the earl of Buchan would not be gentle.

'The whore,' said my husband evenly, noting every detail of the countess's disarray. 'The gallant Lady Buchan! The lady who preferred a traitor's bed to that of her husband. The lady who dared put a crown on her lover's head and thought to call him her king. I trust you will think the delights you found in your lover's arms fair recompense for what will happen now, madam.'

His words were like repeated thrusts of a dagger.

'I have a little surprise for you, lady,' he sneered. 'I hear you love your country, is that not so?'

He looked enquiringly at the woman before him but she said nothing, just glared at his feet through a tangle of hair.

'No words then, madam? A pity, for soon you'll regret the chance to converse with someone. I intend to remove you from the land of your birth. Ah, that hurts, doesn't it, my lady? I thought it would.'

At his words the countess had jerked her head up and looked my husband straight in the eye. He smiled thinly.

'But, I am a merciful man, am I not Lady Buchan? I shall afford you a pleasant view of the Scottish hills to give you comfort in the days ahead. I have prepared a small house for you, madam. Nothing of great size, just a little latticed cage.'

There was the sudden sound of indrawn breath from two of the men.

'A cage,' he went on, 'some four feet measured on each side, not large, but cosy enough. And this cage will hang on the walls of the castle at Berwick which is now an English castle on English soil. From there you will see your precious Scotland and the people of my realm will see you. I hope they are kind to you, my lady Buchan, for you will hang there, in your cage for many years until the fire in your belly has grown cold.'

I closed my eyes. How could anyone devise such a savage punishment for a young woman? I tried to imagine how much four feet would be. Not large enough to lie full length. I stared blankly at the young woman who appeared dazed by the severity of her punishment. I wondered if it had been my husband's idea or that of the cuckolded earl of Buchan.

I could not hate a woman who would have to live exposed to the wind and the rain, year after year with no shelter and no comforts, jeered at by the people of the town and tormented by anyone who chose to do so. It was a savage cruelty.

The other woman was Sir Robert's sister, Mary. I barely heard as my husband condemned her to the same fate as the countess of Buchan, a cage hung on the walls of Roxburgh Castle. It was said she had encouraged her brother in his rebellion and had spoken harsh words against my husband.

By now the women were huddled together, weeping in great distress, knowing that soon they'd be parted and their years of solitary punishment would begin.

The only prisoner left was the girl. She was not one of those girls on the brink of womanhood, almost ready for the marriage bed. She was a child, thin and terrified. Her lank brown hair straggled over her ragged gown and her skin seemed tightly stretched over her shoulders. She clutched a small doll in her hands, a mean little thing made of carved wood. She looked barely old enough to be betrothed. She was given a push by one of the guards and sent sprawling. She hauled herself up and squatted down in front of my husband, her face pointing at the floor, not looking at him.

'Marjorie, daughter of the traitor, Sir Robert Bruce, by his late wife, Isabel of the House of Mar, taken at Tain with Sir Niall Bruce and others,' said my husband's clerk, rolling up his parchment. This was the last prisoner to be dealt with today and the man was clearly glad to be rid of such unpleasantness. From the look on his face he had as little appetite for this savagery as I had.

The child began to weep large silent tears.

'The devil's spawn,' said my husband, looking with some disappointment at Sir Robert's daughter. 'The young of the serpent.'

He turned to his clerk once more.

'Where did I say?'

'The Tower,' said the man without looking at his roll. He knew the punishment well enough.

'Ah yes, the Tower. A fearsome place, child. Your father will not rescue you from there. It is too far distant and its walls are too high and too thick. People do not escape from the Tower. They remain there until they rot.'

I couldn't believe my husband meant to send this child to be locked away in a room in the Tower. And I was right. That was not what he had in mind at all. He bent down and peered at the figure on the floor.

'A latticed cage, like the others.'

'No, my lord!'

I couldn't allow this to happen. I couldn't see this child sent to live in a cage in the Tower where she'd join my husband's other beasts: his lions and bears, locked away from prying eyes, displayed to him and his friends whenever he had the fancy.

He turned to look at me. He didn't seem angry merely surprised. I thought he'd be driven into a fury because I hadn't forgotten our quarrel at Stirling two years ago.

I rose from my seat and knelt in front of him. My hands were trembling as I bent down and kissed his feet in the most abject way possible. I raised my head and looked deep into his eyes.

'My lord,' I whispered. 'As you love me, do not do this. I know you are not an unworthy man. I know you for the noble and merciful king that you are. Send her to a priory, my lord. Do not place her in a cage.'

I hadn't meant to cry but as I knelt on the hard cold stone I felt tears gather on my lashes. I bit my lip waiting for the tirade to start. I bent my head knowing he would never strike me. He never had, not in all the years of our marriage. There was complete silence other than snivelling from the child behind me. After what seemed like hours but which could only have been a few moments, my husband leaned over and raised me to my feet.

'You are right, my lady,' he said slowly. 'I *am* merciful. The child is too young. I had thought her to be better grown.'

He considered for a moment then turned to his clerk. 'Have her taken to the Gilbertine priory at Watton, near Beverley. It is a suitable place for a traitor's daughter. Doubtless the girl will learn the error of her father's ways amongst the nuns at Watton.'

He rose to his feet and waved to his men-at-arms.

'Take the prisoners out. I've seen enough.'

Together we walked from the chapter room back to my chamber. My husband settled himself down in front of the fire. One of his attendants hurried with a small fire pot for him to warm his hands. It had been chilly in the chapter room and his face had taken on a bluish tinge. Even wrapped warmly in my fur-lined cloak I'd felt frozen to my bones.

"Well, wife,' he said. 'Your pleas worked this time. But remember, I don't expect to hear your voice raised when Sir Robert Bruce is brought in.'

'Do you have him?' I said, trying not to show my fear.

'No, but we will. De Valence will catch him.'

I sat and stared at the fire, at the flames flickering round and over the logs, and thought of the days long ago when he and I had been happy. I thought of our children and I thought of Sir Robert, so very far away, not knowing what horrors were being visited upon his women. As the servant piled more branches onto the blaze, I prayed silently that it would be a long time before he knew.

16

The days were getting shorter and the first frosts had appeared, crisping the ground and lacing the stunted apple trees in the priory garden with white. Soon it would be time for the Christmas festivities and afterwards we would go to Carlisle for the parliament. Nobody felt in a joyful mood. My husband was still gripped by the pain in his guts and making matters worse than they already were, Ned had disobeyed his father and gone south.

'I won't have any of you leaving,' his father had growled, when Ned suggested his journey overseas. 'We haven't caught Bruce yet. He's loose out there somewhere in the hills and the glens.'

Ned sighed. 'Bruce has gone to ground. Our spies told us he took ship from the west. He won't be back. You've successfully butchered all his followers so what support would he have? There's nothing to keep us here and the tournament in Ponthieu will be a grand affair, just what we need after months of campaigning.'

He rose, knowing the longer he delayed the more objections his father would find.

'I need you here,' continued my husband. 'A prince's place is by his father's side, not gallivanting off with a load of fools to some charade of pretty knights who've never fought a proper campaign in their lives. I repeat, you are *not* to go. You have duties to perform. His Holiness is sending one of his cardinals to finalise the peace terms we made with the French and I need you there to greet the man when he arrives at Dover. Cardinal Pedro will not expect to be met by a servant. He will expect recognition of the importance of his visit and it would not be wise to antagonise His Holiness, it never is. You can bring the cardinal to Carlisle for the January parliament. That should keep you busy.'

'I don't need something to keep me busy, father, and I thought we were having second thoughts about the French marriage.'

'Second thoughts!' I gasped. 'But it's all arranged. The betrothal was binding. It was part of the agreement. You told me.'

My husband turned to look at me, pursing his lips in annoyance.

'Twelve month ago His Holiness was pressing us to bring forward the wedding,' he said. 'If necessary we were to use a proxy, but neither my son nor I were keen. And now, well now things are different, and it is a very delicate matter.'

I turned to my stepson and touched his sleeve,

'Ned?'

Ned looked uncomfortable.

'His grace, my father and I,' he began hesitantly and then stopped, looking for help from his father.

'The marriage with your brother's daughter is not in our best interests at present,' said my husband, his voice tinged with annoyance. 'There have been approaches from Castile, from Don Enrique, and certainly a marriage there

325

might suit us better. My son is agreeable as he has no great desire to marry your niece.'

I couldn't believe what he was saying. I'd set my heart on this marriage.

'The cardinal is your brother's creature so we must tread carefully,' continued my husband. 'We don't want him thinking we are unwilling to proceed but on the other hand we mustn't let ourselves be pushed into an alliance which would not benefit us. My son is a prize and we don't want to waste him on the wrong girl.'

I said nothing for there was nothing to be said. If my husband and my stepson had decided against the French marriage there would be nothing I could say to change their minds. I thought of my little niece alone at my brother's court and wept silent tears.

Ned said no more on either subject, but two days later, together with Humphrey, Piers Gaveston, Roger Mortimer and a dozen or so of the younger knights in his household, slipped away in the early morning hours before my husband had risen. The night before he'd said a fond farewell, kissing my cheeks and holding my hands. I had tried to get him to change his mind but he was adamant and I was caught between two stubborn men: my husband and my stepson.

My husband was furious.

'I'll teach those young whoresons a lesson,' he thundered. 'Send me Langton, send me my clerks. I'll deal with men who think they can defy me like this.'

Afterwards, with great satisfaction, he told me what he'd done. Writs had been sent out for the arrest of some twenty-two men for imprisonment in the Tower and confiscation of their lands.

'Let them see what it's like to be landless and friendless and shut in one of my dungeons,' he said, his voice rising, getting more and more enraged. 'I am the one who gives the orders, not my son. I am the king. They think because they come from noble stock and fancy themselves as fighting men they can do what they like, but I'll show them how shallow their titles are and who holds power in this realm.'

He sat down and started to chew his fingernails, something I hadn't seen him do in a long while. My heart bled for him. He was gravely ill. He was losing control of his younger men and he knew it. Despite everything I still loved him but any feelings he had for me had long since disappeared, Affection was too shallow an emotion to survive the horrors of the last few months and his illness allowed him no appetite for lust.

He'd not visited my bed since before Eleanor was born and if I was truthful, I was glad. To embrace him with love would be hard when I was revolted by his actions. A divide had opened up between us which I was unable to bridge, however much I tried. Always before, I'd told myself I knew nothing of war and must be guided by one who did, but the savagery which he'd inflicted on Sir Robert's women had been unforgivable. Maybe God could understand and forgive, but I could not.

I thought of my little Eleanor and wondered what I would say to her in the years ahead if she should ever ask about the fate of Sir Robert's women. I looked into our future for comfort, but what I saw was as cold and as bleak as the rain-lashed world beyond the high stone walls of Lanercost Priory.

I received a letter from my stepson asking yet again for my help in his dealings with his father. His friends who had accompanied him overseas were naturally alarmed at the prospect of being landless and in the king's disfavour. They had asked Ned to intercede on their behalf. Ned, naturally, had preferred to approach me.

'They are only young, my lord,' I said, as I sat peaceably at my husband's side with one of his torn shirts in my lap. 'Your captains are so diligent there was little fighting for the younger men and they became bored.'

'A man should never complain of being bored,' growled my husband. 'He should thank God he is still in one piece and not strewn in bits around the battlefield.'

Ii was hard to make him understand how a young man might believe a pretend battle at the tournaments was better than nothing.

'Your son has suggested a tournament at Wark,' I said brightly. 'That would be a wonderful thing. We would see if your new knights could defeat the older, more practised men. You're always saying experience is superior to youth and this would be an opportunity to test your belief. The elderly lord Mortimer of Chirk against his nephew. That would be a sight to see.'

'No,' said my husband. 'There will be no tournament.'

'But my lord, think how ...'

'I said, no,' he shouted. 'Did you not hear me the first time? My son is a fool and he plays me for a fool as well. Do you know what they are saying?'

'No, my lord,' I said meekly, knowing when to be quiet.

'They are saying that my son – *my son*, the heir to the throne - has sworn a pact with that Gascon knave, Piers Gaveston. They are brothers-in-arms, sworn to fight and protect each other. And the fool has vowed to share all his possessions with this nobody. He doesn't just favour him with a few valuable trinkets. Oh no! He chooses to give him half of everything he possesses. Why have I been cursed with such a son? What have I done to deserve this? Have I not been a good father? Have I not given him everything a son could want?'

'You have, my lord,' I murmured.

'See how he repays me. He raises up this cur to think he is my son's equal.'

I didn't know what to say. Ned had behaved outrageously. I knew he was fond of Sir Piers but to make him his brother-in-arms was foolish. Piers Gaveston could never be my stepson's equal, they were far too many poles apart: one born to wear a royal crown, the other born to serve.

'My lord,' I said when he had calmed down a little. 'Perhaps it would be wise to make an example of young Gaveston but to forgive some of the others, the less culpable men. Then you will be seen as not only merciful but also wise and strong.'

He thought for a moment. I had chosen my moment well, as I had learned over the years. His physician's new potion was giving him relief from the pain and I thought it possible he might be brought round to my way of thinking. I knew he regretted his hasty actions and would like to find a way to mitigate the harsh sentences he had imposed on his young knights without appearing to appear weak.

'Yes, yes. You are right, as always. But what shall I do about Gaveston? You realise that if I died tomorrow, my son would share the governance of this realm with him. He's that much of a fool.'

'My lord,' I said, putting my hand on his. 'Please do not speak about dying. We will have you well again by the spring, and you have many more years ahead of you. This is just a winter sickness. And as for your son? We will teach him better ways.'

Christmas was a muted affair. The evergreen boughs were brought into the priory church, my women and I prepared an entertainment for everyone's enjoyment and my husband's minstrels did their best but nobody felt much like dancing or making merry. The only good news we had was word from Humphrey: Elizabeth had been safely delivered of another son and this time, he said, the child would live. A healthy babe, the noisiest anyone could remember and bawling for his milk like the true de Bohun he was. They had called him John.

I smiled as my husband told me the news. If little John lived this would be his twelfth grandchild. How wonderful to be part of such a large family. With Joan's child to be born in the spring and her eldest daughter newly married, I could see an endless ever-growing nursery full of children.

News also reached us of the death of the elderly earl of Norfolk, Roger Bigod, but this was no surprise as he'd been gravely ill for many months. I didn't expect my husband to mourn the death of this old man, but surprisingly, he was sad and dispirited. As he'd said to me at Burstwick, all his comrades who'd fought beside him were dying, and soon there would only be him.

My husband was too ill to go to Carlisle for the parliament. The potion had ceased to be effective and he spent hours doubled up in agony from the disease in his gut. Nothing his physician prescribed seemed to lessen the pain.

Once he realised he couldn't travel he sent for his treasurer. He needed the bishop to open the parliament for him and spent hours instructing poor Walter Langton on what should be said and even more importantly what should *not* be said. He was determined that the Crown's rights must be upheld and that interference whether from His Holiness or his own subjects must be squashed. And he demanded the bishop come regularly to report on his progress.

'It's only ten miles,' he said to me when I dared to suggest that the bishop looked tired. 'In my youth I could ride four times that distance and still fight a man to a standstill at the finish.'

We had few visitors and, with most of the men gone to Carlisle, it was a lonely time. I sat with my husband but he was morose and disinclined to make conversation so I busied myself with my sewing or occasionally in reading. I visited the scriptorium and spent useful hours in the infirmary talking with the herbalist, and in this way passed the time through the worst of the winter, waiting for something to happen or someone to come.

I watched the horsemen ride up the muddy track towards the priory. There were eight of them and before they reached the outer walls I could see the familiar figure of my husband's treasurer hunched within his hooded cloak. It had been raining all week and the rivers were running high. Great pools of water had collected everywhere: in the yards, at the foot of the steps, in front of the doors to the church, everywhere. Rain had even seeped in under the shutters and dripped down the walls of my room.

As soon as he was dry, the bishop came to my husband's chamber. I sat near the candle stitching my husband's tunic where a seam had come loose, while the two men huddled together over the fire discussing the various disputes which had arisen at the parliament. It was quite restful in the chamber, with the fire crackling and the low tones of the men's voices. In the distance I could hear the chanting of the brothers in the priory church and occasional noises from my husband's men in the courtyards outside.

His Holiness's cardinal had, it seemed, met with a lot of complaints from our Englishmen who didn't take kindly to what they considered as interference in England's affairs. Apparently, they looked at the cardinal and saw a servant, not of His Holiness, but of my brother, and that didn't incline them to trust him.

Eventually the conversation was finished and the bishop rolled up his parchments, but he made no move to go. The fire had died down to a mass of glowing embers and the shadows in the room had become deeper. My husband leaned back in his chair and closed his eyes. The bishop seemed on the verge of saying something but then stopped. There were another few moments of silence before he spoke again.

'There is another matter, your grace,' he said, speaking slowly as if drawing the words out one by one with bone tweezers. 'A delicate matter.'

'Yes,' said my husband wearily, opening his eyes. 'What is it?'

'It concerns your son, your grace, the prince, Lord Edward.'

'Langton, I know who my son is, you don't have to tell me. What of him? What has he done? Has he been speaking in an insolent manner again, like he did last year? I thought he'd put that behind him.'

'No, your grace,' said the bishop quickly. 'It isn't anything like that.'

He paused again.

'Well?' said my husband impatiently. 'What is it?'

The bishop eased himself forward onto the edge of his chair and fingered his rolls of parchment. He was biting his lips.

'Lord Edward,' he said at last. 'Lord Edward has asked me to put a request to your grace.'

There was another long silence. The bishop didn't continue. My husband shifted in his seat. He didn't care to sit for long periods these days, he preferred to lie down.

'What is this request? And why couldn't my son come in person? Why all the mystery? Does he want me to increase his allowance because if he does, he is going to find that my purse is empty as far as he is concerned. He's been given the lordship of Aquitaine and he already has his Welsh estates. What more does the profligate boy want?'

'No your grace, the Lord Edward is not requesting

an increase in his allowance, although I must say he does seem to spend liberally for one so young. I've heard tales which would make your hair stand on end, your grace. But then, as you often say, young men are not what they were. Not that I'm saying anything against the Lord Edward.'

'Langton,' said my husband. 'Stop dithering and tell me what my son wants.'

The bishop looked as if he wished he was a hundred miles away, anywhere but here in the chamber with my husband. I wondered what Ned had done.

'Your grace,' said the bishop. 'Lord Edward has asked me to ask your grace to arrange for the County of Ponthieu, which as your grace well knows is in Lord Edward's hands, being part of the estate of his late mother, her grace the Lady Eleanor, the queen, God rest her soul.'

'What is he fussing about Ponthieu for?'

The bishop looked deeply uncomfortable.

'The Lord Edward wishes to make a gift of the County of Ponthieu to his friend, Sir Piers Gaveston.'

At that moment a half-charred log crashed onto the embers of the fire sending a shower of sparks up into the air. My husband opened his mouth and then closed it again. He looked as if he couldn't believe what he was hearing.

'Please repeat that, Langton, just in case I misheard what you said.'

'Lord Edward wishes to make a gift of the County of Ponthieu to Sir Piers Gaveston, your grace. He says he wishes to bestow this gift upon Sir Piers as his dearest brother.'

'God's bones! The imbecile! The idiot! The ...'

For probably the first time in his life, my husband was lost for words.

'I'm sure the Lord Edward would have come himself, your grace, but ...'

Even the bishop couldn't think of a sufficiently worthy excuse for Ned sending my husband's treasurer to his father with this outrageous request. Ponthieu was one of England's last remaining lands across the seas. My husband's first wife had inherited the county from her mother and she in turn had passed the lordship to her only surviving son. To give it away to anyone would be unheard of, but to give it to a mere knight, a member of one's household, was so unbelievable I knew my husband was having difficulty in comprehending what Bishop Langton had told him.

Unfortunately we all three knew that this was just the sort of thing that Ned would want to do. I could imagine him in a fit of generosity offering this wonderful gift to his dearest friend. He would toss it to him in the way another man would toss a coin to a beggar. He wanted to raise Sir Piers up in the world and what better way to do it than by bestowing a gift of land upon him. Gold was one thing, but land was far superior.

My husband buried his head in his hands. I knew how unwell he was feeling as his skin had turned a horrible shade of grey. He raised his eyes and said to his treasurer, 'Tell my son I wish to see him. I shall write a note for you to take when you leave.'

'And Ponthieu?' hesitated the bishop.

'God's bones, Langton! Don't try my patience. Bring the prince to me.'

The bishop departed next morning but before he reached the river I saw another visitor riding up the slope. I recognised the livery, it was one of Aymer de Valence's men,

The only word we'd had since the autumn, when the last of Sir Robert's followers had been dispatched to meet their fate, was that someone had collected the Martinmas rents from the tenants in Carrick. Our spies thought this proof that Sir Robert might be on the move again but nobody knew for certain. Ned was of the opinion that he was still in Ireland while Ralph thought it more likely he was in Norway, with his sister. My husband kept his own counsel on the matter, as did I. I hoped this time the news would be good.

I was to be disappointed. The news was unremittingly bad. Sir Robert was at large in the isles off the western coast and his armies were on the march. From my husband's point of view the only bit of cheerful news was the capture of two of Sir Robert's younger brothers. Without thinking twice he condemned them to hang at Carlisle and sent a stern letter to Aymer de Valence, castigating him for his failure to capture the Scottish king. It seemed that whatever de Valence did, however many other men he killed or captured, without Sir Robert on his knees my husband would not be satisfied.

There was no sign of spring either in the world outside or in my husband's heart. He was in a vile humour and I kept out of his way for fear his ill temper would alight on me. I was sorry for his attendants, but most of them had been with him for many years and were well used to his furies. He threw things, cursed and found fault with everyone, even with the kindly prior, who by now must have thought we'd outstayed our welcome.

It was a burden to have my husband's household descend on such a little priory for so long a time. I hoped we'd not plundered their resources to the point where they'd not have sufficient to see them through the winter and reminded myself to ask the bishop when he returned if something was being done to help. I couldn't help but notice how the brothers seemed less pleased to see me and how my husband's men had begun to squabble with the priory's lay servants: small matters like the use of salt, or the spilling of ale.

It was into this brew of bad temper and strained relations that my stepson and my husband's treasurer returned two weeks later. The weather had closed right in and the unremitting rain had turned the countryside to a sea of mud. I head the noise of their arrival and made sure the chamberlain had arranged for wine and food and fires. But no amount of care on my part could avoid the coming crisis.

My husband had dressed himself in his regal finery for the occasion. His attendants trimmed his hair and beard and carried him to his chair, the one with the magnificently carved back he used when passing judgement on unfortunate prisoners. He sat on a velvet cushion to give him some relief and further cushions were piled at his back, but his crimson fur-lined mantle lay in loose folds over them. What Ned and the bishop would see was not a sick and ailing father but the imposing figure of the powerful king of England ready to rule on his son's request.

Ned looked cocky and self-assured as he strode into the chamber. He wore a fine blue quilted tunic with silver embroidery on the front and a scarlet cloak, lined with lambswool and edged with miniver. His fingers were covered in rings and he wore a jewel-studded belt slung low about his hips. He looked magnificent. He was followed by my husband's treasurer, clad in clerkly black, with his arms, as usual, full of parchment rolls. As they crossed the floor, my husband, who would have taken in Ned's gaudy attire in one cursory disapproving glance, did not even give his son time to open his mouth.

'Why did you send this man here with your request?' he said, nodding at the bishop who was attempting to make himself look as small and insignificant as possible. 'Why did you not come yourself?'

I could see Ned's confident manner melt away in the heat of his father's fury but he raised his chin and tried to appear brave.

'I thought your grace might prefer to have time to consider my request before I came in person. I thought ...'

'You thought?' bellowed my husband. 'You thought? You've never had a considered thought in your life. Not one. And who is this person to whom you propose giving your birthright? Is he some worthy noble, some baron who has served our cause for a lifetime? No! He's a man who's not even been a knight for twelve months. A nobody! A useless covetous churl.'

Ned blanched under the force of his father's anger but he was not going to give way. I could see the muscles tighten in his jaw.

'I shall give the County of Ponthieu to my brother, Sir Piers Gaveston.'

'Brother?' shouted my husband. 'That conniving fool isn't your brother.'

'He is,' said Ned defiantly. 'We are sworn in blood to each other, to be brothers until death. And brothers we shall be.'

'You bastard son of a bitch,' shouted my husband. 'You have no idea of what it means to be a man destined to be king. It would be better for all of us if your true brothers had lived.'

Ned's face was drained of colour.

'But they didn't live, did they? And now all you've got is me.'

'I have two other sons.'

Ned blinked in alarm. I don't think it had occurred to him that Thomas or Edmund could be a threat. But he continued to stand his ground.

'Piers is worthy of this gift. He is a true and loyal brother.'

'He's a servant! God's bones! If I was not afraid of breaking up this kingdom you would never enjoy one yard of your inheritance.'

'Ponthieu is mine,' replied my stepson stubbornly. 'It is mine to give away as I please.'

'And what makes you think you have the right to give away your lands? You've not gained an inch of this kingdom. It's all been my doing. I've given my life to winning it and keeping it together while all you've ever done is idle your time away making merry with your so-called friends. Has it never occurred to you to ask why they would want to be your friends? What do you think they see in you? I'll tell you what they see - a fool. A fool who casts away his birthright as if it was a worthless bauble. They are nothing but bootlickers, hanging on to your stirrup irons, hoping to gather up your gleanings. Have you not one ounce of sense?'

'You are wrong.'

'Wrong!' screamed my husband, rising to his feet. 'A king is never wrong, and unlike you, I know what it is to be a king.'

With that he took a step forward and struck Ned hard across the face.

I gasped and made to go forward, but a hand on my arm, stopped me. It was one of my women.

'You whoreson,' said my husband through gritted teeth. 'You foul stinking son of a bitch. As God is my witness, I shall disinherit you before I let one foot of my kingdom fall into your hands.'

Ned held his hand across his mouth which was bleeding from the blow. He unwisely took a step towards his father as if to retaliate but my husband grabbed him before he could raise his fists. It was a most unseemly tussle. My husband had hold of Ned's hair and was shaking him like a disobedient pup. He gave Ned a shove which knocked him to the ground, then proceeded to kick his son until he was exhausted and cast himself back into his chair. Nobody in the chamber went to the aid of either my husband or my stepson. Nobody dared move.

Ned struggled to his feet wiping a hand across his bloodied mouth. He looked at his father with eyes which shone with contempt and then without waiting to be dismissed, bowed stiffly, turned his back on his king and walked out of the chamber.

My husband banished him. At the beginning of March he had decided he was well enough to journey to Carlisle and it was there, in front of everyone that he pronounced the sentence of banishment on Sir Piers Gaveston. I was surprised at the severity of the sentence but of course it was not really Sir Piers he was punishing. The punishment was designed for Ned. Nothing could hurt him more than being separated from his beloved brother "Perrot".

'You shall leave these shores no later than three weeks after the day of the next tournament, and you shall return to your native land of Gascony where you are to remain at my pleasure until such time as you may be recalled by your king. You shall have no contact with the Lord Edward, Prince of Wales, during this time, nor shall you set foot in any other part of our realm.'

It was a sentence borne of sorrow more than anger and could have been so much worse. Sir Piers kept his head bowed during the pronouncement, his face totally inscrutable. I glanced at Ned who was white-faced. His eyes were panic-stricken but his shoulders were steady and he did nothing to make his friend ashamed of him or to let his father see how much he was being destroyed.

The younger men in the hall, particularly those who had absconded with Ned to the tournament in Ponthieu, seemed taken aback at what was happening. But amongst the others, the older men, I sensed a degree of satisfaction. There were many who didn't like Piers Gaveston, who took advantage of his position as Ned's special friend.

Although he could be immensely funny he was also rude, and men didn't appreciate being the butt of his jokes. I wished Ned had chosen someone else to be his closest friend, someone like Roger Mortimer. He was a steady young men of impeccable lineage. But of course, as every woman knows, the heart loves, not where it is directed but where it chooses.

It was late that night when my stepson came. I was almost ready for bed but when my women told me Lord Edward was at the door I rose from my knees, put on my warmest robe and asked for more logs to be thrown on the fire.

He was drunk. Not just slightly tipsy but sullenly, miserably, hopelessly drunk. I should have realised straight away that his visit spelled trouble. He didn't seem to care about the impropriety of his coming to my chamber nor of the disreputable sight he presented to my women.

I was glad my husband had no idea his son was here. Sadly we had little to say to each other these days and as his illness still prevented him from being with me as a husband I didn't think it likely he would choose this night of all nights to come to my bed.

Ned's clothing was all awry, his jacket open, his undershirt pulled out, as if he had been brawling, and he was unsteady on his feet. The first thing he did was pour himself a cup of wine then collapse heavily onto the chair by the fire before I even had time to ask him to sit.

'Have you not had sufficient this evening?' I asked gently, seating myself carefully beside him.

'No. There isn't enough wine in this dammed castle for that,' he said, slurring his words slightly. 'And it would take more than a few miserable cupfuls to get rid of this pain. Drowning is what I'd like to do. Now, wouldn't that be fun, lady mother? To drown in good Bordeaux wine. The very best. Just what a man needs.'

'Ned, you're drunk.'

'I know. But isn't it wonderful to drink and smother sorrow so that nothing hurts anymore? Not one single solitary bloody thing. Would you like some wine, dear lady mother? Something to dull your own pain?'

He lurched sideways carelessly offering me his cup so that wine slopped over the rim, spilling down the front of my nightgown.

'Sorry.' He tried ineffectually to mop the dampness with his sleeve, but I pushed his hand away, most unwilling to have him handling me in that fashion. It had been too long since a man's hand had touched my person and I felt unwelcome sensations stir at his closeness and the feel of his fingers on my breasts.

'Go away, Ned.'

'Sorry. I didn't mean to offend your person.'

He hiccupped loudly, and slumped his head onto his chest. I decided that for my sake as well as his, I must be brisk and businesslike. I must play the stern stepmother not the sympathetic friend.

'Ned, you must stop this. You are upset. There's nothing you can do but accept your father's ruling in the matter of Piers Gaveston.'

He jerked his head up. His face was white and drawn, a slight flush on his upper cheeks, and he looked at me out of a pair of red-rimmed eyes. I thought at first it was the wine, then realised with a shock that he'd been crying.

'Upset? Upset about my brother Perrot? Is that the word to use? No my lady mother, I'm not upset. How could I possibly be upset? I thought you of all people would understand. You see, lady mother, the truth is, I'm dying. That is what it is. Didn't you know? I'm dying. Inch by inch until there's nothing left of me, nothing but an empty shrivelled husk, no use to man or beast. That whoreson father of mine has ripped out my heart.'

I looked at him and was consumed by his pain and his despair.

'But what would you know?' he went on, wiping a grubby hand across his eyes leaving streaks of dirt on his handsome face. 'You've never loved anyone in your life. How could you possibly understand what it means to love someone when you're married to that, that ...'

In his drunkenness, Ned couldn't find a word hurtful enough to describe his father.

'You've never felt like I do so you can't possibly understand.'

He turned his face away, staring bleakly into the flames. 'You see, lady mother.' He spoke slowly now, softly and caressingly, 'He is everything to me. You might think him very ordinary, just another man, but to me he's the brother I never had. He is the sword by my side and the fire which warms my hearth. Oh, you may smile, but there is nothing in this world more precious to me than Perrot. He is everything. He's my entire world, and he's leaving me.'

Tears trickled down his cheeks.

'Everyone leaves me in the end. Everyone. Nobody stays. You don't know what it's like to be always alone.'

His face was a picture of despair.

'Ned.' I moved closer and took his hand in mine. 'It feels like this now but please believe me, it will pass.'

He looked at me in fury and snatched his hand away.

'No it won't. It'll never pass. Pain like this doesn't pass, it pierces you through to the quick. It's like love. Love doesn't pass, does it? It endures for ever. But you don't understand at all. Why should you?'

'Ned, my dear.'

'Why do you keep calling me that?' he said bitterly, pushing me away from him. 'You don't care.'

'I do care for you, dearest Ned,' I said, grasping his hand again and pulling him against me. His hair was soft and smelled of soap. I felt the warmth of his skin through the fabric of my nightgown and longed to comfort him as I would Thomas or Edmund, but remembered just in time that this was a grown man I held in my arms. I might think of him as a son of mine but he was really no kin to me at all. Any physical closeness would be dangerous for us both. However much I wanted to hold him fast - and I did - it would be unwise.

'You don't.' His voice was muffled against my shoulder. 'I thought you'd love me and be my mother, but you didn't love me. You never did. He was always there, taking you away from me, keeping you for himself, taking you to his bed and leaving me alone. I wanted you to love me but you didn't. You'll never know how much I wanted you. It was so much, so very, very much.'

I felt myself shaking as his tears soaked the skin on my neck and he clutched blindly at my arms, his face burrowing deeper into the silk folds of my nightgown.

Gently I pushed him away once more, detaching his arm from round my neck. The situation was fast becoming perilous, turning into something dark and sinister which my mind fought against. I should have known how he'd felt, and in the deepest recesses of my mind I had, but in my pride at the attention he'd always paid me I'd failed to notice him becoming a man.

I was only a little older than him, and he'd wanted me for himself. He resented his father's ownership of me as he resented his father's control over his own life. I recalled the gift of the ruby ring four years ago. At the time I'd thought it merely the generous gift of a kind boy. But I should have realised he was no longer a boy with a boy's needs. He was a man with a man's needs.

'Perrot understands,' he muttered. 'Perrot loves me. He says he loves me and I believe him.'

His voice trailed off into a jumble of unintelligible words. Soon he would be insensible and although it was one thing to entertain him in my chamber, I could always make some excuse. But if he crumpled at my feet, what would I do then?

I rose quickly, signalling to one of my women to summon Ned's man who was waiting outside. Together we hoisted my stepson to his feet. He was still mumbling but by now his words were completely incomprehensible. The man put Ned's arm across his shoulder and his arm round Ned's body.

'Take him back to his apartments,' I said. 'Don't let him wander about in this state. It would be unfortunate if his grace were to see him like this.'

Indeed, it would be more than unfortunate if my husband

saw him in my chamber at this hour with his clothes all pulled about and me in my nightgown, but that was a worry which I would tuck away and refuse to consider. For the moment I had to think what to do about my stepson.

Alice had hinted to me of the depths of Ned's feelings for Piers Gaveston, but I hadn't taken her seriously. I had no idea how deep or how dangerous their attachment might be, but whatever it was, it was wholly inappropriate. A king's son, the heir to the throne, could never be intimate with a low-born knight. It was unthinkable.

Like a nervous filly I shied away from that word "intimate" for it had another more sinister meaning that rang as clear as a bell in my ears. I knew nothing of these things. I'd heard bawdy talk, occasional comments by some of my women who were probably as ignorant as me, but nothing more. And anyway, two men like that? It was a sin against God and the Church, a sin of impurity against nature, a mortal sin. It simply could not be true. Theirs must be a love like that of David and Jonathan, a pure, brotherly love which transcended earthly desires. Then I thought of Ned's red eyes and the desperation in his voice and I wasn't so sure.

The following day my husband had his son and Piers Gaveston brought to him in the castle chapel and there in the presence of God, with their hands laid upon the Host, they swore to obey his order. Sir Piers would leave and the prince would remain.

With this unpleasant duty done, my husband turned his attention to his campaign against the Scots and I was burdened once more with information of Aymer de

Valence's tortuous progress across the hills and through the glens in pursuit of Sir Robert and his men. The news was not good. Our army had attacked Sir Robert's army near a place called Loch Trool and were beaten back. My husband was in despair. But the bad news from the north was nothing compared to the news which came to us from the south, from Kent.

The man rode into the castle on a sunny morning when I was feeling happier than I had for many a day. Ned had gone with Piers Gaveston to see him safely off on his voyage into exile. Of course his father didn't want him to go, but I persuaded him it was for the best and would make Ned more compliant if he was allowed this time to be alone with his friend.

My husband was feeling unwell and had retired so the messenger was sent to Bishop Langton who sent him to me. I had no warning. Nothing prepared me for the shock. When I saw the Gloucester livery I assumed this was news of Joan's birthing and took the letter eagerly. Then I noticed the black tunic and my mouth went dry.

'Who is it?' I asked, my voice full of fear.

'My Lady Joan,' he replied. 'The countess. These nine days past. Her and the child she was carrying.'

I undid the seal. It was from Eleanor who'd been with her mother at the end, when they knew she was dying. She wrote that Joan had suffered much but was now at peace. She asked the king, in his infinite kindness, to inform her brother who was in the Lady Marguerite's keeping, and her stepfather whose whereabouts were unknown to her.

My husband was surprisingly sanguine about Joan's death.

'She was a difficult child and she grew into a difficult woman. Eleanor and I often wondered what we'd done to deserve such a daughter. We gave her everything but she was never satisfied.'

He lay staring into the darkness beyond the candlelight, thinking of his daughter.

'I was angry with her about de Monthermer. It was her idea of course. De Monthermer's a good captain but she'd have been better off marrying Count Amadeus and we'd have benefitted from the alliance. I could have killed the pair of them, I can tell you. There she was, standing in front of me, bold as brass, telling me she'd married this squire in her husband's household, this *base-born* squire, and no, she couldn't possibly marry the count of Savoy.'

'I know,' I said gently. 'I know.'

'Poor girl,' he said. 'Poor little Joan. They're all gone: my Eleanor, Alphonso, John, young Henry, Nell and all those little girls, and now Joan.'

He was becoming very melancholy so I drew up my chair beside him and talked to him of his grandchildren. This always gave him pleasure for they were mostly far away which meant they didn't try his patience. He liked the idea of his granddaughters growing up, a cluster of pretty girls with red-gold hair and childish laughs, all being made ready to take their places as wives of his favoured men. And his grandsons: tall and strong like young Gilbert de Clare, all there to follow in his footsteps.

After he'd fallen asleep I tiptoed away and went down to our private chapel feeling the need to pray and be alone.

The candles on the altar burned steadily, filling the tiny space with a golden glow. The walls gleamed red, green and gold in the candlelight and the ceiling above shone with a multitude of silver stars. The chapel had been made beautiful by my husband, and I loved it dearly.

I knelt in front of the statue of Our Lady, thinking of Joan and of her kindness to me all those years ago when I first came to England as a frightened young bride. I vowed I would be especially loving to Isabella when she came - if she came. The hours passed and when I'd exhausted my prayers and my thoughts I rose and walked slowly back to my chamber thinking how, with Joan's death, nothing would be the same again.

16

SUMMER 1307

I prayed daily for my husband, spending hours on my knees until the skin was rubbed raw and my bones ached. I offered my suffering as a small sacrifice to God for the easing of my husband's pain, but Our Lord was deaf to my pleas and my husband's agony continued. The end was near and however much I wanted him to live I knew there could not be many more weeks left. Everyone knew it, even the Scots. Rumours were spreading through the towns and villages that the English king was already dead, and people said openly that God had destroyed his power and victory would go to King Robert. They said the prince was not the man his father was. Even our own men were beginning to lose heart.

After two defeats for Aymer de Valence's men in late spring, my husband had given orders for more men to join a muster at Carlisle in the middle of July. He was determined our armies should press on and was convinced Sir Robert would be caught.

He sent word to Ned to return immediately but my stepson failed to arrive. I didn't know where he was or what he was doing. Piers Gaveston had left Dover in early May laden with costly gifts from Ned, that much we knew. But it was now the middle of June and there was still no sign of the prince.

I was summoned to my husband's chamber. He was

surrounded by physicians and attendants and looked extremely ill. His face was grey and shrunken, the papery skin stretched tight over the bones in his cheeks. His eyes were closed but when he opened them I could detect fire somewhere in the depths. He would fight this to the bitter end and death would not defeat him as long as he had one single breath left in his body.

'My son has not come,' he said to me as I made myself comfortable beside him. 'But my army must leave and it is not fitting it should do so without its leader.'

'My lord,' I said. 'You cannot mean to go yourself. You are far too sick. You must rest.'

He held up his hand.

'I hear they say I am dead so I must show them I am not. Otherwise what hope will our men have?'

'My lord, such a journey will be impossible and your litter would ...'

'A king cannot lead his men to war in a litter. Think how that would look.'

'By the love of the Virgin, you cannot mean ...?'

My hands flew up to my mouth in horror at what he meant to do.

He looked at me with infinite sadness in his eyes. 'I shall ride in front of my men as I have always done. I shall don my armour and ride out like a king because what else is there for me? It is who I am.'

I could think of nothing to say. I knew him too well to argue. He might listen to me about his children or about some merciful gesture he was prepared to make but on this, his mind was made up, and nothing I said or did would make any difference.

*

Next evening as the sun was going down, when all the candles were lit and I was preparing for bed, there came a knock at my door. It was my husband's youngest attendant, a lad of about ten. He stood there, clutching his hands, shifting awkwardly from foot to foot, trying not to look at the women beyond the threshold.

'Your grace,' he began nervously. 'His grace, the king, has requested your presence in his chamber.'

'Is he worse?'

'No, your grace. He simply wishes for your presence.'

I thought of my delicate satin slippers and the silk nightgown, hastily covered with a woollen mantle. Not the clothes for wandering around at night with one of my husband's servants, but if my husband needed me then I would go. I wrapped my mantle closely round my shoulders and followed the boy down the stairs and through dimly lit rooms and across the hall. Outside my husband's chamber were two armed guards leaning wearily against the walls but they jumped to attention when they saw us coming. The boy opened the door and stood back while I entered the room. My husband was lying in the depths of his great bed. I thought he was asleep so tiptoed softly not wishing to disturb him but as I drew nearer he opened his eyes and smiled.

'Thank you for coming,' he said quietly, his voice rasping in his throat. 'I trust you had not retired to your bed for the night.'

He was finding it difficult to speak and I had to lean close to hear what he was saying.

'No, my lord. I had yet to say my prayers. But you know

I would come. You are my lord and I am ever obedient to your wishes.'

There was a small matter of constraint between us. In the past year we'd not been close and had shared no intimate conversation. I hardly knew what to say to him now that we were alone and it was difficult to see in this old sick man, the husband who'd been my companion in the past. His hand clutched his chest and he appeared to be in some distress.

'Shall I call one of your servants, my lord? Or your physician?'

'No.'

For a moment he said nothing more, then, with a small movement of his hand he lifted up the heavy coverlet.

'Will you share my bed one more time, wife?' he asked, looking at me with his tired old eyes.

All of a sudden I began to weep. I didn't even know the tears were lurking there, waiting to be shed, but at his words and the look on his face I remembered all the nights we'd spent together, all the good times, the happy times, and I was stricken with the knowledge that it was gone. The past year had been an agony for us both but if I could put it behind me I would be able to remember what had gone before.

'I cannot offer you much,' he began.

'But you have given me everything already,' I said. 'What is there to left to offer?'

Tears were blinding my eyes and running down my cheeks. I slipped off my mantle and my slippers and climbed carefully onto the bed beside him. He was dreadfully wasted. I hadn't realised quite how much flesh he'd lost until I laid my body against his. It seemed as if there was nothing but bones beneath his nightgown.

'As long as you are not expecting a night like those we enjoyed at Leeds,' he whispered.

I gave a great sob and tried to hide my face from him.

'I'm sorry there'll be no more babies, my little pearl,' he said quietly. 'We have our two boys and our queen of the may, but I know you wanted more.'

'What is there if I don't have you,' I sobbed. 'Without you there is nothing. I'm sorry, I didn't mean to weep. I meant to be brave and strong.'

'You will be. I know you will. In the years ahead you'll find strength. Speak to our children of me.'

We lay for several minutes holding each other, saying nothing. Then he turned his head on the pillow.

'Little pearl.'

'Yes, my lord.'

'Pray for me.'

'I shall pray for you every day for the rest of my life, until my dying day, for you have been my whole life.'

'And care for my son.'

I knew who he meant. I'd no need to ask for there was only one of his sons who needed my care just now.

He slept a little, but when he woke he was in a great deal of pain.

'You'd best call my physician, wife,' he gasped, gritting his teeth against the agony in his belly.

I slipped from the bed and ran to the door. Within minutes the chamber was full of men carrying armfuls of towels and I was no longer wanted.

I closed the door behind me and went upstairs to our

little chapel. I knelt in front of the statue of Our Lady and tried to find the words but nothing came. My mind like my heart was empty.

Soon after dawn I stood on the castle steps as I had many times before - a lady saying farewell to her lord as he set off for war. It was a warm morning, yet I was shivering and felt chilled. I'd dressed myself in my finest gown so that his last sight of me would be joyful. As I pulled my cloak tightly around my shoulders, my thoughts slid unbidden to the hundreds of times I'd clothed myself for his delight in my favourite green brocade gown which he admired or the scarlet and gold surcote worn over the blue silk. All these garments I'd worn to please him. I had little interest in fashionable clothes, unlike most women, yet my husband had a keen appreciation of the cut of a gown.

His men assisted him to his great black warhorse and with agonising slowness he half-climbed and was half-hoisted into the saddle. He straightened his back. He wasn't going to let his men see him slumped like a sack of corn. In his armour, the scarlet overtunic emblazoned with the golden leopards of England, he looked as magnificent as he had always done. Beneath his helmet, his hair was white, his face gaunt, yet he was still a warrior king and I knew there would never again be one like him.

Lord de Lacy was there as was Guy de Beauchamp, two of his greatest friends now that the earl of Surrey was gone. Aymer de Valence and the earl of Lancaster were close by and to the rear I saw Humphrey on his bay stallion. Slowly the group of horsemen turned and began to file across the courtyard and out under the gatehouse and down the hill towards the road to the north-west.

As I watched the huge army fall in behind the line of men and horses, I wanted to cry out for him to come back, but of course I did no such thing. I'd been raised to be the wife of a great man and I knew how to behave. I watched his figure gradually disappear in a cloud of dust behind the shoulder of the hill until he was no more. Then, and only then, I walked back up the steps, went straight to my chamber, and once I was alone with my women, I lay on my bed and wept.

I couldn't sleep and became hollow-eyed with exhaustion but one night when he'd been gone a week, I heard the sonorous ringing of the bell for Matins and then fell into a dreamless slumber. I was woken by full daylight and the sound of a herald's horn. Moments later six horsemen came riding fast under the gatehouse and clattered into the courtyard. I was out of bed and making myself ready, frightened to stay where I was, yet afraid to go and see who had come. I'd barely covered my hair when a knock came at the door. It was Lord de Lacy.

He signalled for my women to leave us and waited until they'd gone before he turned his attention to me. He began to speak but he had no need for I already knew why he'd come.

'I bring sad news, my lady,' he said from somewhere a huge distance away, his words echoing in my ears. 'Yesterday afternoon, his grace, the king was commanded by God.'

He held out a sealed letter.

'This is for you,' he said gently. 'It is necessary you have an official document.'

I took the letter, feeling the parchment stiff and smooth beneath my fingers, seeing the red seal dance in front of my eyes. Once I opened the letter there would be no more hope and what I already knew to be true, would be real. I must have looked bewildered because he came, removed the letter and placed it on the table. Then he took my hands, something he'd never done before.

'Sit down, my lady. You look as if you might fall. Come, sit here and I'll fetch you some wine. It's good for shock, they say.'

'Thank you, Lord de Lacy,' I said steadily. 'But I shan't faint; you need have no fear.'

Nonetheless he poured me a cup of wine and insisted I drank it. I wanted to comfort him so I did as he asked. I had no idea what to say or what to do as the whole of my world had been destroyed in that one single moment. What was I supposed to say? What was I meant to do? A thousand words and thoughts chased themselves round in my head.

'The prince,' I said at last. 'He must be told.'

'You must not worry over these matters, my lady. The royal messenger is already on his way to London. We believe the prince is there.'

'How long will he take?'

'Four days if nothing goes amiss, and the prince should return straight away, God willing.'

'Lord de Lacy.'

'Yes, my lady.'

'My husband. Please, Lord de Lacy. Tell me. Where did

358

he die? So that I know. I would very much like to know.'

'Of course, my lady. We were not gone far, only to the shores of the firth, to a little place called Burgh-by-Sands, on the flat land near the Solwaeth. Yesterday was a fine clear day and his grace could see the land of the Scots on the other side of the water. It wasn't any distance but we made camp. Then his men went to give him some food. They raised him up and he died in their arms. It was over in an instant. May God have mercy on his soul.'

Poor Lord de Lacy. He was overwhelmed by sudden unexpected tears, unbidden and shameful, and yet I could understand. He was exhausted and bereft. He'd seen his friend, the king, die in front of him, and then ridden hard to Carlisle to pass on the awful news. And he wasn't a young man. In my grief I felt some consolation that my husband had known the comfort of men's arms about him in his last moments, that his friends had been with him, that he had not died alone. It had been a good death.

'Lord de Lacy,' I said. 'Is there anything I should do or anyone I should inform? Are there duties I should undertake? I am afraid I'm very ignorant of these matters. I've never before lost a husband.'

'No-one will be told other than those who need to know,' he said quietly. 'We've given orders that the death of his grace is kept secret until the prince arrives and is made king. It would be dangerous if the Scots heard that the king is dead and the kingdom unguarded.'

'Are there many who know?'

'No, only those of us who were there. The bishop of Lichfield, has been summoned from Wentworth but I've given him no reason. However, he's not a stupid man and will be certain to guess. His grace, God rest his soul, made Langton the executor of his will, so we need his presence because nothing can be done without him. There are only three letters telling of his grace's death: one for the prince, one for you, my lady, and one which I have with me as surety for my actions.'

'So we must wait.'

'Yes. Until the prince arrives.'

'Lord de Lacy?'

'Yes, my dear lady.'

'The embalming?'

'It is all taken care of. His grace left clear instructions. Don't forget, he himself went through this when his queen died not twenty years ago.'

He stopped in a sudden awareness as to what he should not be saying to me. I was only the second wife, barely a queen at all.

'You mustn't worry about these matters, my lady,' he said more gently.

'Thank you,' I said in a small voice, feeling more and more as if I was disappearing. There was nothing for me to do and soon I would be invisible. I would no longer be the wife of my husband, no longer the first lady in the land, no longer anyone of importance at all.

Nobody needed me now that my husband was gone and I was beginning to wonder if he had ever needed me either. He had given his instructions to others and left nothing for me to do. His men would manage everything and his officials would make the funeral arrangements. It would doubtless be one of those grand ceremonial affairs with much pomp and glitter, and I wondered if there'd be any part for me to play or if I'd be placed at the back away from the eyes of all my husband's people. For what had I ever been but the sister of a foreign king bought as the price of peace. I'd never been of much importance and the peace which I was supposed to bring to our marriage had been too fragile a thing to withstand the brutal assaults on it by my brother's mischief-making with the Scots.

Later, I knelt in our private chapel and tried to pray but the words wouldn't come no matter how hard I tried. My head was full of images of him: of his eyes and his hands, of him playing with our boys, tossing them up in the air until they screamed with laughter. The little things: the shared meals, the games we'd played through the long winter evenings, his joy when we went hawking, and the nights when I'd watched him sleeping. The times we'd knelt side by side in candlelit churches, praying for the souls of his father and his mother and for the soul of his beloved first wife.

Yesterday had been the feast of the translation of St Thomas, a celebration of the day when the bones of the blessed martyr were carried from his tomb to his shrine at Canterbury. How pleased my husband would have been, to depart this life on such an auspicious day.

I lost count of the days until Ned came. I think it was ten but it might have been more. Although no announcement had been made and no-one had been told of my husband's death, everybody knew. It had not taken more than a quarter of a day for the news to sweep through the castle and by evening everyone from the steward to the spit boy was aware that the world had changed. It was as if a spell had been cast over us as we waited anxiously for my stepson to arrive.

Nothing could be done, no plans could be made and nobody knew where they would stand with this new king. Would their position be safe or would they be cast out? Many had not been on good terms with Ned and I sensed their nervousness as the days passed.

Then one morning, out of the pall of gloom which covered the castle there came a ray of light. Servants began making preparations. Rooms were swept, cartloads of supplies were brought in and a smell of roasting meats rose from the bowels of the castle. I could feel the anticipation, the fear, the joy, the excitement. I heard trumpets, and the next moment Ned and his retinue swept into the courtyard. All my husband's men rushed out to welcome the prince who was now the favoured one, the one who would be God's anointed.

He didn't send for me. I sat and waited but no word came. In the past he would come to my rooms, laughing and playful, greeting me with kisses and embraces, but now he was king I would have to wait upon his pleasure.

Some hours after his arrival I saw another messenger, one I didn't recognise, gallop under the gatehouse. By then the courtyards were full of people unknown to me so I didn't realise the importance of this man to Ned.

'He's returned from over the seas,' enthused my youngest maid, imparting the latest gossip she'd heard from the kitchens. 'Says his master is Sir Piers, that Gascon knight who left a while back. He's very handsome, my lady, and they say he's not yet married.'

Next morning I was summoned to attend my stepson in his privy chamber. My feet were heavy as I walked down the familiar steps heading to the apartments where my husband had carried out his royal business. The white veil I wore protected me from the interest of my stepson's men and the curious stares of his servants.

Ned was sitting in my husband's great carved chair looking extremely pleased with himself. There were no signs of sadness but considering how they'd parted this was not surprising. I couldn't expect him to grieve for his father when they'd been on such bad terms.

He was picking at a bowl of sugared almonds, popping the pretty-coloured sweetmeats into his mouth one by one. He didn't rise but sat watching me as I walked across the floor.

'My lady,' he said, pursing his lips. 'The dowager queen. Except you weren't truly a queen, were you? You never had a coronation. But my father was not a man to be careful of your honour. He was far more interested in slaughtering the Scots. However you can be assured that any wife of mine will have a magnificent coronation, for how else can she possibly be a queen.'

I couldn't believe what I was hearing. There were no words of consolation, no acknowledgement of my overwhelming grief, just this spiteful tirade against his father.

'Ned.'

'I think it better you call me, your grace.'

'Of course, your grace.'

He smiled at me happily.

'What shall I call you? I can hardly continue calling

you lady mother, not now I'm your king. How about my lady dowager?' he suggested. 'No, that doesn't sound right either.'

He sat thinking, staring at me with his blue eyes which had become darker in the months since I'd last seen him. The flecks of gold which used to lighten his gaze had vanished and in their place were depths of hidden anger, of ice and fire. The warmth of the boy prince had gone for ever and I was unsure what to make of this flint-eyed stranger in front of me.

In many ways he was the same young man who'd left in the spring, fired with fury at his father's intemperate exiling of his friend. But I sensed a hardness in him, as if he'd been tested and forged stronger in the flames of some inward struggle. I was glad for I'd always feared he was too soft and too easily hurt. This new Ned was a different person - more determined, less kind and clearly not going to allow himself to be any man's cat's-paw.

'It's awkward being a widow, isn't it?' he mused, selecting another sweetmeat from the dish. 'Mary said our grandmother found it particularly difficult. She wanted to control our father and interfere in his dealings with the French. You can imagine how angry that made him so he and our mother contrived to send her to Amesbury where she took the veil. I suppose you'll do the same. It's what widows do, isn't it? And no king likes to have his mother, or worse, his stepmother, looking over his shoulder, trying to interfere at every step. It would make for very bad feelings and neither of us wants that, do we?'

'Of course we don't,' I said. 'I would never dream of interfering in your life, your grace. You are the king and you and your council must rule as you see fit. I never interfered in your father's dealings and it wouldn't occur to me to interfere in yours. I hope to retire to my dower lands to be close to my children. Your father, God rest his soul, asked that ...'

'My father is dead and I make the decisions now,' he snapped.

'Of course you do, and I will go wherever you wish, your grace,' I said, bending my head so that he couldn't see the hurt in my eyes.

'Now let's talk of pleasanter things. Piers will be here soon. Is that not the best of news?'

It came as no surprise that he'd sent for his friend. I doubted he'd hesitated for a moment once he'd received news of his father's death. I could imagine the joy he must have felt but wondered what was in Piers Gaveston's mind as he took ship back to England. Pleasure at having his exile cut short, naturally, but had there also been a thrill of anticipation at the rewards which were now certain to come his way?

I realised, as my husband had, that Gaveston was master in the relationship between these two young men. Ned relied on him overmuch. It might not have mattered if he'd been other than he was but a king needs to be forceful and Ned, we had both known, was too easily persuaded. Again, it might not have mattered if Piers Gaveston had Ned's welfare in mind, but I'd seen both here and at my brother's court how easily men are seduced by the lure of wealth and power and I doubted if Piers Gaveston would be any different.

It was a long miserable journey we made that August back through the dusty lanes of England. The funeral cortege was led by Bishop Langton and followed by my husband's friends and hundreds of men from his household.

Ned accompanied us for the first few miles, but before the end of the second day he turned round and headed back to Carlisle. The new king needed to attend to his father's army which was still encamped ready to set out across the border. I bade him a tearful farewell, tentatively reminding him of my husband's words at Westminster the previous year and how Ned had vowed to complete his father's vision of a single land, united under an English king.

By the time our sad procession arrived at Waltham, the trees were shedding their leaves in sorrow, spreading them like a carpet of tears upon the ground. My husband's embalmed body lay within the abbey, high on his bier, dressed in his red and gold robes of state with a gilded crown upon his head and a sceptre in his hand. He was surrounded by a hundred candles which would burn throughout the long days and nights until it was time to bring him home to the Island of Thorns and seal him forever within his tomb.

17

At some time during those endless weeks of mourning Ned returned to Westminster. They told me he had made the decision to abandon his father's campaign against the Scots and ride south to make preparations for the funeral. But even before he and his retinue reached the Island of Thorns, the first marks of my stepson's rule were being felt.

Walter Langton, the bishop of Lichfield, my husband's friend, his treasurer and executor of his will, was arrested and thrown into prison, accused of diverting the king's treasure to his own household, of extortion and securing wrongful judgements, of selling off royal woods and lands. The list of wrongdoings raised against him was lengthy. This was no surprise. My stepson had never forgiven the bishop for that occasion on the road to Chichester when they'd quarrelled.

This, I realised with a sense of foreboding, was the start of Ned's sweeping from power of all my husband's friends and advisors. Anybody whom Ned did not like would be dismissed, regardless of their usefulness. No wonder the men at Carlisle had been frightened and were now hastening to ingratiate themselves with my stepson.

Even more shocking than this brutal clearing out of his father's stable was Ned's resurrection of the ancient earldom of Cornwall which had belonged to my husband's cousin. Ned gave it to Sir Piers Gaveston. I was at the archbishop's house with my stepson when he told me.

'Earl of Cornwall?'

'Yes,' said Ned. 'Had you not heard? I thought everyone knew. It was the first thing I did as soon as Piers arrived at Dumfries. With the disgrace he'd had to endure on my behalf he deserved a reward, don't you think? And of course I was so very pleased to see him.'

I thought of the day my husband and I had talked of the earldom of Cornwall for Edmund and how nothing had been done until it was too late.

'Were the council in agreement?' I asked, amazed at the sheer stupidity of my stepson.

'They grumbled. What else would you expect? They didn't like having their noses tweaked but it was only the old nitpickers like Warwick and de Lacy who complained. My friends were perfectly content with my decision, and even Cousin Thomas raised no objection. I thought he'd rant and rave but he didn't. He gets along well enough with Piers which is odd because Piers is incredibly rude about him in private.'

'So they all signed?'

'All except Guy de Beauchamp. He stormed out, shouting I had no right to lift someone out of the gutter and make him equal to men of great standing like himself. I told him that Piers had never been in the gutter since his father was a man of some importance in Gascony.'

I wondered if these men who could trace their lineage back through their fathers and grandfathers to the time of the Lionheart or perhaps as far as the Conqueror, were really as content at Piers Gaveston's elevation as Ned believed.

Of course the whole thing was totally improper but Ned seemed to revel in it all the more because of that. I was not surprised the earl of Warwick had refused to sign and rather wished the others had refused as well. I was horrified at what Ned had done but I'd promised my husband to care for his son and that is what I would try to do.

The attendance at Mass next morning was sparse and I was surprised not to see Ned. As I walked back through the hall I noticed a small boy fast asleep in the hearth. The steward gave him a none-too-gentle kick to stir him awake and I was struck by a memory of men who sleep in the heather. I wondered where Sir Robert was now and how he did. I had forgotten him these past months, and was sure he never gave me so much as a passing thought for who was I to him? I had done private penance for my thoughts of that autumn but still wondered how it was possible to love a man as I had loved my husband and yet feel attraction to another.

That evening I asked what arrangements Ned thought proper for his father's tomb.

'He has requested a black chest. What do you think of that?' said my stepson. 'No adornment, no effigy, no gilding, nothing. It's totally unfitting for the father of the king of England and Piers and I considered over-ruling his wishes but the archbishop warned me against such a move. He said it was sinful to go against the last wishes of the dead.'

'It could be impressive,' said the earl of Cornwall, currently languishing against the wall by the hearth, examining the many jewelled rings on his fingers. 'It would be like the tombs of Arthur and Guinevere at Glastonbury. Not my sort of thing, I prefer glittering splendour. But then, people are different, are they not, *mon ami*?'

He flashed a smile at my stepson, who grinned happily back.

On an overcast morning in the middle of October, with birds flying low above the shoreline and a thin mist rising from the river, my husband's black marble coffin on its black-covered hearse was brought to the Island of Thorns.

They carried him in procession, resting first at the churches within the city and then finally along the rutted track past the archbishop's house to the great abbey church at Westminster. It was here on the Friday after the feast day of St Luke that we buried him beside his father's magnificent glittering tomb, near the canopied wonder of that of his brother, Edmund, and close to the body of his beloved Eleanor. His old friend Anthony Bek, the bishop of Durham, who had lent us his palace the previous summer, led the funeral service, and it was some comfort to know that my husband was being laid to rest by a man who had known and loved him.

Everyone came. From far and near, from over the seas, from places I'd never even heard of. They came to bid farewell to my warrior king. Some had been his enemies, others his friends, some had barely known him only his reputation. But they came to honour him. My brother Louis travelled from Paris and my husband's daughter Margaret crossed the sea from Brabant to say farewell to her father.

Elizabeth and Mary stood either side of me, all three of us heavily veiled. Elizabeth's hand sought mine as we heard the eulogies in praise of my husband. I listened and wondered how little any of us had really known him. They described him time and again as a valiant fighter, fearless and warlike, a man with no equal, a knight in armour, an outstanding warrior from his earliest years, in tournaments most mighty, in war most pugnacious. All this I knew. But they also called him illustrious, and strenuous in all things, and how among Christian princes there had been none to match his courage and his sagacity. They compared him to Arthur and Alexander, to Brutus and the Lionheart, and even to Solomon.

One eulogist asserted, 'We should perceive him to surpass all the kings of the earth who came before him. Entirely without equal.'

They spoke of his piety, as the most Christian king of England. One cleric was moved to declare, 'O Jerusalem thou hast lost the flower of thy chivalry.'

And they talked of his willingness to dispense justice to all lest he lose the favour of God and man, and of his prudence in the governance of his realm where he took counsel from both good and wise men.

The more they spoke the less I recognised this man they were praising. Where was the joyful friend, the tender lover? Where was the angry father and the vengeful king? They were painting a picture which held no shades of light and dark, only the bold, glowing illuminations of a history which would be repeated down the years; a lament for a king as his peers saw him: bold, courageous and warlike.

I knew, more than most, that there had been another

side: the gentle, delightful man who enjoyed music and reading and games of love; the husband who liked practical jokes and teasing conversations, whose skill at chess was second to none and who after a day out with his falcons, liked nothing better than to sit with me by the fire and tell me of his day. This was the man I remembered.

Later, Louis took my hands in his.

'Dearest little sister,' he said kindly. 'What will you do now you are no longer a wife? You are still young. Will you remarry? Has your king got plans for you?'

My heart lurched. I had never for one moment considered remarrying. How could any man take the place of my husband? It was unthinkable.

'It is too soon,' I said quickly. 'It is not something I wish to consider.'

'It may not be your choice,' said Louis, 'Your king may need your help just as Philip did. But our brother says you may prefer to take the veil. You've done your duty and given your husband sons and Philip, at least, is content to let you please yourself.'

Next morning I was summoned to the king's presence. He eyed me as I came towards him and made my reverence. I remembered to lower myself and use the correct form of words but it felt wrong. This was Ned and I had loved him as a son.

'Now all this pageantry is over, I have no further need of you, my lady. You may retire to your castle at Marlborough and do whatever it is you wish to do there.'

He was being deliberately distant and unfriendly.

372

'My boys, your grace? Edmund and Thomas?'

'My brothers shall remain with me.'

He must have seen my stricken face and the tears in my eyes.

'They are old enough or did you plan to keep them hidden behind your skirts for ever?'

'No, your grace. But may I keep my daughter?'

'My sister will remain at Amesbury. She is in my care now and I will say where she is to stay. Do I make myself clear?'

I lowered my head. 'Yes, your grace.'

'And when I marry my wife will need women to serve her so my nieces will leave your household.'

Two of Joan's de Clare daughters were in my care but now it seemed I was to lose them too.

'You will live quietly so you won't have need of them. I plan to give Margaret to Piers as a wife.'

I gasped. I couldn't help myself. This was totally inappropriate. Margaret de Clare was my husband's granddaughter and Piers Gaveston was nothing but a parvenu, a common upstart Gascon.

Ned smiled. 'I've also given him the castle at Berkhamsted.'

I shivered. Berkhamsted was mine and had been mine since the day I first married. Why had he taken it away from me?

'You must understand, my lady, that Berkhamsted has always been part of the earldom of Cornwall, and while my father may have felt he had the right to remove it from his dead cousin's estates and give it to you, my lawyers inform me that he was wrong. I sent them to pore over their dusty tomes and eventually they agreed with me that the manor of Berkhamsted does indeed belong to the earl of Cornwall. So there we are. I know you won't begrudge it to Piers because you have so much and he, poor boy, has so very little.'

So this was the way things would be from now on. I could see no happy resolution in the years ahead. Ned was utterly determined to plough his own furrow without regard to anyone else other than his beloved Perrot. I couldn't see Philip's daughter managing to navigate a course through the dangerous waters of my stepson's obsessive love for this man and I didn't know how long the goodwill of my husband's friends would last. But whatever lay in the years ahead would be nothing to do with me, Ned had made that abundantly clear.

I lowered myself once more and murmured a farewell. I kissed his hand and made to leave but he stopped me. He walked over to where I stood near the door and lifted my fingers to his lips.

'I could have loved you,' he said. 'If they hadn't given you to him you could have been mine and I would have been a good husband. You have no idea how much I wanted you in those early days when you had eyes for no-one other than him. But *he* didn't want you. He wanted your sister. He needed a truce and His Holiness was pushing hard. He thought he'd get the beautiful Blanche but he had to make do with you.'

I felt cold. My husband hadn't wanted me, he had wanted my sister and despite his protestations this was something I'd always known.

'It's not very pleasant to feel second-best, is it?' said Ned, looking at me with a little mocking smile. 'But I understand. I know what it's like. All my life I was the son my father had to make do with, the son who lived when all the others died. I wasn't good enough for him so he put me to one side and ignored me, I who could do so much but whom nobody loved.'

As I hurried away I noticed Lord de Lacy standing quietly in the shadows, waiting for an audience. He put out his hand and touched my shoulder.

'He loved you, my lady,' he whispered. 'It was in his nature to love women but he prized you above all. Don't listen to the king, he only wishes to wound you.'

I would go home. I would turn my back on the glittering splendour of the royal court and slip back into the shadows. I would not remarry. There would be no second husband. I had known this on the day we laid him to rest on the Island of Thorns, and I knew it now. I had always known. Loving my husband as I did, I could never take another. It was a simple truth - when my husband died, all men died for me.

EPILOGUE

It is a cool March morning in the year of Our Lord 1318, the eleventh year of the reign of the English King Edward, the second of that name. In the shadowy depths of the church of St Mary at Southwark, built on the south bank of the river just across from the city of London, a tall man of about thirty years or more is weeping. Dressed in an immaculate tunic of black cloth-of-gold, he stands alone. His friends know better than to disturb him at a time like this and his wife he has left in her chamber retching uncontrollably into a silver basin.

Through his tears he can see the thin, wasted body resting on its velvet bier in front of the high altar, surrounded by the glow of a hundred beeswax candles. He wanted her dressed in purple and gold, proclaiming his right to acknowledge her as his mother although it was well known she was only his father's second wife, but she herself requested the simple habit of a Franciscan nun: rough, grey and poor. Despite this unattractive garment there is something magnificent about her - a purity, an aura of sanctity, of love.

'Why did you leave me?' he whispers. 'I pretended I didn't need you, I didn't care, but it wasn't true. The others mean nothing to me. They are there to stem the loneliness, to fill my life with noise and gaiety, to stop myself from going mad. But that's all they are, just friends, nothing more. I don't love them. Not the way I loved you. There was only ever you and Perrot.'

Tears fill his eyes until all he can see is a blur of shadows and flickering light. The kneeling women, the paid widows who surround the body, see no-one and hear nothing. A low rhythmic chanting fills the church, rising and falling in perpetual waves, as the brothers pray for the soul of the dead woman.

Tomorrow they will carry her in procession across the bridge to the church of the Greyfriars at Newgate, the one she endowed with her own money. She requested that she be buried there and he will ensure her wishes are carried out. It is the least he can do for someone who, despite everything, was beloved of them all. Thomas and Edmund will attend. His brothers are sad as one would expect, but young men of that age are careless of the old and don't fear death, not like he does.

His father never feared death but he won't think about his father today. He has spent too much time trying to forget the old man to think of him now. And yet she told him he must forgive his father.

'He loved you and only ever wanted the best for you,' she said.

That was the last occasion he saw her, at their Christmas celebrations. She claimed she wanted to visit Isabella and the children and of course Thomas and Edmund, the boys she gave up to him so long ago. She looked pale and ill, but he wasn't expecting her to die. Not so soon.

'You are very dear to me,' she said that last evening as they sat together by the fire. 'You always have been. I may have misjudged you in the past but when I'm gone I pray you won't forget me.'

Of course he won't forget. If you love someone, you never forget.

WHAT HAPPENED AFTER EDWARD I'S DEATH?

In January 1308 Marguerite attended the marriage of Ned to Isabella of France in Boulogne where, in secret, she offered help to those who wished to remove Piers Gaveston from her stepson's side. Afterwards she retired to her castle at Marlborough and devoted the rest of her life to helping others.

Marguerite and Edward's daughter, Eleanor, died in the priory at Amesbury in 1311. She was five years old. Marguerite died in February 1318.

The relationship between Ned and Piers Gaveston ended in tragedy. In the summer of 1312, after two unsuccessful attempts to get rid of Gaveston, the earls of Lancaster, Warwick and Hereford arranged to have him abducted and killed.

Alice continued to live apart from her husband and they were never reconciled. She had no children. Elizabeth and Humphrey had at least seven children. Elizabeth died in childbirth in 1316. Humphrey was said to be heartbroken.

In the summer of 1314 Robert Bruce and the Scottish army defeated the English army of Edward II at Bannockburn, paving the way for an independent sovereign Scotland.

ACKNOWLEDGMENTS

I could not have written this book without help and among the many hundreds of books and websites I consulted I would particularly like to mention the following which proved invaluable:

G.W.S. Barrow	*Robert Bruce*
Marc Morris	*A Great and Terrible King: Edward I and the Forging of Britain*
Ian Mortimer	*The Time Travellers Guide to Medieval England*
Kathryn Warner	*edwardthesecond.blogspot.com*

I would also like to thank Frances Kline and Ken Cooper for their assistance with editing; Jackie, Jane, Kat and Ken of the writing group for advice and sustenance; and Richard, as always, for his patience with me being marooned somewhere in the fourteenth century.

Also by Caroline Newark

THE FAIR MAID OF KENT

It is 1341 and Joan, the beautiful young cousin of the king of England, is poised on the brink of marriage with the earl of Salisbury's son. While plans are made for the king's continuing war against France the families gather to celebrate the wedding. But the bride is in tears. For unknown to everyone, Joan has a secret and it is one so scandalous, so unspeakably shocking, that discovery could destroy this glorious marriage and place the lives of those Joan loves in danger.

Faced with a jealous and increasingly suspicious husband Joan must tread a careful path precariously balanced between truth and deception, where love is an illusion and one false step could spell disaster.

From the glittering court of Edward III to the lonely border fortress of Wark and the bleak marshlands before the walls of Calais *The Fair Maid of Kent* tells the story of an enduring love in a dangerous world where a man may not be all he seems and your most powerful enemy is the one you cannot see.